ONE
NIGHT

LATIN HEAT

ONE NIGHT OF
CONSEQUENCES COLLECTION

October 2017

November 2017

December 2017

January 2018

February 2018

March 2018

ONE NIGHT
LATIN HEAT

JENNIE
LUCAS

ABBY
GREEN

KIM
LAWRENCE

MILLS & BOON

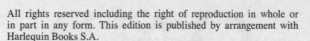

Published in Great Britain 2017
By Mills & Boon, an imprint of HarperCollins*Publishers*
1 London Bridge Street, London, SE1 9GF

ONE NIGHT: LATIN HEAT © 2017 Harlequin Books S.A.

Uncovering Her Nine Month Secret © 2014 Jennie Lucas
One Night with the Enemy © 2012 Abby Green
One Night with Morelli © 2014 Kim Lawrence

ISBN: 978-0-263-93169-3

09-1117

Our policy is to use papers that are natural, renewable and recyclable products and made from wood grown in sustainable forests. The logging and manufacturing processes conform to the legal environmental regulations of the country of origin.

Printed and bound in Spain
by CPI, Barcelona

UNCOVERING HER
NINE MONTH
SECRET

JENNIE LUCAS

*Massive thanks to my editor Kathryn for being
so elastic with the deadline on this one!*

Jennie Lucas grew up dreaming about faraway
lands. At fifteen, hungry for experience beyond
the borders of her small Idaho city, she went to
a Connecticut boarding school on scholarship.
She took her first solo trip to Europe at sixteen,
then put off college and travelled around the
U.S., supporting herself with jobs as diverse as
gas station cashier and newspaper advertising
assistant.

At twenty-two, she met the man who would
become her husband. After their marriage, she
graduated from Kent State with a degree in
English. Seven years after she started writing, she
got the magical call from London that turned her
into a published author.

Since then life has been hectic, with a new writing
career, a sexy husband and two small children,
but she's having a wonderful (albeit sleepless)
time. She loves immersing herself in dramatic,
glamorous, passionate stories. Maybe she can't
physically travel to Morocco or Spain right now,
but for a few hours a day, while her children are
sleeping, she can be there in her books.

Jennie loves to hear from her readers. You can
visit her website at www.jennielucas.com, or drop
her a note at jennie@jennielucas.com.

PROLOGUE

HE SEDUCED ME EASILY. He broke down my defenses as if they were paper. You wouldn't have been able to resist, either, believe me.

After so many years of feeling like a ghost in my own home, invisible, unloved, I think I would have fallen into his arms for one dark glance—one husky word. But Alejandro gave me so much more than that. He looked at me as if I were the most beautiful woman on earth. Listened to me as if every word on my lips was poetry. He pulled me into his arms, made me burst into flame, kissed my grief and cares away. After so many years of living in a cold gray world, my life exploded into color—because of him.

There was no reason why the Duque de Alzacar, one of the richest men in Spain, would want someone like me—plain, poor—rather than my beautiful, wealthy cousin. I thought it was a miracle.

It was only later that I realized why Alejandro had chosen me. He hadn't seduced me out of love—or even lust. It was many months before I realized the selfish reason that had caused him to overwhelm me with his charm, to dazzle me, to make me love him.

But by then, it was too late.

CHAPTER ONE

THE GRAY, LOWERING sky was falling like a shroud across the old colonial city of San Miguel de Allende when I heard the words I'd feared in nightmares for the past year.

"A man was here looking for you, Señora Lena."

Looking up at my neighbor, I staggered back, clutching my five-month-old son in my arms. "What?"

The woman smiled, reaching out to chuck the cooing baby's pudgy chin. "*Gracias* for letting me watch Miguelito for an hour. Such a pleasure…"

"But the man?" I croaked, my mouth dry. "What did he look like?"

"Muy guapo," she sighed. "So handsome. Dark-haired and tall."

It could be anyone, I told myself desperately. The old silver mining town in central Mexico was filled with American expatriates who'd moved here to enjoy the lovely architecture and take classes at the famous Instituto. Many single women had come here to start new lives, pursuing new businesses as artists and sculptors and jewelry makers.

Like me. A year ago, I'd arrived pregnant and full of grief, but I'd still managed to start a wonderful new life. Perhaps this dark stranger was looking for a portrait of his sweetheart, nothing more.

But I didn't believe it. Fear was cold inside me. "Did he give his name?"

Dolores shook her head. "The baby was fussing in my arms when I answered the door. But the man was well dressed, with a Rolls-Royce. A chauffeur. Bodyguards, even." Her smile spread to a grin. "Do you have a rich new boyfriend, Lena?"

My knees went weak.

"No," I whispered.

It could be only one man. Alejandro Guillermo Valentín Navaro y Albra, the powerful Duke of Alzacar. The man I'd once loved with all my innocent heart. The man who'd seduced and betrayed me.

No. It was worse than that.

"He's not your boyfriend, eh?" My neighbor's voice was regretful. "Pity. Such a handsome man. Why did he come looking for you, then? Do you know him?"

Beads of sweat broke out on my forehead. "When was he here?"

She shrugged, looking bemused. "A half hour ago. Maybe more."

"Did you say anything about—about Miguel being my son?"

Dolores shook her head. "He didn't give me the chance. He just asked if you lived in the house two doors down. I said yes. He pulled out his wallet and asked me not to mention his visit, because he wanted to surprise you. Can you imagine?" She flourished some bills from her apron pocket in delight. "He paid me a thousand pesos for my silence!"

Yes. I could imagine. I briefly closed my eyes. "But you told me anyway," I whispered. "Bless you."

She snorted. "Men always want to arrive with a flourish of trumpets. I thought it better for you to be prepared." She looked at my shapeless white sundress and plain sandals with a moue of disapproval, then at my long, casual ponytail and makeup-free face. She sighed. "You have a good figure, but in that dress you look like a marshmallow. You don't make the most of yourself. It's almost like you don't *want* to be noticed!" She shook her head. "But tonight you must be at your most irresistible, your most sexy, *sí?* You want him to want you!"

No. I really didn't. Not that he would want me anyway, now his evil plan had succeeded. "He's not my boyfriend."

"So picky!" She made a *tsk* sound. "You don't want *this* billionaire, you don't want *that* one—I tell you, wealthy, handsome men are not so thick upon the ground as you seem to think!" Dolores glared at me. "Your son needs a father. *You* need a husband. Both of you deserve every happiness." Her expression turned suddenly sly. "And the man at my door looked like he would bring a *lot* of happiness to a wife. Every night."

"No doubt," I said over the razor blade in my throat. It was true. Alejandro had brought me intense joy for one summer. And a lifetime's worth of anguish since. "I should go."

"*Sí.* It's almost Miguel's nap time, isn't it, *pequeño?*" she crooned.

My baby yawned, his fat cheeks vying with his sleepy dark eyes for cuteness. Those eyes just like his father's.

I exhaled, running a hand over my forehead. I'd allowed myself to think we were safe. That Alejandro had given up looking for me. *I should have known.* I should have known better than to start sleeping at night, to start making friends, to start making a real home for myself and my son. *I should have known they would someday find me....*

"Lena?" My neighbor frowned. "Is something wrong? You do not seem happy."

"Did you tell him when I'd be back?"

"I wasn't sure when you'd be done, so to be safe I said four o'clock."

I glanced at the clock in her brightly painted front room. It was only three. I had one hour. "Thank you." In a burst of emotion, I hugged her, knowing that she'd been kind to me—to both of us—but I would never see her again after today. "*Gracias,* Dolores."

She patted my back. "I know you've had a hard year, but that's in the past. Your life is about to change for the better. I can always feel these things."

Better? I choked back a laugh, then turned away before she could see my face. *"Adios...."*

"He'll be your boyfriend, just wait and see," she called after me gleefully. "He'll be your husband someday!"

My *husband.* A bitter thought. I wasn't the one Alejandro had wished to marry. He wanted my wealthy, beautiful cousin, Claudie. It was the whole reason he'd seduced me, the poor relation living in the shadows of Claudie's London mansion. If he and Claudie wed, together they'd have everything: a dukedom, half of Andalucía, political connections across the world, billions in the bank. They'd have almost limitless power.

There was just one thing they could never have.

My eyes fell on my baby's dark, downy head. I clutched Miguel tightly against me, and he gave an indignant cry. Loosening my grip, I smoothed back his soft hair.

"Sorry, I'm so sorry," I choked out, and I didn't know whether I was begging my son's forgiveness for holding him too tightly, for tearing him away from his home or for choosing his father so poorly.

How could I have been so stupid? How?

Hurrying down the small street, I glanced up at the heavy gray sky. August was the rainy season, and a downpour was threatening. Cuddling Miguel against my hip, I punched in the security-alarm code and pushed open the heavy oak door of my brightly painted home.

The rooms inside were dark. I'd fallen in love with this old colonial house, with its tall ceilings, its privacy, its scarcity of windows on the street. I could not have afforded the rent in a million years, but I'd been helped by a friend who'd allowed me to live here rent-free. Well—I thought of Edward St. Cyr as a friend. Until a week ago, when he'd—

But no. I wouldn't think of that now, or how betrayed I'd felt when the friendship I'd come to rely upon had been revealed for what it was.

I'm tired of waiting for you to forget that Spanish bastard. It's time for you to belong to me.

I shuddered at the memory. My answer had sent Edward scowling from this house, back on his private jet to London. There was no way I could remain in this house, living rent-free, after that, so for the past week, I'd looked for a cheaper place to live. But it was hard to find any place cheap enough for the income of a new, self-employed artist. Even here.

San Miguel de Allende had become my home. I would miss the city's cobblestoned streets, growing flowers in my garden and selling portraits in the open-air *mercados*. I'd miss the friends I'd made, Mexicans and expats who'd welcomed an unmarried, heartbroken woman and her baby, who'd taped me up and put me back together.

Now I took a deep breath, trying to steady my shaking nerves. "I can do this," I whispered aloud, trying to make myself believe it. I knew how to grab passports, money and clothes and be out of here in five minutes. I'd done it before, in Tokyo, Berlin, Istanbul, São Paulo and Mumbai.

But then, I'd had Edward to help me. Now I had no one.

Don't think about it, I ordered myself, wiping my eyes. I'd go on foot and hail a taxi on the street. Once at the station, my baby and I would take the next bus to Mexico City. I'd use the emergency credit card Edward had left and fly to the United States, where I was born. I'd head west. Disappear. Once I found a job, I'd pay back Edward every penny.

I'd raise my child in peace, in some small town in Arizona or Alaska, and this time, I'd make sure Alejandro would never, ever find me....

A lamp flicked on in the foyer.

Alejandro was sitting in a chair across the room, staring at me with eyes that burned like fire.

I halted, choking out a gasp.

"Lena Carlisle," he said in a low voice. "At last."

"Alejandro," I breathed as terror racked through me. My hands instinctively tightened on my baby in my arms. "What are you— How did you..."

"How did I find you?" He rose to his feet, tall and broad-shouldered. "Or how did I get in to your house?" His voice was low and husky, with only the slightest accent, blurred from growing up in Spain, followed by years of running a billion-dollar business conglomerate from New York and London. "Do you really think any *security system,* no matter how expensive, could keep me from being where I wanted to be?"

He was even more handsome than I remembered. Seeing him in the flesh, after a year of being tormented by sensual dreams, made my knees tremble. I clutched Miguel closer, willing myself not to faint.

Alejandro's cold eyes never left mine as he walked toward me. He was dressed in black from his well-cut coat to his glossy Italian shoes, draped in *power.*

"What do you want?" I choked out.

He looked from me to my yawning, drowsy-eyed baby.

"Is it true?" His voice was deadly quiet, but the words burned through my heart. His face was grim. "Is this my baby?"

His baby. Oh, God. Please, no. I stumbled back in blind panic.

"My men are outside. You won't even make it to the street...."

I ignored him. Grabbing the wrought-iron handle, I

pulled open the heavy, weathered oak door and started to run. I stopped.

Six hulking bodyguards stood outside my house, in a semicircle, in front of the expensive sedan and black SUV now jamming the slender residential lane.

"Did you think," Alejandro said softly behind me, "that when I finally found you, I would leave anything to chance?"

He stood close behind me, so close I caught the scent of his cologne. So close I could feel the heat emanating from his powerful body. Briefly closing my eyes, I shivered at being so close to the man who had once possessed me, body and soul.

Unwillingly, I turned back to face the ghost who still haunted my heart. His hot black gaze held mine, and in the dark embers of that fire, I was lashed by memories I'd tried so hard to forget. I'd loved him hopelessly from the moment he'd first come to call on my beautiful, wealthy cousin. I'd watched from hallways, made them tea, organized their dinner parties. I'd done it all with a smile, any and all work my cousin required, ignoring the ache of my heart when she bragged after he left that she was going to catch the uncatchable Spanish duke. "He's nearly in my grasp!" Claudie had crowed. "I'll be a duchess before the year is out!"

Then, to everyone's shock, he'd suddenly jilted her.

For me.

He was the first man who'd ever noticed me—really noticed me—and I'd fallen like a stone beneath the sensual onslaught of his power and glamour and dangerous, sexy charm. For six reckless, miraculous weeks in London last summer, Alejandro had held me in his arms, and I felt as if I owned the world.

Memories of the hopes I'd had, the naive girl I'd been, ripped through me now like a torrent of blows. Alejandro's expression was stark, but I could remember his playful smile. The intensity of his dark gaze. The sound of his husky voice whispering sweet words in the night. I could remember hot kisses, and the feel of our naked bodies intertwined in his London hotel suite. In the back of his limo. And once, against the wall in the back stairs of the Carlisle mansion.

Our affair had seemed as infinite as the stars in the sky. But on that bright summer day when I finally gathered the courage to tell him I was in love with him, his smiling face had changed in front of my eyes.

"*Love me?*" Alejandro had repeated scornfully. "You do not even *know* me."

Two minutes later, he was gone, leaving me bereft and bewildered. But the broken, truly broken, came later...

Now, Alejandro took my hand, glancing up and down the quiet Mexican street.

"Come back inside, Lena. We have much to talk about."

Feeling the electricity of his hand wrapped around mine, I looked up with an intake of breath.

He was so close now. Touching me. My lips parted. He was somehow even more devastatingly handsome than I'd remembered. He had the kind of face that could break a woman's heart into a million pieces, to little shimmering fragments of gray dust, leaving you too dazed with his power and beauty to feel anything but gratitude as he lazily destroyed you.

Without my notice, he led me back into the foyer. Reaching over my head, he towered over me, his arm brushing against my hair, his body pressing against mine. I shivered, clutching my baby close. But he merely closed the heavy door with a sonorous bang behind me.

The hard-edged billionaire duke, in his sharply tailored clothes, stood out starkly against my comfortable, bohemian home, with its warm tile floors and walls I'd decorated with homemade paper flowers and my own paintings, one of the Parroquia de San Miguel, but the rest of my baby, the first from when he was just six days old.

Looking down at me, Alejandro said softly, "Is what Claudie told me true? This baby in your arms—it is mine?"

Trembling, I pulled away. Gathering my wits, I glared at him. "Do you really expect me to answer that?"

"It's an easy enough question. There are only two possible answers." Reaching out, he stroked my cheek, but there was no tenderness in his gaze. "Yes. Or no."

"You'd be a horrible father! I won't let my sweet boy be turned into a heartless bastard like—"

"Like me?" His voice was dangerously low. His dark eyes gleamed in the shadowy foyer. "Is that what you really think of me—after all we once shared?"

Caught in his gaze, I trembled. Once, I might have believed so differently. I'd managed to convince myself that beneath his wealth and power and aristocratic title, Alejandro was decent and good. Like generations of women before me, I had seen what I wanted to see. I'd been blind to the truth, until, against my will, the blindfold had been torn from my eyes.

"Yes. That's what I think of you."

A strange expression flickered across the chiseled planes of his face, an emotion I couldn't identify before it swiftly disappeared. He gave me a sardonic smile.

"You are right, of course. I care for nothing and no one. Least of all you, especially after you and your cousin have gone to such lengths to blackmail me over this child."

"Blackmail you?" I gasped. "You're the one who deliberately seduced me, and got me pregnant, intending to steal my baby away so you could raise him with Claudie!"

He grew very still.

"What are you talking about?" he ground out.

My body was shaking with emotion. "You think I didn't

know? When I found out I was pregnant, you'd already left me and gone back to Spain. You wouldn't return my calls. But fool that I was, I was still desperate to share the news, because I hoped you might care! So I begged Claudie for enough money to fly to Madrid. I was scared to tell her why I needed the money. She'd planned so long to marry you. But when I told her I was pregnant, she did something I never imagined."

"What?"

I took a deep breath.

"She laughed," I whispered. "She laughed and laughed. Then she told me to wait. She went into the hallway, but she left the door open and I heard her call you. I heard her congratulate you on your brilliant plan! *Thanking* you, even! How brilliant you were, how clever, to seduce her lowly cousin, the poor relation, to provide the heir you knew she could never give you! Now the two of you could get married immediately." My voice turned acid. "Just as soon as her lawyer forced me to sign papers terminating all my parental rights."

"Yes. She called me." His eyes narrowed. "But I never…"

"'Don't worry, I'll get Lena to sign her baby away,' she said!" My voice trembled as I remembered the terror I'd felt that day. "She asked you to send over a few security guards from your London office, just in case I tried to fight!" My voice choked and I looked away. "So I ran. Before either of you could lock me away somewhere for the duration of my pregnancy and try to steal my child!"

Silence fell. His eyes narrowed.

"From the day, from the *hour* Claudie told me you were pregnant, I've had investigators trying to track you down, chasing you around the world. Yes, she had some crazy idea that it was her inability to have children that kept me from marrying her. She was wrong." He came closer. "I raced to London, but you were already gone. And ever since, you've always managed to disappear in a puff of smoke whenever I got close. That, *querida,* is expensive. And so is this." He motioned at the high ceilings of the two-hundred-year-old colonial house. "This house is owned by a shell company run out of the Caymans. My investigators checked. So why don't you just admit who's helping you? Admit the truth!"

Something told me not to mention Edward St. Cyr. "And what's that?"

"Once you found out you were pregnant, you knew I would never marry you." His voice softened, his dark eyes almost caressing me. "So you came up with a different plan to cash in, didn't you? You struck a deal...with your cousin."

Whatever I'd expected, it wasn't that. I stared at him. "Are you crazy? Why would Claudie help me? She wants to marry you!"

"I know. After you disappeared, Claudie told me she knew exactly where you were, but that you refused to let me see the child until we could guarantee a stable home. Until I married her."

My lips parted in shock. "But I haven't spoken to Claudie for a year. She has no idea where I am!" I shook my head. "Did she really try to blackmail you into marriage?"

"Women always want to marry me," he said grimly. "They think nothing of stealing or cheating or lying for it."

I snorted. "Your ego is incredible!"

"It's not ego. Every woman wants to be the wife of a billionaire duke. It's not personal."

Of course it is, I thought unwillingly, my heart twisting in my chest. How could any woman not fall in love with Alejandro, and not want him for her own?

"But what I want to know is..." His voice became dangerously low. "Is this baby in your arms truly mine? Or is it just part of some elaborate plot you've set up with Claudie?"

My head snapped back. "Are you asking me if my son is some kind of *stunt baby?*"

"You would be surprised," he said tightly, "how often in life someone pretends to be something they are not."

"You think I'd lie about this—for money?"

"Perhaps not. Perhaps for some other reason." He paused. "If you were not working for Claudie, perhaps you were working for yourself."

"Meaning what?"

"You hoped that playing hard to get, disappearing with my child, would make me want to pin you down. To marry you." He lifted a dark eyebrow. "Not a bad calculation."

My mouth had fallen open. Then I glared at him. "I would never want to be your wife!"

"Right."

His single small word was like a grenade of sarcasm exploding all over me. For an instant my pride made me blind with anger. Then I remembered the dreams I'd once had and my throat went tight. I took a deep, miserable breath.

"Maybe that was what I wanted once," I whispered. "But that was long ago. Before I found out you'd coldheartedly seduced me so you could marry Claudie and steal my baby."

"You must know now that was never true."

"How can I be sure?"

He shook his head. "I never intended to marry Claudie or anyone."

"Yes, you said that. You also told me once that you never intended to have children. And yet here you are, fighting for a DNA test for Miguel!"

"I do not have a choice." His expression changed as he said sharply, "You named the baby Miguel?"

"So?"

"Why?" he demanded, staring at me with a sudden suspicious glitter in his eyes that I did not understand.

"After the beautiful city that took me in—San Miguel became our home!"

He relaxed imperceptibly. "Ah."

Now I was the one to frown. His reaction to our baby's name had been so fierce, almost violent. Had he wondered if I'd named him after another man? "Why do you care so much?"

"I don't," he said coldly.

My baby whimpered in my arms. Fiercely, I shook my head as I hugged him close, breathing in Miguel's sweet baby scent, feeling his tiny warm body against me. I nuzzled his head and saw tears fall onto his soft dark hair. "If you didn't get me pregnant on purpose, if it happened by accident and you don't want a child...just let us go!"

His jaw tightened. "I have an obligation...."

"Obligation!" I cried. "To you, he's just someone to carry on your title and name. To me, he's everything. I carried him for nine months, felt him kick inside me, heard his first cry when he was born. He's my baby, my precious child, my only reason for living." I was crying openly now, and so was my baby, either in sympathy or in alarm or just because it was past his nap time and all the adults arguing wouldn't let him sleep. Miguel's chubby cheeks were red, his eyes swimming with piteous tears. I tried to comfort him as I wept.

Alejandro's expression was stone. "If he's my son, I will bring both of you to live with me in Spain. Neither of you will ever want for anything, ever again. You will live in my castle."

"I'd never marry you, not for any price!"

"Marriage? Who said anything about that?" His lips twisted. "Though we both know you'd marry me in a second if I asked."

Stung, I shook my head furiously. "What could you offer

me, Alejandro? Money? A castle? A title? I don't need those things!"

He moved closer to me, his eyes dark.

"Don't forget sex," he said softly. "Hot, deep, incredible sex."

In the shadowy hacienda, Alejandro looked at me over the downy head of the baby that we had created. My breasts suddenly felt heavy, my nipples tightening. My body felt taut and liquid at once.

"I know you remember what it was like between us," he said in a low voice. "Just as I do."

I lifted my gaze to his.

"Yes," I whispered. "But what use are any of those things really, Alejandro? Without love, it's empty." I shook my head. "You must know this. Because the money, the palaces, the title—and yes, even the sex… Have those things ever made *you* happy?"

He stared at me. For a long moment, there was only the soft patter of the rain against the roof, our baby's low whimper, and the loud beat of my aching heart.

Then abruptly, for the first time, Alejandro looked, really looked, at our son. Reaching out, he stroked Miguel's soft dark hair gently with a large, powerful hand.

As if by magic, our baby's crying abruptly subsided. Big-eyed, Miguel hiccupped his last tears away as father and son took measure of each other, each with the same frown, the same eyes, the same expression. It would have been enough to make me grin, if my heart hadn't been hurting so much.

Suddenly our baby flopped out a tiny, unsteady hand against Alejandro's nose. Looking down at him in surprise, Alejandro snorted a laugh. He seemed to catch his breath, looking at Miguel with amazement, even wonder.

Then he straightened, giving me a cold glare.

"There will be a DNA test. Immediately."

"You expect me to allow a doctor to prick my baby's skin for a blood test, to prove something I don't want to be proved? Forget it! Either believe he's your son, or—better yet—don't! And leave us in peace!"

Alejandro's face looked cold and ruthless. "Enough."

He must have pressed a button or something—or else he had some freaky bodyguard alert, like a dog whistle I couldn't hear—because suddenly two bodyguards came in through the front door. Without even looking at me, they kept walking through the foyer, headed across the courtyard toward the bedroom I shared with Miguel.

I whirled on Alejandro. "Where are they going?"

"To pack," he replied coolly.

"Pack for whom?"

A third bodyguard who'd come up silently behind me suddenly lifted Miguel out of my arms.

"No!" I cried. I started for him, arms outstretched, but Alejandro held me back.

"If the DNA test proves he is not my son," he said calmly, "I will bring your son back to you, safe and sound, and I'll never bother either of you again."

"Let me go!" I shrieked, fighting him—uselessly, for with his greater power and strength, his grip was implacable. "You bastard! You bastard! I will *kill* you! You can't take him from me—Miguel! *Miguel!*"

"You are so sure he is mine?"

"Of course he is yours! You know you were my only lover!"

"I know I was your first…."

"My only! *Ever!* Damn you! *Miguel!*"

Something flickered in Alejandro's eyes. But I was no longer looking at him. I was watching as the bodyguard disappeared through the door, my baby wailing in the man's beefy arms. I struggled in Alejandro's grip. "Let me go!"

"Promise to behave, Lena," he said quietly, "and I will."

How I wished I could fight him. If only I had the same power he did—then we'd see who gave orders! If I had his physical strength, I would punch him in the face! If only I had a fortune, a private jet, my own bodyguard army…

My lips parted on an intake of breath.

Edward.

Would he help me? Even now?

That wasn't the question.

Would I be willing to pay the price?

"I don't want to separate you from the baby," Alejandro said, "but I must have the DNA test. And if you're going to fight and scream…"

I abruptly stopped struggling. Nodding, I wiped my eyes. "I'll come quietly. But please," I said softly, looking up at his face, "before you take him to Spain, could we stop in London?"

He frowned. "London?"

I nodded, trying to hide my eagerness—my desperation. "I left something at Claudie's house. Something precious. I need it back."

"What is it?"

"My baby's legacy."

He lifted a dark eyebrow. "Money?"

"And also," I said on a wave of inspiration, "if we could talk to Claudie, together, we could force her to admit how she played us both. Then maybe we could actually trust each other, going forward…."

Alejandro rubbed the back of his head, then nodded. "That would be better. And to be honest, there are a few things I'd like to discuss with your cousin myself."

His voice was grim. I believed him now when he said he didn't want to marry Claudie. Maybe Alejandro hadn't deliberately planned to get me pregnant after all.

But I'd been right about one thing. He still planned to steal my baby. He intended to keep Miguel at his side, to raise him as his heir in some cold Spanish castle, until he turned him into some heartless, unfeeling bastard like himself.

And Alejandro didn't intend to marry me. So I'd be powerless. Expendable.

"So we have a deal?" Alejandro said. "You'll allow the DNA test, and if he is my son, you'll come with us to Spain?"

"With a stop in London first."

"Yes. London. But after that, Spain. I have your word?"

"I honestly hate you," I whispered with feeling.

"I honestly do not care. Do I have your word?"

I glared at him. "Yes."

He looked down at me in the shadows. For a moment, there was a current of electricity between us, sparking in the shadows of the room. His fingers tightened. Then he abruptly released me.

"Thank you," he said coldly, "for being so reasonable."

Hiding the cold determination in my heart, I left him without a word, and nearly sprinted toward my baby.

Alejandro thought he owned me now. But I wasn't as helpless as he thought. I had one card left to play, if I was willing to pay for it.

Was I?

For my son?

Yes. I was.

CHAPTER TWO

THE FIRST TIME I saw London, I was a grief-stricken fourteen-year-old, newly orphaned, just arrived from New York. My grandmother, whom I'd never met, sent her driver to collect me from Heathrow. The sky was weeping and gray. I remembered trembling as I walked up the steps of the tall white mansion in Kensington, a house roughly the same size as my entire apartment building in Brooklyn.

Brought in by the butler, I'd found my grandmother sitting at her antique desk in the morning room. I stood in front of the fireplace for some moments, my eyes stinging and my heart aching, before she finally looked up.

"So you're Lena," she'd said, looking me up and down, from the lumpy coat my mother had made before her hands grew frail in illness, wasting away like her heart since my father's death six months previously, down to my feet crammed into cheap, too-small shoes that had been all my loving but sadly unskilled father had been able to afford. "Not much of a beauty," she'd said crisply, with some regret.

It was raining in London today, too.

As Alejandro's driver waited, holding open my door, I shivered, looking up at the white mansion. I felt suddenly fourteen again. Except now I was going to face my cousin.

Claudie and I were the same age, but she was so different in looks and manner that we could have been born on opposite sides of not just the Atlantic, but the universe.

When I'd first come to the house—devastated by the loss of both my mother and my father within six short months—I'd tried so hard to make my beautiful, spoiled cousin like me, but she'd scorned me on sight. She'd been determined to drive me from the house. Especially once grandmother died and she saw the terms of the will. And she'd finally gotten her wish. She'd won....

"What are you waiting for?" Alejandro said impatiently. "Get out of the car."

"I changed my mind. I don't need to go in."

"Too bad. You're going."

He looked far too handsome and rested. He'd slept and showered on his private jet. He was in a fresh suit. I, on the other hand, hadn't slept at all since yesterday. After an interminable visit to a private hospital in San Miguel de Allende, where he'd paid a small fortune for the DNA test, we'd gotten on his private 747 and I'd spent the long flight walking back and forth in the cabin, trying to calm Miguel enough to sleep. But the cabin pressure hurt his ears, and only my continual walking soothed him. So I'd gotten exercise, at least, using the aisle of Alejandro's jet as my own private treadmill.

But there'd been no shower for me. I felt groggy, sweaty and dirty, and I was still wearing the same white cotton sundress I'd worn in Mexico. There was no way I was going to face my cousin like this.

It was bad enough letting Alejandro see me.

He'd barely said ten words to me on the plane; in fact, he'd said just five: "Want me to hold him?" Of course, I refused. I hadn't wanted to give up possession of my baby, even for a moment. Even thirty thousand feet in the air, when there was no way for him to run off. The DNA test had proved the obvious—that Alejandro was Miguel's father—but I was fighting his emotional and legal claim with every cell and pore.

Now, as Alejandro looked at me in the backseat, the difference between his sleek gorgeousness and my chubby unattractiveness was so extreme I imagined he must be asking himself what he could ever have seen in me. Which begged the question: If he hadn't deliberately seduced me last summer to create an heir, then why on earth had he?

I licked my lips. "Alejandro," I said hesitantly. "I…"

"Enough delay," he growled. "We're going in."

I looked at my baby, tucked into a baby seat beside me in the back of the limo, now sleeping in blessed silence. "You go. I'll stay here with Miguel." Which would also be the perfect way for me to sneak to Edward's house, at the end of the street.

"Dowell can watch him."

I glanced at the driver doubtfully. "No."

"Then bring Miguel with us."

"Wake him up?" I whispered, scandalized. I narrowed my eyes. "Of course *you* wouldn't worry about that. You're not the one who spent the whole flight walking in circles trying to make him sleep."

Alejandro set his jaw. "I offered to take him…."

"You could have offered again." I was dimly aware that I sounded irrational. There was no way he could have taken Miguel from me on the jet except by force, which wouldn't exactly have gone over well, either. My cheeks got hot. "It doesn't matter."

He lifted a dark eyebrow. "You do know how to take care of Miguel better than I do."

His tone told me whom he blamed for that. "I had no choice. I thought you were going to steal him from me."

"So you stole him first?"

I blinked. I hadn't thought of it that way before.

"You could at least have called me directly," he ground out.

Now, that was unfair! "I tried! You wouldn't take my phone calls!"

"If I'd known you were pregnant, I would have." His jaw tightened. "You could have left a message with Mrs. Allen...."

"Leave a *message* with some faceless secretary at your London office to let you know, oh, hey, I'm pregnant with your baby? Seriously?" I lifted my chin. "You should have just taken my damn call!"

Alejandro stared at me, his lips pressed in a thin line. "This argument is over." He turned away. "Unlatch the baby carrier and lift it out of the seat. That won't wake him up, as you know perfectly well."

My cheeks burned slightly. Yes, I'd known that. I'd just been hoping *he* wouldn't.

When I didn't move, Alejandro started to reach around me. With a huff I turned and unlatched the seat. Miguel continued softly snoring in sweet baby dreams, tucked snugly in the carrier with a soft blanket against his cheek.

As the driver closed the door behind us with a snap, I stood on the sidewalk, staring up at the cold white mansion.

I'd never wanted to return to this house. But there was one silver lining. I hadn't been lying when I'd told Alejandro I wanted to come back for Miguel's legacy. Something I'd been forced to leave behind that had nothing to do with the inheritance I'd lost.

As I looked up, the soft drizzle felt like cobwebs against my skin. Like memories. Like ghosts.

"What now?" Alejandro was glaring at me as if I wasn't his favorite person. I couldn't blame him. He wasn't my favorite person right now, either.

Although at this moment there was one person I liked even less. I swallowed.

"I'm scared," I whispered.

He stared at me. "Of Claudie?"

I nodded, not trusting my voice.

"You don't need to be scared," he said gruffly. "I'm here

with you now." Reaching out, he took the baby carrier from my trembling hands. "Come on."

Alejandro carried our sleeping baby up the stone steps and knocked on the imposing front door.

Mr. Corgan, the longtime butler, opened the door. His jowly face was dignified as he greeted Alejandro.

"Good morning, Your Excellency." Then he glanced at me and his eyes went wide. "Miss Lena!" He saw the sleeping baby in the carrier, and the usually unflappable Mr. Corgan's jaw fell open. "It's true?" He breathed, then glanced at Alejandro, and the mask slipped back into place. Holding open the door, he said sonorously, "Won't you both please come in?"

He led us into the elegant front salon, with high ceilings and gilded furniture. Everything looked just as I remembered—vintage, French and expensive. I'd been allowed in this room only a handful of times, the last being when I'd begged Claudie for money to fly to Spain. The day my life had fallen apart.

Mr. Corgan said, "I regret that Miss Carlisle is…out…at the moment, but she has a standing order to welcome you at any time, Your Excellency, if you care to wait."

"Sí," Alejandro said coldly. "We will wait."

"Of course. She will be so pleased to see you when she returns. May I offer refreshments? Tea?"

Alejandro shook his head. He sat down on the pink striped couch near the window. He seemed incongruous there, this dark, masculine Spaniard with severely tailored black clothes, in a salon that looked like a giant powder puff, with the powder made of diamond dust.

He set down the baby carrier on the white polished marble floor beside the sofa. I swiftly scooped it up, and exhaled in relief now that my sleeping baby was safely back in my possession. I followed Mr. Corgan out of the salon and into the hallway.

Once we were alone, the butler's mask dropped and he turned to face me with a happy exclamation.

"We missed you, girl." He hugged me warmly. I closed my eyes, smelling pipe smoke and brass polish. Then I heard a crash and pulled back to see Mrs. Morris, the housekeeper, had just broken a china plate in the hallway. But she left it there, coming forward with a cry.

A minute later, both of them, along with Hildy, the maid, were hugging me and crying and exclaiming over Miguel's beauty, his dark hair, his fat cheeks.

"And such a good sleeper, too," Mrs. Morris said approvingly. Then they all looked at each other. I saw the delicate pause.

Then Hildy blurted out, "Who's his father, then?"

I glanced back at the salon, biting my lip. "Um…"

Hildy's eyes got huge when she saw who was in the salon. Then she turned to Mr. Corgan. "You were right. I owe you a fiver."

His cheeks went faintly pink as he cleared his throat with a *harrumph.* "I might have heard some of your conversation with Miss Carlisle the day you left, Miss Lena." He shook his jowly head with a glare. "It wasn't right what she did. Driving you from the house a year before you would have got your grandmother's inheritance."

I was surprised for only a second. Then I gave a wry smile. Of course they knew. Household staff knew everything, sometimes even before their employers did. "It doesn't matter."

"But it does," Mrs. Morris said indignantly. "Miss Carlisle wanted your inheritance and the moment she convinced you to move out of the house, she got it by default. Just a year before it would have finally been yours!"

I pressed my hand against my temple as emotions I had spent the past year trying to forget churned up in me.

When I turned eighteen, I could have left for college,

or gotten a real job. Instead, I'd remained living in this house, working as a sort of house manager/personal assistant for my cousin beneath her unrelenting criticism as she tried her best to drive me away. I'd had a small salary at first, but even that had disappeared when she'd lazily announced one day that she was cutting the salaries of the staff by twenty percent. "They don't need it," she sniffed. "They are lucky, working all day in my beautiful house. They should be paying *me!*"

Mr. Corgan and Mrs. Morris and the rest had become my friends, and I knew they had families to support. So I'd given up my salary rather than see them suffer. Leaving me virtually destitute for years, in spite of working eighteen-hour days.

But I hadn't minded, not really, because I'd known all I had to do was remain in this house until I was twenty-five, just a few months from now, and I would have gotten the huge inheritance once destined for my father, before he'd been cut out of the will for the crime of marrying my mother.

Eight years ago, when my grandmother lay dying, she'd clutched his old teddy bear and dissolved in tears I'd never seen before as she remembered the youngest son she'd once loved best. She'd called for her lawyer.

If Robert's child proves herself worthy of the Carlisle name, my grandmother's will had read, *and she still lives in the house at the age of twenty-five, she may claim the bequest that would have been his.*

But now it had all reverted to Claudie. I hadn't cared a whit about the money last year, when I'd feared my baby would be stolen from me. But now...

"The house hasn't been the same without you, Miss Lena," Mr. Corgan said.

"Half the staff resigned after you left," Mrs. Morris said.

"She's been intolerable without you to run interference."

Mr. Corgan shook his head grimly. "I've worked for this family for forty years, Miss Lena, but even I fear my time here is nearing an end." Leaning closer, he confided, "Miss Carlisle still insists she'll marry your duke."

"He's not my duke...."

"Well. He's the only man rich and handsome enough for *her,* though she says she'd marry any rich idiot who'd make her a duchess...." Glancing back over his shoulder, he coughed, turning red.

Turning, I saw Alejandro standing in the doorway of the salon. I wondered how much he'd heard. His face was half hidden in shadow, his expression inscrutable.

"Did you change your mind about the tea, Your Excellency?" Mr. Corgan gasped, his face beet red.

Alejandro shook his head. His eyes were dark, but his lips quirked at the edges. "We rich idiots prefer coffee."

The butler looked as if he wished the earth would swallow him up whole. "I'll get it right away, sir...."

"Don't bother." He looked at me. "Did you get what you came for?"

He'd heard everything, I realized. He thought I'd come for my inheritance. He thought that was the precious thing that had brought me here. It wasn't.

I turned to Mrs. Morris urgently. "Did she throw out my things?"

"She wanted to," she said darkly. "She told me to burn it all. But I boxed it all up and left it in your attic room. I knew she'd never bother to go all the way up there to check."

"Bless you," I whispered, and hugged her. "Stay and have coffee," I called to Alejandro. "I'll be back in a few minutes." I started up the stairs, carrying my sleeping baby with me.

Climbing three floors, I reached the attic. It looked even more desolate than I remembered, with only one grimy window, an ancient metal bed frame and stacks of boxes. Setting down the baby, I went straight for the boxes.

"What are you looking for?"

Hearing Alejandro's husky voice behind me, I turned. "These boxes hold everything from my childhood."

He stepped inside the attic room, knocking his head against the slanted roof. He rubbed it ruefully. "I can see why Claudie wouldn't come up here. This place is like a prison cell."

"This was my home for over ten years."

His dark eyes widened. "This room?" He slowly looked around the attic, at the rough wood floors, at the naked lightbulb hanging from the ceiling. "You lived here?"

I gave a wistful laugh. "From the time my parents died when I was fourteen, until I left last year when...well. It looked nicer then, though. I made decorations, paper flowers." A lump rose in my throat as I looked around the bare room where I'd spent so many years. The bare mattress on the metal bed frame where I'd slept so many nights. I gently touched the bare lightbulb and swung it on the cord. "I had a bright red lampshade I bought from the charity shop on Church Street."

"A charity shop?" he said sharply. "But you're Claudie's cousin. A poor relation, I know, but I'd assumed you were well paid for all your work...."

This time my laugh was not so wistful. "I was paid a salary after I turned eighteen, but that money had to go to—other things. So I started earning a little money doing portraits at street fairs. But Claudie allowed me so little time away from the house..."

"*Allowed* you?" he said incredulously.

I looked at him. "You heard about my inheritance."

"How much would it have been?"

"If I was still living in this house on my twenty-fifth

birthday, a few months from now, I would have inherited
thirty million pounds."

His jaw dropped.

"Thirty…"

"Yes."

"And you left it all?"

"To protect my baby. Yes."

"To protect our baby, you sacrificed more money than
most people see in a lifetime."

He sounded so amazed. I shook my head. "Any mother
would have done the same. Money is just money." I glanced
down at Miguel, and a smile lifted my cheeks as I said
softly, "He is my life."

When I finally looked up, his dark, soulful eyes were
looking at me as if he'd never seen me before. My cheeks
went hot. "I expect you think I'm an idiot."

"Far from it," he said in a low voice.

He was looking at me with such intensity. Awkwardly,
I turned away and started digging through the top box.
Pushing it aside, I opened the one beneath it.

"What are you looking for?" he said curiously.

Not answering, I pulled out old sweaters, old ragtag cop-
ies of books I'd read and reread as a teenager, *Rebecca, A
Little Princess, Jane Eyre.* Finally, at the bottom of the box,
I found the three oversize, flat photo albums. "Thank you,"
I whispered aloud when I saw they hadn't been burned, or
warped from being left to rot in the rain or scribbled on
with a venomous black marker, or any of the other images
I'd tormented myself with. Pressing the albums against my
chest, I closed my eyes in pure gratitude.

"Photo albums?" Alejandro said in disbelief. "You
begged me to come to London for *photo albums?*"

"I told you," I said sharply. "I came for my baby's
legacy."

"But I never thought…" Frowning, Alejandro held out his hand. "Let me see."

Reluctantly, I handed them over, then watched as he turned through the pages of the top album, at old photographs pressed against yellowing adhesive pages beneath the clear plastic cover.

"It nearly killed me to leave them behind," I said. "It's all I have left of my parents. My home." I pointed to a picture of a tenement building where the ground floor was a butcher's shop. "That was our apartment in Brooklyn."

He turned the page. "And this?"

My heart twisted when I saw my mother, young and laughing, holding a ragtag bouquet of flowers, sitting in my father's lap. "My parents' wedding day. My dad was a student in London. He fell in love with a waitress, an immigrant newly arrived from Puerto Rico. He married her against his family's wishes, when she was pregnant with me…."

Alejandro looked at me for a long moment, then silently turned more pages. My babyhood flashed before my eyes, pictures of me as a tiny baby, getting bathed in the sink, sitting on a towel on the kitchen floor, banging wooden spoons against a pot and beaming with the same chubby cheeks that Miguel had now.

Finishing the first album, Alejandro handed it to me without a word, and thumbed through the second book, then the third. My childhood passed swiftly—learning to ride a bike…my first day at school…

"Why are you interested?" I said haltingly. "Is it—to make fun of me?"

"To make fun?" He looked at me with a scowl. "You think I would taunt you about having a happy childhood?" He shook his head. "If anything, I envy you," he said softly, looking back at the pages that my tenderhearted mother had made for me when I was a child. Right up to the very last photo, of my father at Christmas, sitting beneath the tree wearing a Santa hat, smiling lovingly at the camera as he held my mother's homemade gift of a sweater. Two months later, he was dead. There were no more photos. The last few pages of the album were blank. Alejandro said softly, "I have no pictures of myself with my mother. None."

I blinked. "How is that possible? I mean, I'd think you'd have a million pictures taken…."

He abruptly looked at me. Without answering, he closed the photo album and handed it to me.

"Perhaps you're not who I thought you were."

"Who did you think I was?"

"Exactly like all the other women I've ever dated. In love with the idea of being a rich duchess." He looked down at me, his dark eyes infinite and deep as the night sky. "But I'm starting to think you're different. A woman who would willingly leave thirty million pounds… You were actually in love with me, weren't you?"

My breath got knocked out of me.

"That was a long time ago."

Our eyes met, and I suddenly had to get out of the attic. I picked up Miguel's baby carrier with one arm and carried the albums with the other. "I'll be downstairs."

Without looking back, I fled, rushing down the flights of stairs. My teeth were chattering, and I was shaking with strange emotion. *Edward,* I reminded myself. The other reason I'd come to London. I had to get his help before Alejandro could bully me into going to Spain. Although it actually wasn't going to Spain that frightened me. It was never being able to leave again. It was being separated from my baby. It was being completely under the control of a man who'd almost destroyed me once, just by making me love him.

As I reached the bottom of the staircase, I heard a car door slam outside. Through the windows, I saw a flash of purple.

Claudie had come home.

I turned to where Hildy was loitering at the bottom of the stairs. "Hildy!"

"Oh, hello," she said, blushing when she saw me. "I was just dusting the banister, Miss—"

"My cousin is here. Please." Grabbing Hildy's arm, I whispered, "I need you to take a message to Edward St. Cyr."

"Edward St. Cyr?" Hildy's eyes nearly popped out of her head. "Mr. St. Cyr himself? Are you serious?"

"Tell him I need to see him," I said with more assurance than I felt.

"Here, miss? You know he and Miss Carlisle hate each other…."

Hearing my cousin fumbling at the door, I shook my head. "Tell him…the Princess Diana Playground in thirty minutes."

With a quick, troubled nod, Hildy hurried toward the back door. Just in time, too. The front door slammed.

"Well. Look who's back."

My cousin's voice was a sneer. Warily, I turned to face her for the first time in a year.

"Hello, Claudie." She was wearing a tight, extremely short bandage dress, the kind you might wear to a club if you wanted a lot of attention, in a vivid shade of purple that almost matched the hollows beneath her eyes. "Late night?" I said mildly.

She glared at me.

"If you came to beg for your inheritance, forget it. My solicitors went through the will with a fine-tooth comb," she ground out. "You'll never…." Then she saw the baby and gasped in triumph. "You brought the brat here? I knew you'd see reason." She rubbed her hands together in glee. "Now I'll either make him marry me, or else I'll—"

"You'll what, Claudie?" Alejandro said coolly from the top of the stairs.

My cousin looked up, speechless for the first time in her life. But she recovered almost instantly. Smiling up at him, she put her hand on her hip, setting a pose that showed her figure to advantage, wearing her six-inch heels and skin-tight purple dress, trailing a cloud of expensive perfume. Her gorgeous, long blond hair tumbled over her shoulders, emphasizing the bone structure of her sharp cheekbones.

But as she licked her big lips, beneath her smile, her eyes were afraid. "Alejandro. I didn't know you were here."

He came down the stairs, looking down at her. He stopped in front of her. Even though she wore such high heels, he was still taller.

"You lied to me, Claudie," he said pleasantly. "Lena wasn't holding my baby hostage. You were."

She visibly trembled, then tried to laugh. Reaching into her crystal-encrusted bag, she got out a pack of cigarettes. "Darling, I don't know what kind of lies my precious cousin might have told you, but…"

He grabbed her wrist almost violently.

"Do not," he said coldly, "smoke near my son."

"*Your* son," she breathed, searching his gaze, then ripped her arm away. "Are you so sure of that?" Her beautiful blue eyes hardened. "How do you know he's yours? You should have seen all the men who used to come through here, Alejandro—trooping up to Lena's bedroom every single night—"

A little gasp escaped me, like an enraged squeak.

Alejandro lifted an eyebrow. "Then they must have been lost, on their way to *your* room, Claudie."

Her eyes narrowed. "I don't like what you're implying—"

"We did a DNA test," he said, cutting her off. "The baby is mine."

For a moment, she stared at him. But you could almost

see her gather her forces. "He doesn't have to be." She looked from him to me. "If you don't treat him like your son, no one else will."

"You think I would abandon my own child?"

"Fine," she said impatiently. She flung a skeletal finger toward my sweetly sleeping son. "We can take her baby. She's nobody, Alejandro. She won't be able to stop us…."

With a gasp, I protected the baby carrier with my body.

"Just think." Claudie swayed her hips as she walked toward Alejandro with her hypnotic red smile. "Just think how perfect our future could be." She started to wrap her arms around him. "With your money and title, and my money and connections…the two of us could rule the world."

He looked down at her coldly. "Do you really think I'd want to rule the world, if the price would be marriage to you?"

Shocked, she let her arms fall to her sides.

"You used Lena for years as an unpaid slave," he said, "then threatened to take her baby, for the sake of stealing what you wanted—her inheritance. And then you tried to blackmail me into marrying you!"

She licked her lips. "I…"

He held up his hand sharply, cutting her off. His voice was deep and harsh. "For the past year, you've lied to me, saying if I ever wanted to see my child, I had to marry you. Blaming Lena, making me think she was the one to blame. For that, you deserve to go to hell. Which I hope you will find—" he gave her a sudden, pleasant smile "—very soon. *Adios,* Claudie." Scooping up the baby carrier, he turned to me gravely. "Shall we go?" Without another word, he walked out the front door.

"Alejandro, wait," Claudie gasped, but I was the only one left to hear. *"You."* Her face as she turned to look at me really did look like a snake's. Or maybe a dragon's—I could almost see the smoke coming out of her nostrils as her blue, reptilian eyes hardened. "You did this!"

For the past decade, I'd dreamed of what I would say to her if given the chance, after all my lonely years, crying alone in my attic. All the subtle and not so subtle ways she'd insulted me, used me, made me feel worthless and invisible for the past ten years. But in this moment, all those things fled from my mind. Instead, the real question came from my heart.

"Why did you hate me, Claudie?" I whispered, lifting my tearful gaze to hers. "I loved you. You were my only family. Why couldn't you love me? Why wouldn't you let me love you?"

My cousin drew herself up, all thin gorgeousness.

"Why?" She lit her cigarette with shaking hands. "Because you're not my real family." Taking a long draw on her cigarette, she said in a low, venomous hiss, "And you're not good enough for Alejandro. Blood always tells. Sooner or later, he will be embarrassed by you, just as I was. He'll take your child and toss you in the gutter, like you deserve."

My mouth fell open as her poisoned dart hit me, square in the heart.

"It didn't have to be this way," I choked out, and I turned and fled, still holding my photo albums against my chest, like a shield.

Outside, a sliver of sun had split through the dark clouds, through the rain. Stopping on the sidewalk, I turned back and looked up at the Carlisle mansion for one last time.

"Goodbye," I whispered.

Then I climbed into the limo, where the driver waited with my door open, and he closed it behind me.

"Enjoy a tender farewell?" Alejandro was already in the backseat, on the other side of Miguel, who had woken and was starting to whimper.

"Something like that," I muttered, trying to surreptitiously wipe my tears.

"I was surprised. It's not like you to let me walk off with—" His voice cut off as he saw my face. "What's wrong?"

"Nothing," I said. Turning to my baby, I pressed his favorite blanket against his cheek and tried to comfort him. Tried to comfort myself. My baby's tears quieted and so did his quivering little body, as he felt the hum and vibration of the car's engine beneath him. His eyelids started to grow heavy again.

"What did she say?" Alejandro said. Frowning, he looked closer at my face. "Did she…"

There was a sudden hard knock on his window. Miguel's little body jerked back awake, and his whimpers turned to full-on crying. Alejandro turned with a growl.

Claudie stood by the limo, her eyes like fire. "Open this window!" she yelled through the glass.

Alejandro's expression was like ice as he rolled it down a grudging two inches. She leaned forward, her face raw with emotion.

"We could have ruled the world together, Alejandro, and you're throwing it all away—for that little whore and her brat!"

Alejandro said softly, his face dangerous, "If you ever insult either my son or his mother again, you will regret it."

Claudie looked bewildered. To be fair, she'd insulted me for so long she'd probably forgotten it wasn't nice.

"But Alejandro…" Her voice had a strange begging sound I'd never heard from her. "You'll never find someone with my breeding, my beauty, my billions. I love you…."

"You love my title."

Her cheeks flushed red. "All right. But you can't choose her over me. She's…nothing. No one."

I swallowed, blinking fast.

"Blood always tells," she said. "She's not good enough for you."

Alejandro looked quickly at my miserable face. Then he turned back to Claudie with a deliberate smile.

"Thank you for your fascinating opinion. Now move, won't you? I need to take Lena shopping for an engagement ring."

"You're—what?" Claudie staggered back. I gasped. Miguel was crying.

The only one who looked absolutely calm was Alejandro. Turning away from her, he sat back in the plush leather seat, and said to Dowell, "Drive on."

Claudie stared after us, looking stupefied on the sidewalk, and almost forlorn in her tight club dress and bedraggled mascara. Looking back at her through the car window, I felt a strange wave of sympathy.

Because I, too, knew what it felt like to be left by Alejandro Navaro y Albra.

"You didn't have to be so cruel," I whispered.

"Cruel?" he said incredulously. "You defend her, after the way she treated you?"

"She's still my cousin. I feel sorry for her...."

"Then you're a fool," he said harshly.

I stroked my crying baby's cheek. My lips creased sadly. "Love makes us all fools."

"She doesn't love me. She doesn't even know me."

"That's what you said to me, too," I said softly. I met his gaze. "I wonder if any woman will ever truly know you."

For an instant, I thought I saw hunger, even yearning in his dark eyes as he stared down at me. Then the expression shuttered, leaving me to decide I'd imagined it. But even then, he continued to look at me, as if he couldn't look away.

"What are you staring at?" I put my hand to my messy ponytail, feeling suddenly self-conscious. "I must look a mess."

"You look…" His eyes slowly traced over my hand, up my arm, to my neck, to my lips. "You look like a woman who cares more about her baby than a fortune. Like a woman who works so hard and so well—for free—that she's beloved by the entire household staff. You look," he said softly, "like a woman who feels sympathy, even for the coldhearted creature who tried to destroy her."

"Are you—complimenting me?"

He gave a low laugh. "If you're not sure, I must be losing my touch."

I flushed. Turning away, I took a deep breath. And changed the subject. "Thank you for bringing me back to London. For these." I motioned toward the photo albums. "And for giving me the chance to finally ask Claudie something I've wanted to know all my life. I always wondered why nothing I did was good enough to make her love me." I looked out the window at the passing shops of Kensington High Street. "Now I know."

Silence fell.

"Are you all right?" he asked.

I nodded over the lump in my throat.

"I know how it feels," he said in a low voice, "to be alone."

"You?" I looked at him sharply, then gave a disbelieving snort. "No, you don't."

His dark eyes were veiled. "When I was young, I was good friends with…our housekeeper's son. We were only six months apart in age, and we studied under the same governess. Friend? He was more like a brother to me," he said softly. "People said we looked so much alike, acted so much alike, we could have been twins."

"Are you still friends?"

He blinked, focusing on me, and his jaw tightened. "He died in the same crash that took the duke, the duchess. The housekeeper. Twenty-three years ago."

"They all died in the same crash?" I said, horrified.

He looked down. "I was the only one to survive."

I thought of a young boy being the only survivor of a car accident that took his parents, his best friend. That made him a duke at the tender age of twelve. I couldn't even imagine the loneliness. The pain. Reaching out, I took his hand and whispered, "I'm sorry."

Alejandro drew away. "It was a long time ago." I saw tension in his jaw, heard it in his voice. "But I do know how it feels."

I swallowed, feeling guilty, and embarrassed, too, for all my complaining when he'd suffered worse, and in silence. "What was his name? Your friend?"

He stared at me, then his lips lifted slightly. "Miguel."

"Oh." I gave a shy smile. "So that's why you don't mind that I named our baby Miguel—"

"No." He seemed to hide his own private smile. "I don't mind at all."

I frowned, looking at him more closely.

His expression shuttered, and his dark eyebrows came down into a scowl. "His surname, however…"

I sighed. "I thought you might want to change that. But don't worry." I gave an awkward smile. "I won't hold you to your marriage proposal."

His eyes were dark and intense. "What if I want you to hold me to it?"

My lips parted in shock.

"What?" I said faintly.

His dark eyes challenged mine. "What if I want you to marry me?"

"You don't want to get married. You went on and on about all the women who tried to drag you to the altar. I'm not one of them!"

"I know that now." Leaning his arm across the baby seat,

he cupped my cheek. "But for our son's sake, I'm starting to think you and I should be…together."

"Why?"

"Why not?" He gave a sensual smile. "As you said, I already broke one rule. Why not break the other?"

"But what has changed?"

"I'm starting to think…perhaps I can trust you." His eyes met mine. "And I can't forget how it felt to have you in my bed."

Something changed in the air between us. Something primal, dangerous. I felt the warmth of his palm against my skin and held my breath. As the limo drove through the streets of London, memories crackled through me like fire.

I remembered the night we'd conceived Miguel, and all the other hot days of summer, when I'd surrendered to him, body and soul. I trembled, feeling him so close in the backseat of the limo, on the other side of our baby. Every inch of my skin suddenly remembered the hot stroke of Alejandro's fingertips. My mouth was tingling, aching….

"That's not a good reason to marry someone. Especially for you. If I said yes, you'd regret it. You'd blame me. Claim that I'd only done it to be a rich duchess."

He slowly shook his head. "I think," he said quietly, "you might be the one woman who truly doesn't care about that. And it would be best for our son. So what is your answer?"

My answer?

I remembered the darkness I'd fallen into the last time Alejandro wanted me—then stopped wanting me. I'd never let myself be vulnerable to him ever again. I couldn't. He'd almost destroyed me once. I could never live through that again.

Sooner or later…he'll take your child and toss you in the gutter, like you deserve.

I couldn't give him control over me, ever again. I

couldn't be tempted. My only hope was to get away. My only hope was...

Oh, heaven...what time was it?

"I need to..." As I saw the time on the dashboard of the limo, my heart nearly burst in panic. "Stop the car!" I leaned forward desperately toward the driver. "Let me out!"

Looking confused, Dowell pulled over on the side of the busy road.

"What are you doing?" Alejandro demanded, looking at me as if I was crazy. I felt crazy.

I unbuckled our baby, who'd just stopped crying and was looking drowsy. "Miguel needs a walk to help him sleep...."

"Is that a joke?"

I didn't answer. Cradling our baby, I stepped out on the sidewalk in front of Kensington Palace, and started running into the park, toward the playground. Toward Edward.

CHAPTER THREE

THE PRINCESS DIANA PLAYGROUND was in the corner of Kensington Gardens, just north of the palace. It was still early, and the playground had just opened, but in the midst of August holidays it was already starting to fill with children of every age, laughing and whooping as they raced toward the teepees and leaped on the ropes of the life-size pirate ship. It was a magical place, as you might expect of a children's playground, near a palace, based around a Peter Pan theme and named after a lost princess.

But I was here desperate for a different kind of magic. Protection.

Edward St. Cyr had protected me more than once. We'd first properly met three years earlier, when I'd been walking up from the Tube late at night and I'd passed a group of rowdy teenagers on Kensington High Street. I'd been weighed down with groceries, and tried to keep my head down as they passed. But some of the boys had followed me up the dark street, taunting me crudely. As one started to knock the grocery bags out of my hand, there'd been a flash of headlights on the street and the slam of a car door, and suddenly a tall man in a dark coat was there, his face a threatening scowl, and the young men who'd scared me fled like rabbits into the snow. Then he'd turned to me.

"Are you all right, miss…?" Then his expression had

changed. "But wait. I know you. You're Claudie Carlisle's cousin."

"Yes, I…"

"You're all right now." He'd gently taken my trembling hand. "I'm Edward St. Cyr. I live a few streets from here. May I give you a ride home?"

"No, I couldn't possibly. I…"

"I wouldn't mind a walk myself," he said briskly, and with a nod to the driver of his Rolls-Royce, he'd insisted on walking me home, though it took ten minutes.

"Thank you," I'd said at the door. "I never meant to impose…."

"You didn't." He'd paused. "I remember what it's like to feel alone and afraid. Will you let me check on you in the morning?"

I'd shaken my head. "It's truly not necessary."

"But you must." He'd lifted a dark eyebrow. "If for no other reason than it will annoy your cousin, whom I've despised for years. I insist."

Now, as I looked out at Kensington Gardens in the distance, I saw the paths where we'd once walked together, he and I. He'd been kind to me. We'd been—friends.

Or had we? Had he always wanted more?

I'm tired of waiting for you to forget that Spanish bastard. It's time for you to belong to me.

I shivered. When we left Mexico yesterday, I had been prepared to make any sacrifice to save my baby from Alejandro. Even if the price would have been going to bed with a man I did not love.

But now I was starting to wonder if that was truly necessary. Perhaps Alejandro was not entirely the heartless monster I'd once feared him to be….

"You shouldn't have run."

Hearing Alejandro's dark voice behind me, I whirled around. "How did you catch up so fast?"

He was scowling. "Did you think I'd let you disappear with Miguel?"

"I didn't disappear. I…"

"Had some kind of baby emergency?" He folded his arms. "You ran for a reason. And we both know what it is."

Could he have somehow found out about Edward St. Cyr? The two men were slightly acquainted. And far from being friends. I didn't think he would take it well. I bit my lip, breathing, "I…"

"You panicked because I asked you to marry me," he accused.

Oh. I exhaled. "We both know you weren't serious."

"We both know I was."

"You won't be, once you have a chance to think about it. You don't want to get married. You said so a million times."

"I never intended to have a child, either," he pointed out, "so there was no reason to marry. But now… You heard what Claudie said. Marrying you will make clear to the whole world that he's my son. That he's my heir. Right or wrong," he said tightly.

Right or wrong? Meaning I wasn't good enough? That Miguel wasn't? My eyes narrowed. "I don't love you."

"I can live with that," he said sardonically. "We both love our son. That is the only love that matters."

"You're wrong," I said stubbornly. "My parents loved me, but they also loved each other, till the day they died. I remember how they looked at each other…."

"Most people are not so fortunate," he said harshly. "I've spent a year pursuing you, Lena. I don't want to fight over custody now. I don't want to worry, anytime you take him for a walk, that you might try to run away with him. I want this matter settled between us, once and for all."

Ah. Now we were getting down to it. "You mean I should give you total control over me, body and soul, so you can avoid the inconvenience of a custody battle?" I said incredulously, then shook my head. "This idea of marriage is just a momentary madness with you—it will pass…."

My voice trailed off as I saw Hildy on the edge of the playground, frantically signaling.

Alejandro frowned. "What is it?" He started to turn his head. "What are you…"

"On second thought, let me think it over," I said quickly. Touching his arm, I gave him a weak smile. "So much has happened since yesterday. Maybe I'm too exhausted to think straight." I pointed toward the outdoor café at the front of the playground. "Could you…please…get me some coffee?"

Alejandro's dark gaze flickered over my bedraggled dress, the dark circles under my eyes. "Of course, *querida*," he murmured courteously. Turning away, he started toward the outdoor café.

The instant he was gone, I rushed to meet Hildy.

"Where's Edward?" I said desperately.

She was already shaking her head. "Mr. St. Cyr wasn't home. They said he's in Tokyo."

Of all the bad luck! "Can I borrow your phone?"

"Yes…." She reached into her pocket, then looked up, her mouth a round *O*. "I didn't bring it! It's still at home!"

Alejandro was already handing over money at the café. I saw him pick up two coffees from the counter. No time.

My shoulders fell. "Thanks anyway. You'd better go."

"Good luck, miss…."

Defeated, I looked out across the green park, deep emerald beneath the lowering gray London sky. I suddenly wondered what the weather was like in Spain. Warm. Sunny. Blue skies. With the chance of a hot, seductive Spaniard demanding that I share his bed.

No! I couldn't let myself think about it! Just sharing custody of Miguel would be bad enough. I would never, ever be Alejandro's lover! And certainly not his wife!

"Here." Alejandro handed me a white paper cup that warmed my hands. The coffee smelled like heaven. I took a sip, then sighed with appreciation as I felt the heat melt me from the inside. It was sweet, and creamy.

"You remembered how I liked it," I said in surprise.

He took a sip of his own black coffee, and gave a wicked grin. "That's how all women like it."

"That's not true!"

He shrugged. "It's mostly true. Cream and sugar will calm a woman down every time."

I glared at him. "You are such a—"

"A heartless bastard?" He paused, then tilted his head. "Do you still think I'll be such a disaster as a father?"

He sounded wistful, even—hurt? No. Impossible. A man like Alejandro had no heart to injure. But still, guilt rose in me, making my cheeks burn. "Maybe you're not *completely* evil." I looked down at the cup. "You did get my coffee right. Even though you're completely wrong with your stereotype about women liking cream and sugar."

"Obviously," he agreed. He tilted his head. "Your arms must be getting tired from holding Miguel all this time."

"A bit," I admitted sheepishly. "He's starting to get too heavy to carry like this for long."

Finishing off his coffee, he threw the empty cup in the trash and reached out. "Give him to me."

I hesitated, then handed him over. I watched anxiously, but Alejandro was careful, holding him, even turning Miguel around so he could see the world around him. Alejandro caught my look. "How am I doing?"

"Not bad," I said grudgingly.

"Would you care to walk?" He lifted a dark eyebrow. "Since he needed a walk so badly that you almost jumped out of a moving car. This taking babies on walks must be a serious business. Or else you had some other reason for coming here that you don't want me to know about."

I looked at him sharply. Did he know something? Or was he just fishing?

He gave me a bland smile.

I shrugged. "It was what you said. Pure panic at your marriage proposal." I took a sip of coffee. "Kind of like how you reacted last year when I told you I loved you. Instant disappearance." For a moment, we stared at each other. Then I turned away. "Yes. Let's walk."

The rain had eased up, and though gray skies were hovering, eager children of all ages, speaking many different languages, were now playing everywhere as we strolled past the pirate ship.

"So what is your answer?" he said casually, as if he'd been asking me out for a movie.

"About what?"

He looked at me.

"Oh." I licked my lips. "That."

"That."

"Be serious."

"I'm trying to be. But I've never asked any woman to marry me before. I'm starting to think I must be doing it wrong. Do I need to get down on one knee?"

"Don't you dare."

"Then what is it?"

I'm afraid you'd make me love you again. The cold knot near my heart, which had started to warm on the edges, returned to ice. "Come on," I mumbled, looking at the ground. "We both know that I'm not exactly duchess material."

"Are you trying to let me down gently?" he demanded. He stopped, leaning our baby against his hip as he looked at me. "Is there someone else? Perhaps the person who helped you flee London last year, and travel around the world?"

"It's not like that."

"When a man protects a woman," he said grimly, "it is exactly like that."

"How do you know it's a man?"

"By looking at your face," he said softly. "Right now."

I looked away. My throat hurt as I took another sip of the rich, sweet coffee, watching all the mothers and fathers and smiling nannies hovering on the edge of their children's delighted play. Some of them looked back at me. They probably imagined we were a family, too.

But we weren't.

I would have given anything if Alejandro could have been a man I could trust with my heart. A regular guy, a hardworking, loving man, who could have been my real partner. Instead of a selfish playboy duke who didn't know the meaning of love, and if married would plainly expect me to remain a dutiful wife imprisoned in his castle, raising our child, while he enjoyed himself elsewhere. Why shouldn't he? If love didn't exist, I could only imagine what he thought of fidelity.

"Why did you seduce me, Alejandro?" I blurted out.

He blinked. "What?"

My voice trembled as I looked up at him. "If you weren't trying to get me pregnant to provide an heir for you and Claudie, why did you seduce me? Why did you even notice me?"

"I don't understand."

"Are you really going to make me spell it out? Fine. You're—you—" I waved my half-full coffee toward him "—and I'm..." I indicated my white dress I'd worn for thirty-six hours now, wrinkled and possibly stained with baby sick I didn't know about, and I shivered in the cool morning air. "I believed Claudie's story last year because, for the first time, everything made sense. There was no other reason for you to... I mean, why else would a man

like you, who could have any woman in the world, choose
a woman like…"

Reaching out his hand, he cupped my cheek. "Because I
wanted you, Lena. Pure and simple. I wanted you." Looking down at me, he said in a low voice, "I've never stopped
wanting you."

My lips parted. I trembled, fighting the desire to lean
into his touch. The paper cup fell from my hand, splashing coffee across the grass. But I barely noticed. Craning
back my head, I blinked back tears as I whispered, "Then
why did you break up with me like that, so coldly and completely? Just for telling you I loved you?"

Alejandro stared at me, then dropped his hand. "Because
I didn't want to lead you on. I'd promised myself I'd never
have either wife or child…."

"But why?" I said, bewildered. "Why wouldn't you want
those things? You're the last of your line, aren't you? If
you died without an heir…you would be the last Duke of
Alzacar."

"That was my intention," he said grimly.

"But why?"

"It doesn't matter anymore." He looked down at Miguel
in his arms. "Fate chose differently. I have a son." His dark
eyes blazed at me, filled with heat and anger and something
else…something I couldn't understand. "And I will protect
his future. Right or wrong."

"You keep saying *right or wrong*. What is wrong about
it?" I narrowed my eyes. "If you're trying to imply that he's
not good enough—"

"Of course not," he bit out.

"Then it's me—"

He shook his head impatiently, his jaw tight. "I'm talking about me."

The great Duque de Alzacar, admitting some kind of
fault? I blinked. I breathed, "I don't understand…."

"What is there to understand?" he said evasively. "Now that I am a parent, my priorities have changed. Wasn't it the same for you, when Miguel was born?"

I hesitated. It was true what he said, but I still had the sense he was hiding something from me. "Yes-s...."

"We have a child. So we will do what is best for him. We will marry."

"You didn't want to marry me in Mexico."

"That was when I thought you were a liar, a thief and probably a gold digger. Now my opinion of you has improved."

"Thanks," I said wryly.

"Why are you fighting me? Unless—" He gave me a sharp, searching gaze. "Are you in love with someone else?"

The image of Edward flashed in front of my eyes. I wondered if Alejandro would still keep his improved opinion of me if he knew I'd been living in another man's house. It would look sordid, even if the truth had been so innocent. At least—innocent on my side. Swallowing, I looked away.

"I'm not in love with anyone." My voice was barely audible over the noisy children at play.

His shoulders relaxed imperceptibly. "Then why not marry me?" His tone turned almost playful. "You really should consider it for the jewels alone...."

I gave a rueful laugh, then looked at him. "I'd never fit into your world, Alejandro. If I took you at your word and became your wife, we'd both be miserable."

"I wouldn't be."

I shook my head. "Your expectations of marriage are lower than mine. It would never work. I want—" I looked down as my cheeks turned hot "—to be loved. I want what my parents had."

Alejandro abruptly stopped. We were in the far back of the playground now, in a quiet overgrown place of bushes and trees. "But what about our son? Doesn't he have some rights, as well? Doesn't he deserve a stable home?"

"You mean a cold, drafty castle?"

"It's neither drafty nor cold." He set his jaw. "I want my son, my heir, to live in Spain. To know his people. His family."

I frowned at him. "I thought you had no family."

"My grandmother who raised me. All the people on my estate. They are like family to me. Don't you think he deserves to know them, and they should know him? Shouldn't he know his country? Where else would you take him— back to Mexico?"

"I loved it there!" I said, stung.

"We will buy a vacation house there," he said impatiently. "But his home is with his land. With his people. With his parents. You of all people," he said softly, "know what it means to have a happy, settled childhood, surrounded by love."

I sucked in my breath. I felt myself wavering. Of course I wanted all those things for my son.

"You'll be a duchess, honored, wealthy beyond imagining."

"I'd be the poor stupid wife sitting at home in the castle," I whispered, hardly daring to meet his gaze, "while you were out having a good time with other, more glamorous women…."

His dark eyes narrowed. "I have many faults, but disloyalty is not one of them. Still, I can understand why you'd immediately think of cheating. Tell me—" he moved closer, his sardonic gaze sweeping over me "—did you enjoy having the use of Edward St. Cyr's house? His jet?"

My eyes went wide. My mouth suddenly went dry.

"How did you find out?" I said weakly.

"Before my jet left Mexico, I told my investigators to dig into the layer of the shell company that owned the house in

San Miguel. If it wasn't Claudie who helped you," he said grimly, "I intended to find out who it really was."

Well. That explained why he'd stopped asking. "Why have you pretended all day you didn't know?"

His handsome face looked chiseled and hard as marble beneath the gray sky. "I wanted to give you the chance to tell me."

"A test?" I whispered.

"If you like." His eyes glittered. "Women always find the quality of danger so attractive. Until they find out what *danger* really means. Tell me. Did you enjoy using St. Cyr's possessions? His money? His jet? How about his bed? Did you enjoy sharing that?"

"I never shared his bed!" I tried not to remember the husky sound of Edward's voice. *It's time for you to belong to me.* Or the way he'd flinched at my reaction—an incredulous, unwilling laugh. He'd taken a deep breath. *You'll see,* he'd whispered, then turned and left. Pushing the memory away, I lifted my chin. "We've never even kissed!"

"I see." Lifting an eyebrow, Alejandro said scornfully, "He helped you out of the goodness of his heart."

That might be pushing it. I bit my lip. "Um…yes?"

"Is that a statement or a question?"

"He's a friend to me," I whispered. "Just a friend."

Alejandro looked at me more closely. "But he wants more, doesn't he?" The sweep of his dark lashes left a shadow against his olive skin, his taut cheekbones, as he looked down at our baby in his arms. After all this time, he still carried Miguel as if he were no weight at all. He said in a low voice, "I won't let my son keep such company. Because I, at least, have clear eyes about what *danger* means."

"And I understand at last," I choked out, "why you suddenly want to marry me."

He narrowed his eyes at me. "Lena—"

"You say he is dangerous? Maybe he is. But if it weren't

for Edward St. Cyr, I don't think I could have survived the darkness and fear of the past year. He was there for me when you deserted me. When you left me pregnant and alone and afraid."

His face turned white, then red. "If you'd given me the chance—"

"I did give you a chance. You never called me back." I took a deep breath. "I know now you weren't the monster I thought you were. But I'll never be able to trust you like I did. It's lost. Along with the way I loved you."

Silence fell, the only sound the children playing on the other side of the trees. I heard their shrieks of joy.

When Alejandro spoke, his voice was low, even grim. "Love me or not, trust me or not, but you will marry me. Miguel will have a stable family. A real home."

I shook my head. He moved closer.

"You promised to come to Spain, Lena," he said. "You gave your word."

I threw him a panicked glance. "That was when—"

"Ah. You hoped you could break your promise, didn't you? Perhaps with St. Cyr's help?"

My silence spoke volumes. His dark eyes hardened. "You gave me your word that if I brought you to London, you would come with me to Spain."

He was right. I had. Now, I felt so alone and forlorn. Alejandro was starting to wear me down. To break my will. To remind me of a promise I'd never wanted to keep.

"It will only lead to misery," I whispered.

"Wherever it leads," he said softly, "whatever we'd once planned for our lives…you are part of my family now."

"Your family. You mean your grandmother?" I shivered, imagining a coldly imperious grande dame in pearls and head-to-toe vintage Chanel. A little like my own grandmother, in fact. "She will hate me. She'll never think I'm good enough."

He gave a low laugh. "You think you know what to expect? A cold, proud dowager in a cold, drafty castle?"

"Am I wrong?"

"My grandmother was born in the United States. In Idaho. The daughter of Basque sheep ranchers."

"Idaho?" My mouth fell open. "How did she…?"

"How did she end up married to my grandfather? It is an interesting story. Perhaps you can ask her when you meet her." His lips twisted grimly. "Unless you intend to break your promise, and refuse to go to Spain after all."

I swallowed, afraid of what it would mean to go to his castle. Surrounded by his family and friends. Surrounded by his *power*. How long could I resist his marriage demand then?

"Enough. You always spend too long in your mind, going back and forth on decisions that have already been made. End it now." Reaching into his pocket, Alejandro pulled out a phone and dialed a number. He pushed it into my hand. "It's ringing."

"What?" I stammered, staring down at the phone. "Whom did you call?"

"My grandmother. If you are breaking your promise to me, if you are truly not willing to bring Miguel to Spain to meet her, tell her now."

"Me? I can't talk to your grandmother!"

"No. *I* can't," he said coldly, "because I love her. *You* have no feelings for her whatsoever, so you should have no trouble being cruel."

"You think I'm cruel?" I whispered as the phone rang.

His eyes met mine. "Tell her she has a great-grandchild. Introduce yourself. Tell her I've asked you to marry me. Go on."

I stared at him numbly, then heard a tremulous voice at the other end of the line.

"*¿Hola?* Alejandro?"

It was a warm, sweet, kindly voice, the sort of voice that a grandmother would have in a movie, the grandmother who bakes cookies and is plump and white-haired and gives you hugs and tells you to eat more pie—or in this case, more paella?—because food is love, and she loves you so much that you're her whole existence, her light, her star. It was the type of voice I had not heard since my parents had died.

"Alejandro?" The woman sounded worried now. "Are you there?"

"It's not Alejandro," I replied, my voice unsteady. "But he asked me to call you. I'm a…friend."

"A friend?" The sweet tremulous voice gasped, her accent definitely American. "Has he fallen sick? Was he in an accident?"

"No, he's fine…."

"If he were fine, he'd be calling me himself, as he always does." A sob choked her voice. "You're trying to break it to me gently. But you can't. First I lost my children, then my…" Her voice broke. "Alejandro was all I had left. I always knew I would lose him someday. That sooner or later—" another sob "—fate would catch up with me and…"

"Oh, for heaven's sake!" I cried in exasperation. "Alejandro's fine! He's standing right by me!"

She sucked in her breath. Her tone changed, became curious. "Then why are you calling me on his phone?"

"He…wanted me to tell you the happy news." Glaring at Alejandro, I kept my voice gentle as I said, "You're a great-grandmother."

"A—" her voice ended in a gasp. A happy gasp. "Alejandro has a child?"

"We have a five-month-old son. I'm the baby's mother."

"You're American? Canadian?"

"Born in Brooklyn."

"Why didn't he tell me before? What's your name? Have we met?" She didn't seem like the snooty duchess I'd imagined. She continued eagerly, "Did you elope? Oh, I'll never forgive Alejandro for getting married without me—"

"He didn't tell you because—well, he wasn't sure about it. For your other question, we're not married." I gritted my teeth. "And we have no plans to be."

"You have no—" She cut herself off with an intake of breath. Then changing the subject with forced cheer, she said, "So when can I meet my great-grandson? I can hardly wait to tell my friends you're coming to live in the castle. The pitter-patter of little feet at Rohares Castle at last!"

"I'm sorry. We're not going to live in Spain."

"Oh." I heard the soft whoosh of her whimper. "That's... all right." She took a deep breath. "So when are you coming to visit so I can meet him?"

I bit my lip. "I don't know if we can...."

"I understand," she sniffled. "It's fine. Just send me a Christmas card with the baby's picture, and...it's fine. I've had a good life. I don't need to meet my only great-grandchild...."

My own fear of spending time with Alejandro, of allowing him more power over me, suddenly felt small and selfish compared with letting her meet Miguel—and even more important, allowing my son to have the family I myself had yearned for. What did I have, a heart of stone?

"All right." With a sigh, I accepted the inevitable. "We'll come to Spain in the next day or two. Just for a visit, mind!"

But even with that warning, her cries of joy exploded from the phone. I held it away from my ear, glaring all the while at Alejandro. "I'll let you talk to Alejandro," I told her, then covering the mouthpiece, I handed him the phone and grumbled, "I hate you."

"No, you don't." He took it from my hand, looking down at me seriously. "I'll win your trust, Lena. And then..."

"Then?"

He gave me a sensual smile. "You'll be my wife within the week."

There are many different kinds of seduction.

There's the traditional kind, with flowers, chocolates, dinner by candlelight. That's the way Alejandro had seduced me last summer. He called the Kensington mansion, asked for me, invited me to dinner. He showed up at the door dressed in a tux, his arms full of roses—to Claudie's rage—and greeted me with a chaste kiss on the cheek.

"You look beautiful," he'd murmured, and took me to the best restaurant in London. He asked me questions, listened aptly and physically grew closer and closer, with the innocent touch of his hand, the casual brush of his body against mine. He held my hand across the dinner table in the candlelight, in full view of the other patrons, looking at me with deep soulful eyes, as if no other woman had ever existed. Afterward, he took me to a club. We danced, and he pulled me into his arms, against his hard, powerful body. Closer. Closer still, until my heart was in my throat and I started to feel dizzy. In the middle of the dance floor, he lowered his head and kissed me for the first time.

It was my first kiss, and as I closed my eyes I felt the whole world whirling around me. Around us.

When he finally pulled away, he whispered against my skin, "I want you." I'd trembled, my heart beating violently, like a deer in a wolf's jaws. He'd looked down at me and smiled. Then took me back to his rooftop terrace suite at the Dorchester Hotel.

There had been no question of resistance. I was a virgin in the hands of a master. He'd had me from the moment he kissed me. From the moment he showed up at my door in a sleek tuxedo, with his arms full of roses, and told me he wanted me in his low, husky voice. He'd had me from the moment he'd seared me with the intensity of his full attention.

That was the traditional way of seduction. It had worked once, worked with utterly ruthless efficiency against my unprepared heart. But I knew the moves now—that is to say, I knew how they ended. With pleasure that was all too brief, and agony that was all too long.

But there are many different kinds of seduction.

Alejandro had decided we wouldn't leave immediately for Madrid, but would spend one night in London, resting at his usual suite of rooms at the Dorchester. He told me it was because the baby and I both looked tired. I was immediately suspicious, but as we left the park, he did not try to kiss me. Even after we'd arrived at the luxurious hotel, he did not look deeply into my eyes and tell me I was the most beautiful woman on earth, or pull me out onto the rooftop terrace, overlooking Hyde Park and all the wide gray sky, to take me in his arms.

Instead, he just ordered us lunch via room service, then afterward, he smiled at me. "We need to go shopping."

I frowned at him, suspecting a trick. "No, we don't."

"We do need a stroller," he said innocently. "A pushcart. For the baby."

I could hardly argue with that, since we'd left the umbrella stroller back in San Miguel. "Fine," I grumbled. "A stroller. That's it."

"You're very boring."

"I'm broke."

"I'm not."

"Lucky you."

"I can buy you things, you know."

"I don't want you to."

"Why?"

I set my jaw. "I'm afraid what they'd cost me."

He just answered with an innocent smile, and had his

driver take us to the best shops in Knightsbridge, Mayfair and Sloane Street. He bought the most expensive pushcart he could find for Miguel, then pushed it himself, leaving the bodyguards trailing behind us to hold only shopping bags full of clothes and toys for the baby.

"You said just a stroller!"

"Surely you wouldn't begrudge me the chance to buy a few small items for my son?"

"No," I sighed. But Alejandro kept pushing the boundaries. All the bodyguards who trailed us were soon weighed down with shopping bags.

"Now we must get you some clothes, as well," Alejandro said, smiling as he caught me looking wistfully at the lovely, expensive dresses. I jumped, then blushed guiltily.

"No. Absolutely not."

"It's the least I can do," Alejandro replied firmly, "considering it was because of me that you lost your inheritance."

"That wasn't your fault..." I protested. He looked down at me with his big, dark, Spanish eyes.

"Please let me do this, *querida*. I must," he said softly. "Such a small thing. You cannot deny me my desire."

I shivered. That was exactly what I was afraid of. That if I couldn't deny him this, I wouldn't be able to deny him anything. And soon I'd be putty in his hands again, like a spaniel waiting for her master with slippers in her mouth.

I'd end up married to a man who didn't love me. Who would ignore me. And I'd spend the rest of my life like a ghost, haunting his stupid castle.

Wordlessly, I shook my head. He sighed, looking sad.

I was proud of myself for sticking to my guns. But as we walked through the expensive shops, Alejandro saw me looking at a pretty dress a second too long. He gave one of his bodyguards a glance, and the man snatched it up in my size.

"What!" I exclaimed. "No. I don't want that!"

"Too bad," he said smugly. "I just bought it for you."

Irritated, I tried to foil Alejandro's plan by carefully *not* looking at any of the beautiful clothes, shoes or bags as we walked through the luxury department store and designer boutiques. But that didn't work, either. He simply started picking things out for me, items far more expensive and flashy than I would have picked out for myself. Instead of the black leather quilted handbag I might have chosen, I found myself suddenly the owner of a handbag in crocodile skin with fourteen-karat-gold fittings and diamonds woven into the chain.

"I can't wear that!" I protested. "I'd look a proper fool!"

He grinned. "If you don't like me choosing for you, you have to tell me what you want."

So I did. I had no choice.

"Dirty blackmailer," I grumbled as I picked out a simple cotton sweater from Prada, but his smile only widened.

The salespeople, sensing blood in the water, left their previous customers to follow eagerly in our wake. The size of our entourage quickly exploded, with salespeople, bodyguards, Alejandro, me and our baby in a stroller so expensive that it, too, might as well have been made of rare leathers and solid gold. Other people turned their heads to watch as we went by, their eyes big as they whispered to each other beneath their hands.

"I feel conspicuous," I complained to Alejandro.

"You deserve to be looked at," he said. "You deserve everyone's attention."

I was relieved to return to his suite of rooms at the Dorchester, even though it was so fancy, the same suite Elizabeth Taylor had once lived in. I was happy to be alone with him.

And yet not happy.

It took a long time for the bodyguards to bring up all the packages. Even with help from the hotel staff.

"I didn't realize we bought so much," I said, blushing.

Alejandro gave a low laugh as he tipped the staff then turned back. "You hardly bought anything. I would have given you far more." He looked down at me. Running his hand beneath my jaw, he said softly, "I want to give you more."

We stood together, alone in the living room of the suite, and I held my breath. Praying he wouldn't kiss me. Wishing desperately that he would.

But with a low laugh, he released me. "Are you hungry?"

After I fed Miguel and tucked him to bed in the second bedroom, we had an early dinner in the dining room, beneath a crystal chandelier, on an elegant table that would seat eight, with a view not just of London, but of the exact place where, last summer, he'd pressed me against the silver wallpaper and made love to me, hot and fast and fierce against the wall.

All through dinner, I tried not to look at that wall. Or think about the bed next door.

I told myself he wasn't trying to seduce me. Maybe he wasn't. Maybe it was just my delusion, reading desire in his dark, hot glances. It had to be me. He wouldn't actually be intending to...

Alejandro suddenly smiled at me. "You are tired. It has been a long day for you."

"All that shopping," I grumbled. He grinned, taking an innocent sip of his after-dinner coffee.

"I meant before that. Mexico. Claudie. Your sleepless night on the plane..."

"Oh." I yawned, as if on cue. "I am a little tired."

"So go take some time for yourself. Take a nap. A shower. Go to bed. I will take over."

"Take over?"

"With Miguel." As I blinked at him in confusion, he lifted a dark eyebrow and added mildly, "Surely you can trust me that far—as far as the next room? If there is any problem, I will wake you. But there won't be. Go rest."

I took a long, hot shower, and it was heaven. Putting on a soft new nightgown straight from the designer bag, I fell into the large bed, knowing that someone else was watching our child as I slept, and I wasn't on call. That was the most deliciously luxurious thing of all.

When I woke, early-morning sunlight was streaking across the large bed, where I'd clearly slept alone. Looking at the clock, I saw to my shock I'd slept twelve hours straight—my best night's sleep in a year. I stretched in bed, yawning, feeling fantastic. Feeling grateful. Alejandro...

Alejandro!

He couldn't possibly have stayed up all night with the baby! He must have left. Jumping out of bed in panic, I flung open the bedroom door, terrified that Alejandro had spirited away our baby and left me behind.

But Alejandro was in the living room, walking our baby back and forth, singing a Spanish song in his low, deep voice, as Miguel's eyes grew heavy. Then Alejandro saw me, and he gave me a brilliant smile, even though his eyes, too, looked tired.

"*Buenos días, querida.* Did you sleep?"

"Beautifully," I said, running my hands through my hair, suddenly self-conscious of my nightgown, which in this bright morning light looked like a slinky silk negligee. I tried to casually cover the outline of my breasts with my arms. "And you?"

"Ah," he said, smiling tenderly down at his son. "For us, it is still a work in progress. But by the time we are on the plane to Madrid, after breakfast, I think our little man will sleep. He's worn himself out, haven't you?"

I stared at the two of them together, the strong-shouldered

Spaniard holding his tiny son so lovingly, with such infinite care and patience, though he'd clearly kept Alejandro up most of the night.

Miguel looked up with big eyes at his father. They had the same face, though one was smaller and chubby, the other larger and chiseled at the cheekbones and jaw. But I could not deny the look of love that glowed from Alejandro's eyes as he looked into the face of his son.

I'd been wrong, I realized. Alejandro did know how to love.

He just didn't know how to love *me*.

Turning back, Alejandro gave me a big grin, filled with joy and pride. Our eyes locked.

The smile slowly slid from his face. I felt his gaze from my head to my toes and everywhere in between. His soulful dark eyes seemed to last forever, like those starlit summer nights.

I looked at Alejandro in this moment, and I was suddenly afraid. Seeing him as a father, as a true partner in caring for the tiny person I loved so much, I trembled.

I could handle his gifts. I might even be able to handle the sensual awareness that electrified the air between us. I could keep my heart on ice. I could resist.

But this?

There are many different kinds of seduction. Some are of the body. Some are of the mind.

But others, the most powerful, are of the heart.

CHAPTER FOUR

I'M NOT GOING to lie. A private jet makes travel easier. Especially with a baby. We had a quick flight from London to Madrid. No standing in lines, no fighting for overhead space. And I felt much better than I had on the last flight. I was well slept, showered. My hair was brushed until it tumbled over my shoulders. I'd even put on a little mascara. Arriving in Madrid in my new soft pink blouse and form-fitting jeans, I felt almost pretty.

"Where's your diamond handbag?" Alejandro teased as we left the jet, going down the steps to the tarmac of the private airport, followed by his men carrying our luggage. "Don't you like it?"

I bit my lip. "Well…"

He put his hand on his heart, as if it had been stabbed with grief. "You don't!"

"Don't worry," I assured him. "I'll still use it. I was needing a new diaper bag."

He gave a low laugh, then sobered, his dark eyes resting on mine as he said softly, "I'll have to see if I can find some other gift to please you more."

I shivered at his glance, then looked out the window of the SUV. *He's not trying to seduce me,* I repeated silently to myself. *He's not. He's just trying to lure me into a loveless marriage of convenience—don't fall for it, don't…*

Madrid was beautiful, an elegant, formal city with its

nineteenth-century architecture, spreading regally across the banks of the Manzanares River. All the gray clouds of San Miguel and London seemed a million miles away. Here, the August sky was bright blue, and the Spanish sun burning hot.

Alejandro's driver took us to his penthouse apartment near the Prado, the bodyguards and luggage following in the car behind. We arrived at the flat, which took the entire top floor, and were answered at the door by a middle-aged woman who seemed far too young to be his grandmother. He quickly introduced her as his longtime housekeeper, the only paid staff at the penthouse, Mrs. Gutierrez, who lived on a floor below.

Alejandro walked us around the enormous apartment, with its stark contemporary furnishings and enormous windows overlooking the city. "What do you think?"

"It's beautiful," I said slowly, "but so cold. You can hardly tell anyone lives here." Shivering, I cuddled my warm baby close. "You must not stay here much."

He blinked. "More blunt honesty."

"Was I rude?"

"I can take it." He shifted his weight, then clawed back his thick, dark hair. I wondered what it would feel like to... No! I stopped the thought cold. Oblivious of my inner struggle, he continued with a sigh, "My company is headquartered here. I am in Madrid all the time."

"Oh," I said, looking at all the sharp edges of the furniture, all the glass and chrome. "Um. Well. It's very—masculine."

He lifted a dark eyebrow. "Perhaps it needs a woman's touch."

In my current frame of mind, I wondered if he was talking about more than his apartment. My cheeks went hot and I cleared my throat. "I'm surprised your grandmother isn't here. She sounded so keen to meet her great-grandson."

"You'll meet her tomorrow. I have an event tonight in Madrid, and Abuela doesn't like to leave her roses, or all the people who count on her at the castle."

"The castle?"

"Rohares, near Seville. Where the Dukes of Alzacar have lived for four hundred years."

"Cold and drafty," I sighed.

"Exactamente." He gave me a sideways glance, seeming to hide a smile. "I can hardly wait for you to see it."

"Yeah," I grumbled. "How many rooms?"

"I lose count," he said, and I couldn't tell if he was joking. But at least such a large building would create more space between us. Even this large penthouse felt too…close, when we were together. Every glance, every word, made me more attracted. It was dangerous.

As soon as his grandmother met the baby, I told myself firmly, I'd be out of this country and away from Alejandro. We'd come to some agreement over custody. Preferably one that involved Miguel living with me in Mexico.

Although it would be a shame to separate my son from a father who loved him, just because I was afraid of being hurt….

I pushed the thought away. "You said something about an event tonight?"

"A celebration—a ball, really. Hosted by my company. Starts in—" he glanced at his platinum watch and said calmly "—twenty minutes."

Thank heavens! I wouldn't have to spend the evening with him, trying desperately not to feel tempted! With real relief, I said, "Go and have a good time. We'll be fine. I'll tuck Miguel into bed and maybe read a book until…"

But he was already shaking his head. "Leave you alone with our son, giving you the opportunity to run away again? No."

"Why do you think I'd run away?"

"Why would I think you wouldn't?"

"You could post your bodyguards at the door," I suggested.

"You'd charm them and escape."

He thought I was charming? For an instant I felt flattered. Then I folded my arms. "You could just decide to trust me."

"I will trust you." He tilted his head, looking down at me with amusement. "As soon as you marry me."

"Never going to happen, and believe me, after this momentary madness—or whatever it is—passes, you'll thank me."

"Fine," he sighed, plunking down on the soft sofa in front of a wide-screen TV and a window with a view of the city. He reached for the remote control. "Shall we see if there are any good movies on tonight? Maybe order take-away?"

I stared at him, my lips parted. "You can't miss your own party."

He shrugged. "Yes. It's a pity. Especially since it was to celebrate my company's upcoming IPO on the stock exchange. But I can miss it to watch a TV movie with you. No problem."

"Are you crazy? You can't miss something like that. You're the host! If you don't even bother showing up, what do you think it will do to your stock price?"

"It's fine. Really." He shrugged. "I don't have a date to the ball anyway."

"You honestly expect me to believe you don't have a date—*you?*"

"You have to admit it's kind of your fault."

Now we were getting down to it.

"How is it my fault?" I said suspiciously.

Tilting his head, he looked at me from the sofa. "I *did* have a date for tonight." He stroked his chin thoughtfully.

"A beautiful Swedish swimsuit model, in fact. But when I called her yesterday and explained I wouldn't be picking her up in my jet because I'd just discovered a former mistress had my baby and I had to spend the day buying you presents instead of flying to Stockholm to collect her, well— for some reason, Elsa wasn't interested in flying coach to Madrid to be my date tonight."

I hid a laugh, tried to look mad. "Too bad for you. But it's really not my problem."

He nodded sagely. "You're scared."

"Scared? Of what?"

"Of spending time with me. You're scared you'll be overwhelmed with desire and say yes to everything, and wake up tomorrow morning, in my bed, with a ring on your finger."

In his *bed?* My mouth went dry.

"It's all right. I understand." He fluttered his dark eyelashes outrageously. "You don't trust yourself, because you want me so badly."

It was so true. "That's so not true!"

He lifted his eyebrows. "Then you'll be my date?"

I thought about the type of people I'd be likely to meet at his party. A bunch of wealthy, beautiful, *mean* people. Just like Claudie. "No, thanks."

"Why?" he demanded.

"The baby will wake up at midnight for a feeding…" I said weakly.

"I'll have you back by midnight. Via pumpkin coach if necessary."

"There's no one I can trust as his babysitter!"

"Mrs. Gutierrez raised four children, and has ten grandchildren. She's very trustworthy and experienced, and she's agreed to stay."

"You thought of everything," I grumbled.

"So say yes."

"I won't fit in with your friends, okay?"

"Always so afraid," he sighed. "Of me. Of them. Of your own shadow."

He was clearly taunting me, but I couldn't help but bristle. "Even if I wanted to go with you, it's too late. Your party starts in twenty minutes, and unless you bought a ball gown in London yesterday without me noticing, I have nothing to wear!"

Alejandro smiled. "Did I ever show you our bedroom?"

I shook my head with a scowl. "It's either yours or mine. Not *ours.*"

"That's what I meant," he said innocently. Walking ahead in the hallway, he pushed open a door.

The bedroom was enormous, with an amazing view of Madrid, but sparsely furnished, with only an expensive, masculine bed. And, incongruously, a crib beside it.

But when I looked closer at the bed, I saw a flash of pink. Coming closer, I gasped when I saw a pale pink gown, a delicious confection of flowers and silk, spread across his plain white bedspread. I picked it up with one hand, then dropped it when I saw the tag peeking at me. Oscar de la Renta.

A pumpkin coach, indeed! I whirled to face him. "You bought this yesterday. You always intended to bring me as your date tonight," I accused.

His lips were curved in a sensual smile, then his hands went up in mock surrender. "I admit it." Then he put down his hands, and his expression changed. His dark eyes became intent. Sensual. "I always get what I want," he said softly, searching my gaze. "And I don't give up. When something is difficult to possess, that only makes me want it more."

For a long heartbeat, we stared at each other in his bedroom.

Then I tossed my head, hoping hc couldn't see how my

body was trembling. "Fine. Have it your way. I'll come with you tonight, since it means so much to you. I'll do it for Miguel's sake, so your friends will know he wasn't just the result of some cheap one-night stand. But that's it."

His dark eyes burned into mine. "A cheap one-night stand? That is the last thing you were to me. You should know that by now."

A shiver went down my spine and through my soul. I straightened, locking my knees, and I handed him the baby. "I'll get dressed as quickly as I can."

Thirty minutes later, Alejandro helped me out of the limo, holding my hand as we walked up a red carpet, past the flashbulbs of the paparazzi.

"I thought your company was a metals and real estate conglomerate," I murmured beneath all of the attention.

"It is," he said innocently, "among other things. We recently bought a movie studio. Look." I followed his gaze to see a beautiful movie star whom I'd admired for years just ahead of us in a tight sequined gown. "That's the reason for the paparazzi."

"She is beautiful," I said.

He looked down at me. "You're more beautiful than her on your worst day. Even when you are wearing a dress like a sack and barely brush your hair."

I snorted, expecting mockery. "You are so full of—"

Then I saw his expression, the frank hunger in his eyes as he looked at me, and my mouth went dry.

"Come on," he said roughly. "The sooner we get this done, the sooner we can go home."

I licked my lips, tasting lipstick, which was foreign to me. But in this pale pink ball gown, I didn't feel like myself at all. I might as well have been wearing glass slippers....

Alejandro led me into a large ballroom, filled with people dancing and drinking champagne beneath enormous crystal chandeliers high overhead. I watched as, ten minutes after we arrived, he went to the elevated dais and made a short speech into a microphone, congratulating the staff of his company, and thanking all their investors and friends, which was met by a roar of applause. When he left the microphone, he returned to my side.

"Now the work is done," he whispered, nuzzling my ear. "Let's have some fun."

He took me out on the dance floor, and I trembled, remembering the last time he'd held me in his arms on a dance floor, the way he'd slowly seduced me, until I surrendered in my first kiss. Now, I felt his arms around me, and I shuddered from deep within, feeling his warmth and strength beneath the tuxedo, breathing in his cologne and the scent that was uniquely him. When the music ended after the first dance, I pulled away.

"I—I need some champagne," I said unsteadily.

"Of course," he said huskily, his dark eyes intent, as if he saw through me, every inch and pore, down to my heart and soul.

For the rest of the night, Alejandro was the perfect gentleman, solicitous, getting me champagne, even cheerfully introducing me to the acquaintances who quickly surrounded us.

One of his friends, a German tycoon of some kind, looked me over appreciatively. "Where did you keep this beautiful creature hidden, Your Excellency?"

"Yes, you should have introduced us," a handsome Japanese millionaire said.

"You sure you want this guy, Miss Carlisle?" An actor I recognized from a big summer movie, where he'd gotten revenge against aliens who blew up Paris, gave me a big shiny grin. "You haven't given the rest of us a chance yet."

I blushed. The whole night seemed unreal, as if I were playing a part, with my hair pulled back into a high ballerina bun, wearing the petal-pink ball gown with tiny flowers embroidered over it. Remembering the part I was to play, I glanced at Alejandro. "Sorry. I only want Alejandro."

His relief was palpable. He smiled back at me.

"Awww, so sweet," the movie star said, somewhat ironically. "Well. Whenever the romance is over, feel free to…"

"It's not a romance," a man said behind us. "It's extortion."

Turning, I sucked in my breath. A man stood behind us, dressed exactly like the others, in a sharp black tuxedo. The man I'd been so desperate to see—and yet, oddly, he seemed out of place here. Handsome. But malevolent.

"Edward," I breathed. "I thought you were in Tokyo—"

His eyes softened. "My staff called me. I was glad to hear you'd gone to London to see me. But not so glad to hear who was with you." He glared at Alejandro, his jaw tight, even as he continued to speak to me. "Are you all right?"

"Of course I'm all right," I said, suddenly nervous.

The two men were glaring at each other, both of them straining the size of the ballroom between their shoulders and masculine pride. I had a sudden dismaying flash of two predators, growling over the same female—or the same prey.

Alejandro's eyes narrowed, but with a swift glance at me, he politely put out his hand. "Edward St. Cyr. I know you by reputation, of course."

The words were courteous and cool. Edward took them as the insult they were no doubt intended. Without taking the offered hand, he bared his teeth in a smile. "How gracious of you to say so. I know of you not just from reputation, but also from more…personal sources." He looked down dismissively at Alejandro's hand. "It does seem a little…tacky?…that after dragging Lena to Europe, you'd force her to pose as your date."

"I didn't force her."

"Of course you did," he said roughly. "What is it, some

feeble attempt to project stability for the benefit of future shareholders? Or—no, don't tell me—some attempt to make her love you again?" Smiling his shark's smile, Edward held up his glass of champagne in salute. "You'd think destroying her once would be enough for you. But if anyone would be selfish enough to try for twice, it's you, Navaro."

No respectful *Your Excellency*. Just Alejandro's surname, tossed out with scorn. The entire group, including me, stared wide-eyed as Edward drank down the entire contents of his champagne glass. We looked at Alejandro.

He had dropped his hand, his eyelids now narrowed to slits. "Whatever you might have heard about me, it was a mistake." He glanced at me. "Lena now knows the truth."

Edward lifted an eyebrow. "Convinced her of that, have you?"

"What are you even doing here?" Alejandro's face hardened. "I don't recall sending you an invitation."

Setting his empty glass down on a nearby tray, Edward looked over the ballroom with a small smile. "I have plenty of friends. One was happy to bring me along."

"Who?"

"The Bulgarian ambassador." Edward turned back with lifted eyebrows and said mildly, "Surely you're not going to throw us out and risk an international incident?"

Alejandro looked at a gray-haired, distinguished-looking man across the ballroom, who appeared deep in conversation with someone I recognized from newspaper photos, who'd recently won the Nobel Peace Prize. He turned back with gritted teeth. "What do you want, St. Cyr?"

"I want Lena, since she's asked for me," he said softly. He turned to me, holding out his arm. "Shall we go, love?"

I heard a low, almost barbaric growl, and suddenly Alejandro was in front of me, blocking me from Edward's outstretched arm.

"So it's like that, is it?" Edward said. "She's your prisoner?"

"She's here with me of her own free will."

"*Free will*." Edward's lips pulled back, revealing white, sharp teeth. "Meaning you probably blackmailed her over that baby. You have no real claim on her."

"I have every claim."

"Because she had your child?" He snorted, jerking his chin. "Keep it," he said derisively. "If I'm the man she wants, I will give her more."

I gasped aloud at his cold reference to Miguel. *It?*

Edward couldn't have referred to my precious baby as "it." He couldn't have implied that he could get me pregnant and replace Miguel in my arms, in my life, as easily as someone might replace a new shoe.

Could he?

The black slash of Alejandro's eyebrows lowered. Every line of his hard-muscled body was taut, as if he were barely holding back from attack. He reminded me of a lion, or a wolf, coiled to spring, with only a thin veneer of civilized reason holding him in check—but not for much longer.

The two of them were about to start a brawl. Right here, in this elegant gilded ballroom, surrounded by the glitterati of Spain and all the world. The crowd around us was already growing, and so were the whispers. I wished I'd never started this by trying to contact Edward. Desperately, I yanked on his sleeve. "Please. Don't…"

Edward looked down at me condescendingly. "It's all right, Lena. I'm here now. I won't let him bully you." His eyes were hard, and his broad shoulders were square, like a rugby player's. And the condescending smile he gave me, after the cold, contemptuous stare he'd just given Alejandro, made me wish he was a million miles away. "You're safe. I'll take over."

"*Take over?*" I repeated incredulously.

Just yesterday, I'd wished so ardently for Edward's help. I'd remembered only that a year ago, when I'd needed to escape London, when I'd felt desperate and terrified and alone, I'd been grateful for his strength. But now...

I'd forgotten what Edward was really like.

Forgotten the times he'd visited his house in Mexico after Miguel was born, when he'd seemed irritated by Miguel's cries when my son's tummy hurt or he was unable to sleep. Edward had made several dark hints about adoption, or sending the baby back to Claudie and Alejandro. I'd thought Edward's jokes were in poor taste, but I'd let it go, because I owed him so much.

But now—

Edward was no longer even looking at me. He was smiling at Alejandro, utterly confident—like a dog who couldn't wait to test out his slashing claws and snarling teeth, to prove who was the stronger, meaner dog, in the pretext for a brawl of fighting over a bone—me.

Alejandro's dark eyes met mine. For a moment, they held. Something changed in his expression. He seemed to relax slightly. He drew himself up, looking almost amused.

"Yes, Lena is the mother of my child," he drawled. "And because of that I have a claim on her that you never will. But that's not the only claim. I have one deeper even than that." He glanced at me. "We intended to keep it private for a few days more, as a family matter, but we might as well let everyone know, shall we not, *querida?*"

"Um, yes?" I said, as mystified as everyone else.

Still smiling that pleasant smile, Alejandro turned and grabbed a crystal flute and solid silver knife off a waiter's passing tray. For a moment I froze in fear. Even with a butter knife—heck, even with his bare hands—I knew Alejandro could be dangerous. Boxing and mixed martial arts were hobbies in his downtime, the way he kept in shape and worked out the tension from a hard day making billion-dollar deals.

I exhaled when he didn't turn back to attack Edward. In fact, he rather insultingly turned his back on him, striding through the ballroom, to the dais, as the crowds parted like magic. He climbed the steps to the same microphone where he'd given the speech before. Most of the guests, seeing him, immediately fell silent. A few continued to whisper amongst themselves, staring between him and Edward—and me.

Alejandro chimed his knife against the crystal flute, so hard and loud that I feared the delicate glass might break in his hand. The entire ballroom fell so quiet that I could hear my own breath.

"I know this is a business gathering," he said, "but I must beg your indulgence for a moment. I am, after all, amongst friends...." His eyes abruptly focused on me across the crowd. "I have some happy news to announce. My engagement."

No. My face turned red and my body itched in an attack of nervous fear beneath my pale pink ball gown as a thousand people turned to stare at me. The whispering increased, building like the roll of distant thunder.

"Many of you probably wondered if I'd *ever* get married." Alejandro rubbed the back of his dark hair then looked up with a smile that was equal parts charming and sheepish. "I confess I wondered that myself." His low, sexy voice reverberated across the gilded ballroom. "But sometimes fate chooses better for us than we could ever have chosen for ourselves."

No, no, no, I pleaded desperately with my eyes.

He smiled.

He lifted his champagne flute toward me. "A toast. To Miss Lena Carlisle. The most beautiful woman on earth, and the mother of my baby son..."

The whispers exploded to a sharp roar.

"...to the future Duchess of Alzacar!"

There were gasps across the crowd, the largest of which was probably mine. But Alejandro continued to hold up his flute, so everyone else did, too. He drank deeply, and a thousand guests drank, too. Toasting to our engagement.

Only two people continued to stare at him blankly.

Edward.

And me.

My body trembled. All I wanted to do was turn and flee through the crowd, to disappear, to never come back. To be free of him—the man who'd once destroyed me. Who could, if he tried, so easily do it again—and more, since now our child could be used against me.

But that child also meant, in a very real way, that I was bound to Alejandro for the rest of my life. We both loved Miguel. We both wished to raise him.

Which meant, no matter how fiercely I wished otherwise, and no matter how I'd tried to deny it, I would never be truly free of Alejandro—ever.

Cheers, some supportive, some envious and some by bewildered drunken people who'd missed what all the fuss was about but were happy to cheer anyway, rang across the ballroom, along with a smattering of applause. Alejandro left the dais, where he was stopped by crowds of well-wishers, including the glamorous movie star I'd recognized and two heads of state.

Behind me, Edward seethed with disappointment and fury, "He doesn't own you."

"You're wrong," I whispered. I turned to Edward with tears in my eyes. "He owned me from the moment I became pregnant with his baby."

Edward's face went wild.

"No," he breathed. He started to reach toward my face, then he stiffened as he became aware of all the people

watching us, the strangers starting to hover, no doubt await-
ing their chance to congratulate me on snagging a billionaire duke into illustrious matrimony. Gorgeous, beautiful
women in designer clothes, thin and glossy like Claudie,
were already staring at me incredulously, clearly in shock
that someone like me could possibly have captured the heart
of a man like Alejandro.

The answer was simple. I hadn't.

This was my future. Everything I thought I'd left behind
me in London, all the pity and dismissive insults. Except
it would be even worse. Being described as a poor relation
was practically a compliment, compared with the epithet
that strangers would soon use to describe me: *gold digger*.

It would have been different if Alejandro and I had actually loved each other. Thinking of it, my heart ached. If
he'd loved me, and I'd loved him, I wouldn't have given two
hoots what anyone else thought. But as it was...

"You agreed to marry him?" Edward said incredulously.

"Not exactly." Swallowing over the ache in my throat, I
breathed, "It doesn't matter. Now he has proof he's Miguel's
father, he'll never let him go. And I will never leave my
son. So we might as well be married...."

"Like hell."

Edward grabbed my arm, his eyes like fire. Without
warning, he pulled me through the crowd. I had one single image of Alejandro's shocked face across the ballroom,
watching us, before I was out the side door and down the
hall, pushed into a dark, quiet corner of the empty coatroom.

Edward turned to me, his face contorted by shadows.

"Run away with me," he said urgently.

I drew back in shock. "What?"

"Navaro has no hold on you."

"He's Miguel's father!"

"Share custody of the kid if you must," he said through

gritted teeth. His hand gripped my forearm. "But don't throw yourself away on a man who will never deserve you."

"What are you saying?" I tried to pull away my arm, but his grip was tight.

"He terrified you for a year—got you pregnant just to steal your baby—"

"I was wrong—he didn't! It was all Claudie! She's the one who said it, and I believed her."

"So he's innocent? No way," he said grimly. "But even if he is—even if he didn't do that one awful thing, what about the rest?"

"What do you mean?"

"He made you love him, then he *abandoned* you. Don't you remember how gray your face was for months afterward? How your eyes were hollow and you barely spoke? I do."

I swallowed. "I…"

"Where was he when you wanted to give him everything? When you tried to tell him you were pregnant? He *changed his phone number.* How can you marry him now? How can you forget?"

I flashed hot, then cold. Yes. I remembered.

"And after all that, he gets you back?" Edward pulled me closer, looking down at me in the shadowy cloakroom with a strange light in his eyes. "No. I was there for you. I took care of you. I'm the one who—"

"Get your hands off my woman."

The low voice was ice-cold behind us. With a gasp that must have sounded guilty, I whirled to face him. "Alejandro!"

His eyes were dark with fury as he looked at me. "So this is why you were so reluctant to marry me?"

"No, you—"

"Be silent!"

I winced.

"Don't talk to her that way," Edward said.

Alejandro didn't look away from me. He held his body in a dangerous stillness as he ground out, "You have nothing to do with us, St. Cyr."

Either Edward didn't see the warning, or he didn't care. "Don't I? Who do you think was supporting her this past year? Who held her together after you blew her apart?" Coming closer to Alejandro, he said softly, with a malicious look in his eyes, "Who was at Lena's side at the hospital, when she gave birth to your child? Where were you then, Navaro?"

Alejandro slowly turned to look at him. I saw the hard set of his shoulders, the rapid rise and fall of his breath. I saw his hands tighten at his sides, and knew Edward was about to lose half of his face.

"Stop!" I cried, stepping between them in real fear. "Stop this at once!" I pressed on Edward's chest. "Just go."

He lifted his eyebrows in shock. "You can't honestly choose him over me?"

"Go. And don't come back." I glanced back at Alejandro and knew only the fact that I stood between them kept him from attack. I took a deep breath. "Thank you for everything you did for me, Edward. I'll never forget how you helped me." My jaw hardened. "But it's over."

Edward's face contorted. "You're throwing yourself away on *him?* Just because of some *stupid baby?*"

My sympathy disintegrated.

"That *stupid baby* is my son."

"Dammit, you know I didn't mean…"

But my heart had iced over. Releasing him, I stepped back, closer to Alejandro. "Yes, I choose him. Over you."

"You heard her," Alejandro said roughly. "You have thirty seconds to be out of my building, before security throws you out."

"Sending in your goons, eh?" he sneered. "Can't be bothered to do it yourself?"

"Happy to," Alejandro said grimly, pushing up the sleeves of his tuxedo jacket as he took a step forward, fists raised.

"No!" I grabbed his arm. My hand couldn't even fully wrap around the full extent of the hard, huge biceps beneath his tuxedo. "Please, Alejandro," I whispered. "Don't hurt him. He was good to me, when I had no one else. I never would have survived without him. Neither would Miguel. Please. For my sake."

Jaw taut, Alejandro slowly lowered his fist. "For your sake." His voice was low and cold as he turned to Edward. "Thank you. For protecting what I love."

Love? For a moment I stared at Alejandro, then I realized he was speaking of Miguel.

Edward glared at him. Obviously not realizing he'd just narrowly escaped death, he sneered, "Go to hell." At the door, he turned back and said, "I'll be back for you, Lena."

Then he was gone. And Alejandro and I were suddenly alone in the cloakroom. But my relief was short-lived.

"No wonder he loaned you his house," he said. "No wonder he protected you. He sees you as his. Why does he believe that?"

I whirled to face him. The cold fury in his eyes was like a wave. But there was something else there, too. Hurt.

"He tried to kiss me last week," I admitted in a low voice, then shook my head. "But I just gave a shocked laugh and he left. Whatever he might have hoped, all he ever was to me was a friend—"

"*Friend,*" he said scornfully. "You knew what he wanted."

I shook my head fiercely. "Not until last week, I never—"

"Then you were willfully blind. He's in love with you."

"You're wrong there." Shivering, I crossed my bare arms over my pink strapless ball gown. "If he'd really loved me, he would have loved Miguel, too. But he was always getting annoyed about him. Suggesting things…like I should send him away, farm him out for adoption…"

Alejandro's eyes darkened. "And you were willing to call him a friend? To let him near our son?"

I wanted to lash back at him. To tell him he was being unreasonable, or that I hadn't had a choice. Instead, I said the only thing that mattered. The only thing that was true.

"I'm sorry," I said in a low voice. "I was wrong."

He'd been opening his mouth to say more, no doubt cutting, angry accusations. But my humble, simple words cut him off at the knees. For a long moment, he stared at me in the shadowy cloakroom. Down the hall, we could distantly hear music playing, people laughing. Then he turned away, clawing back his dark hair.

"*Bien*. I wasn't exactly perfect, either," he muttered. Lifting his head, he glared at me. "But you're never to see him again. Or let him near Miguel."

"Fine," I said.

"Fine?"

"He stopped being my friend the moment he called my baby 'it.'"

"So," he said with a casual tone that belied the tension in his shoulders, "did you let him kiss you?"

I gaped at him. "Oh—for heaven's sake!" I stomped my foot against the plush carpet. "I'm not going to say it again!"

"I found the two of you here, talking…"

"And I just saw you talking to an actress in the ballroom. I didn't accuse you of making out! He made a pass at me last week. I refused. End of story."

"Once we are married…"

My cheeks went hot. "Married!" I stared at him, shocked. "Who said anything about marriage?"

Now Alejandro was the one to look shocked.

"I just asked you to marry me!"

"*Asked?*" My voice was acid. "When you asked, I said no. Tonight, you just *announced* it! In front of everyone! You may have asked—I never said yes!"

"We are going to be wed. Accept it."

"I will accept *an engagement,*" I retorted. "I will accept that we need to live in the same town, perhaps even the same house, for our son. A public front, a pretense for Miguel's sake, to make it appear we are actually a couple—that he wasn't just some *mistake!* But nothing more. There's no way I'm actually going to *marry* you. Do you think I would ever give you my body again? Or my heart?"

"I told you," he ground out. "I'm not asking for your heart."

"Then you can forget anything else—I won't give you my body, or take your name! I owe you respect as Miguel's father, but that's it," I said through gritted teeth. "Whatever you might believe, you don't own me, any more than Edward did!"

"I'm not Edward. I'm the father of your child." He grabbed my wrist, looking down at me. "I'm the man you will wed. I don't need your heart. But your body, at least, will be mine."

"No!" But even as I gasped with fury, heat flashed from his possessive grip on my wrist. Electricity crackled up my arm, to my throat, to my lips, to my breasts, down, down, down to my core. Pushing me back roughly against the coats, he looked down at me in the shadows.

"Did you really think," he said softly, "once I found you, I would ever let you go? I gave you up once for the sake of a promise. I gave you up to *do the right thing.* But fate has thrown you back into my arms. Now you will be entirely mine—"

Lowering his head, Alejandro kissed me fiercely, his lips hot and hard against mine, plundering, demanding. I tried to resist. I couldn't let myself feel—I couldn't—

Then I melted as the banked embers inside me, beneath the cold ash of the past lonely year, roared to a blazing fire. My body shuddered beneath his ruthless, almost violent embrace, and I wrapped my arms tightly around him, holding him to me, lost in the sweet forbidden ecstasy of surrender.

CHAPTER FIVE

HIS LIPS SAVAGED MINE, his tongue hot and salty and sweet. I clutched his shoulders, desperate to sate my desire. I'd hungered for him every night, even when I hated him, against all reason, against my will.

Alejandro's hands ran along my bare arms then moved to the tangle in my hair, tilting my chin so he could plunder my mouth more deeply. Long tendrils of hair had pulled free from my chignon. I felt them brush against my naked shoulders as his hard, muscular body strained against me, towering over mine, overpowering me. But it wasn't enough. Not nearly enough…

His hot kisses moved slowly down my neck, as he murmured husky endearments in Spanish against my skin. My head fell back against the wall of coats, and I closed my eyes, feeling tight and dizzy. He nuzzled my bare skin over the neckline of my gown. His hands cupped my breasts straining against the pink silk of the bodice.

So sweet. So hot. My breath came at a gasp, and as my eyelids flickered, the world seemed to spin in whirling patterns of shadows and light, echoes of past love and longing. For over a year I'd longed for him. For all my life, I'd longed for this. And it was even better than I remembered, a powerful drug beyond imagining. Wrapped in his embrace, I forgot myself, forgot my own name, and knew only that I had to have him or die….

A low deliberate cough came behind us. Startled, I turned my head, and Alejandro straightened. The Bulgarian ambassador stood at the cloakroom door, with his wife draped in pearls behind him.

"Excuse us," he said gravely, and stepping forward, he took a black fur coat off the hanger behind us.

I heard his wife titter as they left, "See, Vasil? I told you it was a love match!"

"Poor devil deserves some pleasure, at least," the man's reply echoed back to us, "after the grasping creature tricked him into marriage with a pregnancy."

Shamefaced, I looked up at Alejandro. The air in the cloakroom suddenly felt thin and cold.

"Let me go," I said.

His hold on me only tightened. "Who cares what they say?"

"I care," I whispered.

"Bull," he cut me off ruthlessly. "You're too strong to be ruled by gossip." His hands moved slowly down the bare skin of my upper back, and I shivered, fighting my own desire. "It's this you're afraid of. This." He stroked my arms to my breast, then abruptly pulled me up to stand, hard against his body. "This is all that matters…."

"It's not," I choked out. "There's love. And trust…."

"Love for our son. And trust for your husband. Your partner."

For a second, I trembled. I did want those things. A real home. I'd already accepted that we would need to live in the same town, or better yet, the same house. Why not accept a partnership? We could share a life, a son, even a bed. Would it be enough, without romantic love? Could I live without that? Could I?

For Miguel's sake?

"Maybe I could accept a marriage without love," I said in a small voice. I took a deep breath and raised my gaze to his. "But there is no partnership without trust. Can you promise you've never lied to me? And that you never will?"

I watched as the brief triumph in his eyes went out. "No."

My lips parted in a silent gasp. I hadn't expected that. My heart twisted as I thought how, with just a few hot kisses and the dream of giving Miguel a real home and family, I'd been perilously close to giving up my dreams.

"Well, which is it, Alejandro?" I choked out. "Did you lie to me in the past? Or will you lie to me in the future?"

His jawline tightened. For a moment, his face seemed tortured. Then, as I'd seen happen before, his expression shuttered, becoming expressionless, leaving me to wonder if I'd imagined the whole thing. "Take your pick."

I stiffened. Hating him—no. Hating *myself* for letting him kiss me. Letting him? All he'd had to do was touch me and I'd flung myself into his kiss with the hunger of a starving woman at a piece of bread. "What have you lied to me about?"

"You expect me to tell you the truth about that?"

"Other women?"

He glared at me. "I told you. I believe in honor. Fidelity. No. My lie is about—something else."

"What?"

"Me," he ground out through gritted teeth. "Only me."

Which didn't tell me anything at all! "Fine. Whatever." I glared at him. "You shouldn't have kissed me."

He relaxed imperceptibly now that we were no longer talking about his secrets.

"This isn't the place," he agreed.

"I didn't just mean the cloakroom. I mean anywhere."

"I can think of many places I'd like to kiss you."

"Too bad." My cheeks flamed, but I wouldn't let him distract me. "Take your kisses, and your lies, somewhere else."

"A marriage in name only?" He sounded almost amused. "Do you really think that will work?"

"Since I can't even trust you, let alone love you, there will be no marriage of any kind," I snapped. "And if you keep asking, even our engagement will be remarkably short."

"Why are you trying to fight me, when it's so obvious that you will give in?" he said. "You want to raise Miguel. So do I. What do you expect to do—live next door? In my stable?"

"Better that than your bed."

His dark eyes glittered. "That wasn't how you kissed me."

Heat pulsed through me. I could hardly deny it. I looked away. "Sex is different for women. It involves love!"

He snorted. "Right."

"Or at least caring and trust!" I cried, stung.

"Who is speaking in generalities now?" he said harshly. A cynical light rose in his eyes. "Many women have sex with strangers. Just—as you said—as many women prefer to drink their coffee black, without the niceties of sugar and cream!"

My cheeks flushed. "Fine for them, but—"

"Lust is just an appetite, a craving, such as one might have for *ensaladilla rusa*. No one says that you must be deeply committed to the mayonnaise in order to enjoy the taste of the potato salad!"

I lifted my chin. "Go seduce one of those salad women, then! I don't want you in my bed, I don't want you as my husband and I just regret I'm stuck with you as Miguel's father!"

"Enough." His voice was deadly cold. "You have made enough of a fool of me, making me beg—for the truth about Miguel, for the DNA test, for access to him. I even had to beg you to keep your promise to come to Spain. There will be no more begging, at least—" his eyes glittered "—no more begging from me."

Alejandro had begged me for stuff? I must have missed that. "I never—"

"You will marry me. Tonight."

"Don't be ridiculous!"

"Right now. Choose." His expression had hardened. "A priest. Or a lawyer."

"Are you threatening me?"

"Call it what you want."

I licked my lips, then tried, "Edward would help me. He has money and power to match even yours...."

"Ah." Alejandro came closer, softly tucking back a long tendril of hair that had escaped when he'd crushed me a few moments ago in his passionate embrace. "I wondered how long it would be before Mr. St. Cyr's name made an appearance. That was even quicker than I expected."

My cheeks went hot, but I lifted my chin. "He would still help me if I asked."

"Oh, I'm sure he would," he said softly. "But are you willing to accept the cost of his help?"

I swallowed.

"And the price to Miguel. Think of it." He tilted his head. "A custody war, when each side has infinite resources to pay lawyers for years, decades, to come." He gave a brief, humorless smile. "Miguel's first words after *mamá* and *papá* might be *restraining order*."

I sucked in my breath.

"And the scandal... The press will have a field day." Pressing his advantage, he stroked my cheek almost tenderly. "Miguel will grow so accustomed to paparazzi he'll start to think of them as members of his family. With good reason, for he'll see them more frequently than he sees either of us." He dropped his hand. His voice became harsh. "Is that really what you want?"

"Why are you doing this, Alejandro?" I choked out.

"I won't risk having Edward St. Cyr as my son's future stepfather."

I shook my head. "It will never happen!"

"I'm supposed to believe that? A few minutes ago, you promised you'd never see him again. Now you're threatening to use his wealth and power in a custody battle against me."

He looked at me with scorn, and I didn't blame him. I wiped my eyes. "You're right. I shouldn't have done that—but you're forcing my back against the wall! I have no choice!"

"Neither do I." His sensual lips curved downward. "You think you can control him. You cannot. He's selfish. Ruthless. Dangerous."

I flashed him a glare full of hate. "Are you talking about him," I said bitterly, "or yourself?"

"Yes, I could be dangerous," he said softly. "If anyone tried to hurt someone I cared about. I would die—or kill—to protect someone I loved."

"But you don't love anyone!"

"You're wrong." His voice was low. His lips pressed together in a thin line. "So will it be marriage between us—or war?"

"I hate you!"

"Is that your final answer?"

Tears of hopeless rage filled my eyes, but I'd told Edward the truth. Alejandro had owned me from the moment I'd become pregnant with his child. I would give anything, sacrifice any part of myself, for my son. My heart. My dreams. My soul. What were those, compared with Miguel's heart, his dreams, his soul?

My baby would not spend his childhood in and out of divorce courts, surrounded by pushy paparazzi, bewildered by the internecine battles of his parents. Instead, he would be safe and warm and surrounded by love. He would be happy.

It was all I had to cling to. All I had to live for.

My shoulders fell.

"No," I whispered. "You win. I will marry you."

"Now."

"Fine! I hate you!"

He looked down at me, his expression sardonic. "Hate me, then. At least that I can believe. Far more than your so-called *love*. But you will be my wife. In every way."

Yanking me into his arms, he kissed me, hard. But this time, there was nothing of tenderness, or even passion. Just a ruthless act of possession, showing me he owned me, a savage kiss hard enough to bruise.

Pulling me out of the cloakroom and outside into the warm Spanish night, he called for his driver. The paparazzi were long gone, and the street was quiet, even lonely.

Alejandro took me to the house of a local official, where with a quiet word a certificate of permission to marry was produced in record time. Then to a priest, in a large, empty church, so old and full of shadows it seemed half-haunted with the lost dreams of the dead.

And so Alejandro and I were wed, in that wan, barren church, with only flickers of candlelight and ghostly moonlight from the upper windows lighting the cold, pale marble. My pink ball gown of silk and embroidered flowers, which once seemed so beautiful, now hung on me like a shroud.

There was no wedding dress. No cake. No flowers. And no one, except the priest and his assistant called as witness, to wish us happiness.

Which was just as well, because as I looked at the savage face of my new husband as we left the church into the dark of night, I knew happiness was the one thing we'd never have.

* * *

Alejandro looked across the front seat of the car. "You're going to have to talk to me at some point."

I looked out the window at the passing scenery as we drove south into Andalucía. "No, I don't, actually."

"So you intend to ignore me forever?" he said drily.

I shrugged, still not looking at him. "Lots of married couples stop talking eventually. We might as well start now."

We'd been alone in the car together for hours, but it felt like days. Alejandro was driving the expensive sports sedan, with Miguel in the baby seat behind us, cooing and batting at plush dangling toys. Three bodyguards and his usual driver were in the SUV following us. "I want some private time with my new bride," Alejandro had told them with a wink, and they'd grinned.

But the reason he'd desired privacy wasn't exactly the usual one for newlyweds. I'd given Alejandro the silent treatment since our ghastly wedding ceremony last night. Seething. It wasn't natural for me to bite my tongue. I think he was waiting for me to explode.

He'd gotten me home by midnight as promised. The instant we returned to his Madrid penthouse I'd stalked into the bedroom where my baby slept, and though I couldn't slam the door—too noisy—I'd locked it solidly behind me. Very childish, but I'd been afraid that once Mrs. Gutierrez left, he might demand his rights of the wedding night. Pulling on flannel pajamas, I'd stared at the door, just daring him to try.

But he hadn't. About three in the morning, feeling foolish, I'd unlocked the door. But he never came, not even to apologize for his brutish behavior. There was no way I would have let him seduce me...but my nose was slightly out of joint that he hadn't even bothered to try. Our marriage was only a few hours old, and he was already ignoring me?

I didn't see him until this morning, when he was coming out of the guest bathroom next door, looking well rested and obviously straight out of the shower. His dark hair was wet, a low-slung towel wrapped around his bare hips and another towel hanging over his broad, naked shoulders.

I'd stopped flat in the hallway, unable to look away from the muscular planes of his bare chest, laced with dark hair, or the powerful lines of his body, to the slim hips barely covered by the clinging white terry cloth.

Alejandro had greeted me with a sensual smile. "Good morning, *querida*," he'd purred, then lifting a wicked eyebrow as if he already knew the answer, he'd inquired, "I trust you slept well?"

But I was starting to get my revenge. His lips were now set in an annoyed line as he kept his eyes on the road, pressing on the gas of his very expensive, very fast sedan. "We are husband and wife now, Lena. You must accept that."

"Oh, I do," I assured him. "But we're a husband and wife who happen to hate each other. So perhaps just not talking is best."

Alejandro exhaled in irritation, his hands tightening on the steering wheel. I turned away, staring out wistfully at the scenery of Spain flying past us. In any other circumstance I would have been in awe at the magnificent view. The farmland and soft hills of central Spain were turning to a drier landscape. Lovely thick bushes of pink and white oleander flowers separated the highway, a vivid, wild, unexpected beauty, much like Spain itself.

Oleander. I shivered a little. So beautiful to the eyes. But so poisonous to the heart.

Just like Alejandro, I thought. I wouldn't let him in. Husband or not, I'd never let him close to me. In any way.

We'd stopped only once since we left Madrid, to feed

and change the baby, and to put gas in both cars. Alejandro offered to take a small detour and stop for lunch in Córdoba, to show me the famous cathedral that had once been a Great Mosque. But I'd refused. I didn't want him doing me any favors. Though later I regretted it, because I heard a lot about the famous Mezquita.

As the car flew south, turning on a new road, I blinked in the bright sun flooding the windows. After weeks of rain in San Miguel, and London's drizzle and overcast skies, the Spanish sun had come as advertised, with a wide blue horizon that held not a single cloud. The arid landscape suddenly reminded me of Mexico. Which reminded me of the freedom and independence I'd had so briefly.

And Edward.

I'll be back for you, Lena.

"Stop it," Alejandro growled.

I nearly jumped in the smooth leather seat. "What?"

"I can hear you. Thinking about him."

"You can hear me thinking?"

"Stop," he said quietly, giving me a hard sideways glance. "Or I will make you stop."

"*Make* me—" I snorted derisively, then I looked at him, remembering his last ruthless kiss in the cloakroom. And the one before it, which had been even more dangerous. I remembered how it had felt, surrendering to his embrace, how it had made my whole body tremble with need.

"You're such a jerk," I muttered, folding my arms mutinously. "My thoughts are my own."

"Not if they are of a man like St. Cyr. Thoughts lead to actions."

"I told you, I don't even like him anymore!"

He snorted. "And that is supposed to inspire trust? You've made it plain you did not wish to marry me. Perhaps you're wishing now you took the other choice."

I looked at him. "What other choice?"

"A war between us," he said grimly. He was staring forward at the road, his jaw tight. "St. Cyr would be eager to help you with that."

My arms unfolded. "No." I frowned. "I don't want war. I'd never deliberately hurt you, Alejandro. Not now."

"Really," he said in clear disbelief.

"Hurting you would hurt Miguel." I looked out the window and said softly, "We both love him. I realized the truth last night, even before your marriage ultimatum—neither of us wants to be apart from him." Blinking fast, I faced him. "You're right. We're married now. So let's make the best of it."

"Do you mean it?" he said evenly. I nodded.

"Let's make sure Miguel has a wonderful childhood and a real home, where he'll always feel safe and warm and loved."

His hands seemed to relax a little around the steering wheel. He looked at me. There was something strange in his eyes, something almost like—yearning—that made my heart twist.

"If it's really true you'd never deliberately hurt me..." He seemed to be speaking to himself. "I wish I could..."

"What?"

He shook his head, and his jaw went hard. "Nothing."

What had he been about to say? I looked down, blinking as my eyes burned. Telling myself I shouldn't care. Willing myself *not* to care.

My lie is about something else.

What?

I remembered the stark look in his eyes. *Me. Only me.*

Stop it, I told my heart fiercely. *Don't get sucked in! Keep your distance!*

Silently, Alejandro stared forward at the road. For long minutes, the only sound was Miguel cooing to himself in the backseat, chortling triumphantly as he grasped a soft toy hanging from the top of his baby seat, and making it squeak. I smiled back at my son. He was the reason. The only reason.

"I'm glad you feel that way. The truth is I don't want to hurt you, either." Alejandro tightened his hands on the steering wheel. He glanced at me out of the corner of his eye. "Our son is what matters. We'll focus on him. I'll never leave you or Miguel. Together we'll make sure our son is always well cared for."

Our eyes locked, and an ache lifted to my throat. Turning away, I tried to block the emotion out with a laugh. "Miguel will be a duke someday. That's crazy, isn't it?"

Alejandro turned his eyes back to the road.

"Sí," he said grimly. "Crazy."

I'd been trying to lighten the mood. But his voice sounded darker than ever. "Did I say something wrong?"

"No. You are correct. Miguel will be Duque de Alzacar." I frowned. But before I could figure out what lay behind the odd tension in his voice, he turned to me. "So you forgive me for forcing you to marry me against your will?"

I exhaled.

"It's a very complicated question."

"No. It is not."

Something broke inside me. And words came pouring out.

"You think I was silly and selfish to want to marry for love. But for the past ten years, that dream was all I've held on to." I looked at my hands in my lap. "Ever since I was fourteen years old, I've felt so alone. So unwanted. But then, last year, when I met you…" I lifted agonized eyes to his. "All my dreams seemed to be coming true. It was as if…I'd gone back in time. To the world I once knew. The one filled with love. The world where I was good enough. Wanted. Even cherished."

Alejandro's expression darkened. "Lena…"

"Then you abandoned me," I whispered. "You told me you didn't love me, that you never would." I looked at him. "But I still married you yesterday, Alejandro, knowing that. Knowing you've lied to me in the past and will lie in the future. I married you knowing that the loneliness I tried to leave behind me in London will now follow me for the rest of my life. Only now, instead of being a poor relation, I'm the gold digger who got pregnant to ensnare a rich duke. And everyone will say, weren't you so good and noble to marry me? Wasn't it an amazing sacrifice for you to make me your wife? How generous of you! How kind!"

He glowered. "No one will say that."

I cut him off with a low laugh. "*Everyone* will. And I know there will be days when I'll feel that marrying you was the biggest mistake of my life." I drew a deep, shuddering breath, then met his gaze. "And yet I can't regret it," I whispered. "Because it will make Miguel's life better to have you in his life. Every single day. He will know you. Really know you."

"I wish he could." Alejandro stared at me. His dark eyes were liquid and deep. "I wish I could tell you…"

I held my breath. "Yes?"

His face suddenly turned cold, like a statue. He looked away. "Forget it."

I exhaled, wishing I hadn't said so much.

He drove the car off the main road, then took a smaller one, then turned on a private lane that was smaller still, nothing but a ribbon twisting across the broad-swept lands. Alejandro stopped briefly at a tall iron gate, then entered a code into the electronic keypad. We proceeded inside the estate, which looked so endless and wide, I wondered how anyone had wrapped a fence around it, and if the fence was visible from space, like the Great Wall of China.

Then I saw the castle, high on a distant hill, and I sucked

in my breath. It was like a fairy-tale castle, rising with ramparts of stone and turrets stretching into the sky.

"Is that…?" I breathed.

"Sí," Alejandro said quietly. "My home. The Castillo de Rohares. The home of the Dukes of Alzacar for four hundred years."

It took another fifteen minutes to climb the hill, past the groves of olive trees and orange trees. When we reached the castle at last, past the ramparts into a courtyard surrounding a stone fountain, he stopped the car at the grand entrance on the circular driveway. He turned off the engine, and I could hear the bodyguards climbing out of the SUV behind us, talking noisily about lunch, slamming doors. But as I started to turn for the passenger-side door, Alejandro grabbed my wrist. I turned to face him, and he dropped my arm.

"I am sorry I hurt you, Lena. When I left you last summer, when I refused to return any of your phone calls—I did that for good reason. At least—" his jaw tightened "—it seemed like good reason."

"No, I get it," I said. "You didn't want me to love you."

"No. That's not it at all." He lifted his dark eyes to mine. "I didn't leave because you loved me. I left because I was falling in love with you."

CHAPTER SIX

I STARED AT him in shock.

"What?" I breathed.

A hard knock banged against the car window behind me, making me jump. Turning my head, I saw a plump smiling woman, standing on the driveway outside, dressed in an apron and holding a spoon. She waved at us merrily. I saw the bodyguards greeting her with obvious affection as they went into the grand stone entrance of the castle.

"Another housekeeper?" I said faintly.

"My grandmother," he said.

"Your—" I whirled to face him, but he had already opened his door and was getting out of the car, gently lifting Miguel out of his baby seat. Nervously, I got out of the car, too, wondering what the dowager Duchess of Alzacar would make of me.

"Come in, come in," she said to the bodyguards, shooing them inside. She kept switching from English to Spanish as if she couldn't quite make up her mind. "Knowing Alejandro, I'm sure you didn't stop for any lunch, so everything is ready if you'll just go straight to the banqueting hall…"

"Abuela," Alejandro said, smiling, "I'd like you to meet my son. His name is Miguel."

"Miguel?" she gasped, looking from him to Alejandro.

He blinked with a slight frown, shaking his head. "And this is my new wife. Lena."

"I'm so happy to meet you." Smoothing one hand over her apron, she turned to me with a warm smile, lifting the wooden spoon high, like a benign domestic fairy about to grant a really good wish. "And your sweet baby! I can hardly wait to…" Her eyes suddenly narrowed. "Your new what?"

Coming over to me, Alejandro put his free arm around my shoulders. "My wife."

She lowered her spoon and looked me over, from my long hair to my soft white blouse with the Peter Pan collar, to my slim-cut jeans and ballet flats. I braced myself for criticism.

Instead, she beamed at me, spreading her arms wide.

"Oh, my dear," she cried, "welcome to the family. Welcome to your new home!"

And she threw her arms around me in a big, fierce, welcoming hug.

Shocked, I stiffened. Then I patted her awkwardly on the back.

"But I'm being silly," she said, drawing back, wiping her eyes with her brightly colored apron. "My name is Maurine. But please call me Abuela, if you like, as Alejandro does. Or Grandma. Or Nana. Whatever. I'm just so happy you're here!"

"Thank you," I said, unsure how to handle such immediate warmth and kindness.

"But you—" she whirled on her grandson with a scowl "—you should have known better than to elope!"

Alejandro looked abashed. It was a funny, boyish expression on his masculine face. "We would have waited and had a proper wedding," he said, rubbing his neck sheepishly, "but Abuela, it happened so quickly.…"

"Huh. Don't think you're getting off that easy. We'll talk about it later. Now—" her plump face softened as her eyes lit up "—let me hold that baby."

Ten minutes later, Maurine was giving me a speed tour of the castle, on the way to the dining hall. "The foundations of Rohares date from the times of the sultan," she said happily. "But most of the building dates from the early seventeenth century. It was bombed in the war, then when we came back we had no money and it fell into disrepair." She looked sad, then brightened, smiling up at her grandson. "But Alejandro made his fortune in Madrid, then restored every part of it, made Rohares better than it had ever been before! And here's where we'll have lunch...."

I stopped in the huge doorway of an enormous dining hall that looked as if it came from the late Renaissance, complete with soaring frescoed ceilings, suits of armor beside the ancient tapestries and a stone fireplace tall enough to fit a person inside. And at the center of the huge, gymnasium-size room, there was a long wooden dining table, large enough to seat forty or fifty people, and groaning beneath the weight of the luncheon spread, flower arrangements, and place settings carefully designed with fine china and the brightest decor.

My mouth dropped as I stared at it.

"Cold and drafty, *sí?*" Alejandro said smugly, grabbing a marinated green olive and piece of cheese off the platter on the table. "Just as you said."

"I've never seen anything like this," I breathed. "And the food..."

He gave a low chuckle. "Abuela believes food is love."

"I can see that," I said faintly, staring up at his face.

I left because I was falling in love with you.

My knees were still weak at what he'd said in the car. It was so far from everything I'd ever imagined, I couldn't believe I'd heard him right. "Alejandro..."

"Abuela can be bossy about it, but she loves nothing more than taking care of people, along with her garden and home." He grinned, shaking his head ruefully. "She now has an unlimited budget, a clear schedule—now she's given up her charity work—and infinite time. When it comes to the domestic arts, she is unstoppable."

"Amazing." I looked at him hesitantly. "But Alejandro…"

"Yes?"

"Did you mean what you said?"

His dark eyes met mine. He knew what I was talking about. "Don't be afraid. As you said—much has changed in this past year."

I hadn't realized I'd been holding my breath, but at that, I exhaled, like air fizzing out of a tire. "You're right," I said, keeping my voice steady. "Everything is different now."

"The past is past. Now we are partners, parents to our son."

"Exactly." I looked away. The bodyguards, apparently accustomed to being fed lunch like this by the dowager duchess, were already at the table, filling their plates and murmuring their appreciation.

Maurine suddenly reappeared in the solid-oak doorway, holding Miguel with one hand, a small card in the other. Going to the table, she snatched a card off a place setting, then replaced it with the new card. Turning back, she patted the chair, beaming at me. "You're to sit here, dear."

"Oh. Thank you, Maurine."

Smiling, she looked at Miguel in her arms, and started another peekaboo game. She'd been lost in baby joy from the instant she'd picked him up in her arms, and the love appeared to be mutual. I watched, smiling, as Maurine hid her face with her hand, before revealing it so Miguel could reach out to bat her nose triumphantly, leaving them both in hopeless squeals of laughter. Alejandro watched them, too.

"Thank you," he said quietly.

"For what?"

His dark eyes met mine. "For coming to Spain like you promised."

"Oh." My cheeks flooded with shame to remember how I'd initially refused. "It's, um, nothing."

He turned away, watching his grandmother play with his son. "It's everything to me."

My blush deepened, then I sighed. "I was wrong to fight it," I admitted.

"You? Wrong?" Alejandro shook his head. "Impossible."

I scowled at his teasing tone. "Yes, wrong. I'm woman enough to admit it. After all, Maurine is Miguel's family, too." I looked around the huge banqueting hall, filled with antiques that seemed hundreds of years old. I had to crane my head back to see the wood-timbered ceiling, with its faded paintings of the ducal coat of arms. "And this is his legacy," I said softly. "This will all belong to him some-day...."

Alejandro was no longer smiling.

"Yes," he said. "It will."

For some reason I didn't understand, the lightness of the mood had fled. I frowned.

He abruptly held out his arm. "Let's have lunch, shall we?"

Even through his long-sleeved shirt, I could feel the warmth of his arm. The strength of it. From the end of the long table, I saw the bodyguards looking at us, saw one of them nudge the other with a sly grin. To outward appearance, we must have looked like goofy-in-love newlyweds.

Alejandro pulled out the chair Maurine had chosen for me, waited, then after I sat down, he pushed it in and sat beside me.

Looking down at the table, I saw three different plates of different sizes stacked on top of each other in alternating colors. At the top of the place setting, there was a home-made paper flower of red-and-purple tissue paper, very similar to the paper flowers my mother had made for me when I was young. Beside it was a card that held a small handwritten name, with elegant black-ink calligraphy.

The Duchess of Alzacar
my darling new granddaughter

Looking at it, a lump rose in my throat. "Look what she wrote."

Alejandro looked at the card, and smiled. "Yes."

"She's already accepted me in the family. Just like that?"

"Just like that." He made me a plate with a little of everything, and poured me a glass of sparkling water, then red wine.

"Wine for lunch?" I said doubtfully.

"It's from my vineyard by the coast. You should try it."

"All right," I sighed. I took a sip, then said in amazement, "It's delicious."

"You sound surprised."

"Is there anything you're not good at?" I said a little sulkily. He smiled.

Then the smile fled from his handsome face. His dark eyes turned hollow, even bleak.

"Keeping promises," he said.

The blow was so sudden and unexpected that it felt like an anvil hitting the softest part of my belly. The moment I'd let my defenses down, he'd spoken with such unprovoked cruelty it took my breath away. Reminding me.

Did you lie to me in the past? Or will you lie to me in the future?

Take your pick.

"Oh," I breathed, dropping my fork with a clang against the twenty-four-karat-gold-rimmed china plate.

He'd done me a favor reminding me, I told myself savagely. I couldn't start believing the pretense. I couldn't start thinking we were actually a family. That we were actually in love. I couldn't surrender!

And yet...

"Are you enjoying yourself, dear?" I looked up to see Maurine smiling down at me from the other side of the table, with chubby Miguel still smiling in her arms. "I hope you see something you like!"

"I do," I replied automatically, then realized to my horror that the exact moment I'd spoken the words I'd been looking at Alejandro. Quickly, I looked down at my plate. "What's this?" I asked, looking at one of the dishes, some kind of meat with leeks and carrots.

"*Pato a la Sevillana,* a specialty of the area. Slow-cooked duck roasted in sherry and vegetables."

I took a bite. It was delicious. "And this?"

"*Rabo de toro.* Another classic dish of Andalucía. Vegetables, slowly braised with sherry and bay leaf."

Bull's tail? I tasted it. Not bad. I tried the fresh papayas and mangoes, the *albóndigas,* the fried-potato-and-ham *croquetas.* I smiled. *"Delicioso!"*

"Muy bien," Maurine sighed happily, then turned on her grandson, tossing her chic, white hair. "Though *you* don't deserve lunch. I should let you get fast food at a drive-through in Seville!" She hitched her great-grandbaby higher on her hip against her pinafore apron. "I cannot believe you got married without inviting me to the wedding! My only family! After I waited thirty-five years to see you get married! After the way you used to make me bite my nails over those wretched skinny, self-centered women you used to cavort with!"

"At least I didn't marry one of them, eh, Abuela? Do I not get credit for that?"

"Yes," she sighed. "On that, you did well."

The two of them smiled at each other, and I had the sudden image of what it must have been like for him to be raised by Maurine in this enormous castle. Alejandro had lost his parents even younger than I'd lost mine. My father had died of a stroke, my mother six months later of illness. But Alejandro had lost both parents in a car crash when he was only twelve. He'd also lost his best friend, Miguel, whom he'd thought of as a brother, and even their housekeeper.

My smile suddenly faltered. All this time, I'd moaned and whimpered so much about my own difficult childhood. But Alejandro had barely hinted aloud about his. A very masculine reticence, but enough to make me writhe with shame. No wonder Alejandro had been so determined that our Miguel, his only child, should come back to Spain, his home, and meet his grandmother, his only family, who'd raised him and loved him.

Even though she didn't seem to be one hundred percent loving him right now.

"But still." His grandmother's chin was wobbling. "All I asked was that you let me attend the wedding. It was my one and only chance to see you get married and I…"

"It was the worst wedding ever," I heard myself blurt out.

Both of them turned to face me. She looked amazed. He looked faintly strangled, as if he were afraid of what I might say next.

"It was just the two of us—" I shook my head "—along with the priest and some stranger as witness. There was no cake. No flowers. You didn't miss anything, Maurine!"

"Call me Abuela, dear," she said faintly. Her gaze softened as she looked at me. Whatever anger she was now lavishing on Alejandro clearly did not extend to me. She blinked with a frown, tilting her head. "You didn't have any flowers? Not one?"

"It's not entirely his fault," I said apologetically. "We felt we should get married immediately, without too much fuss, because of…" I glanced at our baby in her arms.

"Ah." A look of understanding filled her eyes. "Yes, of course."

"The legal part is done, but Alejandro was just saying on the drive that he wished we could have a reception, a party of some kind, to introduce me to his neighbors and friends. I mean, he did tell a few people in Madrid that we were engaged—" I looked at Alejandro beneath my lashes "—but that's not the same as celebrating with neighbors and family."

"No, it's not," she said thoughtfully.

Taking a bite of juicy ripe papaya, I sighed. "But we just don't know what to do. I mean, Alejandro is so busy with his company, and of course I have my hands full with Miguel. I wouldn't have a clue how to organize a party anyway, not a big one. So we were thinking we could maybe hire a party planner, maybe from Madrid…."

"A *party planner!*" Maurine gasped indignantly. "My new granddaughter—and my great-grandson, this little angel—introduced to all my neighbors and friends with some dreary, chic party arranged by a paid *Madrileño!*" She put a dramatic hand over her fulsome chest. "I would turn over in my grave!"

Alejandro's eyes met mine. His lips quirked as he said, "But Abuela, you're not dead."

"You're right, I'm not," she snapped. "Which is why *I* will be planning your wedding reception. Oh, there's no time to waste." Turning away with Miguel still in her arms, she hurried from the dining hall, calling, "María! Carmen! Josefa! Hurry! We have a new project—the most important party I've ever done!"

I turned back to my lunch, only to find Alejandro looking at me. He said in a low voice, "Why did you do that?"

The intense way he was looking at me made me feel nervous and fluttery inside. "Do what?"

"You could have told her the real reason for our quick

marriage. That I forced you to marry me, against your will. That I threatened a custody battle."

"Oh." Awkwardly, I looked back at my plate. I took another bite of the *Pato a la Sevillana*. He just waited. Finally, I said in a small voice, "I didn't want to tell her that."

Alejandro came closer, the hard edges of his jaw and cheekbones leaving shadows across his face. "Why?"

My cheeks felt hot. I couldn't meet his eyes.

"Were you trying to protect her?" He was so close now that I could almost feel the heat through his black tailored shirt. My gaze remained down, resting on his shirt just below his ribcage. Just below his heart. His voice was so quiet I could barely hear as he said, "Or were you trying to protect me?"

"You," I whispered.

The only noise in the cavernous dining hall was the distant murmured conversation of the bodyguards sitting at the far end of the table, the clink of silverware against china, the thunk of wineglasses against the wood.

Alejandro leaned forward, his elbow against the long oak table, bringing his face very close to mine. It was almost painful to be that close to so much masculine beauty. Unwillingly, my eyes traced the hard slant of his cheekbones, the rough edge of his jawline. His darkly intent eyes.

And his sensual mouth. That most of all. I watched, unable to look away, as his lips moved to shape a single word.

"Why?"

I swallowed, sweeping my hand to indicate the elaborate decorations and luncheon spread down the long table.

"She loves you. And you love her." I shook my head and blurted out, "All this time I've been moaning about my family in London. I feel so stupid for complaining about my childhood—while all the time, you yourself—"

He put his hand on my cheek. "It doesn't matter now."

Our eyes locked. I caught my breath, feeling the warmth

of his fingertips brushing my skin. Feeling how much, deep inside, I wanted him to touch me. On my cheek. Down my neck. Everywhere. Unwillingly, I licked my lips.

But I couldn't give in. I couldn't surrender. If I ever gave him my body, as I'd done the year before, my heart would follow. And I didn't think my shattered heart could survive when he betrayed me as he inevitably would—hadn't he told me as much himself?

Is there anything you're not good at?

Keeping promises.

I pulled back, suddenly desperate to get away from the dangerous energy sizzling between us.

"You love each other. You're a family." My voice trembled, betraying me. "I want you to be happy."

He suddenly leaned forward, his eyes dark.

"What would make me happy," he said huskily, "is having you in my bed. Right now."

I sucked in my breath. My body trembled.

"No," I whispered.

His dark eyes met mine. "We both know how this will end."

He was right. *He was right.*

"Thank Maurine for me…." Setting down my silverware, I stumbled to my feet, tossing my napkin over my half-empty plate. "I'm done…."

And I ran.

Tears blurred my eyes as I fled the dining hall, into the shadowy hallway. I dodged antique chests and an old suit of armor, only to run straight into Maurine.

"My dear, whatever is the matter?" she said, looking astonished.

"I just need some—some fresh air," I choked out.

"Of course." Looking bewildered, with my baby still smiling and happy in her arms, she pointed to a door down the hall. "That leads to the gardens…."

I ran down the dark hallway, beneath the cool, thick stone walls of the *castillo*. Flinging open the door, I found myself beneath the bright, hot Spanish sun and the softly waving palm trees. I kept going, almost blindly—wanting only to be away from the castle. From the man who owned it.

Just as he now owned me.

But he would not own my heart, I vowed to myself, wiping my eyes. Not my heart and not my body...no matter how he might tempt me otherwise. I couldn't give in. I couldn't....

I ran down the stone path, past green hedges and huge oak trees with soft, full greenery, past a pond and a picturesque gazebo in an English-style garden, past something that looked like a hedge maze straight out of *Alice in Wonderland.* Choking out a sob, I abruptly stopped. I found myself in a rose garden, surrounded by a profusion of colorful blooms, gentle yellow, soft pink, innocent white and a blaze of red like heart's blood.

"Lena."

His voice was low behind me. Shocked, I whirled around.

"How did you...?"

Alejandro stood in front of me, dark and tall and powerful. Colorful roses and the primal green of the garden hemmed us in on every side, like a riotous jungle. "I know this garden. It's been my home since I was a child."

The sun left a frost of golden light against his dark hair, like a halo, tracing down the length of his body, his tanned, olive-toned skin, his sharp cheekbones, his hard-muscled body that moved with such sensual grace.

"I won't sleep with you," I breathed. "I won't!"

His cruel, sensual lips curved.

"We both know you will." I watched, mesmerized, as the words caused his tongue to flick against the edges of his lips, into the warm, dark honey of his mouth. I remembered how it had felt when he'd kissed me last night. My lips still felt bruised, from the sweet remnants of that fire. "You want me. As I want you."

"I won't let you take me because I am *convenient*." I shook my head fiercely. "You can't have me now, Alejandro!"

He came closer, towering above me, our bodies so near they almost touched.

"Can't I?" he said huskily.

I stared up at him, shivering. Sunshine shimmered in the greenery around Alejandro, making the flowers gleam like colorful lights, the roses like tumbled scarlet against the deep forest green, the leaves and thorns and tangling vines.

Reaching out, he stroked a long tendril of my hair. "I wanted you from the moment I saw you in the hallways of that London mansion, watching me with such longing in your eyes." He lifted his gaze. "I wanted you then. I want you now. And I will have you."

His dark eyes were like deep pools, illuminated by streaks of amber in the sunlight. The kind of eyes that make you lose your breath, the kind a woman could drown in.

The kind of eyes that could make a woman forget a whole lifetime of grief and everything she should have learned from it.

He wanted me. The thought was like a flower. Like one of those beautiful, hardy, deeply poisonous oleander flowers I'd seen growing along the Spanish highway.

He wanted me.

"We are married now," he said.

"For Miguel's sake."

"*Sí.* We married for the sake of our son." He followed me, his powerful body intent, with his dark hair and his dark clothes, like a stalking panther. "But that is not why I want you in my bed."

"But I can't trust you—"

He straightened, his face dangerous. "Why do you think that?"

"You said you lied to me and will lie again. You said you're no good at keeping promises...."

Alejandro looked away. "That was about...something else." He looked back at me. "I will always keep my promises to you."

"But how can I believe that?" I whispered, my heart running like a scared deer.

"Because it's true." He moved closer, running his hand down my long, loose hair, down my back. I shivered beneath the soft, seductive touch. Lifting his hand, he stroked my cheek as he whispered, "Be with me. Be my wife."

My whole body trembled, leaning toward him.

"And if you still think you can't trust me..." His fingers gently stroked my cheeks, lifting my chin as he said softly, "Trust this."

Lowering his head, he pressed his lips against mine. I felt his warmth, his power, the strength of his body. I closed my eyes, lost, dizzy with desire. When he finally pulled away, I stared up at him, trembling.

"Please," I choked out. I lifted my gaze to his. *Please don't make me love you.* "Please don't make me want you...."

He rubbed the pads of his thumbs along my swollen lower lip, and gave me a smile that was breathtaking in its masculine triumph. "Too late."

In the distance, I heard Maurine calling from the castle. I twisted my head, listening, and so did he.

Alejandro suddenly cupped my face in his hands. His eyes were dark. Merciless. "Tonight," he whispered. "You will be in my bed. Tonight..." He ran his fingertips down my shoulders, cupping my breasts. I gave a soft gasp, and he returned a sensual smile. "You will be my wife."

CHAPTER SEVEN

TONIGHT, YOU WILL be in my bed.

Tonight, you will be my wife.

The day raced by. I could not hold the hours back. The clock was ticking and when night fell, I knew he would take me, if not against my will, then at least against my heart.

The dinner table was busy and crowded and happy, because apparently Maurine, the daughter of American-Basque sheep ranchers, had gotten into the habit of eating with her entire household staff, many of whom lived in cottages on the edge of the Rohares estate, and their wives and children were always welcome, as well. Freshly made breads, fruit and cheese were spread across the table in a feast that also included meats, stews and seafood paella, and all kinds of desserts, *tortas* to *galletas*.

"You should see it on holidays," Maurine said to me with a smile, when she saw my eyes widen at the crowd that completely filled all the chairs at the table in the dining hall. "Then, everyone invites their extended families as well, and they come from all over Andalucía."

"Where on earth do they sit?"

Maurine's smile lifted to a grin. "We have to bring all the tables out of the attic and extra rooms, and bring in every antique chair we've got, and the old benches and chests."

"Nice," I murmured. I exhaled. "This place is amazing."

"Because of Alejandro." She looked a few places down the table, to where he was holding court with our baby son in his lap, introducing him to the families of household staff. The women were clustered around him, as if to offer obeisance to a visiting pasha. "He is my whole world. I owe him everything."

"I bet he'd say he owes everything to you. And looking at all this—" I looked at the food, at the decorations, at the care taken with all the details "—I'd have to agree."

"Oh, no." She shook her head vehemently. "If not for him, I never would have survived the aftermath of that car crash, when I lost my whole family...."

"I'm so sorry," I murmured. "I heard about that. Losing your son and daughter-in-law, and even the housekeeper and her son.... I can't imagine how awful. But Alejandro lived."

"That's right. Yes." Shuddering, she closed her eyes. "He saved me. I can still see him in the hospital, his little, injured face covered with bandages, his eyes so bright. Bones in his face had been broken, and he'd never look the same, but he was worried about me, not himself. 'It'll be all right, Abuela,' he told me. 'I'm your family now.'" She blinked fast, her eyes sparkling with tears. "He gave me something to live for, when I wanted to die. And more." She shook her head. "He saved this castle. Even at twelve years old, he was determined to win back our family's lost fortune. He knew he could do it. And he wasn't afraid."

"No." Alejandro wasn't afraid of anything. And he always got what he wanted. I shivered, remembering the dark promise in his eyes in the garden. *Tonight, you will be in my bed. Tonight, you will be my wife....* I pushed the memory away. "How did he build a fortune out of nothing?"

"He went to Madrid at seventeen," Maurine said. "Worked eighteen-hour days, three different jobs. He took all the money he earned and poured it into risky investments that somehow paid off. He wasn't afraid to gamble. Or work. It just goes to show that nobility is in the heart," she said softly, almost as if she were talking to herself, "not the blood."

I snorted. "What are you talking about? He's the son of a duke. It doesn't get more noble than that."

Maurine abruptly focused her gaze on me. "Of course. That's what I meant. He's noble by birth."

Was she confused, or was she just confusing me? "Did people give you a hard time because of your background? I mean—" I shook my head awkwardly "—Alejandro said you grew up in the U.S., the daughter of sheep ranchers…"

"Shepherds, actually," she said, with a twinkle in her eye.

"Exactly. You were a regular girl—then you married a duke." I paused, trying to form the right words. "Did all the other aristocrats treat you badly? Did they call you a gold digger?"

"Me? No." She blinked, and her expression abruptly changed. "Oh, my dear. Is that what's been happening to you?"

I felt the color drain from my cheeks. "No, I…"

"Oh, you poor child." Her plump, wrinkled face was sympathetic, her blue eyes kind. She reached over and patted my hand. "Don't worry. You'll triumph over all the ugly, silly words that people can say. Alejandro loves you. And you love him. That's what matters."

Now my cheeks went hot. "Uh…"

"And I'm so happy you're part of our family." She gave my hand a little squeeze, then chuckled. "I was a little worried. You should have seen the women he dated before you. He didn't bring a single one home. For good reason. He knew I'd skewer them."

"I'm the first woman he ever brought home?" I said faintly.

She nodded. Her gaze became shadowed as she looked at Alejandro farther down the table. "I was starting to think he'd never let any woman into his heart. That he'd never let anyone know who he truly is." She gave me a sudden sharp look. "But you know. Don't you?"

I furrowed my brow. Was she talking about a biblical knowing? Otherwise I didn't really understand. "Um, yes?"

She stared at me, then releasing my hand, abruptly turned away. "How did you like the rose garden?"

I shivered in spite of myself. "It is…very beautiful," I managed. "Like paradise. But what were you saying about Alejandro…?"

Maurine's eyes shadowed. She bit her lip. "I can't believe you don't know. But if you don't, he has to be the one to…"

"Querida," I heard Alejandro say behind me. "It is time for bed."

Seriously? He was announcing this in front of his grandmother and the whole table? I turned with a scowl, then saw him holding up our sleepy-eyed son. Oh. He meant Miguel. With dinner served so late in Spain, it *was* past our baby's bedtime, and he was yawning in Alejandro's arms, causing dimples in his fat little cheeks. "Right." I held out my arms. "I need to give him a bath first…."

But Alejandro shook his head. He wasn't letting me escape so easily. "I'll help you. It's time I learned to do these things as well, don't you think?"

The gleam in his black eyes told me he knew I was scrambling to think of a way to avoid being alone with him tonight. Wondering if I could find a door with a lock. Surely there had to be one in this castle, with its choice of approximately five million rooms. I shook my head with an awkward laugh. *"You* don't want to learn how to give a baby his bath and put him to bed, Your Excellency!"

He snorted at that last bit. "A man needs to know how

to take care of his own son." He lifted a dark eyebrow. "Don't you agree?"

"Yes," I grumbled.

"Such a good father," Maurine sighed.

I narrowed my eyes, then gave him a smile. "I'll show you how to change his diaper, too," I said sweetly.

He gave me a crooked grin. *"Excelente."*

A moment later, we were walking down the dark hallways, the noise of the happy dinner party receding behind us, beneath the thick inner walls of the castle.

"This way," he said, placing his fingertips innocently on the base of my spine to guide me. I trembled.

Tonight, you will be in my bed.

Tonight, you will be my wife.

"Our bedroom is in the new wing...."

"New wing?"

"This castle might have been home to this family for four hundred years, but antiques are—how shall I say this?—not my style."

Going up another flight of stairs, still holding our baby protectively with his muscled arm, he pushed open the door at the end of that hall. I followed him inside, and saw an enormous, high-ceilinged room with floor-to-ceiling windows overlooking a balcony. Modern, masculine, stark. With only one real piece of furniture.

An enormous bed.

I stopped. "But where's the crib?"

"I've had the room next door turned into a nursery." To my relief, Alejandro didn't even glance at the big bed, but just kept walking straight into the connecting door that led to the nursery, and its en-suite bathroom.

The bathroom connected to the nursery was as severe and cold as the master bedroom had been, all white marble and gleaming chrome. But it did have an amazing view. Wide windows overlooked the dark vistas of his estate, lit only by moonlight and distant twinkling lights on the horizon.

He stopped, frowning at the marble bathtub. "On second thought, I don't think this is going to work," he said tersely, looking from the enormous tub to the baby in his arms. "He's too small. We need to get a special baby-size tub...."

It was endearing, really, to see how worried he was. "Tomorrow, if you like, we can go get one. For today, it's no problem." Smiling, I took Miguel in my arms. "Since he can't sit up on his own yet, we'll just hold him up. And be careful." Leaning over, I turned on the water. "Having an extra pair of hands will help."

His eyes met mine. "So you don't...mind that I'm helping you?"

"No," I said softly, "I'm glad."

His expression changed. He started to speak, then turned away, sticking his hand in the water. When the temperature was Goldilocks-acceptable—neither too hot nor too cold—he plugged the drain so the bathtub could fill.

Sitting the baby on the marble counter, I started to pull off his clothes and the clean diaper beneath. "Can you grab his baby shampoo? It's in my bag. Oh." I turned. "It's still in the car—"

With a grin, Alejandro held up the baby shampoo from a nearby drawer, along with a white, fluffy towel. "You mean this?"

"Oh," I said. My cheeks went hot. "It was nice of your staff to unpack everything for me, but..."

"But?"

"It's just strange to have someone going through my stuff."

"You'll get used to it. You'll never have to lift a finger again, unless you want to. Especially with Abuela to oversee everything. She enjoys cooking, cleaning, shopping..."

He paused, suddenly looking uncertain. "That is, if you wish that."

I lifted my eyebrows. "If I?"

Alejandro came closer to me.

"You are the duchess now," he said. "As far as the *castillo* is concerned, your rule is now law."

My cheeks went hot. I licked my lips, tried to laugh as I sat on the edge of the bathtub and checked the water with my elbow. "So you mean I could fire everyone, throw out your tenants, buy Maurine a condo in Barcelona, get rid of all the furniture and paint the walls pink?"

But he didn't laugh.

"If you like," he said in a low voice. "Though I'd prefer we keep the staff and tenants. If you decided otherwise, I would need to take care of them some other way."

"Give them all houses and jobs in Madrid?"

"Something like that."

This kind of thinking surprised me. Most of the high-powered CEO types I'd seen in New York and London seemed to constantly need to resole their expensive shoes, due to the wear caused by stepping on all the little people. I looked at Alejandro curiously. "You really feel responsible for them, don't you?"

"Of course. They—" Tightening his jaw, he looked away. "They're my people."

"Oh." I bit my lip. "Maybe you're not entirely the bastard I thought you were."

"But I am," he said in a low voice. He lifted his gaze to mine. "I can't change who I am."

Something about the expression of the chiseled lines of his handsome face made me feel all confused and jumbled inside. For a moment, the only sound between us was the water running into the bathtub, and the soft yawns of our baby.

"All right, fine. The staff can stay." I sighed. "It would probably be easier to just get rid of me, then."

His lips quirked upward. "Never. Sorry."

"Miguel is your responsibility. Not me," I pointed out. "You don't have to worry about me. I'm not…one of your people." I looked away. "I can support myself. Just so you know."

"I do know. I've seen your paintings."

I stiffened. Edward had often patronized my *little hobby*. "What is that supposed to mean?"

"Isn't it obvious? I think you're talented," he said softly. He pointed toward the nursery. "Or didn't you notice?"

Frowning, I went to the door. And I sucked in my breath as I looked around the dark nursery, at the paintings lining the walls.

"You brought them," I whispered. "All the paintings from Mexico…all the pictures I did of Miguel since he was born."

"I wanted them here. With him." He looked at me. "With us."

A shiver went through me from deep inside.

"You are welcome to paint, or do any work you want," he said gravely, "but only if it nourishes your soul. And any money you make is exclusively your own."

"But that's not right. I don't expect you to support me, to support all of us—"

"That is my job," he said firmly, "to financially support you and Miguel and, God willing, other children."

Other children!

I swallowed, breathing hard. It was as if he were offering me everything I'd never dreamed I could ask for. After growing up an only child, an orphan, I'd always secretly yearned to have a large family. Now Alejandro didn't just want to be a father for Miguel. He wasn't offering just financial stability for us both. He wanted to give me more children, too.

And create those children inside me....

No! I had to get ahold of myself. No matter how Alejandro looked at me in the shadows, or how the husky sound of his voice made me tremble. No matter if he seemed to be offering me my dreams. Without love, without honesty, *it wouldn't work.*

I shook my head. "You don't need to do these things out of duty."

"Not duty." His hand cupped my cheek. "It is my honor. And more." His eyes met mine as he said huskily, "It is my pleasure."

My cheeks flamed with heat. Sparks of need crackled down my body from that single point of contact. My lips went dry, and tension coiled hot, deep inside.

Nervously, I pulled away, looking down at the enormous marble bathtub. "Water's ready."

I carried Miguel to the tub, and Alejandro was suddenly beside me, rolling up his long sleeves to reveal his powerful forearms, dusted with dark hair. "Allow me."

Together, we propped him up to sit in the few inches of water. Alejandro held him upright as I lathered up Miguel's soft, wispy dark hair. The baby was already yawning as we toweled him off, and got him into his blue footsie pajamas decorated with baby animals. He was half-asleep as I took him into the nursery, to cuddle him in a rocking chair and feed him before bed. Alejandro sat beside us in a cushioned window seat. His face was in silhouette as he watched us, with the wide view of the moon-swept valley and the distant lights of Seville.

I cuddled our baby close, until his eyes were heavy and his mouth fell off the nipple, though his plump mouth still pursed, drinking imaginary milk as he slept sweet baby dreams.

I finally rose to my feet.

"Can I put him to bed?" Alejandro said. "At least try…."

"Sure," I said softly. I handed him the burping cloth, then the fuzzy cuddle blanket. "But you'll need to burp him first."

"Um…I'm not so sure that's a…"

"You'll be fine." I lifted a sleepy Miguel against his shoulder, over the burping cloth, and showed him how to gently pat his small back. Hesitantly, Alejandro followed suit, until our baby came up with a huge burp, before he softly sighed, and his eyes became heavy again.

Alejandro flashed me a look of triumph. "Ha!"

Seeing him that way, this handsome, ruthless, broad-shouldered man holding his tiny sleeping son—our son—my heart twisted. I smiled, and hoped the dim light of the nursery wouldn't let him see how I was fighting tears.

Against everything I'd once believed, everything I'd once feared, Alejandro was an amazing father. I knew he would take care of Miguel and love him and always be there to catch him if he fell.

"Now what?" he whispered.

"Tuck him into the crib, on his back," I answered over the lump in my throat.

Alejandro moved slowly, careful not to wake Miguel, careful to hold his head. He looked as if he were sweating bullets, like a man under the pressure of disarming a nuclear weapon, as he gently set our baby down into his crib. Leaning over beside him, I placed Miguel's favorite baby blanket, the fuzzy one decorated with elephants, softly by his cheek.

For a long moment, we stood over the crib, watching our son slumber, listening to his quiet, even breathing. Then Alejandro lifted his head to look at me.

Our eyes locked. And what I saw in his face left me shivering beneath the open weight of his hunger. Wordlessly, he pulled me from the room, closing the door behind us.

We were alone. In his bedroom.

I stared at him, my heart pounding. "You have to know— what happened in the garden today was a mistake."

"*Sí*," he agreed. "It was."

He was taking it a lot better than I'd thought he would. I exhaled. "So we won't…"

My voice trailed off as, for the first time, I realized someone had been in this bedroom while we'd been bathing Miguel. My eyes went wide.

A fire now crackled in the fireplace. Candles glowed from the marble mantle. And…no, surely it couldn't be…

Going toward the king-size bed at the center of the room, I picked up one of the scarlet, fragrant petals that had been scattered over the white bedspread.

"Rose petals?" I said dumbly. Turning, I held it up. "I don't understand…."

He gave a low, sensual smile. "Don't you?"

I exhaled. "You arranged this."

"Yes."

"But you just agreed that our kiss was a mistake—"

"It shouldn't have happened in the garden. Or the kiss in the coatroom in Madrid, either. I wanted you. I lost control. That was the mistake." Coming close to me, he shook his head. "But this won't be."

"Don't look at me like that," I whispered.

"Like what?"

"Like…" I licked my lips. "Like it's all you can do to keep yourself from ripping off my clothes and sliding me beneath you…"

"Because, *querida*," he said, cupping my face, "it is. I've dreamed of you for so long…."

"You dreamed of me?" I breathed, remembering all the

nights I'd yearned for him, in hot dreams that had made me ache, only to wake up bereft and cold in the morning.

"Yes. But tonight, *querida,* tonight," he whispered, lowering his head toward mine, "my dreams come true. Not for duty. Not for convenience. But for pleasure. For need." He slowly traced his hand down the side of my body. "There's been no one for me since you, Lena. Did you know that? No other woman I've wanted in my bed. Just you. And now you are mine at last—as I am yours...."

As the fire crackled in the fireplace, I saw the shadows of red and orange move across the hard edges and planes of his handsome, saturnine face.

"It can't be true."

He pulled me into his arms.

"Tonight," he said softly, "will be the first night of forever."

Trembling, I looked up into his dark eyes. I tried to think of something, anything, to send him away from me. I tried to make my body move away, to run. But it was no longer obeying me. My body knew what it wanted. What it had always wanted.

I felt his hands tighten on my back, over the fabric of my blouse, as he pulled me close.

And he lowered his head to mine. I felt the warmth of his breath against my skin. A hard, reckless shiver went up and down my body. Of need. Of desire so great it made me shake.

Because what I wanted now, though beautiful as flowers, could poison my soul, and kill my heart. Just like the oleander...

"Please," I breathed as I felt the roughness of his jawline brush against my cheek. It was all I could do, to keep from leaning into him, kissing him, pulling him hard and tight against me. I wanted him so badly, I could almost have wept from it.

He traced his fingertip very gently from my earlobe, along my cheek, to my full, aching lower lip. "Please?"

"Please…" I tried to remember what I wanted. *Please kiss me. Please don't.*

But he didn't give me time to gather my senses. Lowering his mouth to my ear, he whispered, "You are mine. Forever and always. My pleasure. My duchess. My wife. My lover…"

"No," I whispered. "I can't be…."

"I forgot." He drew back, his eyebrows an amused slash over his heavy-lidded eyes. "You said you do not want me."

"I don't," I said, praying he would believe such a lie.

"I see." He ran his hand down the bare skin to my throat. "So you feel nothing when I do this…."

Trembling, I shook my head.

"And this…" His large hand cupped my breast over my blouse, the tip of his thumb rubbing over my nipple, which pebbled, aching and taut beneath the fabric.

I couldn't speak. I looked up at him, my lips parted, my heart pounding.

"Give in. To me."

"But I don't love you," I choked out, but what that really meant was *Don't make me love you.*

"I do not ask for your heart. But your body—*sí.* Tonight… your body will be mine."

And he lowered his mouth to mine.

His lips were gentle, even tender. One touch, and I was proved a liar. Of course I wanted him. Of course I did.

I sighed, as his kiss deepened, became demanding, hungry. My arms wrapped around his shoulders, pulling him close.

He slowly lowered me back against the enormous bed covered with rose petals. I gloried in the heavy weight of his body over mine, pressing me deep into the soft mattress.

He pulled off my blouse, kissing down my body as

each opened button revealed more of my skin. He lifted me against him, to pull off my shirt. I felt the warmth of his fingertips trailing down my naked arms, down my back. With expert precision, he unlatched my bra with a single flick of his fingers, and my breasts hung free, full and heavy and aching for his touch.

I heard the hoarseness of his breath as he pushed me back against the bed. Cupping my breasts with his hands, he nuzzled between them, lowering his head to one taut nipple, then the other, pulling it gently into his mouth as I gasped with pleasure.

"Wait," I choked out. "I want to feel you—"

Reaching for his shirt, I yanked it hard from his body. I was definitely not as careful as he'd been about the buttons. At least one ripped off entirely and scattered noisily against the floor in my desperation to feel the warmth of his skin. I exhaled when I could at last run my hands over his naked chest, feeling his hard sculpted muscles beneath the light dusting of dark hair. A low groan came from his lips, and he fell against me on the bed, ravishing my lips with his own.

Ohhhh... Deeper, deeper. The pleasure of his tongue against mine, his lips hard and so sweet, made me burn all over, made me lose my mind....

He kissed slowly down my bare skin, working his way to my belly button, which he flicked with his tongue. Unbuttoning my jeans, he rolled them with my panties down my hips, peeling the fabric inch by inch down my legs, kissing and licking and nibbling as he went, until I was naked and gasping for breath.

He kissed the hollow of my foot, then gently pushed my legs wide. From the base of the bed, he looked up at me, spread-eagled across the bed, naked for his pleasure. I quivered with need. If he tried to leave me now—my lips parted. In that moment, I would have done anything—begged, even—to get him to stay.

But no begging was necessary. With a low growl, he removed his own trousers and then fell hard and naked upon me. I felt the length of him, like steel, pressing between my legs. Looking up at his face in the flickering shadows of the firelight, I realized that he wasn't in nearly as much control of himself as I'd imagined. In fact, he was barely keeping himself in check.

"You don't have to hold back," I choked out, pulling him down against me, my hips lifting of their own volition against his. "Please…"

And this time, there was no question what I wanted. But he would not let me control him or set the pace. Shrugging off my grasp, he slid down my body, then parted my legs with his shoulders at my knees. I felt the heat of his breath against my inner thighs. I gasped, reaching my hands out to grip the white comforter beneath me.

Pressing his large hands against my thighs, he spread me wide. He lowered his head and took a long, languorous taste.

My hips bucked beneath his tongue. The pleasure was almost too much to bear. I tried to move away. But he held me fast. He stroked me, licked me, leaving me wet and in the agony of almost unbearable pleasure. His sensual tongue flicked against my taut core, and I held my breath, tilting my head back, my eyes rolling back in my head as I lifted higher, and tighter.

The moment before I would have exploded, he pulled back. I whimpered. I heard his low laugh as he changed position, returning his mouth to where it had been, but pressing his hands beneath my backside to hold me hard against him. Spreading his mouth wide, he worked me with his tongue, going wide, then deep, then wide again. I felt his tongue thrust inside me, and cried out. My back arched against the mattress as he forced me to accept the pleasure, and as he proved to me, against my will, how much more of it my body could endure.

With a single ragged breath, I lifted higher, and higher, but again, just as I was about to explode, he lifted his mouth. He smiled down at me.

By this point I was starting to turn to a mindless mess, somewhere between blubbering and wanting to resort to physical violence, because I knew he was teasing me, forcing me to soar, to coast, then soar higher still.

Abruptly, he lifted my legs to wrap around his tight, trim hips. Rose petals flew up from the bed as he moved me, the flowers leaving a sensual, heady fragrance as they fell back to earth, sliding first against his body, then mine. I felt him pressing hard and stiff and huge between my legs. I exhaled, pressing my fingers into his back, nearly weeping with need.

Again, he started to pull away, but this time, I wouldn't let him go. My fingernails dug into the skin of his back, and I gave a low growl. *"Bien, querida,"* he panted. *"Bien."*

He positioned his hips, and in one rough movement, he shoved himself inside me, hard and thick and enormous, ramming himself to the hilt. That very first thrust made me explode from the inside out. I saw stars as waves of bliss shook through me. I heard a rising animal cry and realized to my shame that it came from my mouth. I fell back against the soft mattress, as if from a far distance, landing a limp heap on his bed.

He froze, still deep inside me in that first thrust.

"You can go on…" I panted, trying to catch my breath. "I already…"

"More," he said, eyeing my face hungrily. "Do it again." Again? Was he crazy? I shook my head. "I can't…"

"Again," he said grimly.

He slowly pushed inside me, this time letting me feel

every inch. He made me stretch for him, as I felt him deep inside. It felt good. But he was holding himself back for no reason. I knew there was no way I could…

Drawing back, he slowly filled me again, and then again. Gripping my shoulders tight with his hands, he rode me. To my amazement, a new tension began to build deep inside me. Different this time. Even deeper. With a gasp, I wrapped my hands around him, feeling the clench and unclench of the muscled cheeks of his backside, feeling the sweat on his skin as he fiercely held himself in check.

His thrusts became rougher as he rode me harder, faster, our sweaty naked bodies sliding against each other. He held my shoulders tight enough to bruise, as he pounded me hard, hard, hard. Deep, deep, deep. My back started to arch again. Seeing that, he sucked in his breath and lowered his lips to mine, kissing me. I felt the flick of his tongue against mine as he rammed into me so deep, and that was it—the brutality and force and lust shook me into an explosion so great I screamed into his mouth.

His self-control evaporated. With a low guttural growl, he shoved into me one last time, and with a gasp and groan, he spent himself inside me.

He collapsed, his body heavy over mine on the bed.

It took long moments for me to return back to earth. When I did, my eyes flew open.

"We forgot to use a condom," I blurted out. I expected him to look horrified. He did not.

"I forgot nothing." He gave me a heavy-lidded smile. "I want to get you pregnant, Lena."

Shock went through me as I stared at him with wide eyes. "But we…"

"I will fill you with my child, *mi esposa*. Try to fight me if you must," he whispered, then his smile lifted to a grin. "It is always a pleasure to battle with you."

CHAPTER EIGHT

SUNSHINE WAS SPILLING from the windows, across our naked, intertwined bodies spread across the bed, the white cotton sheets twisted and tangled at our feet. My first thought when I woke was to think it all had been a dream. Then I saw Alejandro, still sleeping in my arms, a soft smile on his chiseled face.

I caught my breath. My heart beat faster, in a rhythm like music, because joy—pleasure—everything I'd ever wanted had all come true at once.

Slowly, Alejandro opened his eyes, and his smile widened. His expression was open, and young, and he, too, seemed to be shining with happiness. *"Buenos días,"* he whispered, leaning forward to kiss me tenderly on the forehead, *"mi corazon."*

"Good morning." I blushed, looking away, feeling oddly shy.

Reaching out, he lifted my chin and kissed me, until all thoughts of shyness disappeared beneath the mutual hunger building anew between us.

How was it possible? We'd made love three times last night—three times!—and yet he was still brand new. I gloried in his touch, in the feel of his naked, hard-muscled body against mine, his arms holding me as if I were truly the precious names he'd called me. *My pleasure, my duchess, my wife. My lover.*

And now something more. Something new he'd called me for the first time.

My heart...

We made love once more, hot, hard and fast—and good thing about that last bit, because thirty seconds after we'd both collapsed in a sweaty, gasping heap on top of each other, I heard an indignant cry from the nursery.

We looked at each other and laughed.

"I'll get him," I said, starting to rise from the bed.

"No." He put his hand on my shoulder, pressing me back against the soft sheets, and rose from the bed, pulling on a white terry-cloth robe over his hard-muscled body. "You got up last time. Relax. Go take a shower. Take your time."

I came out, hot and clean and pink-cheeked and happy. I got dressed in a soft pink shirt and skirt, and fed the baby as my husband had a shower in his turn.

This was just as I'd always dreamed. No. It was better. Just the three of us...

For now.

My hand slowly fell on my belly. *I want to fill you with my child.* Was I afraid? Yes. But did I also want, desperately want, another baby? Also yes.

So much had changed since the last time I was pregnant. Instead of being a fearful fugitive, I was married now. Settled. With a home.

Would it be so wrong to just let myself be happy? Alejandro was a good father. He was proving to be a good husband. He wanted to take care of me forever. He wanted us to be a family. And the way he made love to me... I shuddered at the memory of ecstasy.

Would it be so forbidden, so foolish, to trust my husband with my heart?

If only I knew the lie he was telling me, or had told, or would tell. He said he'd been faithful to me for a year, that he'd never be disloyal.

Of course, that could be the lie....

My lips pressed together, and I grimly pushed the thought away. I told myself that, since he'd shared so much of his body, surely he'd soon find it irresistible to share the secrets of his heart. And then I forced myself not to think about it.

Denial is a beautiful thing. A woman in love can be very good at focusing on the rose and ignoring the thorn—at least until it draws blood. Over breakfast, I kept smiling at Alejandro over my plate of eggs and *jamón,* my coffee diluted with tons of cream and sugar. And instead of treating me like a lovesick fool, as I no doubt looked like, Alejandro, the dark, dangerous, ruthless duke, did the unthinkable.

He kept smiling back.

"I'd like to take you around the estate today," he said, sipping his black coffee and reading the morning newspaper, "to meet my tenants."

"What?" I nearly dropped the baby rattle I'd been holding out for Miguel, who was sitting in my lap. Chortling, the baby grabbed it in his fat little fist and triumphantly began to shake. "I thought I'd meet them at the wedding reception."

"Abuela told me it will take her two months to plan the reception. We cannot wait that long." His eyes met mine. He seemed to sense my fear, because he gave me an encouraging smile. "You are my wife. It is right that I introduce you to the tenants on the estate. That is the merest good manners."

"But…"

"Besides. Knowing Abuela, the reception will be a lavish affair, to impress acquaintances and friends. I want the first introduction to be private. Personal." He paused. "Many of them have been farming this land for generations. They might have heard rumors. They might think that having a baby first, and getting married second, is a little…"

"Modern?" I supplied.

"Yes. Modern. I don't want them to wonder if this is a real marriage, or if we'll stand the test of time."

"Will we?" I whispered.

"We will," he said seriously, looking straight into my eyes. "And I want them to have no doubt you are here to stay." Leaning forward, he took my hand in his own. "I want them to think well of you, as I do." He looked at me. "Will you meet them?"

Having Alejandro look at me with his deep dark eyes, and hold my hand, and ask me something, in his husky voice, there was no possibility of resistance. No matter how the thought of trying to impress a bunch of strangers and convince them I would make an excellent *duquesa* filled me with dread. What if they thought I wasn't good enough? What if they had such deep doubts, Alejandro changed his mind about me and decided to find some other wife more worthy? "All right," I said hesitantly. "If you think it truly necessary."

"I do." Alejandro's eyes softened as he looked at our baby. "I'd like Miguel to come, as well. Because he is their future. And they are his."

I bit my lip, trying my best not to look nervous. "Right. Four hundred years on this land, right? So it's in Miguel's blood."

"Something like that." Alejandro put down his napkin and rose to his feet. "We'll see the Widow Ramirez first. She was my governess, once."

The thought warmed my heart. "She taught you as a child?"

"Both me and the...housekeeper's son."

"You mean Miguel," I said softly. "Your friend."

"Yes. We played together as children, studied together, fought. It didn't matter that one of us was a future duke and the other just the housekeeper's son. We studied the same subjects, lived in the same house. We both loved Abuela. We were friends. Until Miguel died that day."

"And you survived," I said gently, touching his shoulder.

"Yes. I survived." He turned away. "I'll get the keys."

I finished my breakfast and my orange juice. When Alejandro returned, he said, "Señora Ramirez is no longer as sharp as she used to be, but she still has a lot of influence with the other tenants."

"No pressure," I muttered, my heart suddenly cold with fear. I looked down at my pink shirt and floppy cotton skirt. "Maybe I should change."

He barely glanced at me. "You're fine."

"I want them to like me…."

Alejandro laughed. "Fancy clothes won't make them like you. In fact, if you showed up in a designer dress and five-inch stiletto heels, they'd like you *less*. The farmers respect honesty, hard work and kindness when it's called for. Bluntness when it's not." His dark eyes gleamed. "You should get along just fine."

"Oh, all right," I sighed, sure he was wrong.

A half hour later, the three of us were in his estate vehicle, a black, open-air Jeep, headed over a dirt road that crossed the wide fields and hills belonging to the Castillo de Rohares.

The Widow Ramirez's house was a snug little cottage on the edge of the estate, where she grew organic peaches and persimmons, aubergines and artichokes, and raised goats that produced milk and cheese. Frail and wizened, barely as tall as my shoulder, when she answered her door she looked at me with critical, beady eyes. But by the end of the visit, she was smiling and pushing more of her homemade butter cookies toward me.

"Eat, eat," she pleaded. "You must keep up your strength if you are to give your husband more children."

I felt Alejandro looking at me, and blushed.

"*Gracias,* Pilar," he said, putting his hands on my shoulders. "We wish for more children very much."

"Of course you do," she said, pouring him tea. "I know it was always your desire to have a larger family, growing up so lonely, up in that huge castle, with your older sister off working in Granada. And your mother," she sniffed, "working night and day, when she wasn't distracted by the duke...."

"Sister? What sister? Alejandro is an only child," I added, frowning up at him. "Aren't you?"

He cleared his throat, glancing at his old governess. "You're confused, Pilar," he said gently. "You're thinking of Miguel. Not me."

Her rheumy eyes focused on him. Then she nearly jumped in her chair. "Yes. Yes, of course. That was Miguel. You are El Duque." She abruptly held out a plate to me. *"¿Más galletas?"*

"Yes, please."

She beamed at me. "It makes me so happy you like my cookies. Alejandro—" she looked at him severely "—barely ate one."

He laughed. "I had three."

"Hardly any," she sniffed. She smiled at me. "You should take the example of your wife, and eat four or more."

"Gracias," I said happily, and took another one, buttery and flaky and sweet. "I will need this recipe."

"I'll be delighted to send it to you!"

Shortly afterward, as we rose to leave, Alejandro hugged the widow's small frame gently and looked at her with real love. "Take care of yourself, Pilar. We'll see you soon."

"You, too, M—Alejandro." Shaking her head with a wry smile, she reached up and patted his cheek, then looked down and kissed the top of our baby's head. Looking among the three of us, she said, "I'm so happy for you, my dear. How it's all turned out. You deserve a happy life."

Leaving her cottage, we got back into his open Jeep, tucking Miguel into the baby seat in the backseat. As we drove across the bumpy road, I exhaled in pure relief. Closing my eyes, I turned my face up to the warm morning sun, feeling happy that I'd somehow—I had no idea how—passed the first test. Instead of her tossing me out, she'd fed me cookies. And I'd pretty much eaten all of them. What can I say? They were delicious. I really did need that recipe.

Smiling, I turned to look at my husband. "She was nice."

"I'm glad you think so." He was looking at me with a strange expression, as if he wanted to say something. I frowned, and I parted my lips to ask what he was thinking. Before I could, he looked away.

"We'll visit the Delgado family next."

For the rest of the day, as my confidence built, I spoke with all of the tenants on his estate. They seemed relieved and happy that I spoke Spanish, though they took pleasure in teasing me mercilessly about my accent. They adored the baby, and all of them praised my new husband to me, even when he was out of earshot. One after another, they told me stories of his noble character, his good heart.

"The land was neglected, and El Duque brought it back from the brink…."

"My roof was falling apart, but El Duque helped me fix it…."

"When the crop died, I thought I would have to leave. But El Duque gave me a loan, enough for seed and animals. He saved us, and he himself was only eighteen…."

"He gave my son a job in Madrid, when there were no jobs to be had. José would have left for Argentina." The old woman wiped her eyes. "El Duque kept my son here in Spain, and I'm so grateful. I'll never forget…."

By the time we visited the last house in early evening, I was no longer even nervous. I was relaxed, holding our baby, laughing and chatting with the farmers, complimenting them on their well-cared-for fields and animals, complimenting their wives on their delicious *tartas*. And seeing how they admired Alejandro, how they treated him with such respect. His people did love him.

And by extension, I realized, they were willing to love me, for his sake. And for the sake of our child.

On the drive back home over the dusty road, back to the castle at the top of the hill, we didn't speak in the open-air Jeep. Miguel was sleeping in the back. Finally, I smiled at Alejandro. "That went well, don't you think?"

"Yes," he said shortly.

What could he possibly be mad about now? Biting my lip, I looked at the passing scenery. I was already starting to love Spain, especially Andalucía. The air was warm, dusty from our tires on the dirt road. The sun was starting to fade to the west, leaving a soft golden glow across the fields. I felt the warm breeze against my skin, the air scented by honeysuckle and bougainvillea and the jacaranda trees in bloom.

But Alejandro didn't say a word. He pulled the truck in front of the garage. Getting out, he opened my door. When I stepped out of the Jeep, he pulled me into his arms. I looked up at him, biting my lip. "Alejandro, didn't I do—all right?"

"All right?" he said huskily. I saw the warmth in his deep brown eyes. They held the same glow as the soft Andalucían morning. "I am proud of you beyond words, *mi corazon*. You made them love you. As..."

He cut himself off, but as I looked up at his face, my heart started to pound. "They loved me for your sake."

"No." He shook his head. "They loved you only for yourself. Your warmth, your smile, your..." Reaching down, he stroked my cheek. Something seemed to stretch tight between us, making me hold my breath. His hand trailed down my hair, down my back. "Come upstairs with me," he whispered. "Right now..."

"But dinner…"

He lowered his head to mine in a deep, passionate kiss, taut and tender, slow and sweet. I clutched his shoulders, lost in his embrace.

Miguel gave a plaintive whine from the back of the Jeep, and Alejandro released me with a rueful laugh. "But Abuela will be expecting us for dinner."

"Yes." I shook my head with a snort. We'd been fed at literally every house we visited. "I won't be able to eat a bite. I'm not the least bit hungry."

"Funny. I'm starving." He gave me a dark look that made my body burn, and I knew he wasn't talking about food. He sighed grumpily. "But you're right. Dinner has been arranged. We wouldn't want to disappoint Abuela…."

"No. We wouldn't." I took our baby out of the truck, and we went upstairs to give Miguel his bath. Alejandro left to dress for dinner tonight, as Maurine had requested. I fed our baby, cuddling him in the rocking chair as he drifted off to sleep, plump and adorable in his footsie pajamas, holding his soft blanket against his cheek. I finally tucked him into his crib, then went to the master suite next door.

I felt dusty from the road, and was tempted to take a shower, but feared that would make me late, which would be rude. Especially since Maurine had insisted tonight's dinner was special somehow. So I just brushed out my hair and put on a long slinky dress and high heels. She'd asked us to dress up for dinner tonight, though what made tonight different from the other nights, I had no idea. I put on some red lipstick and looked at myself in the mirror. I looked so different, I thought. I barely recognized myself. I tossed my hair, seeing the bold new gleam in my eye—and liking it.

Smiling, I went downstairs. But as I walked down the sweeping stairs, voices echoed from the shadows of the stairwell below.

"You should tell her the truth." Maurine's voice was uncharacteristically sharp.

"No," Alejandro answered coldly.

"She's your wife—"

"She cannot know. Not yet. Perhaps not ever. I don't know if I can trust her."

"But this is your life we're talking about!"

"Not just my life. Also yours. And Miguel's. She could destroy us all if she—"

Then they looked up and saw me. I shaped my mouth into a bright smile, as if I hadn't heard anything, as if my heart wasn't pounding.

"You look spectacular, *mi esposa*," Alejandro murmured, and held out his arm. He was dressed in a dark tailored shirt and trousers. "May I escort you to dinner?"

I nodded. But as we walked down the hallway toward the banqueting hall, the happiness that had been building inside me all day had suddenly gone *pfffft* like a balloon.

What was he hiding?

It was growing harder to push the question from my mind. Even denial will carry you only so far. My recent happiness suddenly felt like a house of cards waiting to fall.

I'd felt such incandescent joy, being in his arms last night. Being by his side today, meeting his neighbors and the people who mattered to him. Being introduced, with pride, as his wife.

Every moment I spent with him, I was falling deeper and deeper into an emotion I'd sworn I'd never feel for him again. Especially since I knew he was lying to my face. I was walking straight into heartbreak, only this time, I'd have no one to blame but myself.

Abruptly, I stopped in the middle of the hallway.

He frowned down at me. "What, *querida?*"

I looked at him, my heart aching. "I need to know what you're hiding from me."

Setting his jaw, he shook his head.

"I wish I'd never told you," he said harshly. Dropping my hand, he looked at me with cold eyes. "Should we spend dinner apart?"

He was ruthlessly ending the conversation. Swallowing back tears, I shook my head. He held out his arm again.

We walked, the only sound our footsteps against the flagstones. "I wonder why Maurine insisted that we dress up for dinner tonight," I said over the awkward silence. "I just saw her wearing an old cardigan and jeans…."

We entered the banqueting hall, and my voice cut off.

It was completely empty of other people. The only light came from the blazing fire in the enormous stone fireplace. Tall tapered candles lit the table. Beneath the high, timbered ceilings, the shadows and fire made the room breathlessly romantic.

I blinked, bewildered. "This is why Maurine wanted us to dress for dinner…?" Then Alejandro gave me a sensual smile, and it all clicked into place. "You arranged this," I breathed.

He shrugged. "I spoke with her before we left this morning, and she agreed newlyweds need time alone."

"But what about dinner for everyone else?"

"They already ate." He came closer, his dark eyes intent. "And I'm glad," he said huskily. "I want you to myself."

I stared at him, still conflicted about the way he'd coldly cut off my earlier question. Going to the table, he poured us each a glass of red wine that sparkled like a ruby in the firelight.

"Manzanilla wine. From my vineyard."

As we sat next to each other at the end of the long table, near the fire, I felt my anger starting to be melted by his nearness. The dinner was probably delicious, but I ate mechanically, barely tasting it. Alejandro moved his chair closer. He did not try to touch me. He started asking me questions, asking what I thought of Spain, how I liked the estate, how I liked the baby's nursery. He asked me how I'd first started painting.

"My father taught me," I said softly. "He always wanted to be an artist. But once he got married and had a family, he had to try to earn a living...." I gave a rueful laugh. "He was never good at earning money. But we loved him, just as he was."

Alejandro leaned forward, his elbow on the table, his chin resting on his hand, listening to every word. He focused his attention on me, as if nothing and no one else existed.

I knew how this worked. I'd seen it before. And yet I still could not resist. With every breath I felt him seducing me, drawing me in closer. Against my will, my heart started to warm.

The enormous banqueting hall, usually chilly inside the castle even on a hot summer day, was growing increasingly hot. I found myself leaning forward, asking him questions in my turn, and all the while wishing he would kiss me, and hating myself for wanting it. Finally, I could bear it no longer.

"Why can't you tell me your secret?"

"Put it from your mind," he said harshly. "Or go."

"Fine," I said tearfully. I stood, turning away.

He grabbed me by the wrist.

Slowly, Alejandro rose from the chair, his body grazing mine as he fully stood, towering over me. My head tilted back to look at his face. He was bigger than me, stronger by far. But it wasn't his strength that overwhelmed me, but the stark vulnerability I suddenly saw in his hard, handsome face.

"This is all you need to know," he whispered.

He pushed me against the edge of the stone fireplace, holding my wrists above me, kissing my lips, my throat.

Closing my eyes, I tilted back my head as waves of desire crashed over me.

"I want you, Lena," he whispered, his voice husky, his lips brushing my earlobe. *"Te deseo."*

I shivered. Then remembered why I was mad at him and tried to pull away. "I—I am dusty and sweaty from the road." I gave a casual laugh that no one would believe, least of all me. "I rushed downstairs because I didn't want to be late." He continued to kiss my face, and I closed my eyes, breathing, "But I should…really…go take a bath…."

"Bien," he purred. "I'll join you."

My eyes flew open. "A shower, I mean, not a bath," I stammered. "There's not much room in the shower for two…."

He ran his hands down my back, holding me against him. "Just enough."

He kissed me, and beneath the sensuality of his embrace, I sighed, and my lips parted. My body melted into his, my soft curves pressing into his hard angles as if his body had been made for mine.

Lifting me into his arms as if I weighed nothing at all, he carried me upstairs to our private, luxurious bathroom, where he gently set me on my feet. His dark eyes never left mine as he slowly pulled off my dress, then my bra, then my panties.

When I was completely naked in front of him, he wrenched me hard against him and kissed me deeply, hungrily. I desperately began to unbutton his shirt, then his trousers, until he, too, was naked.

Pulling away, he turned on the water in the shower. I glanced back longingly at the bed, but it was in the next room and seemed a million miles away. He kissed me again, and I gasped against his lips, his naked body hard against mine. Steam lifted from the hot water of the shower, making the luxurious bathroom of white marble and silver a magical, otherworldly place of ice and snow.

Except for the heat. Every inch of me felt warm, bursting with fire.

Alejandro pulled me into the shower. He pushed me away from him firmly, and I whimpered.

"Patience," he said, and I could almost hear his smile. He was still in control. Unlike me...

With agonizing slowness, he washed me in the shower, tangling shampoo in my hair, rubbing soap over my body, scrubbing every inch of me. I felt him stroke my full, naked breasts, my waist, my hips, the soft hair between my legs. I closed my eyes, swaying on my feet. I felt hot and unsteady as he caressed my hair, down my earlobes, my neck. I left handprints in the glass wall of the shower, against the white steam.

Turning me around to face him, he ran his hands down my breasts, over my belly, over my hips and thighs. Hot shooting streams of water poured over us both.

And he knelt before me. Gently parting my thighs, he pressed his face between my legs.

I gasped. His lips were tender and sensual and warm. His tongue slid against me, inside me, the merest breath of a stroke, hot and wet beneath the warm water.

I closed my eyes, pressing my hands against the glass wall behind me.

His hands slid around me, holding me firmly against his mouth. He teased me with the tip of his tongue, soft and light against the most sensitive part of me, then spread me wide and lapped me, until I tossed back my head, slapping my long wet hair against the glass as I shook all over. The hot, steamy water poured over us both as I felt his hands—his tongue—slide over my wet, pink skin.

For an intoxicating eternity, he teased me, bringing me almost to an explosion of pleasure beneath the steamy pulse of the shower, then backing away the very second before I would have exploded into bliss. It might have been seconds or hours, that he seduced me with this sweet torment....

When my need was too much to bear, and I was shaking so hard I could barely breathe with desire, Alejandro turned me around, pressing me against the glass, my bottom resting against his hard, thick length.

"You're mine," he growled in my ear. "Say it."

"I'm yours," I breathed, pressing my arms against the glass.

"Again."

"I'm yours!"

"Forever."

"Forever," I whispered.

He thrust inside me roughly, deep and hard, and I gasped.

I forgot everything in the overwhelming pleasure of having him inside me. *Pleasure* was not a big enough word for it. I melted, lost myself, found myself, until he exploded inside me, and I soared.

Afterward, both of us were panting and spent, and he abruptly turned off the water. He opened the shower door and toweled me off. Without a word, he lifted me in his arms and carried me to our enormous bed. Looking back, I saw the trail of water he'd left across his stark floor.

Clinging to my husband's naked chest as he carried me, I felt as if I were in another time or place. I wondered dreamily about other lovers who'd done this, hundreds of years ago, in this very castle, when the sultan ruled.

Setting me down naked on our bed, he looked down at me. I smiled up at him, blinking tears of emotion, of anger and joy all mixed up together.

Climbing beside me, he held me, kissing my temple tenderly. Our bodies intertwined, his wet skin sliding against mine. My hand stroked the hardness of his chest, laced with dark hair. He held me tight. My eyes were heavy, and started to close.

I'd told him the truth in the shower.

I was his.

Now and forever.

Because I love him....

The realization hit like a bolt of lightning, causing my eyes to fly open.

I was in love with him, and there was something he was keeping from me. A reason he was lying. A secret he thought would hurt me.

I was in love with my husband.

But if I knew the secret he hid from me, would that love be destroyed?

CHAPTER NINE

THE NEXT FEW weeks fled by in a blur. We spent our days doing the work of the estate, talking to tenants and managing the house. I started painting in the garden in the morning, and played with our baby on the floor of Alejandro's home office as he worked on the computer and spoke on the phone to employees around the world.

"I begrudge them every hour," he told me, stroking my cheek. "I would rather spend it with you."

My heart sang as the birds did, flying free through the lush green trees, across the wide blue Spanish sky. But eventually, Alejandro had to go on a business trip. "Madrid?" I pouted.

He laughed. "Granada."

"Isn't that where the Alhambra is?" I said eagerly, picturing the famous Moorish castle. "I'll come with you!"

He shook his head. "It will be a one-day trip, there and back. Very boring. Stay here with Miguel. Paint. Enjoy your day." He kissed my temple and said huskily, "I'll be back before bedtime."

Then he kissed me *adios* until my toes curled.

But after he'd gone, all the fears and shadows came back crashing around me, without Alejandro's warmth and strength to hide behind.

Was he really going to do business in Granada, as he'd said? Or was he there for some other reason?

Was this his lie?

Don't think about it, I ordered my trembling heart, but it was impossible, now that I loved him.

I feared knowing the truth.

I feared never knowing it.

"Dear?" I heard Maurine's tremulous voice. "I wonder if I could ask you a favor?"

"Of course," I said, desperate for distraction.

She smiled at me. "You are such a talented artist. I love the paintings you've done of my roses. You are the only one who's ever done them justice." As I blushed, she continued, "Alejandro's birthday is next month. Would you do a portrait of me and Miguel, in the rose garden…?"

"I'd love to!" I exclaimed, my mind immediately filled with painting materials, size and composition. I went into Seville for supplies, and by late afternoon, after Miguel's nap, the three of us were outside. I propped up an easel in front of where they sat on a bench, surrounded by greenery and red, yellow and pink roses.

The warm Spanish sun filtered golden light over the garden as I painted the portrait of the dowager Duchess of Alzacar and her great-grandbaby, the future duke.

Maurine's lovely white hair was like a soft cloud around her twinkling eyes and smiling face. I drew her outline in loose strokes. That was easy, compared with the challenge of the wiggling, giggling baby in her lap. But I'd painted and drawn my son so many times over the past six months, I knew his chubby face by heart. I could have done it blindfolded.

I smiled to myself, picturing how happy Alejandro would be at the gift, reaching up to adjust the floppy pink hat I was wearing to keep the sunlight out of my eyes. Maurine chattered nonstop, while entertaining the baby in her lap. She told me how she'd first fallen in love with her husband, who'd had a title, "though it seemed useless enough, with no hope of returning to Spain, with the political situation," and absolutely no money or marketable skills. "It's so much easier to know how to work when you've been raised to it. My husband had spent his adult life sleeping in the spare rooms of rich friends from his Eton days."

"Sounds like my father. He wanted to work, but didn't know how."

"It's the upbringing, I think. Even when we finally returned to Spain, with the Navaro fortune lost, Rodrigo had no idea how to pay for the upkeep of this castle. It's not like the old days, when a duke could simply demand peasants give him tribute." She gave a soft laugh. "He was desperate to keep the title and the land, for the sake of his family's history. I loved him, so I did my best to help." She looked away, blinking fast. "I sold oranges from the orchard and gave castle tours. Sadly, our son was no better with money—the earning of it, I mean, not the spending of it. By the time Alejandro became duke, the roof of the castle was caving in, we were mortgaged to the hilt, and I was beginning to think I'd spend my elderly years begging on the streets, or selling oranges at street corners."

I laughed. "As if Alejandro would ever allow that." I smiled, remembering his bossy ways when he'd informed me that taking financial care of us was his job. "He, at least, had no trouble figuring out how to make money."

"No." She smiled, playing patty-cake with the baby. "But of course, his background is so different. He didn't have an overbearing father constantly telling him how an aristocrat was supposed to behave. The small silver lining of having no father at all, I suppose...."

"No father?" Frowning, I lifted the brush off the canvas. I looked around the easel. "But Alejandro's father was the duke. Your son."

Maurine looked up at me sharply, her face oddly pale. "Oh, yes. Of course."

I gave a laugh. "Is the sun getting to you, Maurine?"

"I'm an old woman. I get confused." Her blue eyes suddenly wouldn't meet mine. "But you're right. I think I've been in the sun too long."

She rose to her feet, still holding Miguel, who looked happy to be moving at last after so long sitting still. "I'm a little tired. I'll have the staff bring you some lemonade. And maybe look for Alejandro's hairbrush. Yes, his hairbrush…"

She left the rose garden without waiting for a reply. I stared after her, frowning. What did lemonade have to do with Alejandro's hairbrush?

"I thought she would never leave."

With a gasp, I whirled around. The paintbrush fell from my limp hand, landing with a soft thud into the grass.

Edward St. Cyr stood in the rose garden, near the thick hedge on the edge of the forest. Brambles had ripped the sleeves of his dark tailored jacket.

"Edward," I breathed. "What are you doing here?"

He stopped five feet in front of me, looking down at me. His eyes were stark against his tanned face as he gazed at me hungrily. "You have no idea how I've wanted to see your face."

He reached out a hand, but I stumbled backward, my long skirt dragging against the grass. Holding my floppy pink hat against my head, I glanced uneasily to the left and right.

Having him here, in Maurine's rose garden—in Alejandro's castle—felt all kinds of wrong. Like finding a deadly snake amid the lush flowers. "How did you get in here?"

His lips twisted. "It wasn't easy."

"I told you I never wanted to see you again!" I narrowed my eyes. "You must get out of here! Alejandro will kill you if he finds you here!"

"Ah, but he's gone, isn't he?"

I sucked in my breath.

"And as for your precious duke…" A low, guttural curse came from Edward's lips. "I know you don't want him." He looked contemptuously around the lush, sunlit garden, to the stone walls of the castle just beyond the perfectly trimmed green hedges. "I've come to save you from this… prison."

"It's not a prison," I retorted. "It's my home! And Alejandro is no jailer. I…" I licked my lips, then whispered aloud, "I love him."

Edward's eyes narrowed, and his lips twisted downward, giving him an expression that was hard, even cruel.

"He seduced you, didn't he?" He took another step toward me, and I again backed away, knocking over the easel behind me. I gulped as Edward slowly looked me over, from my hat to my long cotton skirt covered with an artist's long smock. "He's got to you." He straightened, and this time his contemptuous glance was just for me, all for me. "You fell for his lines *again*."

I took a deep breath.

"I love him," I said quietly. "In a way I never loved you—and I never will."

His hands tightened at his sides.

"The charming Duque de Alzacar. Beloved by all." His lip curled. "Of course you're faithful to him. But is he faithful to you?"

I drew myself up coldly. "Of course."

"Are you sure?" He lifted a dark eyebrow. "You know, you must know, about the woman he visits in Granada?"

My lips parted. "Woman?"

"Ah," Edward said, smiling. "You didn't know. They have dinner together. Often. He bought her a tavern in the Albaicín district. Sometimes he even plays his guitar there. Singing old Spanish love songs. In front of everyone."

My mouth went dry.

Alejandro hadn't played his guitar for me. Not once.

Licking my lips, I croaked, "There are all kinds of reasons for…"

Edward moved in for the kill. "Sometimes he stays the night in the residence above her tavern. But sometimes," he said softly, "he just goes for a quick visit. For the day." His lips curled. "A bit of love in the afternoon."

The chill turned to ice. I desperately tried to think of a reasonable explanation for why Alejandro hadn't wanted me to come with him today.

I'll come with you!

It will be a one-day trip, there and back. Very boring. Stay here with Miguel.

It was the nightmare I'd imagined when I'd refused to marry Alejandro. Except this was a million times worse.

Because I'd let myself love him.

"Lying to your face." Edward came closer. "He has no shame. He thinks, in his arrogance, that he can have you, as well. He's out enjoying himself—keeping you prisoner…."

"I'm not a prisoner," I choked out.

He lifted a condescending eyebrow. "No?" He slowly looked around the rose garden. "I could make him pay," he whispered. "I could make him regret."

I gasped—not in fear, but in fury. "If you dare hurt him, I'll…"

"*Hurt* him?" His blue eyes suddenly blazed. "*He* is the one you are worried about? Where was his concern for *you* when he left your heart in ashes?" He took another step toward me, his expression changing as he reached toward me almost wistfully. "Where is your love for me, for saving you…?"

I turned away, stepping back out of his reach. My voice was very cold. "I appreciated your friendship—until the moment I realized you had no time for my baby."

"Lena, you can't…"

"If you touch me, I'll scream. And Alejandro will come running...."

Edward moved closer.

"He's not here, though, is he?"

This time, the expression in his face scared me. For a moment, I stared at him, heart pounding. But as I opened my mouth to scream, like a miracle, I heard Alejandro's voice from the other side of the garden.

"Lena? Are you out here?"

I nearly wept with relief.

"I'm here!" I shouted. "I'm here, Alejandro! In the rose garden!"

Shaking, I turned back to face Edward, but he was already gone, melted back into the forest.

"And don't ever come back," I whispered aloud. I prayed I'd never see him again. But I still heard his ugly words.

You know, you must know, about the woman he visits in Granada?

He was *lying,* I told myself. Alejandro told me he'd be loyal, that he'd been faithful for the past year, wanting only me....

But then, I remembered, he'd also told me he was a liar.

When I saw my husband's strong, powerful body push through the trees to me, I nearly wept.

"Querida," Alejandro murmured, kissing my forehead as he pulled me into his arms. "I came back early. I couldn't bear to be away for...but what's this?" He drew back, his handsome face the picture of concern. "You're shaking."

"It's nothing," I said. My teeth chattered. "M-my easel fell."

"Ah." He smiled at me, his dark eyes warm. "Let me take care of that."

"Don't look at the painting!" I cried. "It's supposed to be a surprise. For your birthday."

Good-naturedly covering his eyes, he handed me the canvas. "I didn't see a thing."

I took the painting, slightly smeared from the fall and half-finished, with Maurine and Miguel looking like ghosts. And I wished I'd covered my ears and not heard a thing when Edward had told me about the woman in Granada.

"It has occurred to me," Alejandro murmured a week later, leaning over the sofa where I sat feeding Miguel, "that we never had a honeymoon."

"Honeymoon?" I said, twisting my head to look back at him. I shook my head. "You mean, without Miguel?"

"Don't worry." He brushed the back of my neck with his fingertips, making me shiver. "I'm not thinking Tahiti. That will have to wait. But a single night, just a two-hour drive away, surely you could manage that?"

I hesitated. "I don't know…"

"I promise you'll enjoy it." He stroked my hair, then gently kissed the crook of my neck, the edge between my shoulder and my neck. My shiver turned harder. "We will get a nice hotel. Go out for dinner. I'm thinking Granada…."

"Granada?" I stared at him, and the color must have drained from my cheeks, because he frowned.

"I thought you wanted to see the Alhambra."

I'd dreamed of seeing the famous Moorish castle since I was a child. But I'd spent the past week guarding my heart. Trying to stay distant and cold. Trying not to think about what I didn't want to know. Granada was the last place on earth I wanted to go.

Or was it?

"Maybe," I said.

He smiled, really smiled, for the first time in a week. Since I'd started keeping my distance, even when we were as close as a man and woman could be. "Is that a yes?"

He tilted his head, looking over me slowly with a sensual, heavy-lidded gaze. "I'd be happy to spend time persuading you...."

My body immediately clamored for him to persuade me, hot and sweet and long. But sex wasn't our problem. We made love every night. Physically, we were closer than ever.

Emotionally, the weight of secrets had caused an ocean between us.

You know, you must know, about the woman he visits in Granada?

My smile faded. Like my courage. I shook my head. "On second thought...forget it."

"Why?" His eyes narrowed, and he moved around the sofa with lightning speed. He cupped my face, looking down at me fiercely. "I am trying to make it up to you!"

"What?" I breathed, searching his gaze. "What are you trying to make up for, Alejandro?"

"Whatever has made you so angry at me." His fingertips tightened infinitesimally. "I want you to look at me like you used to."

"And I want to trust you," I choked out, "like I used to."

He stared at me. He'd never heard that tone from me before. "When I was in Granada..."

I held my breath.

He continued, "You were alone with my grandmother. Did she..." He hesitated. "Did she say something?"

"Did she tell me your secret, you mean?" I said bitterly. "No. She is loyal to you."

He abruptly released me and rose from the sofa, his face hard. "Enough. We are taking a one-night honeymoon. You will come with me. You will have a good time."

I lifted my chin defiantly. "Is that a command, Your Excellency?"

"Take it as you wish." He glared back at me, his eyes cold. "I will tell the staff to pack your things immediately."

The drive to Granada was short, especially after Alejandro stepped on the gas of his yellow Lamborghini. But with just the two of us trapped in the small space, it still took far too long. The tension between us was boiling, about to explode.

I forced myself to look at the guidebook he'd bought me about Granada. I tried to distract myself with its history. To choke back my frustration, my hurt, my rage. Because if I let out my feelings, I feared our marriage would end, and so would any chance at happiness. Forever.

I desperately wanted to ask him about the woman.

I desperately was afraid of the answer.

Alejandro did not speak to me. He drove us to a small hotel, a *parador* amidst the gardens of the Alhambra itself, in a building that was once a fifteenth-century convent, and a royal chapel to the kings of Spain, and before that, a palace and mosque of the Moorish emirs. Once there, he seemed angry at everyone. He glowered at the hotel staff. The moment we were alone in the simple, starkly furnished bedroom, he turned on me, and pressed me to the large four-poster bed in a ruthless, unyielding embrace.

All the women's magazines tell you to do one thing. To have self-esteem. To turn away from any man you cannot completely trust. Especially one who has broken your heart before. They say the past predicts the future.

I knew all this, but when I felt his hand stroke my cheek, the sweet satin stroke of his touch sent liquid fire through my veins. I saw the dark gleam of his eyes as he slowly lowered his head to mine, and I could not resist.

He kissed me, and I felt my heart explode in my chest. Felt my taped-together soul shatter again into a million pieces, even tinier than before, in infinite chiming shards that I would never be able to put together again.

I had to ask him. I had to be brave enough to ask, and

be brave enough to listen to his answer—whether he answered with words, or with silence.

I suddenly realized this might be the very last time we'd ever make love....

"Maravillosa," Alejandro whispered against my skin. As he pulled off my clothes, as I pulled off his, as I kissed him, tasting the salt of his skin, I knew that even amid the pleasure, I was tasting the salt of my own tears.

I loved him.

So much.

And I knew—I'd always known, really—how this would someday end.

Through my tears, I kissed him back desperately, letting him pull me into the whirlwind of mingled anguish and pleasure.

But when the heat between us was satisfied, coldness was all that was left. Both of us still naked, he held me against him on the bed. His voice was low.

"Why do you not look at me like you used to? What has changed? What do you—know?"

I looked at him. His face shimmered through my tears.

"Edward came to see me last week. At Rohares."

"What!" he exploded, sitting up.

I held his hand. "I didn't ask him to come. He snuck in. I only spoke with him for a moment. He wanted me to run away with him. When I refused, he told me...you had a woman here. In Granada. That you visited her. That you bought her a tavern. That you even sing to her...."

For a long moment, we stared at each other in the slanted bars of sunlight coming through the window blinds. I could almost hear the pounding of my heart.

Then Alejandro's lip slowly curled.

"I will kill him," he said, and with cold menace, started to rise from the bed.

"No!" Grabbing his arm, I looked up at him pleadingly.

"It's not about Edward anymore. It's about us. You and me." I swallowed, blinking fast as I whispered, "Do you love her?"

He looked down at me.

"Yes," he said dully.

My lips parted in a silent, heartsick gasp. Numbly, I let him go.

"So that is your big secret. The thing I expected from the beginning." I tried to laugh, wiping my eyes. "How very boring."

"It's not like that." Sitting on the edge of the bed, he scowled at me. "You think so little of my loyalty, even after all the time we've spent together?"

"But you said you love her," I whispered. "You've never said that to me. Not once."

I heard his intake of breath. "It's not like that," he repeated, setting his jaw. "Theresa is not my mistress."

"Then what?" I choked out. "What secret could you possibly be keeping, that would hurt me worse than that?"

"I protect the people I love. At any cost." His voice was bleak. I looked at him sharply, and saw the vulnerability in his eyes. The yearning. He took a deep, shuddering breath. "How I wish I could tell you everything."

Our eyes locked. Held. I opened my lips to plead—

He shook his head and rose to his feet. The yearning in his expression shuttered. His face returned to the handsome mask I knew so well—powerful, ruthless and cold.

"Come," he said. "Our time is short."

After a silent luncheon on the lovely terrace of the *parador,* we walked through the gardens of the Alhambra, with their flowers and trees and wide lush pools. As beautiful and varied and wide as they were, they didn't hold a candle to the gardens of Rohares, in my opinion. Though perhaps I was biased. Because the castle had become my home.

Alejandro held my hand tightly as we walked. I didn't

even try to resist. The truth was I wanted the comfort of his hand. It felt warm and strong in mine. Was it wrong of me to still want to believe? To trust him?

Yes. I was a fool. Any of the women's magazines would have called me an idiot for not already being on my way to a lawyer's office. And yet...

We met a guide who took us on a private tour. We walked through the graceful arcades of the Alhambra complex, through the lush terraces with their views of Granada in the valley below, past the blue pools hedged by myrtle, reflecting the wide blue sky. But in spite of the fact that I'd dreamed of visiting the Alhambra all my life, I barely noticed the beauty. As we walked through cavernous rooms, decorated with tile and geometric patterns and arabesques of Arabic calligraphy in plaster, beneath jaw-dropping ceilings soaring high above, of the sun and stars, my mind was scrambling, trying to put the clues together.

Why would Alejandro need to protect Maurine and Miguel? What could the secret be?

We had our picture taken together in the famous stone Court of the Lions, from the fourteenth century.

"No," the guide laughed. "You are newlyweds. Stand closer."

And so Alejandro put his arm around me. I looked up at his face, and again, I saw the yearning in his eyes. The yearning that matched my own.

"*¡Perfecto!* Now you look like lovers!"

As we left the Alhambra, I turned back to look at it one last time. It had been neglected over the years, vandalized, nearly blown up by Napoleon's soldiers. But after all that, it stood tall and proud over Granada. Unbowed. Unbroken. And so beautiful now. So loved.

"We don't need to see any more," I whispered over the ache in my throat.

"You're here. See it all." Silently, Alejandro drove us

down the mountain to the city. We visited the Capilla Real, the royal chapel, getting special permission for a private tour that took us immediately past the long line of tourists outside, past the gypsies begging on the streets and musicians busking along the crowded edges.

In the dark, quiet interior of the enormous stone chapel, I saw the tomb of Ferdinand and Isabella, who together had practically ruled the medieval world in their day, even before they'd sent Columbus in ships to the New World. Together, they'd finally ended seven hundred years of Moorish rule, laying siege to Granada and driving the last sultan, called Boabdil, from the city.

It was said that the reason he gave up without a fight was to prevent the destruction of his beloved Alhambra. And so he spent the rest of his life mocked, and in poverty, a sultan without a throne....

Alejandro came to stand beside me in the cool shadows of the royal crypt. "What are you thinking?"

I looked at him. "How loving the wrong thing—or the wrong person—can ruin your life," I whispered.

"Sí," he said quietly. He turned away. "Come. This place leaves me cold."

Outside the echoes of the shadow-filled chapel, we were hit by the brilliant Spanish sunlight, the noise of tourists laughing and talking, the distant sound of music. Life.

"Enough history," Alejandro said, shaking his head ruefully. "There's an ice-cream shop down the street, the most famous in Granada. The American first lady visited here recently and said it was the best ice cream in all of Spain...."

But I wasn't listening. I was too busy trying to think things through. Eating the ice-cream cone some time later as we walked, I looked at Alejandro sideways beneath my lashes. He was so handsome, so dark-haired and broad-shouldered. The man of my dreams, come to life.

What was the secret? What was it he couldn't tell me, for fear of endangering his grandmother and his son?

We walked through the narrow streets of Granada, and I bought some chocolates and a garden ornament for Maurine, and a small stuffed toy for Miguel, plus a wooden sword and shield he wouldn't be able to play with for at least a year.

I couldn't stop thinking of that last sultan, Boabdil, who'd sacrificed everything, his honor, his fortune, his pride, rather than see the palace he loved blown up into ash.

What would I sacrifice for love?

What would you?

Love me? Alejandro's words floated back to me. *You do not even know me.*

Maybe he'd been right. A year ago, maybe I'd just fallen for his power, his wealth, his influence. His beauty.

But now, as I looked at his face, I loved him for who he really was. The man who took care of everyone. Who was willing to sacrifice himself for those he cared about. As a father. A grandson. A neighbor. A boss.

A husband.

My heart caught in my chest. What was I missing?

Twilight was falling when Alejandro suggested we go out for dinner and drinks. "A…friend of mine owns a restaurant in the Albaicín district."

I looked at him sharply. He nodded.

"Yes," he said quietly, watching me in the deepening dusk. "I want you to meet her."

I was shaking when we walked up the cobblestoned alleys of the Albaicín, the old Moorish quarter on the hillside beneath the Alhambra. We reached a prosperous-looking tavern, filled with people and music. I froze.

"Come on," Alejandro said gently. "It'll be all right." Pulling me inside, he brought me through the crowds to the bar, where he was greeted eagerly by the other patrons.

"Are you going to play tonight, *señor?*"

With a slight smile, he shook his head. "Where is Theresa?"

The man motioned toward the end of the bar with his glass of sangria. With a quick nod, Alejandro pulled me down toward a dark-haired woman.

"Theresa," he said, kissing her on each cheek.

"Alejandro," she exclaimed, returning the embrace. "I didn't expect you so soon!"

I stared at the woman. She wasn't what I'd expected. She had dark eyes and a round, friendly face, and she seemed at least ten years older than Alejandro. She smiled as she turned to me. "And this must be your wife." A big smile lit up her face. "Your Lena?"

My lips parted. *His* Lena?

"Sí." Alejandro put his arm around me. "My Lena."

"I'm so happy to meet you at last!" she said with clear delight. "I told him he had to bring you here. Wait until you hear him play!"

"Play?" I echoed, looking at him.

He blushed. I swear he did. "Yes. I play a little guitar sometimes. No one cares I'm a duke here. They only care how well I play the guitar...."

"Are you that good?"

"Let him show you." Theresa gave me a wink. "Drink orders always go up thirty percent when you sing, Alejandro." She turned to me with a smile. "Go grab a table, if you can find one.... And what will you have?"

"Bourbon," he said. "Rocks."

"Right. Lena?"

"Something light...sangria?"

She chuckled. "Light?"

"Isn't it mostly juice with a bit of red wine?"

She gave a hearty guffaw and glanced at Alejandro affectionately. "Innocent little thing, isn't she?"

"Very," he said quietly.

She sighed, looking back at me, she suggested, "I'll make you a *tinto de verano*. Dash of wine, sugar and a little lime with sparkling water. Trust me. It won't go to your head."

She was right. The delicious concoction was a mixture of tart and sweet and bubbles, with lemon and limes floating beside the ice. I had one glass, then another, then a third, then looked down at my empty plate and realized I'd ordered and eaten a whole plate of dinner without paying the slightest attention.

"What time is it?" My head was swimming. I put my hands to my temples. "She said this drink wouldn't go to my head," I said accusingly.

Alejandro gave a low laugh. "It wouldn't, but you had four of them."

"Four?" I looked with amazement at my empty glass. "They just taste so light. The most delicious wine cooler ever invented."

"You should stop."

I looked at him brazenly. "You should tell me who you really are."

Time suddenly stood still.

"Don't you know?" he said hoarsely. "Haven't you guessed?"

"Don't tell me you're already having your first fight." Theresa was holding out a guitar. "Fix it, *pequeño*. Play."

"Sí!" the people around us clamored, pounding on their tables. "Play!"

Alejandro shook his head. "We're leaving."

But I didn't want to leave. I wanted to see what everyone else apparently already knew. The other side of my husband. The one he'd never let me see. "Will you play?" I whispered. "For me?"

He whirled to look at me. Then he gave a slow nod.

"For you, *mi amor*." He slowly took the guitar in his hand, and there was a burst of cheers and applause. "This is just for you."

Walking across the crowded tavern, past all the tables to the tiny stage, Alejandro sat on a stool. With his guitar in his lap, he said simply into the microphone, "This is for my bride. The mother of my child." He looked at me. "The woman I love."

My lips parted in a silent gasp.

Could he have said…

Surely he couldn't have said…

How strong were those *tinto de verano* drinks anyway?

Exhaling, Alejandro strummed his guitar, and in a low, husky voice began to sing. It sounded very old, and Spanish. He was a good musician, I thought in amazement, really good, far better than any tycoon-slash-duke had a right to be. The music was so heartbreaking and pure that at first, I didn't bother to listen to the words.

Then I did.

Alejandro stared at me from across the room, and sang about a young peasant boy who'd dared to put on the clothes of a prince. He'd gone through life as an imposter, until he died heartbroken, wishing he could see, just one last time, the peasant girl he'd left behind.

Love me? My whole body flashed hot, then cold as his words took on new significance. *You do not even know me.*

I dimly heard the whispers hissing through the room. "That's the Duke of Alzacar—and she must be his new wife—they're obviously in love…." But I just listened to the music, and suddenly, it all fell into place.

Maurine's shaky words. *If not for him, I never would have survived the aftermath of that car crash, when I lost my whole family…. I can still see him in the hospital, his little injured face covered with bandages, his eyes so bright….*

He was worried about me, not himself. "It'll be all right, Abuela," he told me. "I'm your family now."

Pilar's voice. *I know it was always your desire to have a larger family, growing up so lonely, up in that huge castle, with your older sister off working in Granada. And your mother working night and day, when she wasn't distracted by the duke....*

I couldn't breathe. I felt as if I was choking. The walls of the tavern were pressing in. Rising unsteadily to my feet, I pushed through the tables and headed for the door. I saw Theresa's surprised face as I flung it open and headed outside.

In the quiet night, in the empty, cobblestoned alley, I fell back against the rough stone wall and looked up at the moonlight, shaking. I jumped when I heard the slam of the door behind me.

"So now you understand," Alejandro said quietly behind me.

"You're not the duke at all," I choked out, hardly able to believe it even as I said it. "The real Alejandro died in that crash, didn't he? Along with his parents. And your mother—the housekeeper."

"I had to do it." The only sign of emotion was the slight tightening of his jaw, the low tone of his voice. "Maurine had lost everything. And I loved her. Growing up in the castle, she'd always treated me like a grandson. And on that terrible day, the day of the crash, she lost everyone. When she came to see me at the hospital, she seemed to have aged ten years. She was so alone. I couldn't leave her to die in the dilapidated castle, with no one to take care of her...." Swallowing, he looked down at the cobblestoned street. Moonlight left a trail of silver on his dark silhouette as he said quietly, "So I told Maurine I would be her family from now on. Her grandson."

"How is it possible no one knew?"

"Alejandro and I looked very much alike. We were the same age, same build. And after the accident, my face was injured. We used that to explain the difference. Not that anyone asked. People had long since stopped coming to the castle. The duke and his family had chased most of the tenants away by harassing them over rents. Even their old society friends shunned them, since they were always asking to borrow money. Alejandro's parents felt ashamed of how far they'd fallen. Just not ashamed enough to work for something better." He looked up. "My mother was the only servant left, and she hadn't been paid in a year." Taking a deep breath, he said simply, "When Abuela claimed I was her grandson, and pawned the last of her jewelry to pay the transfer-of-title fees, no one questioned it."

"But a few people knew."

He nodded. "Pilar, our governess." He glanced at the restaurant door. "My older sister. Theresa."

My lips parted. "Your sister?"

"Half sister. She's eight years older. She was working in Granada when the accident happened. She rushed to the hospital as soon as she heard, but Abuela convinced her to keep the secret. They have all kept it. Because they love me. And they love Abuela." He looked away. "As I grew older, it felt wrong, stealing Alejandro's title and name. I promised myself that I would never marry, never have a child. The family line, and the family lie, would end with me. I convinced myself that was redemption."

I stared at him, tears now falling down my cheeks in the moonlight. "That was why you said you're no good at keeping promises," I whispered. "Because you had a child. And then you married me. I thought…" I shook my head. "I thought you meant you could never keep your promises of fidelity…."

"That I would cheat on you?" he said incredulously. He came closer, his face blazing with emotion as he reached out to cup my cheek. "From the moment we met, you've been the only woman I wanted. Even for the year we were apart—there was no one else for me. No one."

"But...when I told you I loved you..."

He gave a low, humorless laugh. He shook his head. "You really don't understand, do you? When I promised myself I'd never marry or have a child, I made sure I would keep that promise by only allowing myself to date women like Claudie...cold, sophisticated, heartless women I'd never be tempted to love. You were different. You were the woman I could not resist," he said softly. "You made me break every promise I'd made to myself. I wanted to tell you everything. Where you were concerned, I had no self-control."

I stared up at him, my lips parted.

"When I heard you were pregnant with my child, I was desperate to find you. But once I did, and we were wed, I suddenly knew I'd never be able to tell you the truth. At first, because I was afraid you'd use the information to blackmail me, and try to take my son away. Then because I owed it to Miguel. You were so proud our son would some-day be a duke...."

"I never cared about that!" I said fiercely. "All I care about is you. And Miguel..." I looked up at him with an intake of breath. "Your real name is Miguel."

He gave me a wicked grin. "You can see why I didn't mind our son's name."

My knees shook, because my world was spinning. "But after we were married—surely then you knew you could trust me?"

"You have such an honest heart." He sobered. "I didn't want you to have the burden."

"Burden? Are you kidding?" I gave a laugh that was giddy, almost hysterical. "If you knew what I'd imagined..."

"It's worse than you think." His face had turned deadly

serious. "My grandmother and I both broke laws with our lies. We could be charged with fraud and possibly sent to prison. For myself, I would have been willing to take the risk, to tell you the truth. But Maurine..." He looked down. "I was afraid to take the risk, for her sake. The idea of her in jail..."

A sudden noise down the quiet street, perhaps a cat knocking over a trash can in a nearby alley, caused us both to jump. I looked at him.

"You can trust me. No one will ever know." I swallowed and whispered. "Did you really mean what you said in the tavern?"

"The song?"

"That you—" I blushed a little "—actually—love me?"

His eyes went wide. Then, with a low laugh, he pulled me in his arms.

"Oh, *querida*. I have loved you from almost the first moment we met. Your sweetness, your nobility, your honesty."

"I was so afraid.... I believed all the wrong things...."

Alejandro wrapped his hands around mine. "And now you hold my heart, my life, in your hands," he said quietly. "You have the power to take Miguel from me, to go back to Mexico, to walk away." He lifted his dark gaze to mine in the moonlight. "You own me completely. What will you do?"

"What will I do?" I whispered, tears in my eyes. Putting my arms around him, I pulled him close and pressed my forehead against his heart. "I will love you, Alejandro. Forever."

CHAPTER TEN

WE ROSE FOR a late breakfast the next morning, after a night in our hotel room with much giggling and even more love-making. As eager as I was to see our baby after a whole night away from him, I was also lingering, enjoying every last moment of this brief, perfect honeymoon.

No one would ever be able to part us again.

"I think," Alejandro said thoughtfully as we left the hotel, "that was the best honeymoon I've ever had."

"Best and only," I said.

"No, surely not only. Our marriage will be nothing but one long honeymoon," he said huskily, then to prove it, he kissed me. The kiss soon became so intense and deep that Alejandro muttered something about renting the room for another night, and started to pull me back toward the hotel.

"But we can't!" I protested with a laugh. "Miguel…"

"All right," he grumbled, then his eyes smoldered. "But I'm taking you back to our bedroom as fast as the car will go."

But at my request, we returned to Rohares the long way. He took me to the spot where legend said Boabdil, the last sultan of Spain, took his very last look at Granada, after he was forced to cede it to Spanish King Ferdinand and Queen Isabella.

"Oh, no. I left the guidebook at the hotel," I said sadly,

then brightened. "But I left my name in it. Hopefully they'll find it and call."

"A guidebook? Get another one!"

"It's a souvenir," I whispered, "of the happiest night of my life."

He kissed me, then standing on the hill, we looked back at Granada. "They say Boabdil wept when he looked his last upon his city," I said wistfully. "And his mother mocked his tears. She sneered that he was weeping like a woman for what he could not fight for as a man. Can you believe that?"

"People can say hurtful things to those they love," Alejandro said quietly. "Especially when they're backed into a corner and their own hearts are breaking."

As we drove back home, I suddenly realized Alejandro was right. I thought of all my anguished years feeling lonely in London, wishing hopelessly for my grandmother, my uncle and Claudie to love me. But they could not, because they did not know how. Instead, they'd relentlessly pursued the wrong things, luxury and status and appearance. They'd never known that the only way to gain happiness was not only to follow your heart, but to give it away.

Leaning over, Alejandro took my hand. Bringing it to his lips, he fervently kissed it. My eyes blurred with tears as I smiled at him, thinking how lucky I was.

And that was the moment I forgave my family for not loving me. Sometimes, I thought, you have to make your own family.

Blushing, I said shyly, "So what do I call you now?"

He looked at me. "I've grown fond of Alejandro. I'll let my son keep Miguel." He turned away, facing the road. His hands tightened on the steering wheel. "After we get back, I'm going to talk to a lawyer. I'll see if there's any way to renounce the title without causing risk to Maurine." He looked at me. "But it seems so much to ask of you."

"What?"

"Would you be heartbroken to give up the title of duchess—and know Miguel would never be a duke?"

"Are you kidding?" I gave a low laugh. "I'm happy to give it up. Do you really think I'm duchess material?"

He looked at me seriously. "Yes, *mi amor*. Yes."

"I'm happy as your wife," I whispered. "However that may be." And he squeezed my hand in his.

When we arrived at Rohares Castle, we hugged our baby and Maurine, who immediately started telling us every small detail of their extremely uneventful night, which mostly involved patty-cake and Miguel dozing as his great-grandmother read him Washington Irving's *Tales of the Alhambra*. "So Miguel felt part of the experience, too. It seemed appropriate...."

"Like his name," I said. Smiling, I glanced back at Alejandro. "It turns out I named him after his father."

With an intake of breath, Maurine looked between us. Then she gave a whoop of joy. "Took you long enough," she cried, then hugged us, telling us we wcrc silly to be so emotional as she wiped her own eyes. "So. I, too, have news. The best news of all." Maurine looked between us, beaming. "While thc two of you were on your honeymoon, I did something with your hairbrush...."

The house phone rang loudly from across the great room. Wondering if it might be the hotel calling about my guidebook, I said hurriedly, "Just a minute." Rushing across the room, I answered breathlessly, "Hello?"

"Don't say my name."

Edward?! I gritted my teeth and rasped, "I'm hanging up now."

"If you do, you'll be sorry."

Something about the cool confidence of his voice made me hesitate. "Why?"

"Because I know."

"What?"

"Everything."

A chill went down my spine. I tried to bluff. "Everything about what?"

"About your husband. And the lie he told twenty-three years ago."

The chill turned to ice. "I don't know what you're talking about."

He snorted, then said quietly, "I followed you to Granada. I was in the shadows on the street. When you came out alone from the restaurant, I was going to comfort you. Then your husband followed you out. And gave me all the ammunition I would ever need to destroy him. And that so-called grandmother of his."

Turning, I stared wide-eyed at Alejandro and Maurine across the great hall, where they were laughing together. I gripped the phone. "What do you want?"

"What I've always wanted. You."

"I don't love you—"

"Yes. I know. You love him. So if you want to protect him, this choice should be easy for you. I'm waiting in a car at the castle gate. Call the guard. Tell him to let me in."

"If I tell Alejandro how you're trying to blackmail me, he will kill you."

"I'm sure you're right. Which is why you won't tell him."

"You don't understand! That's not just an expression. He will literally kill you!"

"Let him try," he said flatly. "Tell him, if that's how you want this to go. I'm not afraid. I have nothing to lose." He paused. "Do you?"

I shuddered, trembling, afraid that Alejandro would really kill him, and he'd end up in jail not just for fraud, but for murder. "What do you want me to do?"

His voice was smooth and slick. "Tell him you've changed your mind about your marriage. Tell him you only wanted him when you thought he was a real duke, but now…you're in love with me."

Horror filled my heart. "He'll never believe it—"

"He *will*. That's what frightens you." He gave a low laugh. "Tell him you're going to spend tonight with me, and your lawyers will be in touch about divorce—and custody. That bit about custody is just for you, by the way. I'll let your baby live with us. Doesn't that show how much I care?"

"You never cared about me," I whispered. "If you did, you couldn't do this."

"I took care of you. I saved you. I earned you. Not him."

"I'm a human soul—not some trophy to be won!"

"You should be mine," he said coldly. "Let him watch you leave with me. Make him believe I'm the one you want. And I'll forget what I know. Do it for his sake. And the old woman's."

"Edward, please…"

"Three minutes. Then I'm calling a press conference."

"And he'll kill you!"

"Then Navaro will be in jail for the rest of his life. And your kid will have no father. Or great-grandmother. Make your choice. You say you really love them? Prove it."

The line clicked off.

My whole body shook as I hung up.

"Who was it?" Alejandro said behind me.

"N-nothing. I mean, no one."

"Which is it? Is something wrong?" His eyes were sharp. Of course he knew something was wrong. He saw right through me. Saw my anguished heart.

So how could I break his—with a lie?

And yet—how could I not?

Wide-eyed, I looked across the great hall toward Maurine, who at her age would likely never come back from the shock of a scandal and trial for fraud, much less being sent to prison. I looked at my sweet baby in his baby swing, who would endure the experience I'd feared most—being surrounded by paparazzi—before he lost his father. And Alejandro. I looked at him, hardly able to breathe. If he really did attack Edward as I feared…

I remembered the look in his eyes in Granada when I'd told him that Edward had visited me. I remembered the cold menace in his face.

I will kill him.

"Lena?" Alejandro frowned, coming closer. "Who was on the phone?"

The phone suddenly rang again. I picked it up.

"Your Excellency?" It was the security guard at the gate. "There's an Edward St. Cyr here. He has no appointment. Should I let him inside?"

I took a deep breath.

"Let him in," I said faintly, then hung up the phone. I picked up my handbag. I walked slowly toward my family, feeling as if I was going to die.

But I would die for them. I looked at those three beloved faces, in this beautiful old castle I'd already come to love. My family. My home. Would I do it? To save them?

Yes.

"Where are you going?" Alejandro said.

"I'm sorry." My teeth were chattering. My words were faint. "Our marriage is over. I'll be back tomorrow. So we can discuss c-custody…."

I stopped at the door. Alejandro was staring at me with open-mouthed shock. I was trembling so hard it was all I could do not to black out.

But it was the only way to save him. To save all of them.

I was the one who'd allowed Edward into our lives. I was the one who should pay for that. Not them.

But as I looked into Alejandro's face, I knew that he, too, would suffer. Squeezing my eyes shut, I turned away.

"Edward's come for me," I choked out. "I'm leaving with him now. We both know it never would have worked out with us, Alejandro. Not for long…"

"What are you saying?" he breathed, searching my gaze. "I don't believe you!"

"I'll be back with a lawyer—tomorrow.…" My voice ended on a sob. Whirling around, I fled for the door. Outside, I saw Edward waiting in an expensive SUV. The windows were all rolled down, the engine still running. Sobbing, I climbed in beside him. He gave me a triumphant, cruel smile.

"Wise choice," he said coldly. "Very smart."

"I don't feel smart," I whispered, hating myself, hating this choice already, wanting to do nothing more than jump out of the vehicle. And suddenly, that's just what I needed to do. "No. NO. I can't do this—"

Reaching over me, Edward put on my seat belt. It felt like a restraint.

"You'll soon be free of his influence," he said softly, reaching toward me. "I promise you."

I shuddered at his touch. "Don't!"

With a low laugh, he put down his hand. "Have it your way. I am a patient man.…"

But as he turned the steering wheel and started to drive down the circular courtyard, Alejandro was suddenly there, standing ahead of us, blocking the way to the road.

He wasn't looking at Edward. He was looking only at me. I saw his lips form my name.

"Make him believe you love me," Edward growled in a low voice. "Make him believe."

I licked my lips. I looked at Alejandro's stark face. The anguish in his dark eyes.

And I couldn't go through with it.

"I can't." My voice trembled as I started fumbling with my seat belt. "I can't do this. Let me out of here!"

"Too late," Edward said grimly, holding on to the latch as I tried to fight him.

Alejandro saw us struggling through the front window. Hands clenched at his sides, he started walking toward the SUV, now staring at Edward with narrowed eyes, his powerful warrior's body threatening his murder.

Edward's mouth twisted as their eyes met. He glared back, the same expression of murder in his face.

They both intended to kill or be killed today.

Over me.

With a low, cruel growl, Edward stomped on the gas, increasing speed as he drove the SUV straight at Alejandro, who was unprotected and alone in the castle courtyard.

But my husband didn't turn and run. He didn't back down. Instead, he started running straight at the car—as if a man could play chicken against seven thousand pounds of steel!

I screamed. Grabbing the steering wheel, I twisted it hard to the left. Veering off balance, Edward's SUV crashed into the stone fountain and twisted, then flew, high into the air.

As if in slow motion, I felt us fly up, up, up, at the same time we flipped in sickening circles, around and around. We hit the ground with a bone-jarring crunch and rolled down the long hill, all the way down. Then, with a shudder and metallic groan, the SUV was still.

I wasn't dead. I was upside down, held into the passenger seat by the taut seat belt that had knocked the air out of me, leaving a streak of pain where it crossed my chest.

Panting, I looked over at the driver's seat. It was empty. Edward was gone.

"Lena!" Alejandro cried. A moment later, my door was wrenched open, and suddenly he was there. He yanked open the seat belt, and caught me in his strong arms as I fell.

Cradling me desperately, my husband sank to the ground,

still holding me against his chest. He ran his hands over my body, found no life-ending injury and exhaled, holding me tight against him, rocking me in his lap. "Oh, my love," he choked out. "You're safe. You're safe. For a moment I thought…" He looked at me fiercely. "Don't ever do that to me again!"

"I'm sorry," I wept, pressing my head against his chest. "He learned the truth and said if I didn't come with him, he would ruin your life and Maurine's and even Miguel's. I couldn't risk you going to jail for the rest of your life—"

"I'd rather be sent to jail for a million years," he said hoarsely, "than lose you." I felt his body trembling beneath me. Reaching up in amazement, I brushed away a single tear trailing down his tanned, hard-edged cheek.

Pressing my forehead to his, I whispered, "Thank you for not letting me go."

He cupped my face, looked me straight in the eyes. "Never. We are forever…."

A low growl made us both turn.

"You'll be sorry." We turned to see Edward collapsed on the grass, where he'd been flung from the vehicle, across the hill. "Both of you," he panted, "will be sorry."

Alejandro's hands tightened on me. I looked up at him in terror. "Don't kill him. It's not worth it. Remember you promised you'd never leave me…."

"Kill him?" He looked at me incredulously. "Why should I? Look at him…."

For the first time, I noticed the odd way Edward's arms and legs were stretched out in unnatural directions on the grass. But even his body wasn't as contorted as his face.

"I'll tell the world," Edward panted, "how you all committed fraud. I'll ruin your lives—both of you—the old woman and that baby, too…."

Alejandro glared at Edward, parting his lips to answer. But someone else beat him to it.

"Calm down, dear. You're acting crazy."

Maurine stepped calmly between us on the hill. She peered down at Edward benignly, as if about to offer him cookies at a party, and the upside-down SUV behind us, with its crushed steel doors and a wheel still spinning, was just a decoration, like fairy lights or balloons. "Whatever you think is wrong, Alejandro is my grandson."

Edward gave a hard laugh. "It's a lie." He coughed. "I'll prove it when I get the court order for a blood test...."

"You know, I always wondered." She smiled, then looked at Alejandro, who was still on the ground, holding me protectively in his lap. She gave a brisk nod. "I was about to tell you, before all the fuss broke out. The hairbrush. You're my grandson, Alejandro. Really and truly. The grandson of my heart." She gave us a broad, self-satisfied smile. "Also a grandson of a DNA test."

I felt Alejandro jump. His face was pale.

"What...?" he breathed.

"The silly secret was just causing such a problem between you two." She looked between us severely. "And the way you were botching things. It just was ridiculous. Honestly, I'd always wondered why your mother stayed on as housekeeper for all those years, even when my son wasn't paying her. And then there was that family resemblance.... Anyway. It never mattered to me one way or the other. Until it started to interfere with your happiness." She grinned. "So I took your hairbrush and had a DNA test. You are my grandson, Alejandro. By heart, as you always were. But also by blood."

"No!" Edward screamed. Then he was suddenly quiet. I think he had fainted from pain.

Rather vengefully, I hoped he had. Although I didn't want him to die, of course. I didn't. Really, I didn't.

Alejandro's eyes were wide. "Is this true, Abuela?"

She nodded. "Remain the Duke of Alzacar, and if anyone wants to check if you are my grandson, let them." She looked at him and said quietly, "There is no one left in the family to inherit, if not you. No one you're cheating of his rightful due. And let me tell you something more. You're the finest duke of them all."

I saw him blinking suspiciously fast. He rose to his feet, helping me to rise, as well. He hugged his grandmother, then pulled me into the embrace. When we finally pulled away, I wiped my eyes, then glanced over at Edward, still unconscious.

"We should call an ambulance, do you think?"

"I can see him breathing," Maurine said with a dismissive wave of her hand. "He's fine." She sighed. "But I'll call." She glanced at Alejandro. "And I expect the *policía* will want to come, as well…."

She went toward the castle, and Alejandro looked at me.

"She's right. We have only a few moments before the police arrive," he said quietly. "A choice must be made."

"So make it," I said, trusting whatever he'd decide.

He clawed back his hair. "I am tired of secrets. Tired of lies." He turned to me. "I never want another secret to shadow the light between us."

I nodded, unable to speak over the lump in my throat.

"So." He smiled at me, blinking fast, then gave a decisive nod. He walked over to Edward, who was still unconscious, his legs stretched out at a painful angle. He put his fingertips to the other man's neck, then straightened.

"Is he—dead?" I said. Not hopefully. Really.

He shook his head. "His pulse is strong. He will recover."

"Too bad," I said.

Alejandro looked at me in amazement. Coming back, he wrapped his arms around me. "It's not like you to be bloodthirsty, *mi amor*," he murmured.

"I can be dangerous—" I reached up my hand to caress his cheek "—when it comes to protecting those I love."

"Yes." The corners of his sensual mouth quirked. Then his expression became serious. "But are you brave enough to face what lies ahead? There will be scandal. Or worse. Though perhaps I can protect Maurine...."

"How?"

"I will say that she was distraught over her family's death, and that I tricked her into believing I was her grandson."

"Oh, she won't like that at all."

"No," he agreed. He looked at me, emotion in his dark eyes. "Can you bear it, Lena? The storm that might come? Miguel will lose his legacy...."

"You're wrong." I put my hand on his cheek. My eyes were watery. "His legacy is more than some title. It's doing the right thing, even when it's hard."

"And love," Alejandro whispered, pressing my hands together as he kissed them fervently. "Loving for all your life, with all your heart."

"It's family, always and forever." Looking up at my husband, I smiled through my tears. "And whatever may come—our forever has already begun."

There are all kinds of ways to make a family.

Some ways are big, such as the way Maurine took in an orphaned twelve-year-old boy and insisted on claiming him as her grandson.

Some ways are small, such as when I sent an invitation to my wedding reception to my cousin Claudie.

Autumn had arrived at Rohares Castle, and with it harvest season for our tenants. The summer heat had subsided, leaving a gorgeous swath of vivid colors, of morning mists and early twilight, full of excuses to sip oceans of hot tea with milk in the morning and go to bed early with my husband with a bottle of ruby-red wine. Every night, we lit a fire in the fireplace—and in our bed. And that fire, as months passed, seemed only to get bigger and brighter.

Just that morning, Maurine had caught us kissing in the breakfast room. She'd laughed. "I don't think the honeymoon will really ever end for you two," she said affectionately. Then the doorbell rang, and she'd hurried from the room with a desperate cry: "The florist! Finally!" And we were alone.

I'd given Alejandro a sensual smile.

"Could I interest you in a little more honeymoon?" I said, batting my eyes coyly, to which my husband whispered, "All day, every day," before he kissed me senseless, then picked me up like a Neanderthal and carried me upstairs, back to bed.

Now, the crowded banqueting hall was lit up for evening, bedecked gloriously in autumn flowers in the most beautiful wedding reception I'd ever imagined. Across the crowds of our guests, I caught Alejandro's eye. He smiled back at me hungrily, as if it had been a year since he'd last taken me to bed, instead of just a few hours. His hot glance almost made me forget we were surrounded by family and friends.

"I told you he would be your husband," a voice crowed behind me. "I always can tell!"

"You were right." Turning, I smiled at Dolores, my neighbor from San Miguel de Allende who'd been whisked here from Mexico for the reception. She'd been equal parts impressed and triumphant when Alejandro had sent a private jet to collect her.

I'd sent Mr. Corgan, Mrs. Morris and Hildy a first-class ticket here from London. They were still working for Claudie. "But she's mellowed a great deal since she became Mrs. Crosby," the butler informed me. "He's rich, and that has made her very happy."

But I could see that for myself. Claudie had arrived at

my door swathed in fur, with her brand-new husband at her side.

"I'm going to give you your inheritance back," was the first thing she announced to me. "David said it's the right thing to do. And besides—" she grinned "—we can afford it."

Same old Claudie, I thought. And yet not exactly the same. "Thank you," I said in surprise. I paused, then smiled. "Donate it to charity. Introduce me to your husband?"

She beamed. "I'd love to."

David Crosby was fat, short and bald, but he was indeed very rich, a king of Wall Street. They looked totally wrong together. Until you saw the way they looked at each other.

Claudie told me they'd met through a matchmaking service just for rich people.

"Trophy wives for billionaires?" I guessed.

"After all, Lena," she sniffed, "not everyone can manage to randomly fall pregnant by the love of their lives."

"No, indeed," I said.

"And I'm so happy…" she said wistfully, and I thought that she, too, must have been very lonely in London.

"I'm happy for you, truly," I said, and impulsively hugged her. My cousin stiffened, then let me hug her. I was encouraged. We weren't exactly best friends, but it was a start. And after all, we *were* family….

Pulling away, she wiped her eyes. "At least you dress better now. Your style used to make me physically ill."

Distant family, thankfully.

But Alejandro and I were surrounded by people who cared about us. I looked around at all the people who were here, celebrating our marriage. Thinking with relief about the one who was not.

I still woke up in a cold sweat occasionally, thinking how I'd almost lost everything by getting into Edward St. Cyr's SUV that day.

Edward, sadly, had lived.

Oops, did I say that out loud?

Yes, he lived. From what I'd heard, he'd had an easier time than he deserved. A punctured lung and five broken bones. When the ambulance and police arrived, he'd refused to press charges against anyone, or even talk about the accident. But as he'd been lifted into the ambulance, our eyes had met, and he'd coldly and silently turned his face to the wall. He was done with me. A fact that left me profoundly grateful.

I tried to wish him well, because he had once been my friend.

Okay, but seriously. He'd tried to run over my husband with his Range Rover. That's not the kind of thing I could ever forgive, or forget. So mostly I just tried not to think of it.

Because we had so many other things to be grateful for. As I stood in the banqueting hall of our castle, wearing flowers in my hair and a blue silk gown, I caught Alejandro's eyes across the crowd. And I suddenly didn't see all the princes and farmers, starlets and secretaries, or the happy mix of our neighbors and friends. I didn't see the champagne, or the amazing food, or the flowers hung joyously across the rafters amid a profusion of music and laughter. When I met my husband's gaze, I shivered, and no one else existed.

Alejandro had contacted a lawyer and confessed everything. With the lawyer's advice, he'd thrown himself on the mercy of the court. As Maurine's DNA test had proved, he was the duke's heir, and his only heir at that, and so the group of nobles who oversaw this type of thing decided to allow him to keep his title. He'd also kept the name. Apparently the combination of money and being a direct blood descendant made a big difference. Suddenly, no one was using the word *fraud*.

The scandal was intense, though. For weeks, our castle had been under siege, with crowds of reporters shaking our gates, clamoring for a picture or an interview. But since no one on the estate or in the nearby town would talk, even the scandal died eventually, especially when the Hollywood star I'd seen at Alejandro's party in Madrid had been discovered naked, drunk and belligerent at the base of the Eiffel Tower. Bless her heart. The paparazzi eventually melted away, as our story was old news. Just in time for our reception today, too.

Tomorrow was Alejandro's birthday. His *real* birthday. I would give him the painting of Miguel and Maurine, and show him the brand-new photo album I'd begun for our family. On the back page, I'd tucked in a picture of a sonogram. We were going to have another baby sometime next summer, when the jacaranda trees were in bloom.

I could hardly wait to give Alejandro his gift....

I heard a clank of silverware against crystal. "Everyone. Could I have your attention?" Looking up, I saw Alejandro holding up his champagne glass. "I'd like to thank all our family and friends for coming today...."

"Any time you want to send your private jet," someone shouted.

"Or first-class tickets!"

"Or help me pave my garden path—how's Wednesday?"

There was scattered laughter, and a few tipsy cheers.

Alejandro grinned. "I'd also like to thank my grandmother for doing such a wonderful job designing this party...."

"Darn straight," Maurine said stoutly, holding our smiling baby in her arms. Miguel, though barefoot as he did not like shoes, was suitably dressed in a baby tuxedo.

"I'd like to thank our baby son for sleeping so well at night...."

Darn straight, I echoed, but didn't say aloud.

"But most of all—" Alejandro's dark eyes glowed with tenderness that took my breath away as he looked at me "—I'd like to thank my beautiful wife. Lena. You gave me the family I never dreamed I could have. Just waking up in your arms every morning is a heaven beyond what any mortal man should deserve. But I will spend the rest of my life trying." He held up the flute. "To family. Forever."

"Family forever," everyone cried, with the greatest cheer of all.

"Thank you," I said to them. I blinked fast, smiling with tears in my eyes. "I love you all." I looked at my husband. "Especially you."

Coming through the crowd, Alejandro took me in his arms, and kissed me soundly in front of everyone. And I kissed him back. Oh, boy, you bet I did.

It was crazy. Just a year ago, I'd been so scared and alone. I'd hated Alejandro. I'd thought I would remain a single mother forever.

The disastrous night we were married in Madrid, Alejandro said sometimes fate chooses better for us than we can choose for ourselves. But I think there's more to it.

It's not just fate. You create your own future, step by step, by being brave. By doing the right thing. By telling the truth. By trying your best.

By reaching for the man you love, and giving him the chance to reach back, pull you into his arms and finally show you the man he really is inside—the powerful, infuriating, sexy, compassionate man whom no one else will ever truly know.

Love, like trust, is earned. It is kept, day by day, night by night, as we reveal to each other who we were. Who we are. And most of all, who we hope to be.

* * * * *

ONE NIGHT WITH
THE ENEMY
ABBY GREEN

Abby Green got hooked on Mills & Boon romances while still in her teens, when she stumbled across one belonging to her grandmother, in the west of Ireland. After many years of reading them voraciously, she sat down one day and gave it a go herself. Happily, after a few failed attempts, Mills & Boon bought her first manuscript.

Abby works freelance in the Film and TV industry but thankfully the 4am starts and stresses of dealing with recalcitrant actors are becoming more and more infrequent, leaving more time to write!

She loves to hear from readers and you can contact her through her website at www.abby-green.com. She lives and works in Dublin.

CHAPTER ONE

MADDIE Vasquez stood in the shadows like a fugitive. Just yards away the plushest hotel in Mendoza rose in all its majestic colonial glory to face the imposing Plaza Indepencia. She reassured herself that she wasn't actually a fugitive. She was just collecting herself... She could see the calibre of the crowd going into the foyer: monied and exclusive. The elite of Mendoza society.

The evening was melting into night and lights twinkled in bushes and trees nearby, lending the scene a fairy-tale air. Maddie's soft mouth firmed and she tried to quell her staccato heartbeat. It had been a long time since she'd believed in fairy tales—if ever. She'd never harboured illusions about the dreamier side of life. A mother who saw you only as an accessory to be dressed up and paraded like a doll and a father who resented you for not being the son he'd lost would do that to a child.

Maddie shook her head, as if that could shake free the sudden melancholy assailing her, and at the same time her eye was caught by the almost silent arrival of a low-slung silver vehicle at the bottom of the main steps leading up to the hotel. Instinctively she drew back more. The car was clearly vintage and astronomically expensive. Her mouth dried and her palms grew sweaty—would it be...?

The door was opened by a uniformed hotel doorman and a tall shape uncurled from the driving seat.

It was him.

Her heart stopped beating for a long moment.

Nicolás Cristobal de Rojas. The most successful vintner in Mendoza—and probably all of Argentina by now. Not to mention his expansion into French Bordeaux country, which ensured he had two vintages a year. In the notoriously fickle world of winemaking the de Rojas estate profits had tripled and quadrupled in recent years, and success oozed from every inch of his six-foot-four, broad-shouldered frame.

He was dressed in a black tuxedo, and Maddie could see his gorgeous yet stern and arrogant features as he cast a bored-looking glance around him. It skipped over where she was hiding like a thief, and when he looked away her heart stuttered back to life.

She dragged in a breath. She'd forgotten how startling his blue eyes were. He looked leaner. Darker. Sexier. His distinctive dark blond hair had always made it easy to mark him out from the crowd—not that his sheer charisma and good looks wouldn't have marked him out anyway. He'd always been more than his looks…he'd always carried a tangible aura of power and sexual energy.

Another flash of movement made her drag her eyes away, and she saw a tall blonde beauty emerging from the other side of the car, helped by the conscientious doorman. As Maddie watched, the woman walked around to his side, her long fall of blonde hair shining almost as much as the floor-length silver lamé dress which outlined every slim curve of her body with a loving touch.

The woman linked her arm through his. Maddie couldn't see the look they shared, but from the smile on the woman's face she didn't doubt it was *hot*. A sudden shaft of physical pain lanced her and Maddie put a hand to her belly in reaction. *No,* she begged mentally. She didn't want him to affect her like this. She didn't want him to affect her at all.

She'd wasted long teenage years dreaming about him, lusting after him, building daydreams around him. And that foolish dreaming had culminated in catastrophe and a fresh deepening of the generations-old hostility between their families. It had caused the rift to end all rifts. It had broken her own family apart. She'd realised all of her most fervent fantasies—but had also been thrown into a nightmare of horrific revelations.

The last time she'd seen Nicolás Cristobal de Rojas had been a few years ago, in a club in London. Their eyes had clashed across the thronged room, and she'd never forget the look of pure loathing on his face before he'd turned away and disappeared.

Sucking in deep breaths and praying for control, Maddie squared her shoulders. She couldn't lurk in the shadows all night. She'd come to tell Nicolás Cristobal de Rojas that she was home and had no intention of selling out to him. Not now or ever. She held the long legacy of her family in her hands and it would not die with her. He had to know that—or he might put the same pressure on her as he'd done to her father, taking advantage of his physical and emotional weakness to encourage him to sell to his vastly more successful neighbour.

As much as she'd have loved to hide behind solicitors' letters, she couldn't afford to pay the legal fees. And she didn't want de Rojas to think she was too scared to confront him herself. She tried to block out the last cataclysmic meeting they'd had—if she went down that road now she'd turn around for sure. She had to focus on the present. And the future.

She knew better than anyone just how ruthless the de Rojas family could be, but even she had blanched at the pressure Nicolás de Rojas had put on an ailing man. It was the kind of thing she'd have expected of his father, but somehow, despite everything, not of Nicolás...*more fool her.* She of all people should have known what to expect.

With a shaking hand she smoothed down the glittery black dress she wore. Maddie's meagre budget since she'd left Argentina hadn't run to buying party dresses. Tonight was the prestigious annual Mendoza Vintners' Dinner, and she wouldn't have been able to get close to the place if she didn't look the part. Luckily she'd found some of her mother's dresses that her father hadn't destroyed in his rage eight years before...

At first it had looked modest enough—high-necked at the front. It was only when she'd had it on, aware that if she didn't leave soon she'd miss her window of opportunity, that she'd realised it was backless—to just above her buttocks. All her mother's other dresses needed serious dry-cleaning. This one had somehow miraculously been protected in a plastic covering. So it was this dress or nothing.

Maddie just wished that her mother had been less flamboyant—and taller. Maddie was five foot nine and the dress ended around her mid-thigh, showing lots of pale leg. Her unusual colouring of black hair, green eyes and pale skin was courtesy of a great-great-grandmother who had come to Argentina with a wave of Irish immigrants and subsequently married into the Vasquez family.

So now, as she finally stepped from the shadows outside the hotel and the gentle breeze whistled over her bare flesh, she felt ridiculously exposed. Mustering all the courage she would need for this encounter, she valiantly ignored the double-take glances of recognition she drew, and strode into the luxurious marbled lobby.

Nicolás Cristobal de Rojas stifled a yawn. He'd been working around the clock to ensure this year's grapes would be ready to pick soon. After a mercurial summer, they would either have one of the best vintages on their hands or the worst. He grimaced slightly. He knew bringing in his vintage wasn't the only excuse for driving himself like a demon. That work ethic was buried deep in his fraught childhood.

'Really, darling,' came a dry voice to his right, 'am I that boring?'

Nic forced his attention back into the room and looked down at his date. He quirked a mocking smile. 'Never.'

His blonde companion squeezed his arm playfully, 'I think the ennui is getting to you, Nic. You need to go to Buenos Aires and have some fun—I don't know how you stand it in this backwater.' She shuddered theatrically, then said something about going to the powder room and disappeared with a sexy sway to her walk.

Nic was relieved to be immune to this very feminine display, and watched as male heads swivelled to watch her progress. He shook his head ruefully and thanked his lucky stars that Estella's presence tonight might at least temporarily stave off the more determined of the Mendoza man-eaters. He was in no mood to humour the mercenary women he attracted in droves. His last lover had screamed hysterically at him for an hour and accused him of having no heart or soul. He had no desire to head down *that* path again any time soon.

He could do without sex if that was going to be the outcome. If truth be told, his last sexual encounters had all felt curiously…empty. Satisfying on one level only. And as for a more long-term relationship? He certainly had no intention of even thinking about that. The toxic relationship of his parents had cautioned him from an early age. He was going to choose a long-term partner with extreme care and diligence. Naturally there *would* be a long-term partner at some point in the future; he had a valuable legacy to pass on to the next generation, and he had no intention of breaking the precious cycle of inheritance.

Just then he saw a figure appear in the doorway to the ballroom. Inexplicably his skin tightened over his bones and the back of his neck prickled—the same way it had just now outside the hotel, when he'd felt as if he was being watched.

He couldn't make out the woman's features. He could only make out long, long shapely pale legs and a glittering short black dress which outlined a slender figure. But something about her was instantly *familiar*. In his gut. Midnight-black wavy hair was swept over one shoulder—and then he saw her head turn. Even from where he stood he could see a stillness enter her frame, and then she started to walk…directly towards him.

Ridiculously Nic felt the need to turn and leave. But he stood his ground. As she came closer and closer, weaving through the crowd, suspicion grew and formed in his head. *It couldn't be,* he told himself. *It's been years…she was in London.*

He was barely aware of the hushed murmurs surrounding him, growing louder as the woman finally came to a stop just a few feet away. Recognition and incredulity warred in his head. Along with the realisation that she was *stunning*. She had always been beautiful—slightly ethereal—but she'd matured into a true beauty since he'd seen her last. She was statuesque and slender and curvaceous all at once. An intoxicating package.

Nic hadn't even realised that he'd given her such a thorough examination until his eyes met hers and he saw the pink flush in her pale cheeks. It had a direct effect on his body, causing a hot throb of desire in his groin.

The ennui he'd just been teased about was long gone. Too many emotions and sensations were starting to fizz in his gut—the dominant ones being acrid betrayal and humiliation. *Still*, after all these years. He retreated behind a cold wall of anger. Anything to douse this very unwelcome stabbing of desire. His eyes narrowed and clashed with eyes so green they looked like jewels. He had to exert every ounce of his iron control not to be flung back into time and remember what it had felt like almost to drown in those eyes. The problem was he *had* drowned.

'Madalena Vasquez,' he drawled, not a hint of his loss of composure in his voice, 'what the hell are *you* doing here?'

Maddie winced inwardly and fought to retain her composure. She could remember a time when he'd called her Maddie. The walk from the door to here had felt as if it had taken years, not seconds, and hadn't been helped by the fact that her mother's shoes were a size too big. She was aware of the hush surrounding them, and the whispers—none of which she could imagine were complimentary after the very public way her father had thrown her and her mother out eight years before.

Nicolás de Rojas's mouth became a flat parody of a smile. 'Please accept my condolences on the death of your father.'

Fire flashed up Maddie's spine. 'Let's not pretend you care one iota,' she hissed, mindful of the eavesdroppers. Nicolás de Rojas didn't seem to be fazed by their audience at all, but the grief and futile anger she felt over her father's death nearly choked her.

The man in front of her folded his arms across his formidable chest, making him look even more intimidating. Maddie's skin itched uncomfortably where the dress revealed her back. Her hands were clenched to fists at her sides.

He shrugged negligently. 'No, I can't say I did care. But I can be polite at least.'

Maddie flushed at that. She'd seen in the papers that his father had died some years before. They were both products of generations who would have merrily danced on each other's graves, yet it wasn't in her to glory in someone's death—even an enemy's.

Awkwardly but sincerely, she said now, 'I'm sorry about your father too.'

He arched a brow and his face tightened. 'Are you going to extend that to my mother? She killed herself when she found out your mother and my father had had an affair for years…after your father told her.'

Maddie blanched to hear that Nicolás was aware of the affair. She saw in that instant how much anger his apparent civility was masking as his eyes flashed dangerously and white lines of tension bracketed his sensual mouth.

Her brain felt fuzzy. She shook her head. She'd had no idea her father had told his mother about the affair, or that she had taken her own life. 'I didn't know any of this…'

He dismissed her words with a slashing hand. 'You wouldn't, would you? You were so quick to leave and spend your family fortune running around Europe with your wastrel of a mother.'

Maddie felt sick. This was so much worse than she'd feared. She'd somehow naively imagined that she would say her few words to Nicolás de Rojas, he would respond with something at least civil, and that would be it. But the ancient feud between their families was alive and well and crackling between them—along with something else Maddie didn't want to acknowledge.

Suddenly Nicolás de Rojas cast a quick glance around them and emitted a guttural curse. He took Maddie's arm in one big hand. She was being summarily dragged to the other side of the room before she knew what was happening. He whirled her around to face him again in a quiet corner. This time all civility was stripped away, and his face was lean and stark with displeasure and anger.

Maddie yanked herself free and rubbed her tingling arm, determined not to let him see how shaken she was. 'How dare you treat me like some recalcitrant child!'

'I've asked you once already—what are you doing here, Vasquez? You're not welcome.'

Maddie felt anger surge up at his sheer arrogance and remembered why she was there and what was at stake: her entire livelihood. She stepped forward, dropping her hand. 'For your information I am just as welcome here as you, and I've come to tell you that my father didn't give in to your pressure to sell and neither will I.'

Nicolás de Rojas sneered. 'The only thing you own now is a piece of useless land full of gnarly vines. It's an eyesore. Your estate hasn't produced any wine of note for years.'

Maddie disguised the pain of knowing that her father had let it all go so spectacularly and spat back. 'You and your father systematically pushed and squeezed him out of the market until he couldn't possibly compete any more.'

His jaw clenched at that, and he bit out savagely, 'It's nothing more than was done to us time and time again. I'd love to tell you we spent all our time concocting ways to sabotage your business, but the Vasquez wines stopped selling because they were inferior—pure and simple. You did it to yourselves with no help from us.'

His words hit home with a dismaying ring of truth and Maddie took a hasty step back at his ferocity. She saw his eyes flash indignantly. Her reaction had more to do with his proximity and its effect on her body, and more disturbingly on her memories, than with his anger. She couldn't halt a vivid flashback to when she'd pressed herself so close against him she could feel every taut sinew and muscle. And the evidence of his arousal for her. It had been intoxicating, thrilling. She'd wanted him so badly she'd been begging him to—

'Here you are!'

Nic growled at the woman who had just appeared by their sides, 'Not now, Estella.'

Maddie sent up silent thanks for the interruption and cast a quick glance to see the gorgeous blonde who had been with Nicolás outside the hotel. She backed away but Nicolás grabbed her arm again.

'Estella, wait for me at the table,' he bit out.

The young woman looked from him to Maddie with wide eyes, and then whistled softly before walking away, shaking her head. Maddie dimly thought that she seemed very easy-going for a lover, but then Nicolás was clamping his hands on her arms. Angrily she pulled herself free again, feeling very raw after that too-vivid memory. She was vaguely aware of her dress slipping down over one shoulder as she pulled away, and saw Nicolás's eyes go there for a split second before something hot flashed in the blue depths.

Maddie spoke in a rush to stop herself responding to that look—which she *must* have imagined. This man felt nothing for her except hatred, pure and simple. 'I came to tell you that I'm back and I won't be selling the Vasquez estate. Even if I was do you really think I'd sell to a de Rojas after all we've been through? I'd burn it to the ground first. I intend to restore the Vasquez estate to its full glory.'

Nicolás stood tall, and then he barked out an incredulous laugh, head thrown back, revealing the strong column of his throat. When he looked down again Maddie felt a weakness invading her lower body—and a disturbing heat.

He shook his head. 'You must have done quite the number on your father before he died to get him to leave it to *you*. After you and your mother left and people heard of the affair, no one expected to see either of you back again. I think people would have expected him to leave it to a dog on the street rather than either one of you.'

Maddie's hands clenched. Pain bloomed inside her to think of that awful time and how angry her father had been—justifiably so. She gritted out, 'You have no idea what you're talking about.'

It was as if he didn't even hear her, though. He continued easily. 'It was common knowledge your father didn't have a *peso* to his name by the time he died. Is your mother's Swiss financier husband financing this whim?' His jaw tightened. 'Or perhaps you've bagged yourself a rich husband? Did you find one in London? You were frequenting the right clubs the last time I saw you.'

Maddie's insides burned with indignation. Her hands clenched even harder. 'No, my mother is *not* financing anything. And I don't have a rich husband, or boyfriend or lover. Not that it's any concern of yours.'

Mock shock and disbelief crossed Nicolás's face. 'You mean to tell me that the spoiled Vasquez princess thinks she can waltz back home and turn a bankrupt wine estate around with no help or expertise? Is this your new hobby because the Cannes yacht parties were becoming boring?'

Maddie felt the red tide of rage rise within her. He had no idea how badly she'd fought to prove herself to her fa-

ther—to prove that she could be as good as any man…
as good as her poor dead brother. She'd never have that
chance now, because he was dead too. And she would *not*
let the legacy she'd been bequeathed die with her. She had
to prove that she could do this. She would not let another
man stand in her way as her father had.

Passion resonated in her voice. 'That's exactly what I'm
saying, de Rojas. Stay out of my way and don't expect a
"For Sale" sign to go up—*ever.*'

Just as Maddie was backing away, wishing she wouldn't
have to present him with her naked back, he said chillingly,
'I'll give you two weeks until you run screaming out the
door. You have no idea what it takes to run a successful
wine business. You never worked a day in the vineyard
while you were growing up. It's been years since Vasquez
produced a wine worth mentioning, and your father got
carried away with his overpriced wines. You're in over
your head, Vasquez, and when you realise that it won't matter what price tag you put on that sign because I'll match
it. Purely because I would relish knowing that your family is gone from here for good.'

Maddie hid the dart of hurt; he knew that she'd never
worked a day in the vineyard because she'd told him once.
It had been intimate information which would now be
used against her.

He took a step closer and said chillingly, 'So you see,
eventually that estate will become part of the de Rojas
brand…and by denying it you're merely prolonging your
own misery. Just think—within a week you could be back
in London, sitting in the front row of a fashion show, with
enough money to keep you satisfied for a long time. I'll
personally see to it that you have no cause to return here
ever again.'

Maddie shook her head and tried to swallow the terrifying feeling of stepping off a ledge into the great unknown. She was hurt at the extent of this man's hostility. It hurt more than it should, and that scared her to death.

She couldn't help the emotional huskiness of her voice. 'This is my *home*—just as much as it's yours—and you will have to carry my dead body out before you get me to leave.'

Maddie was bitterly aware, despite her little assertion, that everything he said was right. Apart from his perception of what her life was like. Of that he had no idea, and she wasn't about to enlighten him.

She backed away further and said, 'Don't come near my property, de Rojas…you or any of your people. You're not welcome.'

He smiled mockingly. 'I admire the act, Vasquez, and I look forward to seeing how long you can play the part.'

Maddie finally wrenched her gaze away from his and stalked off—but not before she almost stumbled in the too-big shoes. Gritting her teeth, she prayed silently all the way to the door that she would at least retain the dignity of not losing a shoe in front of the insufferably arrogant de Rojas and the gobsmacked crowd.

Maddie held her head high, and it was only when she finally reached her father's battered Jeep in the car park and locked herself inside that shock hit her and she shook uncontrollably for long minutes.

The awful reality was that he was right—she was on a hiding to nothing, trying to make their estate work again. But she'd be damned if she wasn't going to try. Her father had made long-overdue amends with Maddie, and even though it had come so late, Maddie had always clung to the hope that she would hear from her father. She would have returned here years ago if he'd welcomed her back.

For as long as she could remember she'd wanted nothing more than to work on the estate.

When she'd received the heartfelt letter from her ill father, with his outpouring of regret for his actions, Maddie hadn't been able to help but respond to his plea to come home to try to save their estate from oblivion.

Maddie's relationship with her father had never been close. He'd always made it clear he wanted sons, not a daughter, and had firmly believed that a woman's place was in the home and *not* in the business of winemaking. But he'd made up for a lifetime of dismissiveness while on his deathbed, when he'd realised he might lose everything.

Maddie had been hoping and praying she'd make it home in time to see him, but he'd passed away while she was in the air on her initial flight to Buenos Aires. His solicitor had met her with the news, and she'd gone straight from the airport in Mendoza to his private and lonely funeral in the small family graveyard in the grounds of their estate.

She hadn't even been able to get in touch with her mother, who was on a cruise somewhere with her fourth husband, who was some ten years her junior. She felt very alone now, when faced with the tangible animosity of Nicolás de Rojas and the seemingly insurmountable task of taking on the Vasquez estate.

Legend had it that Maddie's and Nicolás de Rojas's ancestors had been two Spanish friends, immigrants who'd made the long journey to Argentina to make new lives for themselves. They'd committed to setting up a vineyard together but something had happened—a woman had been involved: a love affair gone wrong and a bitter betrayal. As revenge Maddie's forefather had vowed to ruin the de Rojas name. So he'd founded Vasquez wines in direct competition and built it up right next door.

Vasquez wines had become ridiculously successful, decimating the de Rojas name, thus ensuring that the feud thrived and deepened as each generation fought for dominance and revenge. Violence between the families had been habitual, and once a member of the de Rojas family had even been murdered—although it had never been proved that the culprit had been a Vasquez.

Reversals in fortune had happened through the years, but by the time Maddie had been born the two estates had been almost neck and neck in terms of success. The generations-old dark cloud of hostility between the families seemed to have settled into an uneasy truce. In spite of the relative peace, though, Maddie had grown up knowing that she would be punished if she was caught even looking in the direction of the de Rojas vineyard.

Her cheeks stung with colour now when she recalled Nicolás's jeering 'princess'. He'd only ever really seen her on the few social occasions when their families had been forced to mix, when hosts had nervously ensured that they didn't actually mingle.

Her mother had used those opportunities to parade Maddie in the latest fashions, forcing her naturally tomboyish and bookish daughter into the mould of the fashionable daughter she'd really wanted. Maddie's beautiful mother had wanted a confidante, not a child.

Maddie had been so mortified and uncomfortable in those situations that she'd done her best to fade into the background, while at the same time being aware of the very taboo fascination she felt for Nicolás Cristobal de Rojas, six years her senior, who even as a teenager had exuded unmistakable arrogance and virility. The tension and distance between their families had only made him more fascinating and alluring.

Then, as soon as she'd turned twelve, she'd been sent to

boarding school in England and had only returned home for the holidays. She'd lived for those few months, and had endured her mother's determination to parade her as if she was a doll just because it meant she could catch illicit glimpses of Nicolás de Rojas at the annual polo matches or the few social occasions their families shared. She'd look out of her bedroom window and sometimes would see him far in the distance on his horse as he inspected the neighbouring vineyard. To her, he'd looked like a golden-haired god. Strong and proud.

Whenever she'd seen him socially he'd always been surrounded by girls. Her mouth twisted when she thought of the beautiful blonde he'd so casually dismissed just now. Evidently nothing had changed there…

Eight years ago the uneasy truce between their families had exploded into bitterly fresh enmity and had shown Maddie the real depth of hatred between them. The fact that she'd actually challenged Nicolás's perception of her for a few days in time was something she had to forget. Because it had been undone as quickly as it had been done. What would someone like him be more likely to believe? A lifetime of propaganda and erroneous impressions? Or the briefest of moments fuelled by lust which had quickly been soured for ever?

Maddie shook her head and forced her trembling hand to start up the engine. She had just enough diesel to take her back to the small town of Villarosa, about thirty minutes outside Mendoza. No doubt someone of Nicolás's standing had a suite in the palatial hotel tonight, where he would be accompanied by his long-legged golden companion, but Maddie had nowhere to go except a crumbling homestead where the electricity had been cut off months ago and where she and a loyal skeleton staff depended on an ancient generator for power.

Maddie swung out of the hotel car park and reflected miserably that there must be plenty of de Rojas ancestors laughing down at her predicament right now.

CHAPTER TWO

Nic was stuck in a trance. All he could see in his mind's eye was the bared expanse of pale, slim back and the tumble of jet-black hair against her skin as Madalena Vasquez walked away. She'd stumbled slightly in her shoes, and it had made her look achingly vulnerable for a moment—before she'd recovered and swept out of the ballroom with all the hauteur of a queen. She'd had no right to look affronted at his taunting *'princesss'*, for that was what she had always been.

When she'd been much younger she'd reminded him of a fragile porcelain doll, and he hated to admit it now but she'd always fascinated him with her unusually pale colouring and green eyes. There had been moments—the memory of which burned him now for his naivety—when he'd believed she'd been uncomfortable in their social milieu, when she'd looked almost sick as her mother pushed her to the fore. He'd sensed that beneath the delicate exterior lurked something much more solid.

Nic's mouth firmed. Well, he had first-hand experience of exactly how solid she was beneath that ethereal beauty. As if he needed to be reminded of the kind of person she was. Once she'd challenged his preconceptions of her, but it had all been an act.

She'd shared her mother's temptress nature—an earthy

sensuality that could ensnare the strongest of men. His heart thumped hard. It had ensnared his father before him, and then, a generation later, *him*. She'd only been seventeen. Humiliation burned Nic at recalling it, and he couldn't halt the flood of memories—not so soon after seeing her close up and in the flesh for the first time in years.

One evening he'd been inspecting the vines which were closest to the Vasquez estate; they always had to be ever vigilant in case of sabotage. That particular evening Nic had been weary and frustrated…weary of his mother's constant melancholy—never properly diagnosed as the depression it had been—and his father's caustic cruelty and habitual violence. At the dinner table his father had been drunkenly ranting about how the Vasquez run of success was threatening their sales. Nic had always firmly believed you made your own success, but, constrained by his authoritarian father, he hadn't been able to implement his own ideas.

Something had made Nic look up to the small hill which acted as a natural boundary between the two estates, and he'd seen a feminine figure with long black hair astride a huge stallion. *Madalena Vasquez.* Looking right at him.

His weariness had morphed instantly into burning irrational anger—at her for making him think about her, wonder about her, when she was forbidden. She also represented the dark and tangled feud which he had never really understood.

The supercilious image she presented on her horse had only galvanised him further and, giving in to an urge stronger than he'd been able to resist, Nic had spurred his horse to a canter and headed straight for her—only to see her whirl around and disappear.

He could still taste the urgency thrumming in his blood eight years later—to catch her and see her up close. Never once in their lives had they been allowed to speak to one another. Although he'd seen the way she would look at him from a distance and then glance away with artful shyness.

Finally he'd caught another glimpse of her, low down over her horse, hair streaming in the wind. She'd been cutting through the landscape like a bullet. With increasing urgency he'd thundered after her. It had been on the very edge of both their estates that he'd eventually seen her riderless horse, tied to a tree. She'd come to a remote part of their land where orchards had been planted. And then he'd seen her standing in a clearing of trees, as if she'd known he'd follow her.

More mesmerised by her flushed cheeks and that glossy fall of hair than he'd cared to admit, Nic had swung off his horse and come to stand in front of her. His anger had dissolved like snow on a hot stone. The very forbidden nature of what they were doing had infused the air around them.

'Why did you follow me?' she'd asked suddenly, her voice low and husky.

Nic had spoken on an unthinking reflex. 'Perhaps I just wanted to see the Vasquez princess up close.'

In that instant she went white as a ghost, her eyes like two huge wounded emeralds.

She backed away and Nic put out his hands, instantly contrite. 'Wait. Stop. I don't know why I said that... I'm sorry.' He took a breath. 'I followed you because I wanted to...and because I think you wanted me to.'

She'd flushed pink then, the colour rushing into her cheeks dramatically. Without even being aware of it Nic reached out a hand and touched her cheek, fascinated by the way her emotions showed so clearly, feeling its satiny texture beneath his callused palm. A shudder of pure longing went through him—so strong he nearly shook.

She stepped back, biting her lip, looking tortured. 'We shouldn't be here... If anyone sees us...'

Nic saw a tremor go through her slender frame, the way her young breasts pushed against the material of her shirt. Jodhpurs encased long, slim thighs.

He struggled with his control, waves of heat building inside him. She'd speared him with a defiant look then, which confirmed his suspicions that she wasn't as delicate as she had always appeared—as if her little gallop through the wilderness of their lands hadn't already told him that.

'I'm not a princess. I'm not like that. I hate being paraded in public like some kind of mannequin. It's my mother...she wishes I was more like her. They won't even let me go out riding unsupervised. I have to sneak out when they're busy...'

Nic saw her gaze fall to his mouth and her cheeks pinken again. Power and testosterone flooded his body, and he smiled wryly. 'I spend practically every waking hour on a horse...working in the vineyard.'

She looked back up at him, but not before torturing him with an innocently hungry look at his mouth.

'That's all I ever wanted. But when my brother died my father found me helping to pick the grapes one day and sent me inside. He told me that if he ever caught me in the vineyard again he'd take his belt to me.'

Nic winced and his stomach clenched. He knew only too well what the wrath of a father felt like. Gruffly he said, 'Your brother died a few years ago, didn't he?'

Madalena looked away, swallowing visibly before saying, 'He died in an accident when they were crushing the grapes. He was only thirteen.'

'I'm sorry.' And then he asked, a little wistfully, 'You were close?'

She looked back, her eyes suspiciously bright. 'I adored him. Our father was...*is*...prone to rages. One day I angered him, and he would have hit me but Alvaro stepped in and took it. My father wouldn't stop hitting him, enraged at being shown up by his own son. He was only eight at the time...'

Her eyes were swimming with tears. Nic had been the recipient of many a beating in his own time. Acting on an instinct too powerful to resist, he reached out and pulled her to him, enfolding her slim body in his, wrapping his arms around her. The need to comfort her was overwhelming, and completely alien for someone like him who generally held people at arm's length.

She was a complete stranger to him in so many ways, but in that moment he felt a deep kinship. After long moments she pulled back, and with the utmost reluctance Nic let her go.

She said shakily, 'I should go...they'll be looking for me...'

She turned and Nic reached out, gripping her arm with a desperate feeling in his belly. She looked back and he said, 'Wait...meet me here again tomorrow?'

The world seemed to stop turning for an infinitesimal moment, and Nic braced himself for a mocking laugh— some indication that he'd completely misread those few moments.

But Madalena's cheeks flushed red and she said huskily, 'I'd like that.'

They met every day for a week—stolen moments in that secret place where time seemed to be suspended in a bubble and where inhibitions fell away. Nic spoke to her of things he'd never told another soul as easily as if he hadn't experienced years of emotional isolation. Each day he became more and more consumed by Madalena

Vasquez. More and more entranced with her delicate beauty, which he'd discovered hid an earthy sensuality, driving him senseless with growing desire. Yet he managed not to touch her after that first day, when he'd pulled her into his arms to comfort her.

The depth of his need scared him, and the sensual and sexual tension building between them tipped over on that last day. When Nic arrived to find Maddie waiting, he didn't speak and nor did she. The air quivered and vibrated with awareness around them, and then she was in his arms before he'd stretched them out to pull her into them.

His mouth was on hers, and she was clutching him as if she were drowning. He sank a hand into her hair. It felt like liquid silk. He felt her legs shaking against his and slowly they lay down on the downy grass under the shade of the trees, oblivious to their idyllic surroundings. Heat consumed Nic so much that his hand trembled as he fumbled with the buttons on her blouse.

He was no callow, inexperienced youth, but he felt like one as she lay back and looked at him from under long, dark lashes, her cheeks stained red. When he'd opened her shirt and undid her bra to uncover pale breasts tipped with tight pink nipples, he nearly lost it completely.

He was drunk on her by then—drunk on the taste of those sweet breasts, and her soft mewling sounds of response and rolling hips—so he didn't hear anything until she tensed in his arms.

They both looked up at the same moment to see grim figures on horseback, staring down at them. It all became a blur as Nic scrambled to cover Maddie and she stood up behind him. Then they were both hauled unceremoniously out of the clearing by their respective estate employees and brought home...

'Hello? Earth to Nicolás?'

Nic flinched now, as if stung, and looked down to see Estella staring up at him.

She was holding two glasses of champagne. She handed one to him and said, 'Here. Looks like you could do with this.'

He was feeling incredibly raw and exposed, but he schooled his features and took the drink, restraining himself from downing it in one go.

'So, was that woman really one of the Vasquez family? I thought I might have to get a hose to cool things down between you.'

'She's the last Vasquez. She's come back to take over the family business,' Nic bit out tautly, wanting to rid himself of the potent images.

'That's interesting…' Estella mused in a far too innocent voice. 'You're the last in your line too…'

Nic glowered at Estella. 'The only thing interesting about it is that she'll be forced to sell that estate to me and we'll finally be rid of the Vasquez family for good.'

With tension radiating from his tall form he strode away from her and the speculative look on her face. The last thing Nic needed was someone analysing his encounter with Madalena Vasquez. And the last thing the de Rojas estate needed was for its name to be dragged back down into the mire of rumour and innuendo and a resumption of ancient hostilities. The sooner Madalena Vasquez realised the futility of her position and how unwelcome she was, the better for everyone.

'What the hell is he up to?' Maddie muttered to herself, and turned the silver embossed invitation over and back again, as if it might contain a booby trap.

The message was written on one side and simple.

You are cordially invited to a private tasting of
this year's finest wines from the world-renowned
de Rojas Estate.
   Saturday, 7p.m., Casa de Rojas, Villarosa, Mendoza.
   Black Tie.

The invitation had arrived with that day's post, inter-
rupting Maddie as she waded through her father's papers.

She heard a noise and looked up from where she was
sitting at her father's study desk to see Hernan come in.
He was their oldest and most loyal employee, her father's
viticulturist, and his own father had been the viticulturist
before him. He and his wife, Maria, who was the housekeeper, were both working for board alone, even though
Maddie had told them she couldn't be sure when they
might get paid again.

Her father's head winemaker had long since gone, and
Maddie knew that she might have to take over that role
until she could afford to hire someone new. Fresh from a
degree in Oenology and Viticulture, she was lacking in
practical experience but had a burning love for the industry and craved the opportunity. Even if it was a poisoned
chalice.

She swallowed the emotion she felt at the evidence of
Hernan's loyalty now and handed the card to him. He read
it silently and handed it back with an inscrutable look on
his face.

Maddie just arched a questioning brow.

After a long moment the old man said, 'You do know
that if you accept the invitation you will be the first
Vasquez to be invited onto de Rojas land since as far back
as I can remember?'

Maddie nodded slowly. This was huge. And she had no

idea what he was playing at, but she had to admit she was intrigued to see the famed estate.

To her shock and surprise Hernan shrugged lightly. 'Perhaps you should go. Times have changed, and things can't go on as they always have. He's up to something. Of that I have no doubt. Nic de Rojas is infinitely more intelligent than his father, or even his father before him, so he is a dangerous enemy to have…but perhaps an enemy you know…?' He trailed off.

Maddie looked at the card thoughtfully. It had been two weeks exactly since her tumultuous meeting with Nicolás de Rojas, and she still felt shaky when she thought of it. Going through her father's papers since then had shown her the true ugly extent of how far Nicolás de Rojas was willing to go to to get his hands on their estate.

Her father had been bombarded with letter after letter advising him to sell up. Some had been cajoling, almost friendly in tone, and others had been downright threatening. They'd all been issued by the de Rojas solicitor but signed off with the arrogant Nicolás de Rojas scrawl. There'd even been a threatening letter dated the day her father had died.

As much as Maddie wanted to rip up the invitation and send it back in pieces to Nicolás, she knew she couldn't afford to isolate herself now. She needed to see what she was up against.

The party was the next evening.

She put the invitation in a drawer and stood up resolutely, clamping the gaucho hat she'd been wearing back on her head. 'I'll think about it. In the meantime we need to check the eastern vineyard again. It looks like our best prospect of a harvest this year.'

'You mean our *only* prospect,' Hernan said darkly as they walked out to the battered vineyard Jeep.

Maddie tried not to let the sensation of sheer panic overwhelm her. It was far too frequent for her liking, and not helped one bit by the realisation that the monumental task of harvesting their one chance of a wine that year was going to fall to her and Hernan and whatever friends and relations he could persuade to help with picking the grapes.

Her father had been a staunch old-school-style wine-maker, eschewing wholesale modern methods. That was all very well when you were producing top-of-the-line expensive wines in tandem with more affordable table wines, but in later years her father had all but stopped producing for the more accessible market.

Their one tiny glimmer of hope was in the grapes which had somehow survived the neglect of her father to flourish and ripen on the eastern slopes of the vineyard. These were the Sauvignon grapes which made the distinctive white wine which had put the Vasquez name on the map—particularly because red wines were more common in Argentina.

If they could harvest them, and assure investors of the quality and quantity, then perhaps someone would give them the money they needed to get back on track—or at the very least to be able to pay the basic bills again.

Nic was tense as he stood in the open-air courtyard in the middle of his *hacienda*. His focus was on the imposing entrance doorway, which was still admitting a long line of glittering guests who had travelled from all over the world for this tasting. Hundreds of candles flickered in huge lanterns, and waiters dressed immaculately in black and white moved among the guests offering wine and canapés. But all Nic could think was…*would she come? And why had he asked her, really?*

Nic told himself it was because he wanted her *gone*. His belly clenched. It went much deeper than that, and he knew it. Really, what he'd wanted since eight years ago, and since he'd had that electric glimpse of her in that club in London, was to see her broken and contrite. To see that pale perfection undone. To see her as humiliated as he'd felt. To see her as exposed. She'd lured him to expose himself and he'd stupidly believed the act she'd put on.

Her words resounded in his head. *'I was bored. OK? I wanted to seduce you because you were forbidden to me. It was exciting...'*

A smug voice came from his left. 'It'll only be a matter of time now before you can buy out the Vasquez estate.'

Nic took his eye off the door for a moment and looked at his solicitor, who had been a good friend of his parents. His mother's friend more than his father's. He was a small, overweight man, with mean, calculating eyes. Nic had never especially liked him, but it had been easier to retain him than to let him go after his father's death. He made a mental note to instruct his assistant to seek out new legal represention. He'd do his duty and give Señor Fiero a generous retirement package.

A movement at the door caught the corner of Nic's eye, and he looked back to see Madalena Vasquez entering. The instantaneous effect was almost laughable. His whole body tautened, and an urgent need to see her up close again rushed through him, shocking him with its force. He'd never felt that for another woman. Not even a lover.

From here she looked even more stunning than she had two weeks ago. Her hair was up and she was wearing a long midnight-blue sheath. Strapless, it showed off the delicate lines of her collarbone and shoulders. The gently muscled strength of her arms. There was something slightly odd about the dress, though, that he couldn't put his finger on. Much like the dress she'd worn the other night in Mendoza, it was as if it didn't fit perfectly. As if it wasn't hers.

He was so used to seeing women immaculately turned out that he could spot the slight anomaly a mile away, and it didn't fit with what he would have expected of Madalena Vasquez.

'Who is that? She looks familiar.'

'That,' Nic said tightly, irrationally not liking the fact that his solicitor was looking at her too, 'is Madalena Vasquez. She's home and taking over the family estate.'

The solicitor laughed cruelly. 'That place is a mess. She'll be begging you to buy her out.'

Nic moved away from his solicitor and towards Madalena. He couldn't fathom the urge he felt to turn around and punch the older man. It was visceral and disturbing, and the remnants of it lingered as he drew closer and saw that wide green gaze settle on him. Pink flooded her cheeks and he could see the faintest bruised colour under her eyes—signs of fatigue. His chest constricted. Once he'd believed in that artifice, but it was a trick to incur sympathy learnt from her mother. To make a man believe that she was as innocent as she looked. When she was rotten to the core.

Nevertheless his rogue body could not be dictated to by his mind. Desire was hot and instantaneous.

He put a smooth smile on his face and tried to ignore the increasing heat in his body. 'Welcome to my home.'

Maddie tried not to let Nicolás de Rojas see how affected she was just by watching him walk towards her. She felt like snorting incredulously. *Home* was a woeful understatement for this seriously palatial house. Once, a long time ago, her home had been as grand, but now it was a crumbling shell.

She didn't trust his urbane charm for a second. His eyes were like shards of ice and she shivered imperceptibly. Forgetting her resolve to appear nothing but aloof, she blurted out, 'Why did you invite me here?'

Quick as a shot he answered, 'Why did you come?'

Maddie flushed, all of her reasons for coming feeling very flimsy and transparent now. She should have just sent the invitation back in tiny pieces as she'd intended. But she hadn't.

She squared her shoulders. 'I came because it's been two weeks and I want to let you know that I've still no intention of going anywhere.'

Nicolás tipped his head slightly. She barely saw him make the gesture, and then a man appeared at his side.

'Yes, sir?'

'Madalena Vasquez, I'd like to introduce you to my house manager, Geraldo. He will show you around and see that you have everything you need. If you wouldn't mind excusing me? I have some new guests to attend to.'

And just like that he had turned and was walking away. Maddie felt inexplicably bereft, dropped...

The intensity of emotion he aroused so effortlessly was still high. Maddie cursed herself for allowing any hint of vulnerability through. She had to be strong enough to withstand Nicolás de Rojas and his brand of arrogance or she'd never survive.

She turned to the man waiting by her side with a big forced smile. 'Thank you.'

Maddie's head was spinning by the time Geraldo, who had proved to be a charming host, showed her back into the main courtyard, which was now thronged with people. Men were in tuxedos and women glittered in long dresses and jewels.

The reality of the sheer opulence she'd just seen was

a little hard to take in. The home itself—the few main rooms she'd been shown—was exquisitely furnished but also comfortable. Accessible. It was a *home*. And that had affected her deeply. Her own home had always been more like a cold and austere show house, full of dusty antiques. Unfortunately all of them had long since been sold to fund her father's downward spiral.

'I'll leave you here now...if that's okay?'

Maddie swung her gaze back to the pleasant house manager and realised he was waiting for her answer. 'Of course. You must be busy. I'm sorry to have taken you away from your duties.'

He said urbanely, 'It was a pleasure, Señorita Vasquez. Eduardo, who is our head winemaker, will see to it that you taste from the best of our selection of wines tonight.'

Another equally pleasant man was waiting to escort Maddie over to where the wine-tasting tables had been set up. It was only when she looked up and caught the coolly sardonic expression on Nicolás's face, where he stood head and shoulders above the crowd across the room, that she understood she was being effectively herded in exactly the direction he wanted her to go. And being shown exactly what he wanted her to see.

The transparency of his actions and the way she'd almost forgotten what was happening here galled her. So she merely skated her own gaze past his and made Eduardo the focus of her attention as he explained the various wines to her.

After a few minutes Maddie managed to take advantage of someone coming up to ask Eduardo a question and escape, turning instinctively away from the direction where Nicolás de Rojas was holding court with a rapt crowd. She hated being so aware of where he was at any moment, as if some kind of invisible cord linked her to him. And yet, a small snide voice reminded her, as soon as puberty had hit she'd had that awareness of him as a man.

She walked through a silent, dimly lit room full of lux-uriously stuffed couches and rosewood furniture and out onto a blissfully quiet decked area which hugged the out-side of the house. Little pools of golden light spilled out onto the ground, and Maddie went and curled her hands over the wooden fence which acted as a perimeter.

The strains of a jazz band playing for the very select crowd wafted through on the breeze. She smiled cynically. Nicolás de Rojas could have stopped her at the front door and she would have already been in awe of his screaming success and wealth.

The wide gravelled drive, the rows upon rows of well-tended fertile vines and gleaming outbuildings had been enough of a display. That was what she wanted for her own estate—to see it flourishing as it had when she was a young girl, with rows of vines full of plump sun-ripened grapes...

She heard a noise and whirled around. Her heart thumped hard in her chest at the sight of Nicolás de Rojas in the doorway of the room behind her, shoulders blocking out the light, hands in pockets. He was so rakishly hand-some that for a moment she forgot about everything and could only see him.

Maddie called up every shred of self-control and smiled. But it was brittle. Seeing Nicolás's house up close like this had affected her far more deeply than she liked to admit.

'Did you really think that showing off your success would make me scurry to the nearest airport with my tail between my legs?'

His jaw was gritted but he stepped out of the door-way, making Maddie's breath hitch in her throat when his scent reached out and wound around her. She couldn't back away. The wooden posts were already digging into her soft flesh.

'It must feel very dull here after the bright lights of London…not to mention the ski slopes of Gstaad. Aren't you missing the season?'

Maddie flushed deep red. She smiled even harder, hiding the hurt at that particular memory. 'I wouldn't have had you down as a *Celebrity Now!* reader, Mr de Rojas.'

Maddie had long since berated herself that she should have been suspicious when her flighty mother had expressed a desire to see her—even offering to fly her out to meet her in the wealthy ski resort for a holiday. This was the same mother who had refused to help Maddie out because she believed that she'd already sacrificed enough for her daughter.

As soon as she'd arrived at the ski resort it had become apparent that her mother needed her daughter to help foster an image of dutiful motherhood. She'd been intent on seducing her current husband, who was divorced, but a committed and devoted father. Maddie had been too disappointed and heartsore to fight with her mother, and had given in to a cloying magazine shoot in which for all the world they'd appeared the best of friends.

Nicolás answered easily, 'I happened to be on a plane on my way home from Europe. The air hostess handed me the wrong magazine, but when I saw who was gracing the cover I couldn't resist reading all about your *wonderful* relationship with your mother and how you've both moved on *so well* from the painful split with your father.'

Maddie felt sick. She'd read the article too, and couldn't believe she'd been so hungry for affection that she'd let her mother manipulate her so crassly. She pushed the painful reality of her mother's selfishness aside.

'This evening was a wasted exercise on your part, de

Rojas. You've merely made me even more determined to succeed.'

The fact that he thought he had her so neatly boxed up and judged made fresh anger surge up inside Maddie.

'I've just spent two weeks in a house with no electricity, and as you can see I'm not running screaming for the nearest luxury health spa. Now, if you don't mind, it's late and I've got to be up early in the morning.'

Maddie gathered up her dress to stalk off, but at that moment one of her oversized shoes came off and she stumbled. A strong hand closed around one bare arm to steady her and the sensation was electric.

Nicolás didn't let her go, though. She was whirled around to face him again, one shoe on, one shoe off.

He was frowning down at her. 'What do you mean no electricity?'

Maddie was used to being considered tall, but right now she felt positively petite. Bitterness laced her voice at being made to feel so vulnerable, when she had no doubt that was exactly what this man had intended all along. 'We've been using an ancient generator to get electricity in our house since they cut my father off months ago—when he stopped paying the bills.'

Nicolás shook his head. He looked shocked. 'I didn't know it was that bad.'

Maddie tried to pull her arm back but his grip was firm. Panic at her helpless physical reaction galvanised her to say, 'As if you care. You were too busy signing off on your solicitor's letters, doing your utmost to get a dying man to sell up. Do you know that he received the last letter the day he died?'

Now Nicolás looked confused. His hand tightened. 'What are you talking about? I never signed any letters. Any correspondence between my family and yours stopped when my father died. I was too busy rebuilding our own brand and renovating the estate and house.'

'You can spout all the lies you like, de Rojas. This evening was a mistake. I've let down every generation of my family and my father by coming here. It won't happen again.'

Nicolás's hand softened its grip on her arm and Maddie felt ridiculously disorientated, her anger dissipating like mist over a hill. His eyes were intense blue flames that communicated something base and carnal directly to her insides.

His voice was deep. 'But you did come here tonight, and there's something in the air…it brought us together before, and it's still there.'

Maddie felt the sense of disorientation increase. She finally yanked her arm free from his grip, but his words were hurtling her back in time to when he had stood in front of her and said, *'You're nothing but a tempting tease. I was curious to know what the Vasquez princess tasted like and now I know—poisonous.'*

The bitterness and anger of that exchange eight years ago was far too acute, eclipsing everything else. Maddie had not trusted herself with another man since then because of it. She'd held a part of herself private and aloof for fear of getting hurt again, or facing painful revelations. She had to push him back before he guessed how vulnerable she was.

She squared her shoulders and forced herself to look Nicolás dead in the eye. 'I seduced you once, de Rojas. Did you really think this evening would induce me to try and seduce you again? Eight years isn't enough time for you to get over your wounded ego?'

Nicolás stood tall, and she saw him pale beneath his tan. 'You little bitch.'

CHAPTER THREE

MADDIE didn't know where on earth she'd got the nerve to say those words when, if anything, they could be more legitimately levelled at her. She hadn't got over what had happened eight years ago—not by a long shot.

She heard a rushing in her ears, but she ignored it and tossed her head. 'Don't worry. You won't see me again. I think we can safely say this farce is over. I came tonight because I was curious to see what you were up to. You've seriously underestimated me.'

She was turning away again when she forgot that she still had one shoe off. She stumbled into thin air, and would have fallen if Nicolás hadn't caught her and hauled her back against him. One strong arm was wrapped around her ribcage, just under her breasts, and the other was across her shoulders. Adrenalin pumped through Maddie's veins. She immediately tried to remove his arms but they were like steel bands. And they were completely alone.

She had an urge to shout out, but a hand came over her mouth as if he'd read her mind. Panic gripped her— not at the threat of violence but at the threat of something much more potent. The evidence of Nicolás de Rojas's hardening body at her back was liquefying her insides. A silent scream sounded in Maddie's head: *No! Not this, please*. He would expose her vulnerability in seconds if he touched her.

She bit down on the fleshy part of his hand and heard him curse—but not before she'd tasted the salty tang of his skin. Her belly swooped and fire danced along her veins. He moved her effortlessly in his arms and now she was facing him, his arms manacling her to his body, her hands behind her back. She was completely powerless. And, to her absolute disgust, the predominant thing she was feeling was excitement.

'Let me *go*.'

He shook his head, eyes glittering down into hers. Maddie felt as if she'd completely lost her footing. Past and present, everything was mixing, and she felt seriously overwhelmed.

'I'm not finished with you, Maddie.'

Maddie's heart lurched painfully at hearing him use the diminutive of her name. She could remember with painful clarity telling him that she preferred Maddie to the more stuffy-sounding Madalena. He had touched her cheek and said, 'Maddie it is, then…'

He smiled, and it was the smile of a predator, forcing Maddie back to the present moment. 'One thing you should know is that if I've underestimated you, then you've *seriously* underestimated *me*. We have unfinished business— and ironically enough it's got nothing to do with business.'

Before Maddie had even properly taken in his words or read his intent he'd hauled her even closer. His head descended and his hard mouth pressed against hers. For a second Maddie had no reaction except numb shock. And then sensation exploded behind her eyes—hot and urgent.

Desperately she tried to cling onto reality and not let that hot urgency take over her need to stay immobile and unresponsive. But she might as well have been hoping that the sun wouldn't rise in the morning.

Being in this man's arms again was like seeing a beacon of light strobing across a choppy ocean and reacting to it with an unthinking instinct to seek harbour. Maddie felt the inexorable and overpowering urge to follow it, even as everything rational was screaming at her to stop, pull herself free, not to react. But a much bigger part of her was aching all over with the effort it took not to react.

As if sensing her turmoil, Nic freed her hands and lifted his own to her head, fingers caressing her skull, angling her head so that he could better plunder her mouth. His tongue flicked against the closed seam of her lips and at that touch Maddie felt her resistance falling away. Her free hands hovered for a long moment. She knew in some dim place that she should use them to push him away, but when she put them between their bodies and felt the taut musculature of his torso underneath his thin shirt they clung...didn't push.

He growled low in his throat at her capitulation and became bolder, his tongue prising open her soft lips to seek the hot interior of her mouth. The devastation of that simple intimacy made Maddie sway against him. She could feel her breasts crushed against the solid wall of his chest.

One of his hands was on her waist, digging into her flesh, anchoring her solidly against him. She could feel the bold thrust of his arousal against her belly, and between her legs she felt hot and moist.

The world was turning into a hot furnace of sensation and desperate wanting—and then suddenly a cool breeze was waking Maddie as if from a drugged trance and she was blinking up into Nic's impassive face. It looked as if it was carved from stone. Maddie felt like jelly. Her mouth was swollen, her heart beating like a piston. Her hair was tumbling down over sensitised skin.

'You…' She couldn't even formulate a word beyond that.

In a voice so cold it woke her up more effectively than anything else, Nic said, 'What do you want to say, Maddie? You want me to believe this act? That I've effectively rendered you speechless with passion?'

A look crossed his face that was so bitter it took Maddie aback. For a moment she was distracted from her growing humiliation.

'You forget that you already tried that once with me. I'm not stupid enough to fall for it again. You can't, however, deny that you want me. As much if not more than when you were hot and trembling in my arms eight years ago. I could have taken you that day and you would have been with me every step of the way. You might have seduced me out of boredom, but there was nothing bored about your response then—or just now. And you've never been able to handle that reality.'

The sheer arrogance of his tone and expression revived Maddie from the fugue she'd been in. She moved out of his embrace with a jerky movement and saw dark colour flash along his cheekbones.

'I am not interested in your hypotheses, or your take on the past. The past is in the past and that's where it'll stay. *This…*' she waved a hand to encompass what had just happened '…is nothing but evidence that physical chemistry can be dismayingly arbitrary. That's *all*.'

Nic smiled. 'If I hadn't stopped when I had I could be taking you right here, just feet away from one hundred guests, and I'd have had to put a hand over your mouth to stifle your screams of pleasure.'

The sheer carnality of his words made Maddie raise her hand—he'd pushed her too far.

Before it could connect to his smug face he'd caught it in a steel-fingered grip. Shock washed through Maddie in a wave. She'd never raised a hand to anyone in her life. The line of Nic's mouth was impossibly grim.

'I was merely proving that you're no more in control of your desire for me now than you were eight years ago, no matter how much you tried to convince me that you'd found what we had done so abhorrent it made you physically ill. You came here tonight to test me as much as I tested you. My bed is free at the moment...you're more than welcome to join me there and we can indulge this *arbitrary chemistry* until you've come to your senses and decided to sell the Vasquez estate to me.'

Maddie ripped her hand free of his grip and had to curb the urge to try and strike him again. His version of what had happened that cataclysmic afternoon was very different from hers. She knew she'd given him the impression that what they'd shared had disgusted her...and for a while she *had* found what they'd done abhorrent. But not for the reasons he obviously believed.

And she couldn't tell him. As much as she hated him right now, telling him the truth would only expose her even more. He would know that that week had meant everything to her, that she hadn't set out coldly to seduce him just for her amusement. There was no way she could disabuse him of that belief now. It was her only defence against him.

She stood very tall and said frostily, 'You seem to have forgotten that your bed was busy enough only two weeks ago. I think I'll pass, thanks.'

And then she turned and walked out.

To her intense relief he didn't stop her. It was only when she got outside to the main door that Maddie realised that she was barefoot. She certainly wasn't going to go back now for her shoes and risk seeing Nic again. She scrambled into the Jeep as soon as the valet brought it round, and as she saw the lights of the *hacienda* grow smaller in her rearview mirror she finally let out her breath.

She'd been a prize fool to think that Nic de Rojas wouldn't bring up what had happened in the past. He was a very virile and proud man. She knew she'd damaged his ego then…and she shuddered now when she recalled the bitter look she'd seen cross his face just a short while ago. She'd had no idea it would all feel so fresh and unresolved between them.

Even though the events of eight years before had sent out violent ripples, she would have imagined that the actual week which had led to those events had faded in his memory. That the intervening years and the countless affairs he seemed to have had with beautiful women would have made Maddie's innocent and gauche charms fade into insignificance…

The way he'd just kissed her, together with the memory of that week—those heady days when desire had tightened like a steel coil in her belly until she'd begged him to make love to her—made Maddie shake so much that she had to pull over on the hard shoulder or risk a crash. She put her head down on the steering wheel between her hands and tried to empty her mind, but it was impossible… the memories were too potent—especially after what had just happened.

She'd managed to evade her mother and father that day, and take a horse out riding on her own. She'd always instinctively hoped for a glimpse of Nic de Rojas on his own estate, and her heart had almost stopped when she'd seen him just metres away. The intensity on his face had scared her and she'd turned her horse to run, not even sure what she was running from. Perhaps it had been the delicious and illicit excitement thrumming through her blood.

She could remember looking back and seeing that he was following with that same intense expression—and her excitement had spiked to almost unbearable levels. Her whole body had gone on fire. The friction of the horse as it had surged powerfully between her legs had nearly made her cry out she was so oversensitised. By the time she'd reached the remote orchard which straddled both their estates her body had been as taut as a bowstring, humming for him.

That orchard was a favourite spot of hers. A secret place. And then he'd been there, swinging lithely off his horse, full of that taut energy. It had been overwhelming to see him up close at last—nothing could have prepared her for his sheer masculine perfection.

He'd touched her so gently. And they'd spoken. Really spoken. After years of feeling as if no one could possibly understand her Maddie had found a kinship with the most unlikely person: the son of her family's sworn enemies.

That first day when Maddie had tried to leave, her heart had felt heavier than a stone in her chest. Until Nic had asked to see her again the following day. And then the next and the next.

The week had taken on an unreal aspect…dreamy. Those illicit moments under the spreading branches of the orchard trees had become the only reality Maddie wanted. Nic had consumed her, filled her nights with vivid and carnal dreams. By the end of the week she'd been in such physical turmoil—craving him but scared of that craving—that she'd all but thrown herself at him.

He'd kissed her and touched her, and Maddie's face flamed even now to remember the wanton way she'd writhed beneath his hands, begging for more of something she could only guess at.

And then all hell had broken loose.

Huge looming figures on horseback had appeared and smashed apart the idyll. Evidently their regular absences had been noted by keen eyes. Nic had put Maddie behind him and she could remember doing up her shirt with numb hands, panic-stricken as she'd heard the shouts get louder. And then they'd both been hauled out of the trees and marched away. Maddie could remember looking back to see Nic being corralled onto his stallion, flinging his father's men off him, snarling at them.

She'd sobbed out loud when she'd seen one of the men land him a blow to stop him hitting out. But by then she'd been unceremoniously dumped onto her own horse and was being led away.

By the time she'd got home her mother had been waiting, white-faced and seethingly angry. She'd asked, 'Is it true? You were found with Nicolás de Rojas?'

For the first time in her life Maddie had felt the fire of rebellion stir within her, and she had lifted her chin and answered in a strong voice, 'Yes, it's true.'

She'd not been prepared when her mother slapped her so hard across the face that her teeth had rattled in her head. She'd felt blood on the inside of her mouth. In shock she'd lifted a hand to her cheek and stared in horror at this woman who, at the most, had only ever touched her in public, to give an impression of a closeness that didn't exist.

Then her mother had broken down into hysterical tears. Before Maddie had known it, with her face still stinging hotly, she'd been leading her mother into the drawing room and forcing her to take some brandy to calm her down.

Eventually her mother had looked at her and shuddered expressively. Completely bewildered, Maddie had said,

'Mother, is it really so bad that I was with Nicolás? We... like each other.'

That had set her mother off again, and when she'd finally calmed down once more she'd pulled Maddie down onto the couch beside her. 'You cannot see him again, Madalena. I forbid it. Think of what it would do to your father.'

That rebellion stirred in Maddie's breast again—she could no more deny that she wanted to see Nic again than deny her own name. She stood up, agitated. 'That's ridiculous. You can't stop me seeing him. We don't care about the stupid feud. It's gone on long enough.'

Her mother stood up too. 'Madalena, you will *not* disobey me in this.'

Her mother's constant use of her full name, *Madalena*, broke something apart inside Maddie. Years of frustration at having to tiptoe around her father's mercurial moods, brought on by his abject grief for his dead son and her mother's blatant self-interest, made Maddie explode. 'If I want to see Nic de Rojas again there is nothing you can do to stop me.'

An awful stillness came into the room, and Maddie watched as her mother seemed to wither in front of her.

The glass in her hand was shaking so much that Maddie reached out and took it from her, saying with exasperation, 'Mother, your dramatics won't work with me. They might work on Father, but—'

'I'll tell you why you can't see him again.'

Maddie stopped talking. Something about the low tone of her mother's voice had made a shiver go down her spine. 'What are you talking about?'

And then her mother spoke—and broke Maddie's world into tiny pieces for ever.

'Ever since I was a young girl, when our families used

to socialise in Mendoza, I was in love with Sebastian de Rojas…' Her mother's mouth twisted. 'I wasn't from here, so I knew only the vaguest details about the feud between this family and his own…'

Maddie tried to make sense of what her mother had said. 'You were in love with Nicolás's father? But what's that got to do with anything now?'

Maddie's mother sat down again heavily, wringing her hands in her lap. She avoided Maddie's eyes. 'The truth is, I wanted Sebastian to marry *me*. But I was too young, and his family forced him to marry his wife because she'd been picked by his parents… He married her, and they had their son, Nicolás, very quickly.' Maddie's mother's voice broke. 'I thought he was lost to me for ever…until I met your father.' She looked up at Maddie, her eyes anguished. 'Part of the reason I married him was so I could be closer to Sebastian. When he saw me again he couldn't resist taking me back into his bed. We met in hotels, whenever we could…' Her mouth took on a bitter aspect for a moment. 'I wasn't under any illusions. Sebastian got a thrill out of taking the wife of his enemy to bed, but he'd never have jeopardised his reputation by revealing it.'

Maddie was feeling increasingly distant from everything, as if her mother's voice was coming from far away.

'He went to Europe one winter, to see about extending the business, and when he came back I was pregnant with Alvaro—your brother. He cut off all contact, believing that I'd turned my back on him, choosing my marriage over him.'

Maddie's mother's eyes swam with tears—but Maddie couldn't drum up any sympathy. She felt sick at learning the lengths to which her mother had gone just to get her own way. She'd married a man she didn't love just to entice another married man away from his wife and son.

'I don't see what any of this has to do with me not seeing Nic de Rojas again.' Maddie turned to leave the room and heard her mother standing behind her.

'It has *everything* to do with why you can't see him again.'

With the utmost reluctance Maddie stopped and turned around.

Her mother swallowed visibly. 'I didn't stop seeing Sebastian completely. There were a couple of times when I…I managed to persaude him to meet me.' Her mother took in a deep shuddery breath. 'After one of those times I fell pregnant…with you.' Maddie's mother's cheeks flared a deep and ugly red. 'But in that time I'd also slept with your father. The fact is that I can't be sure that Sebastian de Rojas isn't your father.'

Maddie looked at her mother. The words had hit an invisible wall and fallen somewhere between them, where she couldn't take in their horrible meaning.

Her mother seemed to realise that, and said harshly, 'You can't see Nicolás de Rojas again because he could be your half-brother.'

The glass Maddie had taken out of her mother's hand dropped out of hers to the parquet floor, shattering to pieces. She didn't even notice. Numb shock was enveloping her.

The only thing that broke through the shock and horror of her mother's revelations was the inarticulate roar of rage that came from behind them. Maddie's father stood in the doorway, red-faced, apoplectic. His eyes were mad, and he said in a choked voice, 'I knew it. I always knew there was something between you. Was my son even *my* son, or was he also the son of that bastard?'

Maddie's memory after that was hazy. She remembered a lot of shouting and crying. And being dragged roughly up to her room by her father and shut inside. The following day, after a sleepless night, Maddie had snuck out of her first-floor window and gone to find a horse. She hadn't even cared about her father's wrath any more. She'd needed to get out.

To her horror, she'd found that she'd instinctively made for the orchard again. Too overcome with everything, she'd slithered off her horse before she'd spotted that she wasn't alone. Nic de Rojas had stepped out from the shadows of the trees, his face grim.

Her belly had clenched painfully with a mixture of dread and that awful, illicit excitement. Had she been hoping that he would be here, as he had been every other day, despite what had happened? But what had felt so pure and right the previous day now felt tainted and wrong.

'Why are you here?'

He smiled but it was tight. 'I wanted to know if you'd come back.'

Seeing him here like this—when she carried such awful knowledge—was too much. Choking on the words, she said, 'I came to be alone, actually. I didn't want to see you.'

His face tightened and Maddie spoke quickly to stop him saying anything, 'You should leave. *Now.*'

He came up to her, put his hands on her arms. 'I don't believe that you don't want to see me. Are you going to let them intimidate you?'

His touch was too much. Maddie wrenched herself free, hysteria clawing upwards. 'Get your hands off me. I can't bear it if you touch me.'

She'd whirled away from him, bile rising uncontrollably. She was sick all over the grass where they'd lain the day before. Trembling all over, and icy cold, she stood up again to see a white-faced Nic looking at her.

'Please…just go. I don't want to see you again.'

'You could have fooled me yesterday.'

Bile rose again, and Maddie swallowed it down, saying thickly, 'That was yesterday. This is today. And I don't want anything to do with you again.'

He wasn't moving, and Maddie was becoming desperate. She couldn't bear to look at Nic. Not when he aroused such feelings in her, and not when he could possibly be—

Her stomach cramped with horror and she blurted out the first thing she could think of. 'I was bored, okay? I was bored and I wanted to see if I could seduce you. You were forbidden. It was exciting. That's *all*...'

Maddie lifted her heavy head from the steering wheel of the Jeep. The bright lights of a passing car made her wince. Her head felt thick from the onslaught of memories. She cut them off. She didn't need to remember the next bit—the way Nic had become so cold and dismissive. The way he'd told her that she'd tasted like poison.

He'd come close and said, with chilling emphasis, 'I used to think the feud was irrelevant...well, it's just become relevant again.'

Maddie had just wanted him gone, and when he'd finally left she'd sat down and cried and cried until she'd fallen into an exhausted sleep.

When she'd returned to the house hours later she'd found her bags packed and her father waiting with her mother by the car. Without even a word of explanation he'd driven them silently to the airport and left them there. He'd just said, 'You are no longer my wife and daughter.'

Maddie and her mother had boarded a flight to Buenos Aires. When they'd reached her aunt's house in the suburbs she'd turned to her mother and said, 'I want to know for sure who my father is. I think I deserve that much at least.'

Her mother, tight-lipped, had finally agreed, but one of the conditions of getting the DNA sample from her soon-to-be ex-husband had meant that she'd had to sacrifice a generous divorce settlement—something she'd never forgiven Maddie for.

A month after they'd left Mendoza and her home Maddie had gone to a doctor's office in Buenos Aires with the DNA sample and submitted to the test. Two weeks after that she'd got the results and found out that she wasn't remotely related to Nicolás de Rojas, or his father. She was, without a shadow of a doubt, a Vasquez.

The knowledge was cold comfort when she knew that she would take her mother's sordid revelations to her grave, along with the even more painful revelation that Nic had felt nothing more than lust for her. She'd believed that he'd shared an intimate part of himself with her, but it had all been an act to lull her into a false sense of security. When she thought of how beautifully he'd manipulated her, so that she'd been aching for him after only a few days, she felt shamed.

Maddie eventually felt strong enough to start up the Jeep again and continue the journey home. She'd written to her father to tell him about the DNA result, but he still hadn't forgiven her for the sins of her mother...until he'd been on his deathbed. Maddie had to honour his wishes now and do everything in her power to forget about Nic de Rojas and get on with saving the Vasquez estate.

'You left these behind last night, Cinderella.'

Maddie's back tensed at the all-too-familiar deep and drawling voice. Her skin prickled all over. Slowly she looked up from where she'd been inspecting the vines to see a tall dark shape silhouetted against the sun, holding out a pair of shoes.

For a second Maddie blinked uncomprehendingly. She'd hardly slept a wink last night, as every time she'd closed her eyes lurid images and nightmares had beckoned. So perhaps now she was hallucinating from tiredness.

When the shoes and the shape didn't disappear, Maddie scowled and stood up. Reaching for the shoes, she said stiffly, 'You really didn't need to go to the trouble.'

She was feeling dusty in worn jeans, a plain T-shirt and an old pair of riding boots. Thankfully the gaucho hat she wore shielded her from the intense blue of Nic's eyes as well as from the sun. She could see very well from under the shaded brim that he too was dressed casually, in a dark polo shirt and faded jeans which clung to powerful thigh muscles.

'I'm intrigued to know why you're wearing shoes and dresses a size too large.'

Maddie flushed and glared up at him from under the hat, not wholly surprised that he would know her shoe size. Her breath was taken away by his dynamic magnetism and the sheer force of seeing him in the daylight. The blue of his eyes was stark against the olive tones of his skin.

Without even thinking Maddie muttered, 'They're my mother's.'

He arched a brow. 'Your luggage got lost?'

Maddie started to move away from the intensity of his presence and said caustically, 'Yes—all twenty-four of my personally monogrammed designer cases.'

It was only then that she realised what she was doing— and Maddie suddenly realised the magnitude of Nic de Rojas seeing the exent of their pathetic crop. She whirled around to face him again. 'How did you get in here? You need to get off this land immediately. It's private property.'

He made a tutting sound and folded his arms, drawing Maddie's eye effortlessly to his impressive muscles. She looked back up, angry with herself for being so weak.

'*So* rude! And when I went out of my way to show

you such hospitality last night… We're making history, Maddie. The first time anyone in our families has breached the divide.' Then his mouth flattened. 'Apart from your mother and my father's sordid affair, of course, and our own…*unsatisfactory* foray following in their footsteps.'

Maddie felt sick and avoided his eyes. 'That was a long time ago.' She lifted her chin, but something in Nic's face had hardened, and Maddie shivered slightly.

'You're quite the enigma, aren't you, Madalena Vasquez? Somehow I can't really see you as the studious type.'

Maddie went cold for a second, and then recalled her conversation with his head winemaker, Eduardo. Bitterly she remarked, 'You got your employees to report back on our conversations? Or did you bug them and listen in?'

Nic was even more incredulous. 'You're *really* claiming that you did a degree in Oenology and Vitculture in between your frantic socialising?'

Incensed, Maddie hit back, 'Your own hectic social life didn't seem to prevent *you* from becoming one of the youngest Masters of Wine in the world.'

His eyes flashed. 'Been keeping tabs on me, Maddie?'

Maddie flushed and looked down again, and then a deep inner pride made her look back up. She wouldn't let him cow her. She lifted her chin defiantly. 'It's true. I graduated last year with a first-class degree. You can check the University of Bordeaux's records if you don't believe me.'

'Who funded your studies, Maddie? A generous lover? Or perhaps you seduced your way to gaining a First?'

CHAPTER FOUR

MADDIE shook with impotent rage. 'That's right, Nic. I seduced my teachers and lecturers into giving me the degree. I'm *that* good in bed, and they're *that* corrupt.'

Nic flushed. He'd never normally goad a woman like this. But no other woman pushed his buttons like this one did. The problem was that this knowledge was turning everything on its head. If she had indeed graduated with a First from Bordeaux University, it was exploding most of his firmly entrenched opinions of Maddie Vasquez.

Uncomfortable now, he asked, 'Is that where all your money went?'

For a moment it looked as if she wouldn't answer, and on some level Nic couldn't blame her. But then she did. Her voice was stiff.

'I was working on a vineyard in Bordeaux, and the owner there sponsored me through the course.'

She was avoiding his eye. Nic longed to tip her chin up so he could see her eyes but he was afraid to touch her. Afraid that after losing control as he had last night he'd lose it again and have her on her back on the ground right here under the vines.

She looked at him then, and her eyes were spitting green sparks. 'And before you ask—no, I did not sleep with the owner to get him to sponsor me. He runs a scholarship program in tandem with the University of Bordeaux to educate his employees and I qualified for it. It's as simple as that.'

'Lucky you, indeed,' Nic drawled, but desire was an insistent beat inside him, distracting him from these revelations. Maddie's breasts pushed against the fabric of her T-shirt. He could see a sliver of pale skin at her waist, where her top had come untucked from her jeans. Her hair was in a long plait, with loose tendrils trailing over her shoulders and stuck to her hot cheeks. She was more beautiful than any woman he'd seen in a long time. If ever. Something inside his chest twisted painfully.

Last night when he'd held her against him he'd known a large part of giving in to his desire was to prove a point to himself. He'd needed to see her undone. And she had been—she'd been swaying like a drunk person after that kiss. It had taken all of his self-control to appear coherent when his own head had been scrambled to pieces and all he'd wanted was to tip her over his shoulder and carry her to his bedroom like some caveman.

And, while it had made a dark satisfaction go through him to know that she did desire him, it hadn't been half as satisfying as he'd expected. Because he wanted more. Much more. He wanted the ultimate fulfilment of knowing this woman intimately. He wanted to finish what had started that week eight years ago.

Why was he looking as her so assessingly? Maddie didn't like it at all—or the way he seemed perfectly comfortable in her territory.

She crossed her arms over her chest. 'I want you to leave—*now*. You're not welcome here.'

His eyes narrowed on her as if he'd just thought of something. His voice was grim. 'I want to see those letters. The ones you said were signed by me.'

Maddie hadn't expected that. She opened and closed her

mouth, and then realised that she had no reason to deny him this. And it would get him away from the vineyard. 'Fine,' she said stiffly. 'They're at the house.'

She turned and walked to the edge of the row of vines, very aware of Nic behind her. She could see Hernan in the distance, inspecting another row of vines. He made a face, but Maddie just sent him a signal that she was okay. She saw Nic's gleaming Jeep parked alongside her battered one. Naturally he opened the passenger door of his own Jeep, and after a brief internal struggle Maddie took off her hat and got in.

Nic sent an expressive glance to her Jeep and muttered, as he turned and drove away, 'That thing is a death trap.'

Maddie smiled sweetly at his profile. 'Of which you must thoroughly approve.'

He sent her a dark glance, his jaw clenched. 'I don't wish you *dead*, Maddie, just gone. There's a big difference.' He shifted gears expertly and then asked, 'So, how long were you in France?'

Maddie hesitated before answering, loath to reveal anything of her personal life. 'I went there when I was twenty-one, after spending a year in London.'

Nic's mouth tightened. 'That would have been when I saw you in that nightclub.'

Maddie almost flinched when she thought of the disgust on his face that night, as his scathing gaze had raked her up and down before he'd turned on his heel and walked out with a bevy of beauties in his wake. She longed to tell him that she'd only been there because she'd bumped into some old friends from her English school days and they'd insisted that she go with them to celebrate the birthday of a friend.

They'd even loaned her clothes—which was why she'd been wearing a silver lamé sheath which had not left much to the imagination. She had to concede now that she didn't seem to have much luck with clothes around Nic de Rojas.

All she said, though in a slightly defeated voice, was 'Yes.' And she looked out of the window, missing the quick speculative glance Nic sent her.

Nic studied her profile and had the strong suspicion that she was holding something back—but what? Evidently she'd partied hard for a year in London and then moved to France to work on a vineyard. Maybe her money had run out and she'd been forced to that decision? It didn't quite fit, but perhaps she'd decided the bigger prize would be to come home and take over the business.

And perhaps he had underestimated her ambition. He remembered how wistful she'd been when she'd told him that she'd always wanted to work in the vineyard. He'd dismissed it eight years ago as part of her act, but had to concede now that if she had indeed completed a degree in Oenology and Viticulture then she must be more dedicated than he'd given her credit for.

Certainly she was still here and not running for the hills, as she'd pointed out. And she'd been on hands and knees in the earth just now, unafraid to get dirty. He had to admit that he was shocked at the evidence of how run-down the Vasquez estate had become. He'd seen the faint purple bruises of fatigue under Maddie's eyes which her makeup had failed to hide completely last night. What he didn't like was the protective feeling that had struck him when he noticed them.

They were in front of the villa now. It was crumbling, but still held the faded grandeur of its heyday. The reversal of fortune between the two estates was stark now, but Nic ruthlessly pushed down that insidiously lingering protective feeling and got out. There was no sense of triumph at all, which surprised him slightly. He waited for Maddie to lead him into the house.

'Maria, would you mind bringing some coffee, please?'

Maddie sent up silent thanks that Maria was there to greet them. The older woman bustled off again, for all the world as if this were a usual occurrence and she still had her normal job as housekeeper and all that it entailed. It was important for Maddie not to let Nic see how bad things were. If she could maintain an impression of some kind of normality then he might not circle them like a vulture over a dead carcass. She'd given far too much away last night—in more ways than one.

Colour flared into her cheeks at the thought of that kiss, and Maddie showed Nic into the bright yet dusty study, hoping he wouldn't notice. She went straight to her father's ancient heavy oak desk, took out the letters and handed them to him silently, curious as to his reaction. Maria came back with the coffee and Maddie served. Nic had sat down, and was opening the letters and reading them.

Maddie sat down on the other side of the desk and only realised then how shaky her legs were. So far his face was impassive, but when he got to the last letter his nostrils flared and colour tinged his cheekbones. Maddie's stomach tensed. She could sense his anger already.

Finally he looked at her. 'That's not my signature.'

She frowned. 'It's your name on the bottom.'

'I know,' he said grimly. 'But it's not my signature.'

Before she knew what he was doing he'd reached across for a pen and paper. He stood up slightly and scrawled his name with his left hand, swung it round to her. 'I have a very distinctive signature because I'm left-handed.'

Maddie looked at it. It was completely different—and very much him. An arrogant scrawl. She knew deep down somewhere she didn't want to investigate that he wasn't lying. He was too proud, and he wouldn't hesitate to tell her that he had sent the letters if he had. Why would he lie? He hated her and wanted to see the back of her.

She forced down a disturbing emotion and looked at him. 'So, who sent them, then?'

'The early ones *are* from my father and his solicitor. But once he died someone started faking my signature. I think I know who it is but I'll confirm it for myself first, if you don't mind.'

Maddie nodded.

Nic reached out to take his cup, and swallowed the dark strong coffee in one gulp. 'I've taken up enough of your time.'

He stood up, and she rose to her feet as well. To her chagrin, her first response wasn't relief that he was going.

Maddie felt seriously unsettled and more than a little vulnerable as she acknowledged that he *hadn't* sent the letters. She followed him out and said carefully, 'So this means the pressure to force me to sell up will stop?'

Nic turned at the front door and smiled down at Maddie. But any hint of friendliness was gone. It was a cold and hard smile, and reminded her succinctly of who she was dealing with. She took a step back.

'Nothing has changed really, Maddie. I still want you gone so I know we'll never have to deal with a Vasquez again. But there are other means of persuasion than letters. Much more pleasurable means.'

Maddie cursed her gullibility, and the way her belly had quivered when he'd said *pleasurable*. 'I said it once and I'll say it again. It'll be over my dead body, de Rojas. I'm not going anywhere.'

He shook his head. 'And we were doing so well—on first-name terms. Face the facts, Maddie. You need a massive injection of capital to make this vineyard lucrative again, and even then it would take years of good vintages to undo the damage that's been done. Your degree, while commendable, means nothing when you've got no wine or fertile vines to work with. You haven't even got electricity.'

Maddie smiled brilliantly, hiding her panic that she'd told him so much. 'We do have electricity, actually. I managed to pay some money into the account so we're not totally destitute. Now, if you're quite finished with your fact-finding mission, I'd appreciate it if you got lost.'

Maddie took great satisfaction in slamming the door in Nic's face, and only breathed out shakily when she heard his Jeep roaring away. She leant back against the front door and blew some hair out of her face.

Just then Maria appeared from the direction of the kitchen. 'We need more diesel for the generator. It's just died again.'

Maddie could have laughed if she wasn't afraid she'd start crying. She'd told a white lie about the electricity, determined not to let Nic de Rojas know she was so vulnerable. But the fact was that things were much, much worse than even he could ever know. She did need a massive injection of capital, and right now the only option open to her was to look for an investor.

She pushed herself off the front door. She knew exactly who she *wouldn't* be approaching for that help. She shivered slightly when she thought that his *other* methods of persuasion would have a lot to do with showing her just how much she hungered for him, and in the process gain some measure of vengeance for the way she'd rejected him eight years ago. And for the affair between her mother and his father which had wreaked such havoc.

Whatever his meaning, Maddie knew that if she allowed any kind of intimacy between them he would have the power to break her in two—and she could not allow him that satisfaction.

Nic's hands tightened on the steering wheel of his Jeep as he drove away. The knuckles showed white through his skin and he had to consciously relax. He didn't doubt that Maddie was lying about the electricity, and he didn't like the feeling that he was backing her into a corner where she felt she had to put up such a front.

Dammit. Nic slapped a hand on the steering wheel. It was only as he'd been walking out of her father's study that he'd realised the magnitude of what he was doing. He was the first in his family to come to the Vasquez estate and he had done it as unthinkingly as taking two steps forward...because he'd wanted to see her.

That need had transcended the paltry excuse to return her shoes, or to question her about her degree. As soon as he'd come within feet of her he'd wanted her so badly he'd been able to taste it on his tongue. He could remember her scent, and the way she'd tasted all those years before. Despite making sure his bed was a busy place in the meantime. Even if he was blindfolded he knew with grim certainty that he could pick Maddie out in a line-up. And he hadn't even slept with her. Yet.

Damn. He cursed her again. He'd seen the stubborness in every line of her body. He knew it well because it was deeply embedded in him too. A fierce drive to succeed and prevail.

Nic had been a sickly baby and child. His mother had suffered complications during the birth and hadn't been able to get pregnant again. His father had gone slowly mad with grief because the entire legacy of his family's estate rested on the shoulders of this one surviving weedy child.

And, even though Nic had become strong and healthy, his father had never seemed to be able to trust in Nic's ability completely. Nic's mouth twisted—not even when he'd achieved the remarkable feat of becoming a Master of Wine at the age of twenty-eight, when there was only a seven per cent success rate in graduating first time around.

Nic knew now that his childhood frailty had most likely had more to do with his mother's overprotectiveness than anything else, but from as far back as he could remember he'd known that he had to overcome the lethargy and allergies that held him back. And he had done it, slowly but surely, with single-minded determination and a deep desire to see his father look at him without that awful disappointment in his eyes.

By the time he was twelve he'd been bigger than most of the other boys in his class at school. His asthma had disappeared and his constitution had been as strong as an ox's. The doctor who'd used to come and see him had shaken his head and said, 'I've never seen anything like it in my life...'

Nic knew it was no miracle. It had been sheer determination to succeed. No one had ever known about that very dark and personal struggle to be strong and prevail. Until he'd told Maddie one day at the orchard. The words had slipped out of him before he'd even realised it, and even now he could see those huge green eyes, limpid with empathy, causing an ache in his heart.

Nic's hands tightened on the steering wheel again, hot anger coursing through him because he'd once been so gullible. Fooled by a pretty face and a lithe young body. That feeling of kinship...had he been so desperate that he'd conjured it up? The thought had always stung him. As a consequence he'd never let any woman close again;

the minute any lover tried to explore more personal avenues he cut them off.

His avowal to Maddie that he wanted to see her gone for good had far more to do with getting rid of his growing obsession with her than any need to extend the de Rojas empire. She was trouble and he knew it. He wanted her, and yet he knew he had to resist her for his own sanity. But, conversely, he knew that the only way to regain any sense of sanity was to have her on her back, beneath him, bucking against him and screaming for release.

By the time Nic got back to his own home he was seriously irritated. He decided to make the most of his mood and act on his resolve of last night to have a chat with his soon-to-be *ex*-solicitor about the letters. Anger whipped through him again at the thought of what he'd done in Nic's name.

Two days later, Maddie was weary all over. She felt as if she was fighting a losing battle as she drove the Jeep home from Villarosa with a pathetic amount of groceries to feed herself, Maria and Hernan. The petrol gauge was nearly on empty.

For a brief moment she thought how easy it would be just to give in...to call Nic up and say, *Fine—you've won.* She would get enough money from the sale of the estate to keep Maria and Hernan in comfort for the rest of their lives.

Maddie saw the outline of the estate in the distance and her throat grew tight. Despite being shut out of the workings of the vineyard her whole life by her father because she was a girl, she loved it. Ever since she was tiny she'd been fascinated by the whole process. She could remember being carried on her brother's skinny shoulders and reaching out reverently to touch the grapes, in awe of how these plump and bitter-tasting fruits could be transformed into complex and delicious wines.

Her blood sang here. She felt attuned to the earth and the seasons. Its backdrop of the magnificent snow-topped Andes was an image she'd held in her head during the long years of exile from her home. And now that she was back she wouldn't allow Nic de Rojas to run her off again just because he wanted to extend his empire.

But she faced an uphill battle. She'd just left the bank in Villarosa, where the manager had spent half an hour pointing out how impossible it was for him even to think about a business loan in the current economic climate.

The bank had been her last option. Over the past few days she'd gone to other vintners in the area, and one by one they'd all told her they weren't interested in investing. One of them had at least had the honesty to say, 'We simply can't go up against de Rojas. If he sees us investing in you it'll be like waving a red flag. He's too successful and we can't afford to get drawn into your feud…'

So even without lifting a finger Maddie was damned by her poisoned association with de Rojas. For ever.

When she saw his gleaming Jeep and his tall rangy body leaning against the bonnet with arms folded as she drove up to the house, her blood boiled over. She swung out of her Jeep and took out the shopping bags, holding them in front of her like a shield.

He made a movement to help and Maddie grabbed them tighter to her. 'I thought I told you you weren't welcome here.'

He had the gall to smile. 'Are you always so prickly in the evening? I must remember that for future reference. Perhaps you're a morning person.'

Maddie sensed him following her inside. She put down the bags on the nearest table and whirled around, hands on hips. Adrenalin was washing away her recent weariness. 'De Rojas, you're not welcome here. In fact I've heard your name enough in the past few days to last me a lifetime. So please, just *go.*'

Maddie would have physically pushed him, but was too afraid to touch him. Too afraid of her reaction when she could already feel it building up inside her. The insatiable need to drink him in, taste him. He was smartly dressed today, in chinos and a white shirt. Every inch the relaxed, successful vintner. She'd dressed smartly too, for the bank. She'd even splashed out with her fast-dwindling money to buy something that would fit, conscious of Nic's recent criticism.

As if reading her thoughts, he let that blue gaze drop and took in the pencil skirt, court shoes and tailored blouse. And then lazily he returned it all the way to where her hair was in a chignon.

'I like the office look—very demure.'

Maddie's hands became fists. She didn't feel demure. She felt hot. All over.

Before she could say anything else he said, 'Apparently you've been looking for an investor. I can tell by your mood you're not having much luck.'

Maddie choked back a curse and said, as calmly as she could, 'Unsurprisingly the local wine community don't want to upset their vastly more successful neighbour. How does it feel to know you're the don of the area, Nic? Does it make you feel powerful to know that people are too scared to invest because they might incur your wrath? That's hardly going to encourage healthy competition, now, is it? It's very easy to be successful in a vacuum.'

He flushed at that. 'Your father would be able to tell you all about that if he were still alive.' He elaborated. 'Your family was the first to quash any local competition, preferring to keep things simple and just between ourselves. If you'd done your research you'd know that more vintners have sprung up since the demise of your estate than ever before—and I've actually invested in some of them.'

Now Maddie flushed. Once again he was doing—or saying—the opposite of what she'd expected. She didn't like the way he was constantly putting her on the back foot.

His continued coolly. 'I came to tell you that my father's solicitor was responsible for the letters. He was a close friend of my father for many years and, unbeknownst to me, made a promise to him on his deathbed that he would continue to wage a campaign to get your father to sell. I suspect he also had a long-standing crush on my mother, and when she committed suicide he vowed some kind of vengeance on your father for having told her of the affair.'

Maddie sat down on a chair behind her. A sense of futility washed over her. Would the tangled mess that lay between them ever stop sending out poisonous tendrils into the future?

'Thank you for letting me know.' She looked up at Nic and saw something suspiciously like concern on his face, but it was quickly gone so she must have imagined it.

'I've also taken the liberty of paying your electricity bill for the forseeable future.'

Now Maddie sprang up, incensed. 'What did you do that for? I told you we were fine.'

Casually Nic reached out to a nearby switch and flicked it. Nothing happened, and Maddie went puce.

Just as casually he said, 'I knew you were lying. I'm doing it because it's a serious health and safety issue. I can't very well stand by and let an accident happen when I could have helped prevent it. Full power will be restored any time now.'

Feeling impotent with anger, Maddie quivered all over.

She couldn't say anything because when Hernan had gone out to get the generator going again he'd almost tripped and done himself a serious injury in the dark. Nic had her in a bind. How could she jeopardise the safety of her employees so wantonly by refusing this? And yet how could she accept?

'Like I said, Maddie, I just want you gone. I don't want you dead.' He arched a brow. 'Is it so hard to say, *Thank you, Nic*?'

Maddie's voice was constricted with the feeling of impotence, but finally she got out, 'What do you want from me?'

Nic came close to where Maddie stood and she fought not to let him see how she trembled when he got close. His eyes were all too assessing, and she could almost hear his brain whirring.

His jaw clenched, and then he said in a hard, flat voice, 'Dinner with me tonight. At my house.'

Maddie swallowed and fought the urge to run. He wasn't finished with pointing out how far she had to go to catch up. She longed to be able to say no, to refuse. But he had her in a corner, with no room to manoeuvre. The safety of her loyal staff was too important.

Ungraciously, she finally gritted out, 'Fine.'

After an infinitesimal moment when the very air around them seemed to vibrate with awareness and tension, he turned and walked out, leaving Maddie feeling as limp as a dishrag. She sank back onto the chair, her mind churning painfully.

He'd just pulled the rug from under her feet by doing an amazingly generous thing—and now, by asking her for dinner, he was blurring the lines, reinforcing the fact that he threatened her on many more levels than just the professional one.

Perhaps this was Nic's plan? To chip away at all the places where he would show up her weaknesses until he had her exactly where he wanted her. Maddie shivered when an image popped into her head of her lying back on a huge bed, with Nic looming over her like a marauding pirate. She would have to tell him tonight in no uncertain terms that she would repulse any further gesture, and set up a payment plan to pay him back for the electricity.

As if proving a point, suddenly the dark hallway was flooded with light. Maddie looked up and blinked, and then Maria rushed out from the kitchen, her eyes suspiciously bright. She came and hugged Maddie and said emotionally, 'Oh, *niña*, now I know everything will be all right...'

Maddie didn't have the heart to tell her that the sword of Damocles swung over them as much as it ever had.

'Good evening, Señorita Vasquez. Please come in.'

Maddie swallowed her nerves and stepped onto the flag-stoned floor of Nic's palatial hallway. Soft lights sent out a golden glow, reminding Maddie of how seductive it had been here the first time around. She tried to steel herself against it but it was hard.

She followed Geraldo through the now-empty court-yard, with its burbling fountain and flowers blooming out of pots everywhere, and into the main drawing room. He led her to a drinks cabinet and said solicitously, 'Señor de Rojas will join you shortly. He's been held up with a phone call. Please, can I offer you a drink?'

Maddie smiled tightly. 'Sparkling water would be fine.' She fully intended to keep her wits about her tonight.

Geraldo gave her the drink, and then excused himself after telling her to make herself comfortable. Maddie caught a glimpse of her reflection in a framed picture and smoothed down her skirt. It was the same one she'd been

wearing earlier, but she'd teamed it with a dark grey silk
top that thankfully was her own, and fitted. It was loose,
with a wide neck, and she adjusted it now so that it wasn't
falling down over one shoulder. She'd dithered over her
hair and finally tied it up, not wanting Nic to think for a
second that she was trying to seduce him.

She wandered over to a wall that was full of framed
photos. She became more and more intrigued as she inspected what was obviously a history of the de Rojas family.

'Please forgive me for keeping you.'

Maddie's grip tightened on her glass before she turned
around. Nic was standing in the doorway dressed in black
pants and a pale blue shirt, open at the neck. His thick dark
blond hair shone in the dim light, and those blue eyes took
her breath away even now.

Maddie suddenly felt inexplicably shy, and it unnerved
her. She'd had to develop a thick skin to survive these past
few years and she didn't like this new vulnerability that
Nic de Rojas seemed to bring out in her with such effortless ease. 'It's fine. I wasn't waiting long.'

He came towards her then, and stopped near the photos.
He gestured with his head and Maddie had to tear her eyes
off him. 'My family—all the way back to the nineteenth
century, before they left Spain to come here.'

Maddie found herself smiling slightly. 'We have a wall
like this too. I always wonder why my ancestors looked so
fierce in the pictures.'

'Times were hard then…they had to fight to survive.'

Maddie snuck a glance at Nic. Something about the
way he'd said that caught at her insides. At that moment
she had a vivid memory of him revealing to her once how
sickly he'd been as a child, and how hard he'd struggled

to overcome that physical frailty. He was so virile now, so *vital*, that it was almost impossible to believe.

Then he was stepping back and the moment was gone. He indicated with a hand for her to precede him. 'Let me show you into the dining room.'

Maddie moved forward jerkily. She cursed Nic for making her remember things and for putting on this chivalrous act. It was so much easier to deal with him when the lines of battle were clearly drawn.

Nic solicitously pulled out her chair for her, and waited till she'd sat down before taking his own seat opposite. It was a small, intimate table, with candles flickering and lending a far too seductive air for Maddie's liking.

'An aperitif to whet the palate?'

Maddie looked up and fought the urge to adjust her top and let some air get to her skin. She was suddenly boiling. He was weaving some sort of sensual spell over her. And she hated to admit it but she was curious to know about the wines Nic would choose. She was having dinner with a Master of Wine, after all. There were only a few hundred in the world—a very select group.

'Just a small amount. I'm driving.'

He inclined his head and dutifully poured a taster into her glass from a bottle whose label was obscured. It was a white wine. Maddie lifted it and let the clear liquid swirl for a moment before dipping her head and breathing deep. As soon as the bouquet registered she paled dramatically. Nic watched her carefully.

Maddie didn't taste the wine and put the glass down with a trembling hand. She looked at him, willing down an incredible surge of emotion. 'Is this some kind of a joke?'

CHAPTER FIVE

Nic was innocence personified. 'Why would it be a joke?'

Maddie was vibrating with tension now. 'You serve me a Vasquez wine—why? Are you expecting me not to recognise it? Is this a test?'

Maddie put down her napkin and stood up, a little bewildered at how emotional she was feeling, afraid that it was coming partly from that memory just moments ago.

Nic's hand snaked out and caught her wrist. 'Sit down. Please.' When she just looked at him and tried to pull her wrist out of his grip he smiled ruefully. 'I'll admit that I was curious as to whether or not you would know the wine.'

Maddie pulled her wrist free finally but didn't sit down. She looked down at Nic with her most haughty expression. 'Of course I recognise the wine. I grew up watching those very grapes ripen every year.'

Passion made her voice low and fervent. Maddie sat down abruptly—conflicted about how she was feeling. So Nic had served her a Vasquez wine? What was the big deal?

As if reading her mind, he frowned at her now. 'I didn't mean to anger you.'

'No,' snapped Maddie. 'You were just testing me, to

see if I really know my stuff or if I slept my way to getting my degree, is that it?'

Now Nic flushed dark red. 'I don't believe you manipulated your results.'

To Maddie's chagrin, hot tears burnt the back of her eyes and she blinked furiously, only vaguely satisfied when she saw Nic's horrorstruck face. She knew the emotion was coming from a complex mix of bittersweet grief for her father and the overwhelming pressure she was under—not to mention the passion Nic was able to evoke in her so effortlessly.

Exerting a valiant effort to bring herself under control, Maddie picked up the glass again and took a sip. She closed her eyes for a moment, letting the liquid rest in her mouth before slipping down her throat like smooth silk. She opened her eyes again and narrowed a fiery green gaze on Nic. 'If I'm not mistaken this is from the ninety-nine vintage. It won us the Prix de Vin for the best white in New World Wines that year.'

Nic inclined his head, his eyes focused on hers with unnerving intensity. 'You're right. My father bought a case of every vintage of Vasquez wines to analyse them. Exactly as your father did with our wines, I'm sure.'

Maddie nodded, and could feel some equilibrium returning. She looked away for a moment, and then back. 'I'm sorry…it just caught me unawares. That particular wine was always a favourite of mine.' Her voice was husky. 'It reminds me of home. *Here*.' Maddie's fingers pleated the napkin on the table. 'It always made me so homesick whenever I smelt it abroad. People used to order it in the restaurant where I worked, and I would pretend not to know that I should open it at the table just so I could open it first and smell it without anyone watching.'

She looked at Nic, and down again quickly when she saw that gaze, no less intense.

'It used to amaze me to think of this bottle coming all the way from our estate. It made me wonder about the year—had the seasons been kind to the grape? I could always tell just from the smell if it had been good or bad. I can't believe I never got fired for making such a *faux pas*, but the customers always seemed to forgive me.'

Nic watched as candlelight played over Maddie's pale skin, casting her features into mysterious shadows. Her cheekbones stood out. Her lips looked ripe and full. The grey silk of her top lay against her collarbone like the most decadent covering, and the swell of her breasts pushed enticingly against the slippery fabric. He could well imagine the customers forgiving her anything.

He'd never seen anything so sensuous as the way she was cradling her glass. He was transfixed by her natural beauty and her innate earthy sexiness, and all of a sudden he felt as if he was hurtling back in time and out of his depth. The terrain he'd been so sure of was shifting. She was articulating exactly how he felt about the wines he cultivated—each year the vintage *did have* a certain personality, a complexity.

Maddie was about to take another sip when she looked up to see Nic's mesmerised expression. She halted the glass before it got to her mouth. 'What is it?'

He shook his head and colour flared along his cheekbones, making Maddie feel off balance.

'Nothing. I shouldn't have tested you like that.' His mouth quirked in a wry smile. 'You seem to bring out the worst in me.'

Maddie had to fight down a burgeoning sense of lightness. 'I'll take that as a compliment.'

He lifted his glass to hers. *'Salud,'* he said, and then took a deep sip.

The sheer masculinity of his movements while doing something that was inherently delicate made Maddie's toes curl. He was such a *man*.

Much to her relief, their starter was served and eaten largely in silence, with Maddie berating herself for having come over all hysterical just because Nic had fancied giving her some sort of test. And for waxing lyrical about feeling homseick. As if Nic was at all interested in what she thought.

When the main course was served she focused on the meat with single-minded determination, savouring every succulent morsel.

Much to her surprise, they managed to conduct a civil conversation about neutral topics, and when Nic handed her a glass of red Maddie took it without a conscious awareness of how comfortable she'd become.

He said, 'Try this. It's a new blend I'm working on, and this is the first run of wine. I'm not marketing it yet.'

Maddie put down her fork. 'Are you sure you want to be sharing secrets with the enemy?'

Nic's mouth quirked. 'After seeing your vineyard I know I'm in no imminent danger.'

Maddie flushed at being reminded of the painful reality. She raised the glass to her mouth and forced herself to hold Nic's gaze, refusing to be the first to look away. But in the end she had to, because as she savoured the wine she closed her eyes instinctively to try and figure out the various components.

She opened them again and saw Nic watching her. It set a slow fire burning deep inside. Slowly she said, 'Well, it's a classic Malbec…but not like anything I've tasted before—it's got a strain of something else.'

Nic inclined his head. 'Very impressive.'

Maddie had to admit grudgingly, 'I like it. It's not as straightforward as the usual Malbecs—it's got more complexity…a dark side… Pinot?'

Nic smiled. 'I can see how you got your First.'

Maddie felt a ridiculous rush of pleasure go through her just as the attentive staff member came in and took their plates away.

Nic stood up and indicated for Maddie to precede him out of the open French doors to the patio outside. Her belly clenched for a moment—this was where he'd kissed her the other night. Then she saw that a smaller table for two had been set there, with more candles flickering in the breeze.

She almost wanted to back away and insist on leaving. But she was loath to give Nic the satisfaction of knowing that he was getting to her. She moved forward and sat down in the chair that Nic pulled out. Presently the waiter came back and served them both small dishes that held exquisite-looking lemon tart desserts. Nic opened a bottle of dessert wine and poured some for Maddie. Her mouth was already watering at the thought of the tart lemon soothed by the sweet wine.

Feeling churlish at how easily he was entrancing her, she said, 'You really don't have to do this, you know. It's not working.'

Nic smiled urbanely. 'What's not working? You've proved your point, Maddie. You're happier to live in squalor than to come running to me for home comforts. Clearly I underestimated your ability to put up with discomfort.'

Maddie's appetite disappeared and she said tightly, 'You underestimate a lot more than that, Nic. You don't know one thing about what happened when I left here. You seem to have this halcyon fantasy that I went to Europe and spent my time skiing and partying.'

Carefully he said, 'Why don't you tell me what you did?'

Maddie wanted to refuse, to tell him it was none of his business, but she had a desire to make him understand that she was made of sterner stuff, that she wouldn't just turn around and give up. And also a dangerous desire to see him regard her with something besides mockery or disbelief in his eyes...

'When my mother and I left here we left with nothing. My father threw us out and turned his back on us completely.' Her mouth tightened. 'We spent three years in Buenos Aires living with my aunt, who eventually threw us out. In the meantime Mother had been divorced and found herself a rich suitor. She gave me a one-way ticket to London to get me out of her hair.'

Maddie didn't want to elaborate and tell him that her mother had blamed Maddie for being left with nothing in the divorce. Her gaze remained resolutely forward, out into the darkness that encompassed his vast estate.

'I got to London and found work in a restaurant by night, and as a hotel chambermaid by day. The night you saw me in that club was pure chance. I'd never been in it before, or since then.' Maddie blushed when she thought of the picture she'd presented in the revealing dress. She rushed on. 'When I'd made enough money I moved to France and looked for work picking grapes for the summer. I ended up at the vineyard in Bordeaux, where Pierre Vacheron took me in.'

Maddie sent Nic a quick defensive look. 'He found out where I came from, that I had some knowledge of wine, and decided to give me one of the scholarships. I'd most likely still be there if my father hadn't written and asked me to come home. Pierre offered me a full-time job.'

Nic's face was expressionless. 'That magazine article painted a very different picture.'

Considering that since she had divulged so much already she might as well tell him the whole truth, Maddie laid out the bones of the painful reality of her relationship with her flighty and self-absorbed mother. The humiliation of the whole episode was vivid again.

When she'd finished she put down her dessert wine glass and stood up. The full enormity of her naivety was hitting her—to allow herself to think for a second that Nic de Rojas was as urbane and charming as he appeared this evening. With any other woman, yes. With her, *no*. He was just trying to unbalance her, and she was letting him.

'I want you to realise that I won't be easily dissuaded, or seduced by the trappings of wealth.'

Driven by the wave of ambiguous anger he was feeling, Nic said, 'Don't underestimate *my* determination to succeed in this matter, Maddie. I've proved how determined I can be over and over again.'

Maddie fought not to let Nic see how he was affecting her. 'So we're back where we started?'

Nic's gaze grew hot and moved to her mouth.

Maddie moved back, putting up a hand as if to ward him off. *'No...'*

He reached for her easily and pulled her into him. *'Yes. This is where we started—and where we've yet to finish.'*

And he bent his head and took her mouth in a kiss so incendiary and devastating that Maddie had no defence. Especially not after laying herself bare like that. Her hands clung onto his powerful biceps, her whole body arched into his—he was bending her back further and further with the sheer force of his kiss.

Lips ground into teeth which clashed and nipped at soft skin. Maddie tasted blood at one point and didn't know if it was hers or his. Their tongues duelled madly, in a hot swirl. She only wanted *this*. She would have given every-thing up in that moment to prolong it…

And then abruptly Nic put her away from him with both hands. 'Get out of here, Maddie.'

Maddie looked up, shocked, hurt and bewildered. Her chest was aching with the effort to draw breath. She saw the blood on his lip. She'd bitten him.

A need to claw back some control forced her to say shakily, 'With pleasure. I won't whore myself to you for my vineyard, Nic—the sooner you realise that the better.'

Nic stood in a haze of sexually frustrated agony for long moments. On one level he couldn't fathom how he'd just let Maddie go, but then he remembered the way she'd kissed him back, biting his lip in her ardour. And *that*—hot on the heels of her further revelations about her life these past few years—had made him feel unaccountably vulnerable.

He'd assumed Maddie and her mother had been given plenty of money. He'd had no idea that her father had turfed them out with no support, or that her mother had all but turned her back on her too. That she'd had to take two me-nial jobs just to survive.

Nic went over to the wooden perimeter on the decking which wrapped around this side of the house. His hands curled around it tightly and he took a deep breath, still struggling for control. Kissing Maddie just now had re-minded him too vividly of losing himself to her seductive wiles before.

She'd spent a week reeling him in, making him trust her with pathetic ease. Only to reveal in the end how she'd really felt about seducing him. It had made her physically ill. He'd watched the way she'd retched and coughed after he'd touched her. Nic's stomach clenched hard. She must have been very bored indeed to have pushed the limits of what she could endure for the sake of doing something exciting and illicit.

Something very private and vulnerable in him had been destroyed that day. He'd become hardened. Impenetrable. No woman since then had managed to crack his protective veneer, or challenge his cynicism. But the way Maddie had kissed him just now, and the way she'd kissed him the other night—as artlessly and yet as devastatingly as he remembered—was a threat for which he hadn't been prepared.

He'd thought he could handle kissing her, but tasting her again was dangerous—he felt himself slipping and sliding away from everything that held him rooted to reality and sanity.

Nic had developed a mild aversion to being touched after his mother's nervous and overprotective constant fussing, which had been in stark contrast to his father's habitual rages, when he'd used his fists freely. But when Maddie touched him, he couldn't get enough. It galled him now that he found every woman's touch invariably cloying or too possessive, but not *hers*. It made him very nervous to acknowledge that...which was why he'd pushed her back.

Something inside Nic hardened. He *would* have her—but on his terms. He would force her to be honest with him and herself. There would be no drama, regrets or recriminations this time. Only satisfaction and closure.

A couple of days later Maddie was sitting in her father's study and looking at another invitation. It was addressed to her father, and it was for the Annual South American Vintners' Gala Ball in two days' time. It was in a different city each year, and this year, as luck would have it, it was to be in Buenos Aires. So near—but so far.

Maddie sighed. Something like this was just what she

needed—a chance to meet people who only remembered Vasquez as a successful estate. It was the perfect place to look for investors. But she had no hope of flying to Buenos Aires where the ball was being held. She had no money for the flight, and anyway there was a national airline strike.

Just then the phone rang, and Maddie picked it up. She flushed all over when she heard an all-too-familiar deep voice on the other end. Then she felt cold when she remembered the way he'd aborted their kiss and pushed her from him the other night. She hated Nic de Rojas for exposing her weakness and desire like that. For rejecting her.

'Yes?' Her voice was as cold as she felt.

'Did you get your invitation?'

Maddie couldn't help her stubborn streak from rising up. 'What invitation?'

'You're such a terrible liar, Vasquez. I know you're probably looking at it right now and figuring out how to get there so you can sucker some poor investor into taking on your dead-end estate.'

Maddie made a face at the phone, and then said airily, 'Oh, you mean *that* invitation? Yes, I have it…why?'

'Are you going?'

Something in his voice made Maddie's hackles rise. 'Of course I'm going. Why wouldn't I?'

'No need to sound so defensive, Maddie—I was asking because I'm taking a private jet and was going to offer you a lift.'

Maddie's jaw dropped, but she quickly recovered. After the other night she wouldn't accept anything from this man. 'No, thank you.' She injected saccharine-sweetness into her voice. 'I've got alternative arrangements made. I'll see you there.'

She barely heard him mutter something about *'stub-*

born woman' before she cut him off. Maddie's heart was thumping. She'd have to go now. She couldn't afford to show Nicolás any weakness.

By the time Maddie arrived in Buenos Aires, sticky and hot, almost two days later, she ached all over. She'd taken a ridiculously long bus journey from Mendoza, and every bump in the road seemed to be engraved on her nerves.

Maddie hauled her bag behind her and joined the masses of people all making their way to various destinations. Hers was the cheapest hotel she'd been able to find close to the Grand Palace Buenos Aires hotel, where the gala was due to take place that evening.

When she finally found her room and looked at herself in the mirror, she realised that she had a mountain of work to do to make herself look every inch the successful vintner she wanted to portray herself as being.

Nic didn't like the sense of anticipation firing up his blood. This fizzing expectancy. He was used to being in control at all times, and right now he felt off-kilter. He realised that it was because he didn't know where *she* was. He'd almost gone to her home and forced her to come with him on his plane, but a sensation of lingering rawness after the other night had stopped him.

And how the hell had she even got here? He knew it couldn't have been by air because of the strike, which was why he'd ordered the private jet.

Just then he spotted a familiar face in the crowd and he smiled warmly, welcoming the distraction.

Maddie's stomach was in knots. She took a deep breath and stepped into the thronged ballroom. She'd managed to ferret out another of her mother's dresses, and mercifully this one fitted. It was green and shimmery, it fell to the floor, and it was relatively demure, with long sleeves and a high neck. But when she walked one pale leg was exposed, thanks to a thigh-high slit. Maddie had cursed when she'd discovered it; the sooner she could afford to supplement her own wardrobe again, the better.

She'd used her practically maxed-out credit card to buy some cheap shoes and get her hair done in a salon, and now it lay in lustrous-looking waves over one shoulder. She was glad she'd spent the money when she saw how immaculate everyone else looked. She just hoped they wouldn't notice that her emerald earrings had come from a costume-jewellery shop.

And then she saw Nic across the room. Her hands tightened reflexively on the clutch bag she carried in front of her like a shield. She hated the awful feeling of excitement that danced along her veins at seeing him again. He wasn't looking at her, though; he was looking down at the woman in front of him and smiling in a way that made an awful yearning go through Maddie.

And then, to her horror, as if they were connected by some telepathic thread of awareness, he looked up and straight at her. His smile faded. The woman he'd been talking to looked over as well, and Maddie felt her belly hollow out when she recognised the same stunning blonde from the first night she'd seen him again in Mendoza.

Someone came by with a tray full of champagne and Maddie grabbed a glass inelegantly because she could see Nic taking his companion by the hand and leading her towards Maddie. It was as if she was rooted to the spot. She couldn't move, and with everything in her head and heart she cursed him—because he was going to introduce her to his mistress and make her feel like dirt.

He came closer and closer, a curiously intent look on

his face and in his eyes. Maddie was stuck like a deer in the headlights. She'd never felt so alone or exposed. She should never have come…she should have known he'd take any opportunity to humiliate her…

'Maddie, you made it…I'll resist the temptation to ask how you did it.'

Maddie's voice wouldn't work for a long moment. She could feel a curious glance from the stunning blonde, and hot, angry colour seeped into her cheeks. She'd never been in this situation before—having kissed another woman's man. And she was disappointed. Somehow she hadn't expected this kind of behaviour from him.

'…like you to meet someone.'

Like watching a car crash in slow motion, Maddie managed to look at the other woman and smile, but it felt numb. She realised then that the woman was much younger than Maddie had realised—about twenty at the most. Now she felt sick—and also, more worryingly, as if she wanted to gouge her eyes out.

'This is my cousin Estella. You would have met her at the wine-tasting evening, but she had to be in BA for a modelling assignment. She's in high demand. Not to mention that she breaks out in hives after a couple of days in the country.'

The girl looked adoringly at Nic and hit him playfully on his shoulder. 'Hardly hives, Nic. You do like to exaggerate, don't you?'

Maddie was aware that the girl was exquisite, beautiful, and had a sense of humour. And then it sank in properly. *My cousin.*

Maddie forced her throat to work, and tried to ignore the relief flooding her. 'It's nice to meet you, Estella,' she said scratchily.

'You too, Maddie.' She turned her sunny smile back to Nic and said, 'I'd better go and find my date or he'll be sending out a search party.'

'I need to meet this man who is going to pretend that he *won't* be sharing your hotel room tonight.'

Maddie looked at Nic and saw an endearingly stern look on his face. His cousin blushed, but rolled her eyes. 'Yes, Nic, but please don't give him the third degree. He's a nice guy, really.'

She jumped up and pressed a kiss to Nic's cheek, then was gone with a flash of blonde hair and sinuous tanned limbs.

Maddie was mesmerised by Nic's fond gaze after his cousin, so she wasn't prepared when he turned to look at her and his whole visage became noticeably cooler.

'I booked her a room for the night because I don't like her going back out to the suburbs too late. At least this way I know she's safe. Her father was my mother's brother. He died when she was small, so I've become a sort of…father figure for her.'

Maddie's belly clenched at hearing how protective Nic was of his cousin. A bit redundantly she said, 'She seems nice.'

Someone bumped into Maddie at that moment, and she winced. She could feel that she had a bruise on one hip.

'What is it?'

The sudden urgency in Nic's voice made her look up. 'Nothing. I'm just a bit sore after—' She stopped herself there. But it wasn't long before a dawning realistion came into Nic's eyes.

'You took the bus, didn't you?' He shook his head. 'Of all the stubborn—' He stopped and cursed. 'How long was it? Fourteen hours?'

Maddie cursed him, and then admitted painfully, 'Sixteen, actually. We got a flat tyre.'

He shook his head at her and then said, 'I suppose you're here to look for an investor?'

Maddie flushed. 'What other choice do I have? It's find an investor or lose everything to you.'

'You'd be a very wealthy woman.'

Something painful twisted in Maddie's chest at hearing him reiterate that he wanted her gone at all costs. It made her feel very nervous and she lashed out. 'Why can't you get it through that thick skull of yours that it's not about the money? I love my estate and I want to restore it to its full potential.'

Nic's jaw clenched. He opened his mouth, but just then the gong sounded for the gala dinner. Maddie took the opportunity to flee in the ensuing crush, grateful that she didn't feel a strong hand on her arm. She had every intention of talking to as many people as possible and staying away from one person in particular.

All during dinner Nic was aware of Maddie across the other side of the table. She was seated beside Alex Morales, one of the most successful vintners in the US—a man Nic had never particularly liked or trusted without ever having analysed why. It was a gut reaction, and it was becoming stronger by the second.

He couldn't concentrate on the conversations either side of him and he wanted to snarl at the pouting redhead across the table who seemed determined to give him a bird's-eye view of her surgically enhanced cleavage.

All Nic could imagine was Maddie's huge green eyes imploring Morales to invest in her poor vineyard, and he had to physically restrain himself from walking over, plucking her from the chair and carrying her far away.

Maddie looked at her attentive and charming dinner companion incredulously. 'You'd really like to discuss this further?'

The man smiled and oozed charm. 'Of course, my dear.'

He was a little cheesy for Maddie's liking, but she wasn't about to dismiss a potential investor because of a possibly erroneous gut feeling.

She couldn't believe she'd had the good fortune to be seated next to Alex Morales, and that he was interested in learning more about the Vasquez estate. This could be the solution to all her problems. If she could persuade Morales to invest in her she'd be free of Nic's influence.

Maddie had been uncomfortably aware of Nic's gaze on her all throughout the dinner but she'd done her best to ignore him. However, with this exciting development, she couldn't help glancing over in his direction. She hated that she met that blue gaze so effortlessly, as if drawn by a magnet. He was looking impossibly grim. She smiled and his eyes flashed. Maddie knew it was childish, but she was buoyed up to think that her problems could soon be over.

People were already getting up and moving out to the ballroom, which had been cleared for dancing with tables set around the dance floor. Morales took Maddie's hand to guide her from her seat. His touch lingered a little too long for Maddie's liking, but she quashed the flutter of doubt, telling herself she had to explore this opportunity.

He bowed slightly in a disarmingly old-fashioned gesture. 'If you'd excuse me? I have an important call I have to make, but I will be available in about thirty minutes if you'd like to continue our discussion?'

Maddie's eagerness was dismayingly obvious. 'I really appreciate this, Mr Morales.'

'Please…' He smiled, showing glaringly white teeth. 'Call me Alex. Why don't you meet me at my room—say in thirty-five minutes?'

He told her his room number and was turning away when sudden panic gripped Maddie. Their conversation had just taken a turn she really hadn't expected.

She reached for Morales's arm and he turned back, one eyebrow raised. 'Yes?'

Immediately Maddie felt gauche. 'I'm sorry, but… wouldn't it be easier to meet in one of the bars?'

Morales smiled, and it was faintly patronising. 'I have to make the call in my room, so it really would be easier if you came to me. All of the bars will be full and very loud. Of course, if this discussion isn't that important to you…'

His voice trailed off and Maddie picked up his meaning instantly, seeing her chance floating away.

'No, no,' she said hurriedly, telling herself that he sounded reasonable. 'Your room will be fine. Absolutely fine.'

He inclined his head and then walked away. Only to be replaced almost immediately by someone taller and far more disturbing. Maddie tried to walk around Nic but he blocked her.

She glared up at him. 'Yes?'

Nic's jaw was tense and his eyes were flashing. 'I don't trust that man.'

CHAPTER SIX

'Oh, please,' Maddie sneered. 'You just can't bear the thought that someone else might see the potential in my estate and want to invest in me.'

Nic's eyes flashed. 'I think he wants to invest, all right, but it's not necessarily in your estate. Where are you meeting him?'

Maddie went puce. She refused to answer and went to walk around Nic again, but he caught her arm in a big hand. Maddie gritted her teeth against the instant chemical reaction in her body.

He was incredulous. 'Don't tell me you're going to meet him in his room? Is that what that little conference was about?' Maddie went even more red and Nic exploded, 'For crying out loud, Maddie, you're too inexperienced to deal with someone like Morales. He'll chew you up and spit you out!'

Maddie reacted viscerally. Little did Nic know how inexperienced she really was—physically *and* in situations like these. But every ounce of pride demanded that she project an image of confidence. She looked up at Nic and tossed her hair back. She smiled up at him and hoped it had the same slightly patronising edge that Morales had just used on her.

'Do you really think I haven't met men like Morales before now? I know his type, Nic. He just needs to be played a certain way.'

Nic's face flushed and he dropped her arm suddenly, as if it was poisonous. Immediately Maddie felt bereft.

He sounded utterly disgusted. 'Forgive me for thinking for a second that you might be going into a situation you're not equipped to handle. If he's the kind of investor you want, and you're willing to do what it takes, then clearly I've underestimated you *and* your ambition.'

Nic took a step back from her and walked away, leaving Maddie feeling vulnerable and insecure. What exactly had Nic meant by not trusting Morales? She recalled his smooth smile and shuddered a little. Surely even if he came on to her she could just walk away?

Maddie didn't like the way Nic had made her feel slightly ashamed just now, or the feeling, for a brief moment, that he might be concerned for her safety. Maddie wasn't used to anyone else stepping in to fight her battles for her. Her brother had been the only one who'd ever stood up for her, and he'd died a long time ago.

Realising that she was standing and brooding in an empty dining room, Maddie knew she had to move. She glanced at her watch and cursed silently. It was already nearly time to meet Morales. Pushing down the sudden trepidation she felt, Maddie hurried to the lifts.

Nic was standing in one of the hotel bars with some acquaintances when he saw a flash of green out of the corner of his eye and looked to see Maddie disappear into a lift. His stomach clenched so hard for a second that his vision blurred slightly. He couldn't believe that she was actually going through with it. He'd underestimated her, all right. Underestimated her greed and her ambition to succeed no matter what it took.

Nic battled for a long moment with the seething emotions in his gut and then one overriding feeling rose up as he recalled Maddie's defiance just now, and her flushed face. Surely she wasn't doing this to get at *him*?

Nic put down his glass and excused himself. In hindsight, and when she wasn't standing in front of him and scrambling his brain cells with her proximity, her bravado seemed far too brittle.

He quickly got Morales's room number and strode to the lifts, punching the button. And then something stopped him—maybe he had completely misread the way she'd kissed him with such artless fervour? Maybe she changed her method for each man and gave them what she thought they wanted? Maybe she was playing Nic—kissing him the way she suspected would affect him most, reminding him of those gauche responses in the orchard that day?

The lift doors opened and Nic was torn. He couldn't move. Was he really going to go after Maddie and risk exposing himself all over again? He could already see her mocking face when she opened Morales's door. What the hell was he going to say when he *did* get up to the room?

'Nic! There you are. I've been looking for you everywhere. You have to come and meet Louis…he's waiting for you.'

Nic looked down at his cousin, who had just hooked her arm into his, and felt slightly dazed. Suddenly everything came back into perspective and he cursed this bout of uncharacteristic indecision. He felt nothing for Maddie except mistrust and antipathy—along with an annoying level of desire. Estella was someone he loved unconditionally. Who was more important to him?

He smiled down at her and said, 'Lead the way.' And as Estella dragged him in her wake Nic pushed aside all thoughts of the sable-haired witch, telling himself that Maddie was certainly able to handle herself.

He ignored the slightly ominous sound of the lift doors closing again behind him.

Maddie was stuck in a waking nightmare. She had locked herself inside the bathroom in Morales's suite and was shaking all over. She had no idea how much time had passed. But mercifully he'd stopped thumping on the bathroom door and calling her names a few minutes ago.

Carefully she stood up and went over to the sink. She looked at herself in the mirror. Her eyes widened in shock—her hair was a mess, her dress was torn at the neck and blood was oozing from a cut lip. She was still in shock. She couldn't really believe what had happened.

Her first indication that something was wrong should have been the fact that he was obviously more inebriated than he had been downstairs. But at first Morales had been charming. And interested. He'd disarmed her and made her feel as if she was overreacting. She'd tried to ignore the fact that his words were slurring slightly and that he was a little unsteady on his feet.

She'd launched into her spiel about the estate. But then he'd come over to sit beside her and put his hand high on her thigh. Immediately panicked, Maddie had jerked back, dislodging his hand. Everything had changed in an instant. He'd turned into a monster.

In the struggle that had ensued he'd ripped her dress and slapped her across the face. Maddie had somehow managed to push him off her and made for the only route of escape or safety she could see. She had locked herself in the bathroom. Morales had shouted obscenities, and she'd been terrified he'd break the door down. But now, after long minutes, everything was mercifully quiet.

Maddie crept over to the door and listened. Her heart leapt when she heard the unmistakable sound of snoring. With her pulse beating fast, she turned the lock silently and opened the door, half terrified it would smash open in her face.

She saw Morales sprawled on the couch, fast asleep with his mouth open wide. Nearly crying with relief, Maddie crept out—all the way to the main door. Her hands were shaking so badly she almost couldn't open it, and when it did open she all but fell into the corridor. She only realised then that her shoes had come off somewhere along the way in the struggle, but there was no way she would go back and get them now.

Forcing herself to keep moving, she set off to find the lift.

Nic rounded a corner in the corridor where he'd walked Estella back to her room, much to her amusement, and stopped dead when he saw a familiar figure walking towards him. Recognition was like a hot poker in his belly. He knew this was Morales's floor, and hadn't liked to admit that part of his motivation in walking Estella to her room had been for that reason. Had he really been hoping to bump into Maddie making her walk of shame? Well, his subconscious desire had manifested her right in front of him.

Anger rose like a swift tide of lava inside him. And something else much more potent and disturbing. *Jealousy.* An alien emotion because no other woman had ever aroused it in him.

In that moment Maddie looked up and saw him. She stopped dead and froze like a deer in the headlights. Nic heard something inarticulate like a sob coming from her throat, and then she turned and was walking back the way she'd come. Away from him.

All Nic was aware of was her *déshabillé* and mussed-up hair. And then he saw her bare feet. His anger became white-hot. Being barefoot made her look ridiculously vulnerable, but she'd just been— Bile rose in Nic's throat, and before he even knew what he was doing he was pursuing her, driven by dark and angry demons.

When he was close enough to reach out and touch her he stopped, and said with scorn dripping from every word, 'Well? Did you give Morales everything he wanted or just enough of a taste to keep him interested?' Disgust and something else—*disappointment*—lanced Nic in a very vulnerable place.

Maddie stopped too, her shoulders a tense line. She didn't turn around. 'Just leave me alone, Nic.'

Her voice sounded husky and raw, and it made Nic even angrier. She was still playing on his emotions. He reached for her shoulder and swung her round—but when he saw her face the bottom fell out of his stomach.

Instinctively he put his other hand on her other shoulder. 'Maddie…what the hell…? Did Morales do this?'

Maddie tried to look away, or down, but Nic gently tipped her chin up so he could inspect her face. He cursed volubly. Maddie jerked her chin out of his hold and pulled back. The blood on her split lip looked garish against the stark paleness of her face.

'What, Nic? Aren't you going to say I told you so? You did warn me, after all, not to trust him.'

Maddie was struggling to hold it together, to be strong. She couldn't bear it that Nic was witness to her awful humiliation. She'd never felt so frail or weak. Or useless. And she hated the lingering terror that made her want to cling onto his solid strength. She looked down, tears suddenly stinging her eyes.

He sounded tortured. 'When I said I didn't trust Morales, it was a gut instinct. I've never liked him, or his business methods, but I had no idea he was capable of violence.'

Maddie was bitter. 'Well, it would seem your instincts have been proved right.'

He asked then, 'When did he do this to you? After...?'

Maddie looked up at Nic in abject horror, forgetting about her tears. He thought that she'd *slept* with Morales anyway? How low was his opinion of her? Bile rose and she was afraid she'd be sick. And yet who did she have to blame but herself when she'd been so intent on proving to Nic that she was *experienced*?

Suddenly the fight left Maddie. The shock that had been numbing her wore off. The awful shaking that hadn't abated. It seemed to intensify all over her body. 'I didn't sleep with him. That was never my intention.' She shuddered reflexively. 'I couldn't...with a man like that...just to get something. You can call me naive, or whatever you want, but I went to his room believing that we would just talk about business.'

Maddie took a deep shaky breath, and avoided Nic's eye again. 'But then...he was all over me...and I couldn't move or breathe. He'd been drinking. I hadn't realised how much. He ripped my dress and then he slapped me...'

To Maddie's horror she started crying in earnest, great deep racking sobs that seemed to come out of nowhere and she couldn't control them. She felt so cold. Suddenly heat engulfed her and she felt herself being drawn into an embrace of solid muscle. Musky male scent surrounded her. And finally she felt safe. Unbelievably safe.

Maddie was incredibly slender and vulnerable in Nic's

arms, her slim body trembling violently. The protective instinct was almost overwhelming. He wanted to believe her so badly he could taste it.

To see her crushed like this was almost as hard as if she'd been defiant and triumphant. No one could fake the terror he could feel in her body. Nic's vision was red. His father had used to hit his mother whenever she angered him, and Nic had an absolute abhorrence of violence against women. The rage he felt towards Morales scared him with its intensity.

Yet he found it hard to believe that Maddie hadn't known what she was walking into by agreeing to meet him in his room. How could she have been so naive? An experienced woman like her? Had she just been playing out of her league? Not counting on Morales turning violent?

Deep inside Nic was shame and self-recrimination that he'd allowed Maddie to walk into that situation. That he'd let his own pride stop him from following his initial gut instinct to go after her. This woman had him so tied up in knots that he'd prefer to let her be in danger than deal with her. He was pathetic.

Nic held Maddie for a long time, until her sobs had stopped. His hands moved up and down her back, soothing her. *Déjà vu* hit him straight in his belly when he remembered another time and place, when he'd held this woman in his arms after seeing her in tears. He tensed against the inevitable pain that accompanied those memories, but for the first time it didn't come.

She'd stopped shaking and crying, and was as still as a mouse in his arms. He could feel her breath, warm through the flimsy material of his shirt. And just like that the protective instinct was dissolving in a rush of heat and arousal. Her body was moulding against his as if made for him alone. Every curve fitted perfectly into his harder planes.

Nic gritted his jaw, but he couldn't stop his body responding to her proximity, or the way it felt to have her soft breasts crushed against his chest.

When she tensed slightly and shifted, Nic loosened his hold.

Maddie realised that she'd just fallen into Nic's arms like some kind of wilting heroine and felt embarrassed. She pulled back from him reluctantly, swaying a little unsteadily on her feet. Her eyes widened on a point on his chest. 'There's blood on your shirt.'

He barely glanced down. 'It's fine.'

Much to her shame, his touch had stopped being comforting and had become something much more provocative long seconds ago—when the blood had rushed to intimate parts of her body in helpless reaction to being held by him. Her nipples were tight against the lace of her bra even now. Her skin was tingling all over and she felt hot.

He hadn't let her go completely. His hands were on her shoulders, his gaze searching hers. 'Where do you think you're going?'

Maddie met his eyes reluctantly, afraid he might see something of that shameful desire in her eyes. She felt very raw and exposed. 'I should go back to my hotel.' She shuddered reflexively, despite wanting to appear in control of her emotions. 'I want to have a shower. I feel dirty.'

When she moved to pull free of his hands completely Nic let her go, but to Maddie's horror her legs were so weak that they gave way. As if without his touch she couldn't stay standing.

Nic caught her up into his arms so fast her head spun, and he said grimly, 'You're not going anywhere. You're coming with me.'

Maddie tried to protest, but she was too weak. Being

in Nic's arms like this made her feel like the worst traitor for giving in, but she couldn't drum up the will to fight.

She was barely aware of Nic taking her into a lift and it ascending to the top floor, or their walk down the corridor and then a door swinging open onto a dimly lit room with a plush interior and stupendous views over night-time Buenos Aires.

Gently he put her down on a sofa and said, 'Will you be all right for a minute?'

Maddie nodded, feeling guilty. The minute Nic had enfolded her in his arms she'd felt a thousand times better. He stood up to his full height and Maddie watched as he picked up a phone. With his other hand he yanked off his bow tie and shucked off his jacket. He opened the top buttons of his shirt with long, lean fingers, and Maddie's mouth went dry.

He was speaking in low tones on the phone. 'Send up a first-aid kit, please? Thank you.'

He put down the phone and disappeared into the bathroom. Maddie could hear running water, and then Nic reappeared. He squatted down beside her. 'Do you feel okay to have a shower?'

Maddie's skin was still crawling when she thought of that man. She nodded vigorously and Nic helped her up from the couch.

He said, 'There's a robe in the bathroom. By the time you're out I'll have a first-aid kit to see to your lip.'

Maddie went into the steam-filled bathroom and shut the door. She leant back against it for a long moment, until the steam started to make her feel light-headed. Incredibly weary, she undressed and stepped into the shower, letting the hot water beat down for a long time before soaping up her hands and washing herself all over. Finally, when she felt clean again, she got out.

She dried herself and rubbed her hair, leaving it to hang damply down her back. Belting the robe tightly around her body, she cautiously opened the door again to face Nic.

He was standing with his back to her, looking out of one of the huge windows. Maddie's heart picked up its unsteady pace when he turned around to face her. He was drinking amber liquid from a tumbler glass but he put it down, coming towards her.

'Let me see your lip.'

Maddie put a finger to it and winced because it felt so swollen. Nic came and took her chin in his thumb and forefinger, lifting it to the light. Maddie held her breath. His proximity was setting every nerve tingling. She was intrigued and unsettled to see this side of him. He let her go and took some cotton wool and antiseptic from the first-aid kit.

'This might sting a bit.'

He touched the cotton wool to her lip and Maddie sucked in a breath, her eyes watering, but she said nothing.

'At least it's stopped bleeding. It'll have gone down by tomorrow.'

Maddie said, half jokingly, 'You're familiar with split lips, then?'

To her surprise Nic's jaw tightened. He just said, 'I've had a few in my time.'

Then something else caught Maddie's eye, and before she knew what she was doing she'd taken Nic's hand in hers. 'What's happened to your knuckles?' They were badly grazed.

When he tried to take his hand back Maddie held on firmly and looked at him.

Nic answered tightly, 'While you were in the shower I paid a visit to Morales.'

Maddie gasped. 'You hit him?'

Nic's face was hard, making a shiver run through Maddie.

'I stopped myself from knocking him senseless. He's lucky he got away with a bruised jaw.'

Overcome with a burgeoning and volatile emotion, Maddie bent her head and pressed a kiss to Nic's bruised knuckles. She looked up again and said huskily, 'I hate violence, but in this case...thank you.'

Nic's eyes were so blue Maddie felt as if she was falling, even though she was still standing. A taut stillness came into the air around them—until Nic said, 'Morales is claiming that you slept with him.'

For a second Maddie almost didn't understand what he was saying, and then the words sank in—and the way Nic was looking at her. She dropped his hand, suddenly aghast that she'd just kissed it. She'd been looking at him like some lovestruck groupie and he still thought...

Maddie felt sick.

'You think I'm lying.' Her voice was flat. She moved back, conscious of being in a hotel robe with nothing underneath. And of having exposed herself. How could she have forgotten for a moment, just because Nic had been slightly chivalrous and protective, that he still didn't trust her, that he thought the worst of her? He'd done nothing he wouldn't have done for any other distressed woman. She'd just read an ocean of meaning into his actions...

In the ensuing silence Maddie looked away. Even if she reiterated her innocence it would be her word against Morales's. She looked back at Nic again, and said half defiantly, 'What do you care anyway?'

Nic felt a heavy dark weight lodge in his gut. He *had* believed Maddie, out there in the corridor, when she'd been so obviously distraught. But when he'd confronted Morales just now and the man had drunkenly goaded Nic by saying, 'Jealous, de Rojas? Because she slept with me and not you?' Nic had seen red. He hadn't been so angry in years. Before he'd even known what he was doing his fist had connected with Morales's smirking face.

It burned Nic inside to know that he'd been driven to violence—not so much by what the man had done to Maddie as at the thought that she might have actually slept with him.

Just now, when she'd taken his bruised hand in hers and kissed his knuckles and then looked up at him, he'd felt as if he was drowning in those green depths. Losing himself in her. Again. The last time he'd lost himself with this woman she'd annihilated him.

He assured himself that he was not that young man any more. But it was as if she'd peeled back a protective layer of his skin, exposing his innermost self all over again.

Pushing down that heavy weight even further, Nic said coolly, 'I care about the fact that a man abused you. Beyond that it's none of my business.'

Maddie was incredibly hurt by Nic's mistrust, and couldn't believe that she'd been so seduced by a little tenderness. Once again Nic was proving just how naive she was—as if Alex Morales hadn't already drummed it into her.

'You're right.' She hoped she matched his cool tone. 'It is none of your business.'

Maddie went to go back into the bathroom to get her dress.

Nic said from behind her in a curt voice, 'Where are you going?'

She turned around. 'I have to return to my hotel. My bus back to Mendoza leaves at six tomorrow morning.'

Nic emitted a curse that made Maddie blush. And then

he said curtly, 'You're not going back to that hotel. It's too late. And you're coming home with me tomorrow. You will *not* be taking a sixteen-hour bus journey again.'

Maddie felt like stamping her foot. Why couldn't Nic just disapprove of her and let her go?

Volatile emotions were rising, making her voice wobbly. 'I might have believed you care if you hadn't just accused me of sleeping with a man to secure his favour. A man capable of violence! Quite frankly my cockroach-infested hotel room is a more enticing prospect than staying here to suffer your judgemental condemnation.'

Nic slashed a hand through the air. 'Dammit, Maddie, I'll get another room. But you're *not* leaving this hotel— and if I have to lock you in here, I will. Tell me where your stuff is.'

Maddie looked at Nic and fumed—inwardly and outwardly. She put her hands on her hips. 'Damn *you*, Nic de Rojas. You think you're so perfect? How dare you pretend to be honourable when you clearly think me nothing better than a street—'

Nic closed the distance between them in seconds. Suddenly he was too close and Maddie backed away, her pulse leaping in her throat. He was blisteringly angry— but Maddie sensed that it wasn't with *her*. That threw her.

'Your hotel and your room number, Maddie. I'm not going to take no for an answer.'

To her everlasting mortification, when Maddie thought of navigating Buenos Aires to get to her fleapit of a hotel, and that tortuous bus journey tomorrow, she wanted to cry. She was still feeling extremely fragile and vulnerable. Nic thought she had sold herself this evening for her estate, and yet he'd insisted on looking after her—as if she was an unsavoury package he had to take care of. She could

see the glitter of determination in his eyes, and wouldn't
put it past him to lock her into the suite.

She swallowed and gritted out finally, 'It's the Hotel
Esmerelda. Room 410.'

Nic was returning to the suite after booking another room
for himself and getting Maddie's things from her hotel.
He'd wanted to get away from her so that his brain might
start functioning again in a vaguely normal manner.

Deep down he didn't really believe that she'd slept with
Morales...but when she stood in front of him and those
green eyes were on his the need to put up a wall between
them felt like the most important thing. He'd had no defence when he'd seen her so upset and vulnerable, and
the speed and ease with which she got under his skin terrified him.

Nic steeled himself outside the suite door. He had her
one small suitcase in his hands, pathetically light. Any
woman he knew travelled with a veritable entourage to
carry their luggage. But not Maddie.

When he opened the door and went in all was hushed.
He'd half expected to see her standing defiantly where
he'd left her. He explored further and came to a halt. She
was curled up on the couch like a little lost soul, black hair
fanned over her shoulders, her head resting on one arm.

Nic's chest constricted and he put down the bag. He
walked over and bent down beside her, but she didn't
stir. Overcome with a feeling too huge to push down, Nic
tucked some black silky locks behind her ear. She was so
pale, her eyebrows starkly black against her skin. That
garish cut looked even more lurid.

Unable to help himself, Nic bent forward and pressed a
kiss to the corner of her mouth where it was cut.

Maddie was asleep, but in her dreams something amazing was happening. She felt cocooned in safety and warmth and something else—something much hotter. Desire. She dreamt that Nic was touching his lips to hers gently, lingering as if he couldn't force himself to pull away.

Maddie struggled up through layers of consciousness and opened slumberous eyes. She was looking directly into Nic's vivid blue eyes, intent on hers with a seriousness that connected with something deep inside her. She wasn't even sure if she was dreaming or not.

She moved her mouth experimentally, loath to lose that connection of his warm firm mouth on hers. Gently he applied more pressure, and Maddie's lips opened slightly. Her eyes fluttered closed, because the sheer intensity of his gaze was too much. She felt the tip of his tongue exploring, and a deep mewl sounded in the back of her throat. Instinctively she sank back even further into the couch, aware of Nic's broad chest close to her breasts.

The pressure of his mouth on hers became stronger, and a fire started fizzing in her veins. Maddie angled her head and Nic's hands and fingers sank into her hair, cupping her head so that he could stroke his tongue inside her mouth and tease hers.

Maddie felt buoyant. Euphoria was infecting her blood. When Nic's mouth left hers and he trailed his lips down over her chin and neck her head fell back, her belly tightening with need. If she was dreaming she never wanted to wake up. She could feel his head descending and he pulled open her robe. Maddie felt air whistle over the exposed slope of her breast, and her hands were on Nic's shoulders, as if to hold him in place.

She raised her heavy head and looked down to see Nic's own dark blond one close to the pale swell. With his hand he was exposing her breast fully now, and cupping the plump mound with its tight pink nipple. A callused thumb circled the darker areola and then flicked the tip. Maddie sucked in a breath, her hands tightening on Nic's shoulders. Her body was arching towards him, instinctively seeking more.

When his mouth moved down to take the place of his thumb and surrounded her with a moist sucking heat she gasped out loud. Never had she felt such an intense building need within her…at least not since that cataclysmic week after which everything had changed and been tainted.

Her urgency seemed to be transmitting itself to Nic. His mouth became rougher and his hand moved down, sliding under her robe, over her belly and down. His mouth came back up to find hers, but they'd both lost sight of the fact that Maddie was injured—because pain bloomed as soon as Nic's mouth crushed to hers.

It was like a shower of cold water being thrown down on them both. Maddie yelped with pain and Nic sprang back as if shot. Maddie put her hand to her mouth and felt the warm trickle of blood again. She all but scrambled off the couch, feeling totally disorientated. *How* had she ended up kissing Nic?

Maddie wasn't even comforted by the sight of his own flushed cheeks and tortured expression. She went to the bathroom and straight to the mirror. There wasn't much blood. She sucked in a shaky breath and wet the corner of a facecloth to hold it to her mouth. Her eyes were huge and glittering, her cheeks hectic with colour. Her chest was rising and falling as if she'd just been running, and down lower, between her legs, she was slippery, hot and aching. His hand had been so close…those long fingers almost touching her right there. She pressed her legs together as if that would push down the desire.

When she felt a little more in control of herself she went

back outside to see Nic standing like a statue, watching her warily.

'I think I'd like to be alone now.'

Something savage crossed Nic's face, and in two long strides he was right in front of her. 'You wanted it too, Maddie. Don't pretend you didn't.'

Maddie flushed. Okay, so she'd woken up to find Nic's mouth on hers, but the kiss had been supremely gentle. She could remember the moment when she could have drawn back and pushed him away, but weakly she'd wanted to pretend that she didn't have to make the decision to stop and had exerted pressure back, changing it into a very mutual thing.

The hurt of his low opinion of her was still raw. Maddie had to protect herself. For him this was just sexual attraction. He didn't even care that she might have slept with another man only hours before.

Nic reached his hand out as if to touch her lip and Maddie jerked back, making his eyes flash dangerously.

'It's fine. Please, Nic, just go.'

He looked at her for a long moment, a muscle pulsing in his jaw, and then finally he stepped back. 'Eight in the morning I'll come and get you. Be ready.'

Maddie nodded.

Nic turned and walked towards the main door, and then he turned back. Ominously he said, 'We're not done with this, Maddie. Not by a long shot.'

CHAPTER SEVEN

MADDIE was grateful that Nic seemed preoccupied the next morning, and their journey to the airfield was made largely in silence. He'd looked at her assessingly this morning, and Maddie had had to submit to his inspection of her mouth, her chin in his hand as he'd tipped her face up to him.

Just the touch of those fingers to her face had had her heating up inside like an exploding thermostat. He'd let her go and declared, 'The swelling has gone down. A couple more days and you won't even see it.'

Maddie had bitten back the childish urge to tell him that she could have figured that out for herself, but a weak part of her had *liked* his concern. Even if it was only perfunctory.

The small private jet was all cream leather seats and pristinely carpeted luxury. Maddie was intimidated by this further evidence of Nic's wealth. He, however, was nonchalant, his large frame dominating a two-seater couch along one wall. Maddie chose a seat at right angles to Nic.

When they were airborne, and Maddie had turned down the offer of champagne, the silence grew taut between them. Maddie wished she had a book or something to pretend an interest in. She was far too aware of Nic brooding just feet away, and felt like asking snappishly what was wrong.

She risked a glance over and her heart flipped in her chest. Instead of a censorious blue gaze she saw his head tipped back and his eyes closed. His jaw was tense, though, so he couldn't be asleep. She could see the dark fans his lashes made on those defined cheekbones, the faint stubble already forming on his jaw even though he was freshly shaved.

His shirt was open at the neck and Maddie had a tantalising glimpse of dark blond chest hair dusting dark olive skin. She looked back up and blanched when she saw him staring back at her. She'd just been caught ogling him like some lust-crazed teenage girl.

Despite his relaxed pose, Maddie could sense that inwardly he was alert, like an animal poised to strike. Immediately she felt nervous.

'I have a proposition for you.'

Maddie felt even more nervous. She cleared her throat and crossed her legs. 'What kind of a proposition?'

His eyes flicked down briefly to follow the movement of her legs, and Maddie pressed her thighs together unconsciously. Nic took his arms off the back of the couch and moved forward, resting his arms on his thighs.

'I think you've proved how determined you are to save your estate.'

Maddie flushed to think of the awful helplessness she'd felt in Alex Morales's room, how easily he'd dominated her. How easily he could have hurt her far worse than he had.

Defensively she said, 'I wouldn't do what I did last night again. It was stupid.'

Nic shrugged minutely. 'You were just out of your depth.'

Maddie stung at Nic's rebuke, but it was true. She wanted to get them off the subject of last night. It reminded her of too much raw emotion. 'What is it you want to propose?'

For a split second Maddie had an image in her head of Nic kneeling at her feet, looking at her with a tortured expression and asking her to marry him. Hot colour seeped into her cheeks, making his gaze narrow on hers, and Maddie wished she could just disappear.

'You still insist on seeking an investor—you won't sell?'

Maddie tensed. She shook her head. 'I'll never sell.'

'So,' he prodded, 'you'll keep looking for an investor?'

Maddie nodded. 'I have to.'

Grimly Nic said, 'That's what I was afraid of.'

Wary now, Maddie said, 'What do you mean?'

Nic was shaking his head. 'You're not going to find it easy. Morales is undoubtedly making sure your name is muck. If he told *me* last night that you'd slept together, then he'll be spreading the word to others too.'

Maddie felt sick. She wanted to shout and scream her innocence to Nic, but she knew he wouldn't listen to her.

'So…what does that mean?'

Nic said, 'It means that unless you go to Europe and seek out your contacts there you don't have a hope of getting an investor.'

Maddie felt sicker. She had no money for a trip like that, and she couldn't go and ask her old boss for help. He had a flourishing business, but not enough to invest the kind of money she needed. And she'd left him after he'd put her through college. She could hardly ask him for a handout when he'd already been so generous.

Maddie looked at Nic. She felt incredibly bleak. 'So what is this? An exercise in showing me how hopeless my case is?'

Nic looked at Maddie. He had her exactly where he wanted her now. Well, not *exactly*. Where he really wanted her was on her back, underneath him, begging for release. But this was a means to that end. He felt ruthless, but he quashed the feeling. Last night had proved to him how out of control he was around Maddie as soon as he came within touching distance.

He had to have her. But he had to protect himself in the process. He needed to control this vulnerability. And what he was about to propose offered him that protection.

Nic watched her reaction closely as he said, 'I will invest in your estate.'

The colour seemed to leach from Maddie's cheeks at first, leaving her skin like porcelain and her eyes huge. And then, as she took a deep breath, colour rushed back, staining those cheeks red. His groin throbbed in response.

She shook her head. 'No way. You want something. You want to ruin me.'

Nic smiled. 'I have to admit that at first I just wanted you gone…but since you've come home life has certainly been more entertaining.'

Maddie resolutely turned away and crossed her arms over her chest. Nic's eyes were helplessly drawn to where her breasts were pushed up, clearly defined under the thin T-shirt she wore. One long lock of black hair curled down, tantalisingly close to the slope of her breast, and he clenched his jaw. He had to have this woman. He would go insane if he didn't.

Maddie seethed inwardly. So Nic thought she was *entertaining*? She heard a movement and in seconds he'd come to sit in the empty chair opposite hers. His long legs were stretched out on either side of hers, effectively caging her in.

'What do you think you're doing?' Maddie gritted out.

Nic smiled easily. 'I'm going to make you see that you have no option but to give in to my proposal. Unless you

want to see your estate fall apart and your staff left with
nothing after their long years of hard work.'

Maddie's mouth had opened, but now she shut it again.
Hernan and Maria. They had nothing but the security she
provided them with. Not even pay.

As if reading her mind, Nic said softly, 'If you let me
invest in the Vasquez estate, Hernan and Maria will be secure. I will set up a pension plan. Hernan can work on the
vines again. You can hire a new head winemaker.' Before
she could say anything he went on, 'You need new barrels,
and we both know how much they cost. The last I heard
your father was still using a basket press.'

Maddie flushed hotly. Her father had favoured the old-
school methods. Defensively she said, 'The basket press
is coming back into vogue.'

Nic inclined his head. 'I'm not denying that. I use one
myself for certain grapes. But you can't use a basket press
alone. It has to be a sideline to a much more modern operation. It's a luxury—like hand-picking your crop.'

'*You* still hand-pick,' Maddie shot back.

'Yes, I do, but again that's only for certain grapes. Most
of our picking is done by machines now.'

Maddie felt an ache near her heart. What Nic had on
his estate was a blending of the old and the modern, which
was exactly the way she would love to see things run on
the Vasquez estate.

He went on relentlessly. 'Not all your vines are ruined.
You have a hope of a respectable harvest next year if you
take care of your vines now and cut them back. And what
about the vines that have produced something? How are
you going to harvest them with only yourself and Hernan?'

Maddie felt a sinking weight in her belly. She couldn't
take her gaze off Nic's. It was glued there in some kind
of sick fascination. He was chipping away at all the walls

surrounding her, showing her the huge gaping holes where they all threatened to fall down on top of her.

'I'll draw up a contract, so it'll be a legal document. I will invest in your estate, see to the provision of labour and materials, new machinery. I will oversee the production of your first fully functioning harvest, whether that's next year or the year after, and then I will stand back and let you take over.'

Maddie looked at him suspiciously. 'You'll walk away?'

Nic smiled cynically. 'Not without a large share of the profits each year, Maddie, until the investment is paid off. You won't see much of an income for a while, but it'll give you your estate back and protect your staff.'

Somewhere deep inside Maddie a tiny seed of hope and excitement was blooming. What Nic was offering was more than generous.

The tiny seed disappeared at the thought of Nic overseeing everything, being autocratic.

'You'd turn the Vasquez estate into a subsidiary of your own.'

Remarkably, he shook his head. 'That's not what I'm interested in. I quite like the idea of helping foster some healthy competition again, and I'm interested to see how you would develop things.'

Somehow Maddie couldn't see Nic deferring to her judgement. Suspiciously she asked, 'Would you state that in the contract?'

He nodded once. 'Of course. It'll all be laid out in black and white. You can read over it with your own legal people.'

Maddie held back a moment of hysteria. She had no money for legal people. She and Hernan would just have to vet it as best they could. That thought gave her a jolt. Was she already taking this as a given? She hated it that

Nic could manipulate her so easily, but at the same time she wasn't stupid enough to cut her nose off to spite her face.

Stiffly she said, 'I'd have to think about it.'

Nic smiled tersely. 'There's not much to think about, Maddie. I'm offering you a chance to sink or swim.'

After that comment, Nic settled back in his seat and stretched out his legs, trapping Maddie even more. He put back his head and within minutes was snoring softly. Finally Maddie could relax slightly. She uncrossed her arms. Her head was buzzing with all that Nic had just said and offered.

She looked suspiciously at his benignly sleeping face. He had to have an agenda. It couldn't be this simple.

She looked out of the window at the vast pampas lands underneath them. This was what she'd always wanted more than anything—a chance to work on her own estate. It had been denied her her whole life, and when her father had finally offered her the chance it had come too late. And now Nic de Rojas, the most unlikely person on the planet, was offering her a second chance. Not only that, but she had a responsibility to her staff. Hernan and Maria couldn't live on the estate indefinitely. Soon they would want to retire. They were old and weary.

Maddie sighed again, and then finally let her own weariness suck her under into sleep.

'Maddie...'

Maddie woke with a start. She'd been dreaming about Nic. Her cheek was tingling, as if someone had just touched her there. When her eyes focused, Nic was bending down so close to her that she could see the small lines fanning out from his eyes. She felt too hot, and knew instantly that it had been an erotic dream.

Scrabbling back into her seat as far as she could, she saw his jaw clench.

'We're landing in a few minutes. Buckle up.'

Maddie buckled up with trembling hands, relieved that Nic had moved back over to the couch. She could breathe a little easier when he wasn't in her direct line of sight.

They landed softly and within minutes were in Nic's Jeep, heading out of Mendoza and towards Villarosa. Maddie felt as if she'd done ten rounds in a boxing ring—mentally and physically. She snuck a look at Nic's rigid profile. He looked so stern. Had she just imagined what had happened on the plane? Had he really told her he'd invest?

When the familiar lines of the Vasquez estate came into view Maddie breathed a sigh of relief. Nic stopped at the steps leading up to the main door. He indicated the house. 'Renovation of the house would be part of the investment too.'

Maddie's heart thumped. She hadn't imagined it. She looked at him warily. 'Why are you doing this?'

Nic's face was suspiciously expressionless. He shrugged minutely. 'I have the means…and I don't like to see a good vineyard turn to dust.'

Maddie struggled to understand. She couldn't do this unless she knew *why*. She turned in her seat to face Nic. 'But our families…the feud…we've fought for so long. How do I know you're not going to just take me over completely?'

Nic's mouth tightened, and something ambiguous flashed in his eyes. 'You once told me that the feud meant nothing to you.'

Maddie felt very vulnerable thinking of that time. 'You said the same thing. But then…it all blew up again.'

Nic looked impossibly stern. 'Our parents are dead, Maddie. It's just us now. I'm willing to move on if you are.'

Maddie didn't trust him for a second. She saw something else light his eyes and immediately her insides tightened.

'There is one condition to my offer—and it won't be in the contract.'

Instantly Maddie's hackles rose. She breathed out. 'I knew it was too good to be true. So what is this condition?'

After a long moment, during which Maddie's nerves were screaming with tension, Nic finally said softly, 'One night with me, Maddie. One night in my bed to finish what was started eight years ago.'

Maddie looked at Nic disbelievingly. She knew what was between them. It crackled in the air the moment they came within feet of each other, and she'd been moments away from begging him to take her only last night... But somehow she'd been hoping that she could ignore it.

Now Nic had laid it between them. He had made the business proposition about this heat between them. She shook her head. Her throat felt tight. 'Whether you believe me or not, a man offered me a similar deal last night and I turned him down. What makes you think this is any different?'

Nic leant forward, and Maddie couldn't move back any further. The door handle was pressing painfully into her back. Nic was so close now she could feel his breath on her face. He trailed a finger down her cheek and lower, pushing aside the top of her T-shirt to rest it where the pulse was nearly beating out of her skin. His forearm touched her breast, making the nipple spring into aching hardness, pushing against the fabric of her bra.

Nic smiled, and as if he knew exactly what was happening to her body, he subtly moved his forearm back and forth against that turgid peak.

'This is different, Maddie, because you didn't want him.

You want me...so badly I can smell it. And *that's* why you'll do this.'

Panic rose up inside Maddie, almost strangling her. She reached behind her and fumbled for the door handle, almost landing on her backside outside the Jeep in her haste. Nic was out too, and coming towards her. It took a minute for Maddie to realise he was holding out her bag. She grabbed it from him inelegantly.

Nic smiled and just said, 'You know where I am, Maddie. I look forward to hearing from you. That is,' he added softly, 'if you're interested in saving your estate and being honest with yourself.'

And then he got back into his Jeep and drove off, leaving a small cloud of dust in his wake.

For almost a week Maddie battled sleepless nights full of demons and Nic's voice saying, *Be honest with yourself.* She spent the long days facing the fact that without funds she and Hernan could make nothing even of the small harvest they could bring in.

She went round and round in her head, endlessly replaying her last conversation with Nic word for word, and always with a flash of heat she came back to him saying, *'You want me...so badly I can smell it. And that's why you'll do this.'*

She did want him. She couldn't deny that. She wasn't that much of a hypocrite. It scared her the way the days dragged, and how her mind kept returning to him like iron filings to a magnet. She hadn't realised how accustomed she'd become to seeing him, or expecting him to turn up. And when he didn't...she didn't like the feeling of emptiness.

Maddie desperately tried not to think about his *condition* to the investment proposal, but invariably she would

think about it. In a way, the thought of doing it like this…
where the lines were clearly marked in the sand, with no
false emotions involved, no false seduction…should actually make it easier.

Maddie knew that when it came to Nic de Rojas she was
weak. He could have put on an elaborate act, pretended to
seduce her. And she would have fallen for it. She knew she
would have. And in the process she would have shown him
how ambiguous her feelings were for him. This way there
was no ambiguity. She was protected. She would gain closure finally, and shut the door on that part of her life. The
awful memories surrounding what had happened might
finally fade into the background and she could move on.

Maddie weakly blocked out the fact that she'd have to
deal with him every day for a long time to come if she
agreed to this. It would make the prospect of closure all but
redundant. But as the days passed Maddie was no closer
to being able to pick up the phone and change the course
of her life irrevocably.

At the end of the week, late in the evening, Maddie
was sitting in her father's study, brooding that she was
only able to see the documents in front of her because Nic
was paying for the electricity, when Hernan came in. He
looked concerned.

'I'm worried about you…and this place.' He was shaking his head. 'We're backed up against the wall, Maddie.
There's nothing you can do. You'll have to sell up.'

For a moment Maddie clung to that like a life raft. 'But
what about you and Maria?'

She could see how Hernan paled slightly in the dim
light. He shrugged, but Maddie wasn't fooled by his non-
chalance. 'Don't worry about us, *niña*. We can take care
of ourselves. You're not responsible for us.'

Maddie felt hope die and a heavy weight almost crushed

her. She knew how much this estate owed Hernan. He was such a gifted viticulturist that he alone had been responsible for the quality of their grapes, which had allowed her father and his chief winemaker to come up with the successful blends that had led to their wealth and security. She couldn't turn her back on Hernan now, or his wife. And she knew she couldn't turn her back on the very legacy she held in her hands.

'We might not have to sell…'

Immediately Hernan sat up straight. 'What do you mean?'

Maddie laid out the bare facts of Nic's investment plan without mentioning his private little caveat which affected only her.

Hernan looked at her incredulously. 'But…you will say yes, won't you? It's a chance to save the Vasquez name—the *only* chance.'

Maddie looked at Hernan. 'It's such a huge step to take. How do I know I can trust him?'

Maddie knew she wasn't talking about the investment itself now. She was talking about whether or not she could trust Nic not to sleep with her and decimate her completely. She was talking about whether or not she could trust herself not to lose herself completely if she took that cataclysmic step.

Hernan sagged in his seat and suddenly looked ten years older. Maddie immediately forgot about everything. 'Hernan, what is it?'

He looked up eventually, and his face was ashen. 'The truth is, Maddie, Maria isn't well. She needs treatment—treatment that we can't afford.'

Maddie got up and went over and put her arms around Hernan. He said to her with tears in his eyes, 'We didn't want you to worry… We thought the only option would be to sell and we would leave and go to our son in Buenos Aires.'

Maddie immediately shook her head. She knew that Hernan and Maria hated the city. Their lives were here. Their son in Buenos Aires was not well off, and had a family of his own to look after.

'There's absolutely no way you're going anywhere. If I agree to this deal with Nic de Rojas, I'll make sure you're both looked after—and especially Maria.'

Hernan took her hand in his old and worn ones. 'But we don't want to put you under pressure…we're not your responsibility.'

Maddie squatted down so that she could look at Hernan properly. She squeezed his hand and said, 'I know that, Hernan, but you are due something for all your years of service. You deserve medical care, at the very least, and security. I can provide that now.' She took a deep breath. 'I'll call Nic de Rojas tonight.'

Hernan gripped her hand tightly, the sheen of tears still in his eyes, and Maddie felt emotional. She'd done it now. No going back. She couldn't even if she wanted to. These people were more important to her than her own petty personal concerns.

The following evening Maddie was driving over to Nic's estate, an overnight bag in the back. She was so tense she felt as if she might crack apart, and she forced herself to breathe deep. It had been a tumultuous and emotional day.

The previous evening she'd rung Nic and told him she'd agree to the investment with the proviso that he met a condition of her own—that Maria be taken care of with the best medical care as soon as possible. Nic hadn't hesitated. He'd agreed immediately, and it had struck another blow to Maddie's misconceptions about him.

That morning Nic had appeared with his own doctor, who had consulted with Hernan and Maria. Maria had been taken into the best private clinic in Mendoza that very afternoon, and the relief they'd both felt had been palpable to Maddie. She'd been incredibly emotional as she'd watched them leave.

Maddie was aghast at how relieved she'd felt to see Nic arriving that morning, along with intense fizzing excitement in every cell. It had felt as if she hadn't seen him in months, not days. When she'd seen him up close, though, he'd looked a little worn and tired. Maddie had had to quash the ridiculous urge to ask him if everything was all right.

When Hernan and Maria had left Maddie had faced Nic, feeling extremely vulnerable. 'Thank you for taking care of Maria…it was important to Hernan and to me.'

'Don't mention it.'

Reluctantly she'd asked him, there on the steps of the house. 'So what happens now…?'

He'd just looked at her with an expression so intense that Maddie had gone slowly redder and redder.

'You will come to me this evening. Eight p.m.'

He'd said nothing else. He'd walked to his Jeep, got in and left.

Maddie forced herself to concentrate on the road now and tried not think about the night would bring.

Nic was pacing in his office. He did not like to admit how close to panic he'd been by yesterday evening when Maddie had finally rung. The very walls of his house had been closing in on him, and he hadn't liked his clawing desperation to see her again. He'd hated not knowing what she was up to—had she gone looking for another investor? Had she somehow miraculously secured an investor without his knowing?

Nic had agreed as soon as she'd mentioned wanting Maria to be taken care of. He would have agreed to anything except Maddie reneging on their own personal part of the agreement. That she would be his for one night.

One night. Nic stopped pacing and looked out over his vineyard which was disappearing into the dusk, the colours melding and blurring. One night. He could do this. One night was invariably all it took for him to grow bored with a woman. So why would Maddie be different? His conscience pricked. Who was he kidding? Maddie had been different from the moment his hormones had realised she was growing up.

Nic ran a hand through his hair impatiently and turned around. A sheaf of papers sat on his desk. It was the investment contract. It epitomised everything Nic couldn't articulate about this woman who had come back into his life. This woman who he wanted more than the breath he took into his body. He hadn't realised how starved he'd been for her until he'd heard her voice on the phone the previous evening. Even though she'd been cool, he'd been burning up just to hear her.

And then when he'd seen her today…he'd wanted to back her into the wall of the house and take her there and then. His desire was like a wild beast, clawing at his insides.

This contract meant that Maddie would not turn around after tonight and claim that she'd been *bored*, or that she regretted what happened. Because she couldn't. She wanted her estate too badly. And she wanted Nic too badly too—even though he knew without the contract she might deny it. This way she couldn't. He would not be exposed again. Never again.

So why, when Nic looked at the sheaf of papers on his desk, did they seem to mock him?

Maddie looked warily at the big pink box with the red satin bow which sat on the bed as if it might jump up and bite her. She'd arrived at Nic's house and been met by Geraldo, who had greeted her warmly and shown her up to a sumptuous suite of rooms—as if they didn't both know she was there to spend the night with Nic.

He'd indicated to the lavish box on the bed and said, 'A gift from Señor de Rojas. He'll see you in the dining room at eight. If you need anything in the meantime please don't hesitate to call.'

Eventually, aware of time passing, Maddie opened it up and peeled back layers of blood-red tissue paper to reveal what seemed to be acres of dark grey satin folds. She lifted the dress out and gasped. It was stunning. No woman could be immune to the beauty of a dress like this. The material was heavy, and yet as light as a feather. Strapless, it had a ruched bodice and a high waist, and it fell in swathes of satin and chiffon layers to the ground.

More was hidden in the tissue paper in the box: silver shoes with diamanté straps and dark grey underwear, lacy and ethereal. There was also a velvet box, and Maddie opened it to reveal stunning teardrop diamond earrings and a matching bracelet. Something very fragile inside her withered slightly when she looked at the incredible bounty of luxurious goods laid out on the bed. But then Maddie chastised herself. Nic was actually doing her a favour, treating her like a mistress. All she had to do tonight was play a part—perhaps that would help her to stay intact and immune to emotion.

At eight o'clock on the dot Maddie was standing nervously at the door of the room a shy young girl had indicated. The dress felt unbelievably decadent against Maddie's bare legs. She'd put on the underwear simply because she had nothing else to wear that wouldn't ruin the line of the dress. The jewellery felt heavy and cold against her skin.

She'd put on the minimum of makeup and left her hair down—primarily because her hands were shaking too much to do anything more elaborate. Taking a deep breath and trying to remain in a detached frame of mind, Maddie knocked lightly on the door before opening it.

The scene inside was impossibly seductive, with candles flickering and a small table set for two. It was a different room from the one they'd eaten in before, more formal. It took a second for Maddie to register Nic standing by the window, his hands in his pockets. He was dressed semiformally in a white shirt and dark trousers, hair slicked back and damp, as if he'd just had a shower.

'You wore the dress.'

Maddie gripped the handle hard and struggled to maintain her equilibrium in the face of this seductive scene. She bit back the need to remind him that she was just playing the part he wanted. 'Yes, thank you.'

Nic inclined his head and smiled faintly. 'You can let go of the door. I won't bite. I promise.'

Heat bloomed inside Maddie at the thought of Nic's teeth nipping her sensitive flesh. She let the door go abruptly just as a staff member came into the room. After conferring with Nic for a moment the man left again, and Nic walked over to the antique sideboard which held different bottles of drink.

She watched as he poured some champagne into two flutes. He came and offered her one and she took it.

He tipped his glass to hers, eyes unnervingly intense. *'Salud.'*

'*Salud,*' Maddie echoed, and took a sip of the sparkling efferescent drink, tearing her gaze away from Nic's to look around the room.

'Your mouth has healed well.'

Maddie looked back to Nic and instinctively touched the corner where it had split. It *had* healed.

'You look beautiful tonight.'

Something uncomfortable was prickling across Maddie's skin. She wasn't used to this—to compliments. To Nic being so effortlessly urbane around her. She didn't know how to behave. And all she could think of was how beautiful *he* looked.

'So do you,' she answered huskily, and then blushed and looked down. 'That is, not beautiful but handsome.'

Oh, God. Maddie took another quick sip of her drink before she could make a complete blithering idiot of herself. She wasn't sophisticated. Surely Nic could see that?

To fill the yawning gap in conversation Maddie asked if Nic had had any news from the hospital about Maria, and he told her that they were still doing tests. Maria had gone to the local doctor with chest pains and they were concerned that it could be a heart problem.

'Thank you again,' Maddie said huskily. 'Hernan didn't know where to turn, and they couldn't have afforded the kind of care they're getting now.'

Sounding serious, Nic said, 'I pay for health insurance for all my employees. Maria and Hernan will be included in that too.'

Maddie had the suspicion that Nic would have helped them anyway. It made her uncomfortable to acknowledge this, so she said, slightly acerbically, 'Just like I'm going to be an employee?'

He chided her. 'Business partners, Maddie...'

Nic drained his glass of champagne and put it down,

gesturing for Maddie to be seated at the dinner table. It was ornately set, with gleaming silverware and crockery so delicate-looking that Maddie was afraid to touch it. The champagne was fizzing in her blood, making her feel slightly light-headed.

The whole scene was intimidating to Maddie.

Especially when Nic looked so sophisticated and at ease across the table from her.

Discreet staff came in and served them with their starter—a light soup. A sense of panic and claustrophobia was rising inside Maddie, and the soup became like treacle in her throat. It was as if they were both ignoring the elephant in the room. The fact that Nic expected them to have dinner and then go upstairs and have sex. At that moment Maddie couldn't even imagine Nic's expression changing from the stern one he'd had since she'd arrived.

Maddie was aware that her own wish to remain detached was fast dissolving.

More staff arrived to take their starters away. Maddie felt agitated and hot.

Nic frowned at her. 'Are you okay? You look a little flushed.'

It was the dispassionate way he asked that galvanised Maddie. She wanted to scream, *No, I'm not okay!* She stood up abruptly, making some of the crockery knock the wine glasses. It sounded like gunshots. She put out a trembling hand, only realising then how agitated she was. The sparkle of diamonds at her wrist was like cold fire.

'I…I can't do this like this. Pretending that this is normal when it's not.'

CHAPTER EIGHT

Nic was just looking at her. Maddie's skin was prickling all over. She started to take off the jewellery, all but ripping the undoubtedly expensive earrings from her ears and the bracelet off her wrist. Immediately she started to feel lighter.

'All this. It's not *me*. I can't sit here and act like nothing is happening...'

Nic stood too. Someone came into the room with a tray and Nic sent them a glowering look, making them disappear again. He looked back to Maddie, the expression in his eyes feral. 'Something's happening, all right. You will *not* do this, Maddie. It's too late to back out. If we don't have tonight, you have *nothing*.'

Maddie backed away from the table and stumbled slightly. She bent down and took off the shoes with heels like weapons. Her heart was hammering and she craved air, and space, and something more tangible than what was in this room right now.

'If we do this we do it my way. I can't do it like this...' She flung out a hand. 'This seduction scene, it's all fake... we both know that's not what this is about.'

Maddie turned and all but stumbled out through the door, picking up the dress, half running and half walking to the main front door. She heard a curse behind her and

Nic following. She didn't even know where she was going, but she got out through the front door and looked to her left, saw the stables in the distance. Suddenly she knew.

Maddie was in the stables and leading a horse out of a stall, putting a bridle on, when she heard an ominously low, 'What the hell do you think you're doing?'

She took a deep breath, turned to look at Nic and nearly quailed. But she straightened her shoulders. 'I'm not leaving. But if this is happening, it's happening my way.'

Maddie found a box and stepped up to swing herself up on the saddleless horse. Now she was looking down at Nic and her heart tripped. His hair shone dark gold under the lights. A horse whinnied nearby.

He seemed to battle something inwardly, and then he cursed again and she saw him throw off his dinner jacket and lead his own horse out of the stall. It was a massive black stallion. She saw the play of his impressive muscles underneath the thin material of his shirt and something euphoric bubbled up inside Maddie. She kicked her heels and her horse moved out of the stables. Outside, the sun had set a short time before and the sky was a beautiful bruised lilac colour, still quite light.

Rows and rows of vines stretched as far as the eye could see, and in the distance were the huge vats and outbuildings which housed the hub of Nic's empire. Maddie turned in the other direction and kicked the horse into a trot— away from the house, towards the border between their estates.

When she had enough space she picked it up to a canter, and soon she heard powerful hooves behind her. Maddie had always felt free on a horse. She didn't look back, half afraid to see Nic bearing down on her. The cooling evening air caressed her hot bare skin. The satin folds of the dress fell and moved around her legs with the motion of the horse.

She felt the huge black presence of Nic's stallion come alongside her, and then Nic was reaching forward to effortlessly take Maddie's reins and bring her and her horse to a juddering halt. She had to press her thighs tight to its back to stop from falling off.

She spluttered, 'What do you think—?'

'Where the hell are we going?' he asked, anger vibrating from him in waves.

Maddie's mouth opened and closed, her breath coming rapidly. She refused to let herself be intimidated. 'You *know* where we're going.'

For a split second she thought she saw something bleak cross Nic's face, and then it was gone and his eyes spat blue sparks. 'I'm not going there with you.'

Maddie yanked her reins out of Nic's hands. 'If you want me—if you want this night—then we *are* going there.'

Nic looked at Maddie. His breath was searing through his lungs and it wasn't because of exertion. He was burning up. She looked magnificent. He'd been in a daze since he'd seen her arrive in the dining room, more beautiful than any woman he'd ever seen before. When he'd thought she was walking out on him he'd been so panicked it had made him feel weak.

He wasn't in a daze now, though, when he thought of what she was suggesting, and he snarled, 'What *is* this? Some pathetic attempt to be poetic? Well, it's lost on me. I'd sooner have you in my bed. Or back there in the stables would do fine.'

Maddie clamped down on the pain she felt when he spoke so crudely. She shook her head and her horse pranced away a little, sensing her agitation. 'No, it's there...or nowhere.'

Suddenly she'd whirled the horse around and was cantering off at speed again. Nic cursed volubly. There was enough light in the gathering dusk but she could still miss a rock or stone and be thrown in an instant. Giving in, he spurred his own horse on to follow.

When he reached the orchard, *déjà vu* nearly made him dizzy. He'd consciously and unconsciously avoided this place like the plague for years. Maddie's horse was riderless, tied to a small tree, and she was standing there— just waiting. Exactly as she had been all those years ago. Except now she was a mature woman. Her shoulders were bare and white in the dusk, her hair like black satin. Her breasts were full against the silk of her dress.

He swung off his horse, feeling tight inside, and secured him to another tree. He walked towards her. Her eyes were huge. Her face was pale. He felt acutely exposed, but he was reluctant to let her see how much being back here affected him.

Now that she was standing here Maddie couldn't believe she'd made this mad dramatic gesture. She'd acted from a visceral need to break out of that oh, so polite dinner as if nothing was wrong.

Her voice was husky, her senses already reeling at Nic's scent and proximity. 'This is where it started and where it ends. Tonight. For ever.'

Nic looked huge in the gloom. As if he'd grown several inches and his muscles had become even bigger. Once again she had a bittersweet rush of emotion at the knowledge that he'd once been much more vulnerable. But then he came towards her and Maddie's breath caught in her throat.

He stopped a couple of feet away and watched her, and then drawled laconically, 'Well, what are you waiting for?'

His insouciance after the intense anger she'd just witnessed made her want to lash out. For a moment she had believed that coming back here might have affected him emotionally.

She was completely unprepared for this, despite her show of bravado. He thought she'd slept with Morales the other night, so he had the erroneous idea that she was some grand seductress, when she'd never done anything like this in her life. And the reason she'd never done it was standing right in front of her. The scar of that last traumatic day after such a heady, perfect week was etched into her psyche. It had inhibited her from seeking out male company, too scared of rejection and irrationally scared of horrific revelation.

Sudden anger flared that Nic hadn't had to go through any of that…he'd blithely got on with his life. That anger galvanised Maddie to march up to him. She grabbed his shirt in her hands and pulled him down towards her.

Maddie searched blindly and inexpertly for his mouth, eyes shut tight against the reality of what she was doing, telling herself that she could divorce all emotion from this event.

For a long moment Nic seemed just to suffer under Maddie's gauche ministrations, and she nearly sobbed with frustration against his closed lips. Surely he must be realising how inexperienced she was? He couldn't be turned on by this?

But then he took control, and everything changed in an instant. Hard arms of steel wrapped around her, binding her to him like a vice. His mouth opened and grew hard, plundering hers with an expertise that awed her, his tongue tangling hotly with hers, forcing her head back onto his arms. Exposing her throat to him.

Everything within her was becoming languid and hot, while an urgent need clamoured for attention between her legs. Her breasts were swelling against the silk of her dress and her arms were crushed against Nic's chest.

When he finally pulled away she felt drunk. She couldn't open her eyes for a long moment. His hands came up and framed her face. She finally opened her eyes to see two blue oceans right in front of her. Two hot and stormy oceans.

His thumbs traced her cheekbones and then he dipped his head again to hers, his mouth touching more softly this time, teeth nipping gently at her lips, making them sting before soothing them. There was something so unexpectedly tender about this that Maddie could feel the bottom dropping out of the pit of her stomach.

It reminded her of when he'd been so gentle and seductive before…before it had all turned sour. She felt tears prick the backs of her eyes and desperately fought not to let them fall. Nic's mouth caressed and kissed her throat and shoulders, moving down. His hands dropped to her back, moulding her waist and hips, coming down to cup her buttocks through the silk of her dress, lifting her slightly so that his erection was cradled between her legs.

She gasped and tried to pull back, the intimate move suddenly shocking. But he wouldn't release her, those blue eyes blazing down into hers as he subtly moved his body back and forth against her until she was breathing rapidly and moving restlessly against him.

Hunger was rising in her, erasing thoughts of the past, gnawing and desperate. She nearly sobbed with relief when she felt him lower her down to the soft grass underneath the trees, following her. Now Nic loomed over her like a golden-haired god. Eyes devouring her, slipping down, taking in her chest rising and falling rapidly.

He lifted a hand and smoothed the back of it over the top of her bodice. Maddie sucked in a breath when his knuckles brushed the swell of her breast. He reached around underneath her back and found the zip. Maddie lifted slightly to help, sucking in a breath when she felt him pull it down as much as he could.

Slowly he peeled the dress down to expose one breast, and Maddie bit her lip, fighting the urge to cover herself. She could see Nic's cheeks become flushed, his pupils dilating, and a heady feminine energy rushed through her. He *wanted* her. Unconsciously she moved, so that her breast pushed forward, and the ghost of a small smile played around his mouth. Reverently he cupped and moulded the pale flesh, making Maddie close her eyes. A rough thumb rubbed back and forth over one tight, puckered peak.

She didn't even realise she'd said anything until she heard his throaty, 'What do you want?'

She opened her eyes. The lids felt heavy. 'I want...' *You,* she wanted to say, but she stopped. It felt so raw.

'Do you want me to taste you?'

He didn't wait for an answer. He looked feverish now, his eyes glittering fiercely, his big hand and long fingers still caressing her breast and making her want to shout out with frustration and pleasure all at once.

He came over her more fully, pressing her down into the ground, his erection feeling even bigger and harder now. He dipped his head and his mouth unerringly closed around that taut peak, and then Maddie did cry out. It was surrounded with fierce sucking heat. He was relentless, tugging it into his mouth, tongue swirling around it until it was so stiff and tight and sensitised that she cried out again, her hips moving restlessly against his.

Almost roughly Nic pulled down the bodice, fully exposing both breasts now, and paid homage to the other thrusting peak, driving Maddie mad with pleasure. Her head was thrashing back and forth, and she could feel one of Nic's hands move down and start to pull up her dress, bunching it around her thighs. She couldn't speak or think. She could only feel.

He shifted slightly and his fingers touched her where her panties felt damp between her legs. His head came up, and cool air whistled over the wet peak of her breast. Maddie was overheating.

She looked up to see Nic staring at her. His fingers started to move back and forth, pressing her panties against where she was so wet. She moaned. She felt so exposed and yet she craved it.

'You're ready for me, aren't you?'

Maddie nodded, feeling vulnerable all of a sudden. She felt as if she'd been ready for him for years. Aeons.

'Tell me how much you want me right now.'

Maddie couldn't think when he was touching her so intimately. She'd dreamt of this moment for so long and it was overwhelming now to be experiencing it. The words came out. She couldn't stop them. 'I want you, Nic...so much. I've always wanted you...'

His hand stilled for a moment. Maddie couldn't fathom the cynical look that crossed Nic's face.

'You'll say anything, won't you?'

She shook her head, nearly crying out when his hand and fingers started moving again, harder this time, as if he was angry and sensed her hunger. 'I don't—'

She gasped when she felt him slide one finger inside her panties, close to where the secret folds of her body hid the full extent of her desire and vulnerability.

'Yes...you do. But it doesn't matter any more. Nothing matters except this.'

And with a guttural growl he bent his head, his mouth finding hers in a drugging heady kiss while one finger thrust deep inside her damp heat, making her scream into his mouth. Now she was utterly exposed and undone. There was no going back, only forward.

Maddie was barely aware of her hands ripping at Nic's shirt. She only knew that she craved to see his chest, to feel it next to hers, rubbing against her breasts. And all the while his hand was between her legs, which were splayed outwards. One finger became two and Maddie nearly passed out. The pleasure was so intense.

And then he was tugging her panties down, taking his hand away for a moment, putting her legs together to undress her. Maddie felt feverish now. Hot all over.

His shirt was swinging open, his chest broad and tautly muscled. A smattering of dark golden hair covered his pectoral muscles and arrowed down to his pants in a tantalising and utterly masculine line. He sat back for a moment and she saw his hands come to his belt. With wide eyes she lay back and watched as he opened his pants, tore down his zip and yanked them down. His briefs were tented over a long and thick bulge. Maddie could feel nothing but intense excitement.

She vaguely heard foil ripping, and saw Nic's erection spring free as he ripped down his briefs. He rolled on a condom and came back over her, spreading her legs again to accommodate him as easily as if she were a pliable doll. Maddie was vaguely aware that her dress was bunched up around her waist and pulled down under her breasts. She didn't care.

Nic's hand was between her legs again and she cried out at the contact, her chest coming up into contact with Nic's. 'Please,' she sobbed. 'Please…do something.'

She didn't even know what to ask for. All she knew was that she needed *more*.

Nic shifted his weight onto his hands and Maddie's legs fell open wider. She could feel the thick blunt head of his penis as he started to push into her. Her muscles contracted at the alien invasion and her eyes grew wide. She knew she wanted this, needed it, but a sudden instinct that pain was inevitable seized her muscles.

Nic sank in some more, and pain hit like a steam train crashing into her chest. Maddie sucked in a shocked breath. The pain was white-hot.

Nic frowned and cursed softly. 'You're so tight…'

Instinctively, as if Maddie knew that the only way was to go through it, she arched up, forcing Nic to impale her a little more. She cried out at the shocking, rending pain. But her hands were on his buttocks and a fierce determination gripped her.

She looked up into Nic's eyes and saw the dawning understanding. '*Dios*, Maddie…you're not…?'

'Don't say it,' she said fiercely, feeling sweat break out on her brow. 'Don't you dare stop now.'

For a long moment tension gripped them both. The broad head of Nic's shaft was barely inside her and the pain was clearly devastating, but all he could see was her flushed cheeks and that stark determination in her eyes. So many things were hitting him at once, but the biggest one was a feeling of exhilaration. She was *his*. She would become his right now and no one else's.

He thought she'd been playing a part even when she'd told him how much she wanted him. This revelation smashed that assertion to pieces and left Nic spinning off in a direction he couldn't even begin to look at now.

Nic found some control from somewhere and gritted out painfully, 'This is going to hurt…but it won't last, I promise.'

Maddie looked up at him, tousled and flushed and beautiful. She bit her lip and said, 'Okay.'

The trust in her eyes nearly broke him in two, and with

sweat forming tiny beads on his chest Nic gritted his jaw and drove himself into her reluctant flesh. She cried out. Her hands gripped his buttocks fiercely and Nic nearly came right then at the feel of her body clamping so tightly around his.

She was crying in earnest, tears trickling out of her eyes, but still she was not pushing him away. Nic felt weak at her show of bravery. He put his forehead to hers and then pressed a kiss to her mouth. He could taste her salty tears and crooned softly, 'It's okay, *querida*, that's the worst bit…just try to relax…let me move and it'll feel better… I promise.'

Maddie felt light-headed from the pain, but there was something deep within her melting and reacting to Nic's tender words. Something that she'd shut away long ago coming to life again. She felt like a warrior. She wanted to embrace the pain with this man. She pressed a kiss to his shoulder, as if to tell him she trusted him. She couldn't speak.

Slowly she could feel her flesh adapting to his, relaxing ever so slightly from its tight grip around him. He sank in a little more—unbelievably. Eventually she could feel his pelvis snug against hers. And it didn't hurt as much. The pain was being replaced with sensations. Flutterings along nerve-ends.

Slowly Nic started to withdraw, and instinctively Maddie clutched at his tight buttocks as if to stop him. He pressed a kiss to her mouth, which felt swollen and bruised. 'No, sweetheart…trust me…let me go.'

Maddie relaxed her hold and he continued to slide out, so slowly that little exquisite shards of sensation started to flutter through her lower body. When he was almost entirely out he drove in again, and this time his passage was smoother, increasing those flutters.

Maddie's hips moved. She rolled them, forcing Nic to curse and say, 'Stop, Maddie…this is hard enough…I won't last…'

She stopped, in awe of his strength and size, and the extreme gentleness he was showing her. She tried to stay as still as possible as he taught her flesh and her body how to respond to him, but an urgency was building, the pain was being washed away by pleasure. A kind of pleasure she'd never felt before.

Digging her heels into the soft, fragrant earth beside his thighs, Maddie couldn't stop herself from moving—just as Nic's own movements became faster and more urgent. Blood was thundering through her body. Her heart hammered. She was straining, searching for something but she didn't know what.

She felt Nic put a hand between them—right there, near where he was driving in and out with relentless precision. Each thrust getting harder and faster and deeper.

Maddie wrapped her legs around his slim hips, deepening the penetration even more, just as his thumb found her sensitised clitoris and stroked it. Pleasure exploded with unstoppable force inside Maddie's whole body, radiating outwards from that thumb and his own driving flesh. It was like an endless wave, so breathtaking in its magnitude that Maddie was incoherent, bucking wildly beneath Nic as he ground himself into her and shouted out.

His whole body went taut for a long moment, every sinew and muscle locked. She could feel him pulsing and throbbing inside her, and then he was spent, and his whole weight came crashing down, crushing her to the ground.

Maddie wrapped her arms around him and knew in that moment that she loved Nic de Rojas. She'd never hated him. She couldn't. She'd fallen for him from a distance as a lovestruck teenager, and that had become a solid reality when she'd stood before him in this place all those years ago. Now…after giving herself to him completely…it was cemented deep in her cells for ever. And he would break her heart into tiny pieces even as he showed her paradise.

Maddie was barely aware of their journey home along the trail, lit now by moonlight. She was only aware that she was sitting within the cradle of Nic's strong hard thighs on his horse while he held the reins of her own, leading it home.

One arm was clamped around her waist, and she couldn't stop her head from sinking back into his chest as extreme lethargy washed through every bone and cell in her body.

Having Maddie sitting so close to where Nic still ached was a form of torture so delicious he never wanted it to end. His brain was reeling from an overload of pleasure more intense than anything he'd ever experienced or could have imagined. Even the memory of thrusting into Maddie's tight embrace had his libido raging again, and he had to grit his teeth to counteract it.

So many thoughts were vying for dominance. But one superceded them all. *She'd been a virgin.* She hadn't slept with Morales. Even though deep down Nic had believed her, there'd been a tiny part of him unwilling to give up a kernel of doubt. As if the minute he trusted her she'd laugh in his face.

She'd given herself to him more passionately and unself-consciously than the most experienced woman he'd ever bedded. He'd never forget that blazing look of trust when she'd been in such pain but had not shied away from it. She'd embraced it like a pagan warrior.

He'd only become aware afterwards that he'd still been half dressed. His trousers had been around his ankles and he'd bunched her dress around her waist. He'd been like an animal in heat.

Everything was spinning out of Nic's control. His chest felt too full. And yet he couldn't stop his arm from tightening around her even more, or the exultation that whispered through him when her soft breath sighed over his skin.

Maddie only came to again when she sensed she was being carried in Nic's arms through the quiet house. She could barely lift her head. That delicious lethargy was weighing everything down, including her mind, where dangerous thoughts hovered. Everything was still and hushed and quiet.

Maddie looked up to see the stark planes of Nic's face above her. Without thinking about what she was doing, she reached up and cupped his strong jaw. She could feel him grit it against her hand.

Then she heard a door hit a wall, and she was being carried into a dimly lit and unashamedly masculine room. Nic's bedroom. Once again sanity hovered on the edge of her consciousness, but Maddie was a coward. It was as if they were in a bubble and she couldn't bear for the bubble to burst yet.

Nic put her down gently on the side of the bed and Maddie winced when sensitive flesh came in contact with the soft surface.

Immediately Nic was crouching at face level. 'Are you sore?'

Maddie felt inexplicably shy and blushed. 'A little… but it's fine.'

Just looking at him now was making blood rush back to all her extremities. Making her *want* all over again.

Nic pressed a swift kiss to her mouth, and then said, 'Give me one minute and I'll make you feel better.'

She watched speechlessly as he stood up and strode towards the bathroom. She only noticed then that she had all but ripped his shirt off like some demented madwoman. Her heart swelled in her chest, and once again she blocked those dangerous tendrils of reality from intruding.

Nic was back and coming towards her, stripping off his ruined shirt, revealing that huge expanse of glorious, hard-muscled chest. Maddie's insides clenched down low. Lord, he was even more beautiful than she'd thought.

He reached for her and, as if she was full of magnets aligning themselves only to him, she was effortlessly swept into his arms. She curled up tight against his chest, relishing the profound sense of protection in his embrace.

Steam was building up in the bathroom and Maddie could hear the shower running. Gently Nic let her down, and she found her legs to be ridiculously wobbly. They got even worse when he pulled her zip down and tried to pull down her grass-stained dress over her breasts. Instinctively Maddie's hands came up. She looked up into wry blue eyes.

'Don't you think it's a little late for modesty?'

Maddie tried to smile but it felt brittle. Slowly Nic took her hands away and peeled the dress down. Maddie's cheeks flamed. His eyes devoured her hungrily and she watched as he lifted his hands to cup the full mounds of pale flesh. She bit her lip when she felt her nipples responding, growing tight with need again.

In an instant Nic's hands had dropped and he stepped away, saying gutturally, 'I can't stop touching you...'

Acting on instinct, Maddie stepped forward and lifted his hands to cup her flesh again. 'I like it... Don't stop.'

His eyes met hers, and they were blazing. She could feel his hands tremble slightly and a wave of tenderness washed over her.

Nic spoke abruptly, taking his hands away. 'No…if I start now…'

'I won't have you on the floor of the bathroom.'

He quickly dispensed with her dress and his own clothes, and then led her into the huge shower stall and under the powerful spray. Maddie let her head drop back as the water cascaded down, and murmured luxuriously when she felt Nic's soapy hands running all over her.

By the time he was done she was leaning weakly against the wall of the shower and begging him to stop.

With stark need stamped on his face he handed her the soap and said, 'Your turn.'

Lord.

Maddie took the soap and lathered up. Nic rested his hands high, either side of her head, so that he formed a cage around her, and gave her his body. As Maddie smoothed soapy hands over his shoulders and down his chest her eyes grew wide. And when she got lower and saw the proud jutting swell of his erection they got wider. Fascinated, she wrapped one slick soapy hand around him and exulted in his sharply indrawn breath. He was all silky skin encasing pure steel.

As much to distract herself as anything else, she ordered him to turn around and he muttered, 'Spoilsport.'

Maddie faced his back and lifted her hands, but they stilled in horror when she saw the lurid white lines slashing across his powerful muscles. They extended from his neck down to his waist.

As if he'd just realised what she was looking at, he whipped around so fast her head spun.

She felt sick as she looked up into his white face. 'What are those marks?'

He just looked at her for a long moment and said nothing, but he reached for the control and switched the shower off. He stepped out and hitched a towel around his waist, handed her one. She took it wordlessly, a chill skating over her skin.

She stepped out and briskly rubbed her hair, before putting the towel around her own body and following him into his room. He was standing at his window, arms folded, looking outwards. Maddie stopped uncertainly. This was completely uncharted territory.

'Nic?'

She could see his muscles tense even more, and those scars stood out in vivid relief. She had a flashback to that moment eight years before, when his father's men had had to beat him to get him to come with them, and dread turned her blood to ice. She forced her legs to move and stood in front of him. She looked up.

'It happened that day, didn't it? Those men…they beat you?'

Nic was looking resolutely above Maddie's head and his jaw was clenched. Her heart ached.

'What do you care?' he asked coolly.

All signs of passion were gone. Rejection emanated from every tense line in his body. He'd never been more remote. Exactly as he had been that day when she'd gone back and seen him…and hadn't been able to hide her horror.

Maddie was in turmoil. 'I just…I want to know what happened…'

He looked down at her then, and his eyes were like two ice chips. She shivered.

He raised a brow. 'You *really* want to know the sordid details?'

CHAPTER NINE

MADDIE nodded even as her heart thumped. They couldn't be any more sordid than what she'd been through in the aftermath of that cataclysmic afternoon.

Nic's voice was devoid of any expression. 'My father's men brought me back to the house, where they informed him of who I'd been found with and what we'd been doing. My father was angrier than I've ever seen him. He brought me out to the yard in the middle of the stables and ordered the men to hold me down so he could whip me.'

Maddie just looked at Nic. All she could see in her mind's eye was his face when she'd seen him the following day...before he'd turned so icy and cruel. He'd been pale. He must have been in agony, yet he'd come back... to see her. Perhaps he hadn't meant those cruel words he'd uttered? Perhaps he'd just been protecting himself against her extreme reaction.

The revelation made Maddie feel weak inside even as Nic continued in that toneless voice, 'With the benefit of hindsight I can see how making love to his own ex-lover's daughter must have pushed a button or two, though I didn't know that then.'

Maddie started to tremble violently, unable to expunge from her mind the horrific image of him being whipped.

And all because of what they'd done so innocently. The ripples had been catastrophic.

Nic caught her expression. 'You don't have to put on a horrified act, Maddie. I would have thought you'd appreciate the melodrama our actions inspired. Isn't that what you were looking for to alleviate your boredom?'

Melodrama! Boredom! Maddie nearly cried out loud. He had no idea. He'd been horsewhipped. Because of *her*. Maddie couldn't stop her emotions from boiling over. She put a hand over her mouth and fled for the bathroom, just making it to the toilet in time, where she retched over the toilet bowl.

She felt his presence behind her and begged weakly, 'Just leave me alone. Please.'

His voice sounded tight. 'No. Let me help…'

Before Maddie could protest she was being lifted up and a cool wet cloth was being pressed to her face. Nic handed her some toothpaste on a brush and she brushed her teeth. When she was done he took her hand and led her back to the bedroom. Maddie pulled her hand free from his and sat on the edge of the bed.

Nic stood apart and looked down at her, his expression guarded. 'You're an enigma, Madalena Vasquez. You set out to tease me years ago, and when I tell you what happened to me it makes you physically ill.'

His jaw clenched then, as if he was remembering something, and Maddie could see him start to retreat. She knew exactly what he was remembering: her cruel words. She desperately wanted to erase them for ever.

Huskily she said, 'I never set out to tease you, Nic, or to humiliate you. I promise on my father's life I had no plan, no agenda. When you followed me that first day I was terrified—but exhilarated. I wanted you…but I would never have set out to seduce you just for fun.' Her voice grew husky. 'That week... It meant something to me.'

Nic reached out and caught her arms in his hands, pulled her up to face him. He bit out through a clenched jaw, 'Don't try and rewrite history, Maddie. You seduced me because you were bored. That week was a diversion— nothing more.'

Maddie shook her head. 'No,' she whispered. 'It wasn't. I *wanted* to see you again.'

She felt herself teetering on the edge of a precipice. At the last moment she knew she couldn't tell him everything, so she'd furnish him with half a truth. She took a shaky breath. 'When we were discovered that day and I was taken home, my mother was livid. We had a huge fight and she told me about the affair she'd had with your father... My father overheard...'

Maddie comforted herself that what she was saying wasn't a complete fabrication; she was just ommitting certain information.

She went on, 'When I saw you the next day I couldn't tell you about the affair. It was too sordid. I was ashamed, and I was afraid of what would happen if they thought I was still seeing you. I had to make you leave, so I said the most hurtful things I could think of, but they weren't true...'

Maddie felt more exposed than she'd ever felt. She'd just revealed her heart to him. She looked away, terrified he'd see the emotion, see the lie in her eyes. What she *wasn't* telling him. The darker truth.

He released her and tipped up her chin, spearing her with that laser like gaze. 'Before your father came a few weeks after that, and my mother and I found out about the affair, I'd always assumed you and your mother left so quickly because you wanted to get away from here—and *me*.'

Maddie shook her head, her heart aching at the thought of how Nic had interpreted events. She suddenly felt sick again. Maybe Nic already *knew* the awful thing she'd carried with her for so long?

Hesitantly she asked, 'What did my father say to your parents, exactly?'

Nic stepped back, raking a hand through his hair impatiently. His whole body radiated tension. 'It was my mother he wanted to speak to.' He smiled bitterly. 'After all, my father already knew. My father was away that day. I just remember finding her hysterical, ranting about your mother and my father together. I had to get the doctor and he sedated her. A couple of days later she took an overdose of pills and left a note telling my father that she knew everything. It was bad enough having found *us* together, but after my mother's suicide the old enmity was truly alive and well again. Father's rage eventually led to his own heart attack…'

Maddie's stomach churned. It didn't sound as if his mother had elaborated on *everything*. If her father *had* told Nic's mother the full ugly truth she must have taken the information to her grave. Maybe it had been too horrific to comprehend. There was no way Nic's father wouldn't have used that information for his own ends to get back at her father or his son, she suspected, if he'd known.

Maddie couldn't help herself from reaching out to touch Nic's arm. 'I'm so sorry.'

Nic smiled, but it was tight and bitter. 'My mother wasn't exactly stable at the best of times. She most likely suffered from something clinical, like bipolar disorder, but it was never diagnosed. It didn't take much to push her over the edge.'

Maddie felt as if she was treading on eggshells. 'It must have been hard growing up with that…inconsistency.'

Nic emitted a curt laugh and pulled back from Maddie's touch. Her hand dropped ineffectually.

'You could say that. If Father wasn't trying to toughen up his runt of a son, Mother was weeping silently in a corner.'

Maddie's heart clenched at hearing Nic refer to his physical weakness again. Galvanised by something she couldn't name, Maddie said with a touch of defiance, 'Yet you overcame it and proved him wrong…'

Something bleak crossed Nic's face. 'Even then he couldn't respect me. I think it angered him to know that I'd prevailed.' Nic's mouth twisted. 'It just meant that he had to get his men to hold me down to thrash me. He no longer had the satisfaction alone.'

Maddie felt tears spring into her eyes. She'd had no idea he'd been so brutalised by his father.

Nic must have seen the brightness in her eyes and he quickly closed the distance between them, hauling her body into his.

A huge lump was in Maddie's throat, an ache in her chest. Nic looked ferocious.

'I think it's time we stopped talking and remembered what this evening is about…'

Nic's mouth was on Maddie's before she could respond. Tears were running down her face, but he was ruthless, intent on sucking her back under to a place where no words were needed. Maddie eventually gave in, her arms snaking around Nic's neck and the ache in her heart intensifying even as the tears eventually dried on her cheeks and her sobs of emotion became sobs of need and want under Nic's masterful touch.

* * *

When Maddie woke the following morning it took a long time for her to register where she was and what had happened. Her body ached, but pleasurably. Between her legs she was tender and slightly sore.

Maddie groaned. It all came back. The dress; the dinner; the orchard…and back here in Nic's room. She opened her eyes wider and looked around. She wasn't in Nic's room, in his bed any more. Even though dawn had been breaking outside when she'd finally fallen asleep.

He must have brought her back here, to the room she'd been shown into yesterday evening. Immediately Maddie felt vulnerable at the thought of Nic depositing her here while she slept, as if he was done with her. As if he couldn't bear to be with her for a moment longer. And with sick realization, Maddie knew why. He had to resent her for making him open up, for telling her what he had. He'd been through so much. The thought of him returning to the orchard that last day with his back ripped apart from a whip made her want to cry all over again.

A knock sounded on the door, making her flinch. Maddie squeaked something, half terrified it might be Nic—she wasn't ready to see him. Not when she was feeling so emotional. But it was the same girl who'd shown her to the dining room the previous evening. Relief flooded Maddie when she came in with a breakfast tray.

Maddie sat up, acutely self-conscious of her nakedness under the sheet. The girl put the tray on a table and then said shyly, 'I have a message from Mr de Rojas—he says that he will see you at your home this afternoon.'

The contract.

Maddie felt a hard ball lodge in her belly. She thanked the girl and when she'd left got shakily out of the bed, wrapping a towel around her. She went to the window and looked out. The view took in the eastern slopes of Nic's vineyard, with the snow-capped Andes mountains in the distance. It was stunning.

And then she saw him, striding down a row of vines in the distance. She shrank back, even though there was no way he could see her from where he was. But in that moment he looked up in her direction. Maddie ducked, her heart beating furiously. Humiliation burnt her up inside as she huddled there pathetically.

He couldn't even be bothered to come and tell her himself. The night was over. He'd got what he wanted, which was to see her as exposed and rejected as she had made him feel all those years before. If he had felt anything for her once, it was long gone.

Nic cursed himself for looking up at Maddie's bedroom window, and for fancying for a second that he might have seen her. She'd been dead to the world when he'd left her in the bed, her pale skin marked and lightly bruised from where he'd gripped her in the throes of passion.

Even now his blood rushed south, hardening his body, and he cursed out loud. He ripped a grape off the vine and bit into it, wincing slightly. Eduardo, his head winemaker, was looking at him, and Nic suddenly needed to be alone.

He said curtly, 'Another couple of days before we pick these. I'll find you later to check the others.'

Eduardo took the hint and nodded, walking away, and Nic breathed out a sigh of relief. His head was so tangled and snarled up since last night. Maddie was the first woman he'd fallen asleep with, whose touch he'd instinctively sought, wrapping his body around hers as if loath to let her go. *That* more than anything else had galvanised him into bringing her back to her own room to put some space between them.

He hungered for her even more acutely now that he'd

tasted every bit of her. Another first. Usually his desire was dented very quickly.

Last night had veered off the tracks in a big way the moment Maddie had stood up from the dinner table and started taking off the jewellery and shoes. And then…the orchard. Even now Nic could remember the panic he'd felt when he'd realised that was her intention. And yet at the same time something had resonated deep inside him—a need to get out of the falsely polite structure he'd insisted on with the dinner.

When he'd seen her standing among those trees it had felt terrifying, but completely right. As if there could be no other place for them to seek closure, no matter how exposed it made him feel. But all of that had fallen away as soon as he'd started kissing her. And when he'd discovered her innocence…

Nic's insides turned molten even now. She'd been a virgin. She was his and no one else's.

Nic hadn't even realised his hand was full of grapes until he felt the sticky juice oozing between his fingers. He looked at his hand and saw that it was trembling slightly. He recalled the tears in Maddie's eyes when he'd told her about his parents. That effortless feeling of affinity she'd evoked. Exactly as she had once before…

Past and present were meshing dangerously.

Sleeping with Maddie last night should have been a clinical exercise, and it had been anything but. It had morphed into something completely different. It proved to him how dangerous she was—how easily she slipped under his guard and elicited information from him. Exactly as she'd done before.

Even what she'd told him about *her* version of events that week was too huge for him to digest right now. It put a spin on things that threatened everything.

For a moment Nic felt panic steal over him—a completely alien emotion. And then he remembered the contract. Relief flooded him. The contract put a boundary around last night and around *him*. And more importantly it put a boundary around Maddie, keeping her at a distance from Nic.

Maddie was operating at a level of numbness which was working very well for her. She was blocking out the previous night's events, and if some lurid images snuck through her ironclad defences she closed her eyes and meditated on something else until they disappeared.

It was lonely in the house without Hernan and Maria. She'd spoken to Hernan on the phone earlier and had been devastated to learn that Maria would need an operation. Maddie had told Hernan to stay with Maria for as long as he needed. They were hoping that the operation would take place the following week.

Feeling restless, and not looking forward to a visit from a triumphant Nic with the contract, Maddie set out to check the cellars. She needed to start making an inventory of the things she needed. No doubt Nic would expect her to be well prepared for when his funds became available now that they'd be on a purely business footing.

Maddie felt no great sense of excitement that her estate was going to receive an injection of funds. It all felt flat now, meaningless.

When she remembered how she'd felt in Nic's arms last night in the orchard—the wave of love that had come over her—she assured herself that it was just because he'd been her first lover. Heightened emotion.

Maddie resolutely forced Nic from her mind yet again, and concentrated on making notes. More time had passed than she'd realised when she noticed that she was stiff from bending over and squinting at barrel labels. She'd been hoping that she might find a hidden gem of a barrel full of untouched wine, but no such luck.

Then she heard a distinctly bad-tempered-sounding *'Maddie!'*

For a perverse moment Maddie considered hiding among the barrels, as she and her brother had used to do when they'd been small, but she squared her shoulders and called out, 'Down here.'

She heard him before she saw him, and already her skin was tingling and she was remembering—and biting her lip trying *not* to remember. And then he appeared, in a loose shirt and jeans, hair dishevelled, looking so gorgeous that her lower body instantly grew hot and tingly.

Maddie couldn't speak, but it appeared Nic had enough to say for both of them. He strode towards her, eyes flashing with displeasure. 'How the hell does anyone know where to find you? Why don't you have a mobile phone? You could have been anywhere on the estate—'

He broke off and came closer, eyes sparking down into Maddie's, and to her utter chagrin she felt ridiculously emotional and close to tears.

'Well, I'm here, as you can see.' Maddie hated that she was so raw.

Nic seemed to temper his own response. 'I couldn't find you. I looked all over the estate... If anything happened to you—if you fell and sprained an ankle or anything...' He stopped and cursed. 'I need to know where you are.'

Maddie's treacherous heart leapt at *'I need to know where you are'*, but just as quickly she ruthlessly drove down that insidious emotion.

She stepped back and said coolly, 'Let's not pretend you're actually concerned, Nic. You just don't have time to spend looking for a business associate. Did you bring the contract?'

Nic seemed to blanch before her eyes, but then colour rushed swiftly back. His response surprised her, but he seemed to control himself. 'Yes, I did. It's upstairs in your father's study.'

Nic let Maddie precede him out of the cellar, and used the opportunity to get himself back under control. All of his earlier assurances had died a quick death when he'd come to the estate and hadn't been able to find any trace of Maddie anywhere. Panic had escalated as he'd imagined her lying somewhere, helpless. With so much out-of-date machinery in this place anything was possible.

And then, when he had found her, the relief had been overwhelming.

By the time he was following her into her father's study Nic was firmly back in control. He watched as Maddie sat down and pulled the contract towards her. She scanned it briefly and looked up at him with that cool expression on her face. It made Nic's blood boil and his loins ache. He wanted to see her undone again. Right now.

'Hernan won't be back for a few days. I'll have to wait till he gets here to go over this.'

Nic saw Maddie's throat work, the slight pink colour suffusing her skin. *Good.* She wasn't as cool as she looked, after all.

Nic dragged his attention from Maddie's physical response. 'I heard about Maria earlier. She's receiving the best of care, and the physician is confident it's a routine enough operation. He doesn't envisage any complications.'

Maddie said carefully, 'That's good… But this will have to wait until Hernan is back. I can't bother him with it now.'

Nic felt something like relief flow through his system.

A reprieve. He suddenly hated that damn contract. He conveniently pushed aside the memory of the panic he'd felt that morning. All he wanted was Maddie.

Maddie did not like the look on Nic's face as he prowled closer to the heavy oak desk. He put his hands down on top of it and said throatily, 'That's absolutely fine with me. But until the agreement is signed this isn't over.'

Maddie gulped, all pretence of insouciance fleeing. 'What isn't over?'

Nic came around the table and tugged Maddie out of the chair so she was standing flush against his body.

'This.'

And he wrapped his arms around her and pulled her so tightly into him that her curves melded into his hard muscles like the pieces of a jigsaw. Maddie made her hands into fists and hit out ineffectually, but Nic's mouth was on her jaw and trailing hot kisses down her neck to where the pulse was thumping out of her skin.

She groaned weakly. 'Nic...*no.*'

Nic's answer was to bend and lift her into his arms, making her squeal. He looked at her. 'Where's your room?'

Maddie was torn, already breathing heavily, her whole body aching for this man's touch. She knew a thousand and one reasons why she shouldn't do this, and yet the moment seemed fragile and illusory, as if it was a dream. There was a lightness between them for the first time.

'Upstairs, second door on the right.'

Nic's face was grim, but the heat in his eyes mesmerised Maddie. She hated herself for being so weak.

When Nic brought her into the sparsely furnished room with its plain double bed everything seemed to fall away. Past, present and future. There was only now, and this crazy, unexpected reprieve. She could recognise now that she was relieved that she hadn't signed the contract yet. Until she did she was a free woman—not beholden to Nic de Rojas.

Nic was opening the buttons on her shirt, and Maddie lifted her hands to do the same to his. Nic pushed her shirt off her shoulders and down her arms. His went the same way. Nic reached around and tugged Maddie's hair free of its band, so that it fell around her shoulders. In an endearingly gentle moment he spread his fingers through the silky strands of her hair, hands cupping her head, massaging it gently. He tipped her face up to his and something inside Maddie quivered ominously.

'This isn't over...not yet...'

And then Nic was kissing her, drugging her. With deft hands he unfastened her bra, letting it follow their shirts to the floor. Then he was cupping both breasts in his hands, massaging their firmness, trapping her nipples in his fingers, making Maddie moan into his mouth.

He took his mouth from hers and lifted one voluptuous breast so that he could swirl his tongue around the hard tip. His arm had come around her back, supporting her, arching her into him. Maddie's hands were in Nic's hair, mussing it up.

When he deposited her on the bed and opened her jeans she lifted her hips to help him. Her knickers disappeared too, but Maddie didn't have time to be embarrassed. She was too hot, waiting impatiently for Nic to finish taking off his own clothes, revealing his impressively taut body.

Maddie breathed in, sighing with deep-seated pleasure when Nic came down beside her. One hand pushed her thighs apart so that he could stroke with his fingers where she ached most.

Maddie couldn't have articulated a coherent thought

even if she'd wanted to. By the time Nic had donned protection and was pushing into her hot moist core, Maddie knew she would take this for as long as it lasted. And deal with the fallout later.

When Maddie woke much later it was dark outside. She was alone in the bed, and instantly cold when she recalled what had happened. Within minutes of seeing Nic again they'd been in bed. That had *never* been a part of the plan. It was meant to be one night and then she'd sign the contract…except she remembered now that she hadn't signed it. Guilty relief curled through her. It was as if they could ignore the inevitable for as long as the contract didn't exist. But Maddie knew that as soon as it was signed everything would change.

She tensed when she heard a faint noise from downstairs. The kitchen was two floors below her room, but the sounds sometimes carried up. She got out of bed and pulled on her jeans and shirt, smoothing her hair as best she could.

Creeping downstairs, she heard tuneless whistling as she got closer to the kitchen. She stopped at the door and her jaw dropped at the sight before her. Nic was in his shirt, which was buttoned up wrong, and the low-slung jeans with the top button still open, deftly tossing pancakes. His jaw was dark with stubble.

He spotted her and stopped whistling. 'How do you like yours?' he asked. 'With cream or chocolate or strawberries?'

Maddie went in and felt as if she was in some kind of twilight zone. Faintly she said, 'Where did you get all this stuff?'

Nic answered easily. 'I went out.'

Maddie looked at him, aghast. 'What time is it? How long was I asleep?'

Nic consulted his watch. 'It's nine p.m. and you were out for about four hours.'

Maddie blanched. 'You should have woken me.' She looked away, not wanting him to read in her expression or her eyes that she was relieved to see him still here.

Lightly he said, 'You looked far too peaceful.'

What Nic was thinking was that he didn't like how much he wanted to see the delicate purplish signs of fatigue gone from under Maddie's eyes. When he'd woken it had taken all of his restraint not to wake her with a kiss, or pull her back into his hardening body.

He'd come downstairs, and when he'd seen the pitiful state of affairs in the kitchen guilt had swamped him. He'd gone shopping for the first time in years. And as he'd shopped Nic had realised that for the first time in a long time he felt unaccountably lighter.

Without the contract between them Nic had seen a barrier being removed. They could continue this affair... because surely after another couple of nights he'd get that familiar sense of ennui and be able to move on from her?

Nic's jaw clenched now as he acknowledged that if anything his hunger for Maddie was only sharper. He could smell their mingled scent in the air and it was like the headiest of perfumes. Suddenly he wanted to swipe all the ingredients and shopping off the counter and take Maddie there and then.

Maddie sat down gingerly on a stool and watched Nic prepare another pancake. He'd already prepared about six. Half jokingly she said, 'How many are coming to dinner?'

He looked up, and Maddie felt speared by the intensity of his gaze. He smiled a crooked smile. 'I used to make tons of these when I worked in the vineyards in France during a European summer. We had to take it in turns to cook…communal living,' he explained. 'I was doing my Master of Wine course.'

Maddie shook her head. 'That's such an achievement. Your father must have been proud of that…' When Maddie saw Nic tense she cursed herself inwardly. But he spoke after a moment.

'He died just after I got my results. He didn't appear to be impressed.'

Maddie felt exposed at this acknowledgement of the lack of love he'd faced from his own father. Something that was all too familiar to her.

'So, have you made your mind up yet?'

She saw him hold up a jar of chocolate spread in one hand and a carton of cream in the other. To Maddie's intense shock, because she'd never thought of herself as an erotically minded person, she immediately had a vision of Nic putting some chocolate spread on her nipple and then licking it off.

Cheeks flaming, she blurted out, 'Cream and strawberries. Please.'

Nic just looked at her with a knowing glint in his eye and put the chocolate down, saying, 'Maybe you'll try that one later.'

Completely mortified, Maddie said nothing, and waited for Nic to serve her a pancake oozing with cream and strawberries. He handed her a glass of sparkling clear wine and Maddie took a sip, letting the effervescence take her far, far away from the reality that this was very finite and all too transitory.

'Nic, what is this? What are we doing?'

Nic closed his eyes momentarily, as if that might help block out the memory of Maddie's husky voice a short

while before. He'd just pulled on his jeans and shirt and
turned around to see Maddie resting back on her elbows
in the bed, looking deliciously tousled and flushed. The
sheet had barely hidden the curves of her breasts and inevitably, even though so recently sated, his body had started
to hum with energy and renewed desire.

Who was he kidding? Here in his Jeep, driving away,
it was still humming.

Three days had passed now. Three days and heady
nights when time had seemed to blur and lose focus as
soon as Nic drove into the gates of the Vasquez estate.
He had gone there each day, ostensibly to talk to Maddie
about what she wanted to do with the vineyard, but as soon
as he saw her they inevitably ended up in bed. The desire
between them was insatiable.

Damn, damn, damn, damn. Nic hit his fist off the steering wheel.

Maddie was under his skin, in his blood. In the very
place he'd wanted to keep her out, and in a place no other
woman had got close to. Since that week in the orchard,
when he'd come so close to allowing himself to be emotionally vulnerable for the first time in his life, he'd kept
his heart closed off to everyone around him. He'd learnt
his lesson and he'd learnt it well.

Despite that, Nic knew he had to revise his whole memory of what had happened eight years ago. Maddie had
been innocent—not even aware of her own power. Yet
her words still stung. The vehemence with which she'd
uttered them was still vivid and the way she'd been physically sick when he'd touched her. But he had to concede
now that perhaps it had just been overwrought teenage
dramatics in the aftermath of hearing the bombshell news
of her mother's affair.

Her words resounded in his head again like a taunt: *'Nic, what is this? What are we doing?'*

He'd gone back over to Maddie in the bed and taken her face in his hands, pressing a long, lingering kiss to her mouth. When his heart had begun thundering and he'd known he was fast hurtling towards the point of no return he'd pulled back and said, 'Until the contract is signed, *this* is what we're doing.'

She'd stiffened and pulled at the sheet, forcing Nic to stand up.

'And then it's over—just like that?'

Nic had looked down into those wide green eyes and seen something that had made him profoundly nervous. It was a reflection of himself as a younger man, laying himself bare for ridicule. He couldn't go back there—not for anyone.

He'd spoken past a huge constriction in his chest. 'It can't be anything else...not if you want this investment.'

Maddie had paled, but then she'd looked him dead in the eye. 'I just wanted to be sure there was no confusion.'

Suddenly Nic had felt anger rise at her coolness. He'd bent and pressed another kiss to her mouth, only satisfied when she gave a helpless little mewling sound revealing her lack of control.

He'd stood back from the bed. 'I'll be back later, to go over some business details with you.'

With defiance evident in her voice, Maddie had said, 'I'm going into the clinic to see Maria this afternoon. Her operation has been brought forward to tomorrow.'

'Well, then,' Nic had gritted out, 'I'll come and get you and we can go together—after we've discussed business.'

Nic was well aware that once Maria's operation was over and she was in recovery, Hernan would come back to

Villarosa and look over the contract. And Maddie would sign. And this edgy truce between them would be over.

Because Madalena Vasquez was linked to too many emotions and memories for it to become anything else.

CHAPTER TEN

MADDIE felt a vibrating in her jeans pocket, took out the mobile phone Nic had given her, and scowled at it before answering.

All she heard was an autocratic, 'Where are you?' and instantly her insides were melting and blood was rushing to the sensitive parts of her body.

She gritted her jaw. 'I'm at the vats.'

She ended the connection, feeling very shaky. She had been ever since that morning, when Nic had laid it out so baldly—that this affair would last only until the contract was signed and then return to a platonic business relationship. It should be making her feel happy. Surely she wasn't naive enough to think it could be anything else?

Maddie knew that for her own sanity she should be grateful. There was too much history between them. The feud might not exist any more but it had wreaked too much havoc to be healed by them alone...

She sighed now, and nearly jumped out of her skin when she heard a soft, 'Don't fall in.'

Maddie whirled around to see Nic on the catwalk. She'd been so engrossed that she hadn't even heard his Jeep, or his arrival on the steel catwalk. She turned away, scared he'd see how raw she felt. 'I did fall in once...when I was about nine.'

She heard Nic gasp audibly. 'How on earth did that happen?'

Maddie smiled wryly. 'I was playing hide-and-seek with Alvaro, my brother. Hernan was here, helping with the hand-plunging. I was fascinated and leant over too far to have a look…and fell in. Luckily Hernan fished me out again straight away.'

Maddie touched her head and looked at Nic with a wry smile. 'He managed to catch my hair…I was more upset by the pain than by the fact that I could have drowned in fermenting red wine.' She dropped her hand. 'Hernan brought me home and he and Maria cleaned me up. They never told my parents…' Maddie shuddered lightly. 'If they had, my father would have locked me in my room for a week with no food.'

Nic's voice was tight. 'Did he do that a lot?'

Maddie shrugged and picked at some flaking pieces on the huge and now empty vat. 'Sometimes…if something angered him. It was more frequent after Alvaro died. He was an angry man…angry that he had a useless daughter who he couldn't pass his legacy on to.'

Suddenly conscious that she'd been babbling, Maddie changed the subject abruptly. 'These vats are in need of serious upgrading. Father got them in because he wanted to go back to concrete tanks.'

Maddie looked at Nic when he didn't say anything straight away. Then, to her relief, he said, 'We can get rid of them if you like and go back to steel. It depends on which you think is best…'

Maddie followed Nic back down to ground level and they spent the next hour discussing the various merits of upgrading the current facilities or replacing everything with the most up-to-date modern equivalent.

By the time they were on their way to the clinic in Mendoza, Maddie was feeling far more under control.

That control became shakier, though, when she witnessed Nic's concern for Maria and his insistence that she receive the best of care. He was going out of his way for people who hadn't even been his own employees.

Maddie was largely silent on their way back to Villarosa, after leaving a worried but valiantly optimistic Hernan at his wife's bedside. She wasn't prepared when Nic asked, 'What made your father change his mind?'

Half absently she said, 'About what?'

'He threw you and your mother out, turned his back on you. So why did he suddenly leave it all to you?'

Maddie tensed in her seat and Nic looked at her. For a long moment she couldn't speak. All she could think of was that awful afternoon and the horrific things she'd learnt. Feeling bile rise, she blurted out, 'Stop the car, please…'

Nic pulled over into an empty layby that was near a local beauty spot lookout, with the Andes rising majestically in the far distance. But Maddie was oblivious. She stumbled out, feeling as if a huge weight was bearing down on her.

Nic got out too and touched her shoulder. 'Maddie, what is it?'

Maddie jerked back, her eyes wide.

Nic felt Maddie jerk back. She was so pale, and her eyes were…horrorstruck. *Déjà vu* slammed into him. She'd looked at him like that before. She'd flinched like that when he'd touched her.

She spoke thickly. 'There's something…you don't know. Something else that happened after we…after we were caught.'

She whirled around and faced out to the view. They were the only people there, and it was quiet.

Nic felt his insides constricting, growing tight. As if to ward off a blow.

Through a tight jaw he asked, 'What don't I know?'

Maddie stared unseeingly at the view. 'I don't want to tell you,' she said in a low voice.

She felt Nic put his hand on her shoulder again and pull her round to face him. He dropped his hand then, as if loath to touch her, and a sense of inevitability washed over Maddie. Perhaps she did owe him the full explanation? This would bring them full circle.

'Tell me *what*, Maddie?'

Still some part of her resisted. 'I never told you because at first I couldn't. And then…then I didn't want you to have the awful blackness of it in your head, poisoning you like it did me.'

Nic shook his head, obviously completely confused. And then he looked grim. 'Maddie, we're not leaving here until you tell me what this is about.'

Maddie looked around. She felt weak all of a sudden, and went over to sit on the low wall.

Nic's hands were in his pockets. He just looked down at her.

She started hesitantly. 'I didn't tell you everything that happened when I got back to my house…after we were caught. I did start to have a fight with my mother as I told you…she was livid.'

Nic took his hands out of his pockets and folded his arms. 'Go on.'

Maddie focused on a point in the middle distance and drew in a deep breath. 'She told me that I wasn't to see you again, and I told her that she couldn't stop me.' Maddie looked at Nic then, and said softly, 'I wanted to see you again… But then she started to tell me about the affair. I didn't know what it had to do with *us* and I tried to walk out…but then she told me something else…'

Keeping her eyes on his, Maddie relayed to Nic the full extent of what her mother had told her.

'That's why I couldn't see you again…and my father had overheard every word.'

Nic felt as if he'd been punched in the gut. He looked at Maddie stupidly. And then he felt nauseous. It burned its way up, held down only by extreme strength of will.

Maddie stood up, seeing the reaction on Nic's face. 'When we went to Buenos Aires my mother agreed to get a DNA sample from my father. He gave it to her with the proviso that she would get nothing from the divorce. I got the test done and found out that I am…*was* his daughter. But of course it was too late to tell you any of this. Too much had happened. I was still traumatised by the possibility…' Maddie stopped and swallowed painfully. 'I sent a letter to my father, but never heard from him until just before he died.'

Colour was beginning to seep back into Nic's cheeks. He uncrossed his arms and ran a hand through his hair. He couldn't look at her, and Maddie felt it like the sting of a whip.

'My God, Maddie.' Nic went and stood at the low wall and looked out over the view.

Maddie turned to face the same way. She couldn't look at Nic. She bit her lip so hard she could taste blood. 'That last day…I didn't even realise I'd headed for the orchard until I got there. That's why when I saw you I reacted the way I did. How could I have told you what my mother had put in my head? It was too horrific.'

Nic sounded grim. 'Your father must have told my mother. It has to be the reason she took such a drastic step.'

Maddie nodded. 'I suspect so, yes. And I'm sorry.'

'For God's sake, Maddie, it was hardly your fault.'

His curt tone made Maddie flinch. She'd held this knowledge in for so long, and now it was out and she'd tainted Nic's head with it too. An awful helpless shaking started in her legs and rose up, taking over her whole body.

'I'm sorry. I never wanted to tell you—I shouldn't have said anything.'

Maddie heard Nic curse, and then he was turning to her and pulling her into his arms, his hands on her back, pressing her against him, stilling the awful shaking until it was just tiny tremors racking her body. She couldn't even cry.

Nic was rubbing her back now, and her hair, soothing her as if she were a wild unbroken horse.

After a long moment he pulled away and put his hands on her shoulders. He looked her in the eye. 'I'm glad you told me.'

He kept looking at her until Maddie nodded reluctantly. Then Nic took her hand and led her back to the Jeep, putting her into the passenger seat as if she were a child, securing her seat belt. Maddie felt numb, slightly removed from everything.

A grim-faced Nic got in beside her and they drove back to Villarosa. When Maddie saw Nic take the turn for his own estate she said, 'Where are we going?'

He looked at her. 'You're coming home with me tonight.'

The inevitable heat deep within Maddie started to thaw some of the numbness. It felt as if something had shifted between them as soon as she'd uttered the heinous words. When he'd held her just now his touch had been platonic. Maybe he could never desire her again with that knowledge in his head? Even though he knew it wasn't true—it was poisonous.

They got back to Nic's house. Without a word he just took her hand and led her up to his room. Maddie felt incredibly insecure and confused. She pulled free of Nic inside his bedroom door, too many evocative memories crowding her head. 'What are we doing here?' She was ashamed of how badly she wanted him.

He came and stood right in front of her. 'We're going to exorcise those demons right now, right here,' he said.

Maddie looked at him and her heart beat fast. 'What do you mean? How?'

He cupped her face in his hands and pressed close against her, so she could feel his body hardening against hers.

'Like this.'

And then he kissed her. But this was unlike any kiss they'd shared before. It reminded Maddie of how he'd kissed her for the first time—how badly she'd wanted it after the long week of building tension. He'd been so intimidatingly sexy and yet disarmingly clumsy. Like when he'd fumbled with the buttons on her blouse before opening it, and his cheeks had flushed at seeing her breasts.

It was as if past and present interlocked. Maddie was being lowered down onto the bed and Nic loomed over her. He opened her shirt and pushed it apart, pulled down the lacy cup of her bra, forcing her breast to pout up towards him.

Maddie arched her back instinctively, silently begging him to touch her.

He looked at her steadily. 'I've never forgotten how you tasted that day...the sweetness of your skin, your breast. I could have drowned in your scent...'

Maddie ran her fingers through Nic's hair, an unstoppable tide of emotion forcing her to rise up and take his face in her hands, her mouth searching for his. Each touch and moment was imbued with echoes of the past, of the way Nic had touched her that day for the first time.

They passed the moment when they'd been stopped before, and kept going. Clothes were shed and lay in a tangled heap, on the floor or under their hot slick bodies on the bed. When Nic lay between Maddie's legs his mouth was on her breast, one big hand trailing up the outside of her body, luxuriating in her satin-smooth skin, dewed with sweat.

'Nic, please…' she begged, rolling her hips impatiently.

Shifting his big body only slightly, Nic thrust into Maddie, and her whole body stilled as she looked up at him and relished the moment when their flesh joined.

'Keep your eyes open,' Nic instructed gutturally.

Maddie couldn't take her eyes off him as he slowly started to thrust in and out, taking them higher and higher and further away from the ugliness of what had happened.

When Maddie's orgasm broke over her it felt transcendental, spiritual. As if it was washing something away. Nic's gaze was searing her alive, burning into her as his own body crescendoed and his release broke free. Maddie felt the warmth of it inside her and instinctively clasped her thighs tighter around Nic's hips.

After a long moment Nic fell into an exhausted slump beside Maddie. He hugged her close, arms wrapped right around her. All he could think of before sleep and blackness claimed him was how intense it had felt to have no barrier to his release going deep into Maddie, and how tightly her legs had clasped him to her in that moment.

Maddie woke and looked at Nic. He was so much more relaxed in sleep. He was always so tightly controlled. Her heart lurched and she suddenly longed for a time when she would see him relax and smile…and laugh. Perhaps he would…with someone else. Not her. He'd been softer once—she'd seen it in his eyes, along with hope. But she was the reason that softness and hope had been replaced by cynicism. When she thought of how vulnerable he'd been when they'd met, underneath all his arrogance…her rejection must have cut too deep for him ever to forgive.

Maddie didn't want to wait for Nic to wake and react to her presence. She knew something had changed last night. They'd crossed a line. The past had been well and truly dealt with. This affair had always been about old scores, lingering desire… The contract had provided a kind of reprieve, but it would be signed soon and then Nic would be relegating Maddie back to the periphery of his life.

Maddie had to face up to her conscience, which was riven with guilt. She'd slept with Nic using the contract as an excuse because she'd believed that it was the only way she could sleep with him. He'd never have wanted her without the contract. He wouldn't have lowered himself to seduce her just for desire's sake.

She had to get out of there before she forgot that and started wishing and hoping that perhaps…in another world…if they hadn't shared such a tangled history… eveything might have been different.

The fact was that ultimately Nic had got his hands on the one thing he wanted most, and that was the Vasquez estate. In the end he'd prevailed, and got personal revenge into the bargain.

When Nic woke the sun was high outside and he felt completely disorientated. The bed was empty beside him and he closed his eyes. The bittersweet relief that went through him to find that he was alone was palpable.

The last thing he remembered was waking during the night and finding Maddie soft and sexily pliant in his arms.

He'd been hard and aching and she'd woken, pushing her buttocks against him, urging him to take her.

He'd slid into her from behind. It had been quiet and intense.

His head reeled anew when he thought of what Maddie had told him yesterday. He'd acted from some visceral place, bringing her back here to make love in a need to negate the awful words. When he recalled what it had been like to lock eyes with her as they'd made love he felt dizzy, even though he was lying down.

Maddie's revelations put a spin on the past that Nic wasn't sure he could really assimilate. Her reaction that day...he had no defence against it any more, nothing to hide behind. He knew he would have reacted exactly the same—might possibly have been even more brutal than she'd been to him. And the fact that she'd been burdened with the knowledge...it made Nic feel sick.

She'd wanted to see him again. If her mother hadn't told her what she had, the following day at the orchard would have been very different. A cold sweat broke out on Nic's brow as he lay there and contemplated how different things might have been...and could be now. And there his mind immediately shut down. His body was locked with tension.

He'd come full circle with Maddie. They'd reached a truce. He could forgive her now and move on. He'd invest in her estate, help her get back on her feet. And that had to be enough. He simply could not contemplate an alternative, because that meant challenging the walls of defence he'd needed to exist for so long. Since his mother had smothered him with anxiety and his father had brutalised him. And since he'd spent that week with Maddie and felt his heart beating for the first time...

The concept of love had been alien to him until he'd met

Maddie. And then it had become mangled, and had withered inside him after her cruel words and brutal rejection. No matter what he knew about that day now, he couldn't undo the damage. And Maddie was inextricably bound up in all of that, so she could never be a part of his future.

Nic's bones ached when he thought of relegating Maddie to his past. He jack-knifed off the bed and took a stinging cold shower, assuring himself that finally he could move on—but he could only do it by leaving Maddie behind.

Maddie walked out of the clinic feeling tired but happy. Until she saw a familiar Jeep pull into the car park. Unconsciously she started walking faster and put her head down. She cursed when she heard, 'Maddie!'

Slowly she turned around. She didn't feel ready to face Nic yet. It had been two days since she'd left his bed, and she'd not seen him or heard from him. The message was clear: it was time to move on.

She schooled her features into a bland, polite mask. But still when she saw him she couldn't stop that impulse she had to devour him with her eyes. Her heart spasmed, her arms tight across her chest. 'Nic.'

'How is Maria?'

Maddie smiled tightly. 'She's going to be fine. The operation was a success. She'll need to recuperate here at the clinic for a few days, but she's been very lucky. They're very grateful to you.'

Nic waved a hand as if to brush aside the considerable expenses he'd met for Maria's operation and care. 'It was nothing,' he said gruffly.

Maddie's chest felt constricted. 'Was there something else you wanted?'

He looked at her for a long moment, and she felt an icy feeling of foreboding.

'The other night…we didn't use protection.'

Maddie went cold and then hot. She hadn't even thought about it afterwards. Mortified, she babbled, 'It's fine. I got my period today.'

Nic looked grim. 'That's good…'

Wanting to escape, Maddie said, 'Hernan is coming back to the estate tomorrow. He's going to check over the contract, so I should have it signed the day after, if he thinks it's okay.' Maddie felt like a fraud for delaying the inevitable: she'd looked over the contract and it was more than fair—and generous.

Nic nodded. 'I'll come and pick it up myself.'

'Goodbye, Nic.' Maddie turned quickly and headed straight to her Jeep, hating the stinging in her eyes. She knew it was silly, but somehow *now* felt like the moment when whatever link they'd shared for the past eight years was finally broken.

'Maddie—'

Maddie's steps faltered and her breath stopped. Blinking back the moisture in her eyes furiously, she turned around again. Nic hadn't moved. The planes of his face were stark, and he said, 'I'm sorry that—'

Maddie put up a hand, bile rising in her throat at the thought that he was going to give her some platitude. 'Don't, Nic. Just don't. You don't have to say anything. It's done.'

And she turned and half ran, half walked to her Jeep. She and Nic had been seeking some kind of closure and now they had it. Whatever she'd felt move between them the other night had been nothing more than an illusion, a reaction to heightened emotion.

So, she asked herself on the way home through a veil of tears, if this was closure why did it feel so *un*closed?

* * *

Maddie sat looking at the contract. It was early in the morning. She and Hernan had gone over it all last night and he'd concluded that she wouldn't have got a better deal from anyone else. With Nic's investment the entire estate and house would be completely renovated and updated— something her old-fashioned father had fought against all of his life. His resistance was one of the main reasons the estate had fallen apart.

Hernan and Maria would be well protected and looked after. Nic was going to bring in a project manager and a new head winemaker. He would also hire new cellar hands and seasonal grape-pickers, as well as the machinery needed to mass-pick grapes.

Maddie knew she had no choice but to accept this investment—not just for her sake but for the sake of the local economy. The Vasquez estate had long been an employer of locals and it could be again. Not to mention the huge debt she owed Hernan and Maria, who needed support now more than ever. She couldn't deny that she wanted the estate to flourish again. It was just a pity that she wouldn't be there to witness it.

With a heavy heart Maddie picked up a pen and signed on the dotted line. And in doing so she sealed her fate— because she couldn't remain here now. She couldn't renege on this deal, but she also couldn't go on living here, seeing Nic every day, living with his casual dismissal of their affair. She'd sold her soul and heart to him—and she'd used his investment in the estate as an excuse to hide behind.

What had happened between them amounted to nothing more than a ream of paper written in legalese.

Maddie tried to write a note to Nic, but no matter what she said it came out trite and ridiculous. In the end she gave up and simply wrote:

Nic, I am handing full control of the estate and all decisions to Hernan. He is the best person to oversee the work to be done.
Yours, Maddie.

Even that made her scowl. She folded it and put it in an envelope and left it on top of the contract, with her note to Hernan. And then she left her home.

Nic watched the dawn break, casting a pink light over the snow-capped Andes in the far distance. His jaw itched with stubble. His eyes stung. He hadn't slept all night. He hadn't slept since he'd woken in the empty bed the other morning.

The view he now looked upon, which encompassed the vastness of his estate, usually never failed to fill him with a sense of satisfaction, but for weeks now it had failed to move him. He'd become distracted and had lost interest in work—which had been his one *raison d'être* for ever.

Only yesterday Eduardo had had to repeat himself three times before Nic had registered what he was saying, and then Nic had snarled at him like a bear with a sore head. Nic had, of course, apologised profusely—he'd never lost his rag like that before—but the level of control he'd been wielding for years was deserting him spectacularly.

And Nic knew the moment it had started to desert him. When he'd seen Madalena Vasquez walk through the doorway in that hotel in Mendoza. He'd known *then*, even before he'd recognised her, that everything had changed irrevocably.

And just like that, as the pink light spread across the Andes, Nic knew what it meant—and what he had to do if he wanted to gain any sense of control or sanity back. All of this—his struggle with his parents, his health—meant absolutely nothing now. Because from the moment he'd seen Maddie Vasquez on her horse eight years ago and followed her to the orchard, she'd controlled his destiny.

She'd made him trust, and then she'd broken him apart and reformed him with her brutal rejection—which was now so understandable. But she was the only one who could heal him, make him take a chance on trusting again...

From the moment she'd come home he'd been slowly thawing, coming back to life inside and fighting it every step of the way. The pain of it was almost unbearable. But now that pain was as necessary to him as breathing.

Nic hadn't even realised he was moving until he was in his Jeep and driving out of his gate towards Maddie's estate. He barely noticed the one other vehicle on the road—a taxi. When he got to the house it felt silent, and Nic knew with a sick feeling why it felt like that.

He went into the study and saw the notes and the contract. He put the letter for Hernan aside and opened the one for him and read it. Slowly he put it down and picked up the contract. He looked at the last page. Maddie's name was scrawled on the bottom line.

With an inarticulate roar of rage Nic flung the contract against the book-lined wall and the pages went everywhere. He turned and stormed out, eyes wild.

Maddie shuffled forward in the queue at the ticket booth, counting her money. She had just enough. When she got to Buenos Aires she would try to persuade her aunt to let her stay for a couple of weeks while she tried to find a—

'Running away, Maddie?'

Maddie's brain froze mid-thought. She looked around to see Nic standing there, arms crossed across that broad chest. His calm and reasonable tone belied his wild look: his hair was messy, his eyes were bloodshot, and his jaw was stubbled with dark blond beard. And he was utterly, utterly gorgeous.

Maddie quickly turned back to face the queue again, and tried to will down the heat seeping into her cheeks. 'I don't know why you bothered to come here, Nic. And, no, I'm not running away.'

She went forward a few steps and Nic kept pace beside her.

'Could have fooled me. Did you realise you couldn't hack it? That you don't really care for your estate that much, after all?'

Maddie rounded on him, bristling. 'You *know* that's not true. I love that estate.'

'Then why are you leaving?'

Maddie flushed. She was becoming aware of people nudging each other, because inevitably they recognised one of Mendoza's foremost citizens. All they'd have to do was recognize *her* and then they'd have enough fodder to gossip about for months. *De Rojas has run Vasquez out of town!*

Reluctantly Maddie stepped out of the queue and moved away, so people couldn't hear them. She rounded on Nic. 'I don't need to be there for you to invest in the Vasquez estate.'

Nic was grim. 'It's part of the deal.'

Maddie felt like stamping her foot, and emotions weren't far from the surface. 'Nic, I'm leaving, and there's nothing you can do or say to stop me.'

Resolutely she turned to join the back of the queue and start again. Then she heard Nic say rawly from behind her, 'What if I said I don't want you to go, and it's got nothing to do with the investment?'

Maddie stopped, and her breath grew very shallow. She wasn't even aware of the interested eyes of onlookers flitting between her and Nic. She'd misheard him—or he didn't mean what she'd thought he meant.

She took an experimental step forward and heard, 'Maddie, *dammit.*'

And then Nic was in front of her, planting himself squarely in her way. She looked up. The muscle in his jaw was ticking.

'Nic…?'

'I don't want you to go because I've just realised how much I need you.'

Maddie's hands were gripping her bag. Something fluttered ominously in her chest but still she thought he had to be talking about the investment.

'But Hernan will be there. He can handle it…'

Nic nearly exploded. 'I'm not talking about the investment. I don't care about that. I only offered to invest because you seemed so determined to throw yourself in harm's way. And the contract—' Nic stopped abruptly and cursed out loud before admitting, 'The contract was a way for me to have you in my bed without admitting that I was terrified you'd reject me again.'

He reached out a hand and touched Maddie's cheek. She felt his hand trembling. *Déjà vu* washed over her.

'I messed up, Maddie, because I was too cowardly to admit how much it made me *feel* when you came back here.' He shook his head. 'Your rejection that day…it was like having my heart torn out of my chest and ground into the earth. Nothing mattered after that. I closed myself off. In the space of that week I fell for you so deeply…'

Maddie's vision was blurring. She brought her hand up over Nic's on her face and held it there, willing him to trust her. 'Oh, Nic…I'm so sorry that happened. That my mother poisoned my mind…that I couldn't tell you. I wanted you so badly. I fell for you too. And I know that's why you can't possibly forgive me.'

Resolutely Maddie took Nic's hand down and dropped it. She stood back. 'That's why I'm leaving. I'm not strong enough to live near you, loving you, knowing that you're getting on with your life…and you have to move on.'

Nic sounded slightly dazed. 'You love me? Even now?'

Maddie nodded and fresh tears blurred her vision. 'You were always in my heart and thoughts. I told myself when I came back that I hated you for being so autocratic, and for making me believe that what had happened between us eight years ago was pure lust on your part. But it was a lie. I agreed to that stupid contract because on some level I thought it was the only way you'd have me…'

Maddie looked down and wiped at her damp cheeks. She clutched her bag and took a step around Nic—only to feel him take her arm in a strong grip.

She couldn't even look at him. 'Please, Nic…let me go. You can't make me stay. Not now.'

He didn't listen. He turned her around and tipped her chin up. Maddie saw his face and her heart stopped. He looked young…and free of those awful shadows. A smile curled the corners of that beautiful mouth and her heart started again, making her feel light-headed.

Gently Nic asked, 'Have you listened to a word I've said?'

Maddie felt confused. What *had* he said?

Suddenly Nic took her bag out of her hand and dropped it to the ground. And then, before she could take in a breath, he was down on one knee in front of her, holding her hand in his.

Looking up at her with those intensely blue eyes, he said throatily, 'Maddie Vasquez, I love you. I was fascinated by you before I ever met you, and then when we did meet I fell deep into your heart. I've never stopped loving you, no matter how hurt I was, and I only realised that when you came back home. I told myself I hated you, that I wanted revenge...but I wanted *you*. And I wanted your heart. But I was too cowardly to admit it...'

Maddie was stunned into silence, sure that she had to be dreaming. The queue had long since broken up, and they were now surrounded by an avid crowd of spectators. Maddie heard someone close to her sigh theatrically.

'Maddie Vasquez...will you please marry me? I can't move on with my life unless I know you're going to be in it. I want us to have babies and grow old together, to be the ones to bury this ancient feud for ever. I love you.'

Maddie started crying in earnest, emotion rising up within her and making her shake. Nic stood up and pulled her into his arms, cradling her and soothing her. Eventually, when she could, she pulled back and looked up at him. He still looked wild, and trepidatious. She could see the old fear in his eyes—the fear that even now she'd walk away...

She reached up and put her arms around his neck.

She pressed a salty kiss to his mouth and said on an emotional sigh, 'Yes, I'll marry you, Nic de Rojas. How could I possibly do anything else when I love you so much?'

The cheers of the crowd made Maddie bury her head shyly in Nic's chest, and then she felt him lifting her into his arms and striding out into the glorious sunshine.

One year later

'No,' Nic said patiently. 'We *are* married, but my wife has an extensive estate in her own name so she decided to stay a Vasquez. She's a modern woman.'

Maddie's hand was tightly clasped in Nic's. She fought back giggles when he gripped it tighter and they watched the snooty older couple walk away, radiating disapproval at this unconventiality. The people of Mendoza were only slowly coming to terms with a de Rojas/Vasquez union, but the Vasquez estate was well on its way to flourishing again under its own label.

When the couple had gone Maddie laughed out loud, and buried her head in Nic's chest to hide it. His hand was tender on the back of her neck, fingers exerting a gentle pressure, and Maddie finally looked up when she'd collected herself, loving the feeling of languid heat which invaded her bones at his touch, which would turn to something much more urgent given half a chance—even more so now than it ever had.

'Well, Señor de Rojas.' She smiled up at her husband. 'Do you realise that this is our first anniversary?'

Nic frowned. 'But we only got married nine months ago...'

Maddie looked around the sumptuous ballroom of the hotel in Mendoza and squeezed his hand. 'Not that anniversary. I mean this time last year we met again for the first time...'

Nic looked down into his wife's clear and loving green gaze and felt his chest tighten almost unbearably. It happened a lot, this physical feeling of love. That night a year ago—he could remember seeing her shape in the doorway, could remember feeling right then that trouble was in store. And he wouldn't have changed one second of it.

He smiled and took her hand, lifting it to his mouth to kiss the inner palm. Her eyes darkened and immediately blood rushed to his groin. He almost groaned out loud. They were like two rampant teenagers.

His voice was low and husky. 'Happy anniversary, my love…'

Maddie turned her face into his palm and Nic glanced up and cursed softly, wishing that they were alone. He felt Maddie sigh against his hand and looked down, immediately concerned. He saw her wry look and felt her hand come between them, to rest on the very prominent swell of her belly. She was already two weeks overdue.

She grumbled good-naturedly, 'Do you think this baby will *ever* appear? If he takes much longer I'll need a crane to get around.'

Nic smiled wolfishly and wrapped both arms around Maddie, pulling her close. 'I can think of one way we can urge him along…'

Maddie's insides liquefied at the carnal look in Nic's eyes. This past year had been a dream. She loved this man more than she'd even allowed herself to believe possible when she'd first fallen for him.

Maddie asked, 'Can we just leave? Now?'

He pressed a kiss to her mouth and said, 'We can do whatever we want.'

'But your speech…'

Nic looked round and Maddie saw him share a look with Eduardo, his head winemaker. He looked back to Maddie. 'Eduardo will take over. This…' He put his hand possessively on her belly. 'You, *us*—there's nothing more important than that.'

The next day, at five p.m., Nic and Maddie welcomed their son, Alvaro, named after Maddie's brother, into the world.

Maddie, exhausted but happy, looked at Nic cradling his son—all ten pounds eleven ounces of him—and smiled wryly. 'If we could patent your particular method of helping labour along I think we could make a fortune.'

Nic's little finger was caught in a chubby hand, and he looked at his wife and said mock seriously, 'Next time I'll make sure to put much more effort in.'

Maddie groaned softly. 'The way I'm feeling right now, there won't *be* a next time.'

Nic chuckled, and Maddie was glad to see the colour restored to his face. He'd nearly fainted in the delivery room, his torture at being so helpless evident when Maddie was in such pain.

He came and handed Alvaro back to Maddie, who sat up and started to breastfeed. Nic leant close and whispered in her ear, 'Don't worry, Mrs Vasquez. I'll make it so pleasurable next time you won't even think about the pain.'

Maddie looked at Nic and saw how dark his eyes were at seeing her breast exposed like this, their baby suckling furiously. She felt a familiar tugging in her lower body that no pain could diminish—not even a fifteen-hour labour.

She groaned softly and said, 'What have I let myself in for?'

Nic pressed a kiss to her neck and then pulled back to look at her, one hand on his son's head. He just smiled.

* * * * *

ONE NIGHT WITH MORELLI

KIM LAWRENCE

*Massive thanks to my editor Kathryn for being
so elastic with the deadline on this one!*

Though lacking much authentic Welsh blood,
Kim Lawrence comes from English/Irish stock.
She was born and brought up in North Wales.
She returned there when she married, and her
sons were both born on Anglesey, an island off
the coast. Though not isolated, Anglesey is a little
off the beaten track, but lively Dublin, which Kim
loves, is only a short ferry ride away.

Today they live on the farm her husband was
brought up on. Welsh is the first language of many
people in this area and Kim's husband and sons
are all bilingual – she is having a lot of fun, not
to mention a few headaches, trying to learn the
language!

With small children, the unsocial hours of nursing
didn't look attractive so encouraged by a husband
who thinks she can do anything she sets her mind
to, Kim tried her hand at writing. Always a keen
Mills & Boon reader, it seemed natural for her to
write a romance novel – now she can't imagine
doing anything else.

She is a keen gardener and cook and enjoys
running – often on the beach, as living on an
island the sea is never very far away. She is usually
accompanied by her Jack Russell, Sprout – don't
ask, it's a long story!

CHAPTER ONE

SHE HATED BEING late and she was—very.

Her jaw ached with tension. Obviously it served no purpose to get stressed about stuff you couldn't control, like fog at airports, traffic jams or—no, dropping in at the office had been completely avoidable and a major mistake, but it was human nature and she couldn't help it.

Weaving her way neatly in and out of the crowds still wearing her sensible long-haul-flight shoes, Eve flicked open her phone. She was studying the screen, her fingers flying, when a sharp tug almost pulled her off her feet.

Instinct rather than good sense made her grip tighten around the holdall slung over her shoulder. The tussle was short but the thief who grunted and swore at length at her had size on his side; although he was skinny, he was wiry and tall and he easily escaped with her bag.

'Help... Thief!'

Dozens must have heard her anguished cry but nobody reacted until the tall hooded youth—a stereotype if there ever was one—who was shouldering his way through the crowd clutching her bag hit one pedestrian who did not move aside.

She saw the thief bounce off this immovable object and hit the pavement face down before crowds hid him and her bag from view.

She missed the thief shaking his head as he looked up,

a snarl on his thin, acne-marked face aimed at the man at whose feet he lay sprawled. The snarl melted abruptly and was replaced by a flash of fear as he released the bag handle as though it were alight and, lurching to his feet, ran away.

Draco sighed. If he weren't already very late he might have chased the culprit but he was, so instead he bent to pick up the stolen bag, which immediately opened, disgorging its contents at his feet and all over the pavement.

Draco blinked. In his thirty-three years he'd seen a lot and few things had the power to surprise him any more. In fact, only that very morning he'd asked himself if he was in a rut—the trouble with ruts was you didn't always recognise you were in one—but standing ankle-deep in ladies' underwear—wildly sexy lingerie, to be precise— most definitely surprised him.

Now that, he thought, was something that didn't happen every day of the week—at least not to him.

One dark mobile brow elevated, and with a half-smile tugging his sensually sculpted lips upwards he bent forward and hooked a bra from the top of the silky heap. Silk, and a shocking-pink tartan, it was definitely a statement and, if he was any judge, a D cup.

Under his breath he read the hand-sewn label along one seam.

'Eve's Temptation.' It was catchy and the name rang a faint bell.

Had Rachel had something similar in a more subdued colour? He sighed. While he missed the great sex, if he was honest—and he generally was—he didn't miss Rachel herself, and he had no regrets about his decision to terminate their short and, he had assumed, mutually satisfactory arrangement.

Only she had crossed the line. It had started with the 'we' and 'us' comments—*we* could stop off at my parents', my sister has offered *us* her ski lodge as it'll be empty at New Year. Draco blamed himself for allowing it to pass as long as he had, but in his defence the sex had been very good indeed.

Things had finally come to a head a couple of months ago when she had *accidentally* bumped into him in the middle of an exclusive department store on one of the rare occasions when he was able to spend some quality time with his daughter.

It wasn't her appallingly obvious efforts to ingratiate herself with Josie that had stuck in Draco's mind; it was his daughter's comment on the way home.

'Don't be too brutal will you, Dad, when you dump her?'

The worried expression in her eyes had made him re-alise that he'd become complacent, he'd allowed the once clearly defined lines between his home life and the other aspects of his life to blur. It was more important to keep that protective wall around his home life now that Josie was getting older than it ever had been.

The day he had looked at his baby and realised that her mother wasn't coming back he had sworn that this desertion would not affect her; he would protect her, give her security. He had made some inevitable mistakes along the way but at least he hadn't allowed her to form attachments with the women he had enjoyed fleeting liaisons with over the years and risk being hurt when they too left.

'Nice,' he murmured, running his thumb over the fine butter-soft silk.

'That's mine.' Eve's determined gaze was fixed on the pink tartan bra that she hoped was going to be next season's best-seller.

'You're Eve?'

'Yes.' The response was automatic. She could, if she'd wanted, have claimed ownership of, not just the name, but the bra and the brand of which she was justifiably proud, though there was a strong possibility that, as on numerous previous occasions, the information would be received with scepticism.

She understood why: it was all about appearances and she simply didn't look the part of a successful businesswoman, let alone one who was the founder of a successful underwear company that had based its brand on glamour with a quirky edge that not only looked good but was comfortable to wear.

'It was very brave of you to stop that thief running away with my bag. I hope he didn't hurt you.' Her smile faded dramatically as she looked up into the face of the man who was holding her sample. 'I'm very...' She cleared her throat and swallowed, her tongue uncomfortably glued to the roof of her mouth.

There were several other equally disturbing accompanying symptoms, and it was so totally unexpected that it took her a few heart-racing moments to put a name to the frantic heart-pounding, uncontrolled heat rush and visceral clutch that dug into her stomach and tightened like a fist. Even the fine invisible hair on her forearms was tingling in response to what this man exuded, which was—give it a name, Evie, and move on, she told herself sternly—raw sex!

Either that or this was a much less publicised symptom of jet lag!

'Grateful.' For small mercies—I didn't drool, she added silently, refusing to contemplate the mortifying possibility that she had been standing there with her mouth open for more than a few seconds.

Now that she was able to study his face with the objectivity she prided herself on, Eve could see that, though her first impressions were right—he was quite remarkably good-looking; maybe the most good-looking man she'd ever seen up close—it wasn't his face or athletic body that had caused her nervous system to go into meltdown, it was the aura of raw sexuality that he exuded like a force field.

That made sense, because obvious good looks didn't do it for her—they never had—and his were very, *very* obvious! It wasn't that she had anything against cheekbones you could cut yourself on, classic square firm jawlines, overtly sensual lips or eyelashes that long—actually the crazily long and spiky eyelashes framing deep-set liquid dark eyes were kind of nice—it was just that Eve had always liked a face with character belonging to men who spent less time looking in the mirror than she did. And of course being a *man* he didn't have to worry about the thin white scar beside his mouth. It didn't matter that the likelihood was he'd done it doing something as mundane as falling off his bike as a kid; it added to the air of brooding danger and mystery he exuded.

The thought of being considered a hero for just standing still and letting the thief bump into him drew an ironic smile. 'I'll survive.'

Well, his ego would at least—it could obviously withstand a force-ten gale. The uncharacteristically uncharitable thought brought a furrow to her brow but for some reason just looking at him made her skin prickle with antagonism.

Draco gave up the D cup and studied the claimant, a breathless pink-faced female who snatched it from his fingers. The bra couldn't be hers as she was definitely not a D cup. Actually, he was pretty sure she was not wearing a bra at all, and there was a definite chill in the air—well, this was London; when wasn't there? His interested glance drifted and lingered on her small but pert breasts heaving dramatically beneath the loose white shirt she wore.

Eve, catching the direction of his stare, felt her colour deepen even though she knew she was being a bit paranoid.

Nothing could be less revealing than her shirt; anything tighter rubbed the small scar below her shoulder blade that was still a little tender.

'Thank you.' She struggled to inject some warmth into her response and, just to be on the safe side, fastened her jacket, taking care not to put too much pressure on her shoulder. By next week it ought to be healed enough for her to be able to wear a bra again.

'You're actually called Eve?' His curious gaze roamed over her heart-shaped face. If the original Eve had possessed a mouth that lush and inviting he for one would have cut Adam some slack.

'Let me guess—you're Adam.' She sighed as though it was a tired line she'd heard often.

'No, I'm Draco, but you can call me Adam if you want to.'

'A lovely offer but I doubt we'll ever be on first-name terms.' She thanked him again, crammed the last camisole into the bag and snapped it closed then, after tilting a nod in his direction, hurried away.

He's not watching, Eve, so why the hip swaying? she berated herself crossly.

He was watching.

Frazer Campbell, a meticulous man, reached the bottom of the page, readjusted his half-moon specs and began at the top of the page again. Draco's jaw clenched as he struggled to control his impatience.

'I am assuming this is an empty threat?' he asked.

The letter, though sprinkled with pseudo-legal phrases, was written by hand, the writing his ex-wife's, the wording definitely not... Draco strongly suspected that she had received some help with it, and even without the headed notepaper it didn't take a genius to figure out who from. His ex-wife's fiancé, Edward Weston, had got his seat in

Parliament on the family value ticket—so it wasn't hard to see where he was coming from. Selling yourself to the British public as a defender of family values was tough when your future bride had played a very peripheral role in her own daughter's life.

Draco didn't personally know the man, though he'd heard him called a joke on more than one occasion and maybe, if the subject he had chosen to poke his nose into had been any other, he might have been laughing—but he wasn't.

One thing he absolutely did not joke about was his daughter's welfare.

Frazer, older by several years than the man who was pacing the room restless as a caged panther in the enclosed space, smoothed the paper with the flat of his hand as he laid it back on his desk—it had landed there in an angry, crumpled ball.

'It's not really a threat as such, is it?' Edward Weston came across as pompous but he wasn't a total idiot and anyone who threatened Draco would have to be; the wealthy London-based Italian entrepreneur was famous for many things but turning the other cheek was not one of them! Frazer counted himself lucky to call Draco friend—you tended to bond pretty quickly with someone you got buried in an avalanche with—but if he hadn't been, Draco's reputation alone would have made him someone Frazer would have avoided.

The comment earned him a flash from Draco's dark eyes.

'Do you want to hear what I think or what you want to hear?' Frazer's shaggy brows twitched into a straight line as he noticed for the first time what his friend was wearing: full morning suit. 'Your wedding?' he asked cautiously.

'Marriage!' The single word made the speaker's opinion of that institution quite clear, it dripped with such acid scorn.

'Shame—if you were married it would be a perfect solution to the problem. There would be no question of your daughter not having…' he paused to consult the letter and read out loud '…"a stable female influence in her life".' Frazer smiled at his own joke while Draco, his dark eyes glinting not with laughter but with cynicism, lowered his long, lean frame into a chair on the opposite side of the desk.

'I'd sooner move my mother in.' The other man laughed; he had met Veronica Morelli. 'You make a mistake,' Draco continued, 'and you don't repeat it, unless of course you're a total fool.'

Frazer, who was blissfully happy in his second marriage, did not take offence. 'Do you think it's safe to come to a fool for expensive legal advice?'

Draco gave a tight grin that deepened the lines radiating from his deep-set eyes and briefly lent warmth and humour to the dark depths. 'There are exceptions to every rule,' he conceded. 'And I'm coming to you as a trusted friend—I couldn't afford what you charge.'

The older man snorted. Draco Morelli had been born to wealth and privilege, he could have sat back and enjoyed what he had inherited, but he was a natural entrepreneur and to his Italian family's occasional bemusement over the last ten years he had made a series of financial investments that had made his name a byword for success in financial circles.

Under his smile was iron resolve. Draco's short-lived marriage had been by anyone's standards a total disaster but it had given him the daughter he adored so he could never regret it—but to deliberately take that route again…?

It was not going to happen.

He had affairs, just not *love* affairs. He did not dress

things up and recognised that for him sex was simply a basic need; he had proved over and over again that the emotional element was not necessary. It required no effort on his part to maintain an emotional buffer—there were even occasions when he did not much like the women who shared his bed. What did require some effort on his part was keeping his daughter, now a scarily mature and impressively grounded thirteen, as ignorant as possible of his affairs.

'She's talking custody rights or at least Edward is.' His ex's latest was a very unlikely choice for a woman who normally went for men considerably her junior. It was hard to think of a more unlikely couple and Draco doubted it would last despite the ostentatious rock on Clare's finger, but if he was wrong—well, good luck to them.

But he wasn't going to allow his daughter to have her life thrown into turmoil because Clare had discovered her inner earth mother—not on his watch!

'I am fond of Clare—let's face it, it's hard not to be fond of Clare,' her ex-husband conceded. 'But I wouldn't trust her to take care of a cat, let alone a teenager. Can you imagine it…?' He shook his dark head, grimacing at the mental image.

When they handed out the responsibility gene Clare was out of the room. Josie had been three months old when his ex had gone out for a facial and manicure and not come back. Left effectively a single parent at twenty, Draco had had to learn some new skills very quickly—he still was learning.

Fatherhood was a constant challenge, as was resisting his mother's interference. When he'd told the grieving widow that she needed a new challenge in her life, he certainly hadn't intended that challenge to be him! When Veronica Morelli wasn't turning up on his doorstep without warning with large suitcases she was trying to set him up with suitable women—the marrying kind.

'She's asking for joint custody, Draco, and she is the girl's mother.' Frazer held up a hand to stem the eruption his comment invited and continued calmly. 'But, no, given the circumstances and her history I don't think there is any prospect of any court coming down on her side, even if it got that far and she did marry Edward Weston. It's not as if she doesn't have access, very reasonable access, already to Josie.'

Draco nodded. No matter what her faults were, his ex-wife was Josie's mother and she was in her own way fond of her only child. Clare's *fondness* meant months could go by and their daughter would have no contact beyond the occasional text or email from her mother, then she would appear loaded with gifts and was for a time a doting mother, until something else caught her interest.

Draco's objectivity when he thought of his ex-wife was still tinged with cynicism but the corrosive anger had long since gone. He was even able to recognise that it had always been aimed more at himself than Clare, and with some justification when you considered the stubborn sentimentalism masquerading as love that had made him go through with a marriage that had had impending disaster written all over it.

'So you don't think I have anything to worry about?' he asked.

'I'm a lawyer, Draco—in my world there is always something to worry about.'

'Sure, I might walk under a bus.' He glanced at his watch and got to his feet, brushing an invisible speck from the perfectly tailored pale grey jacket. Actually, he was catching a helicopter rather than a bus to the wedding of Charlie Latimer; he found weddings depressing, and boring, but Josie was very excited about dressing up and he was making an effort for her sake.

'Is it true that Latimer is marrying his cook?'

'I haven't a clue.' Draco, who had less liking for gossip than he did weddings, replied honestly while he thought of a pink tartan bra and a pair of big green eyes...

On his way down in the elevator he thought some more about the bra's owner, and he was so involved in the mental images that there was a twenty-second delay before he noticed that the lift door had opened.

Focus, Draco... He did not for a second doubt his ability to do just that; it was a case of prioritising and he was good at that. It had been this ability that had got him past the first few weeks and months after Clare had walked out. He could have carried on being bitter, twisted and generally wallowing in a morass of self-pity; he could have allowed himself to be defined by that failure.

But he hadn't.

After that reminder, keeping his libido on a leash was relatively simple and he told himself that Green Eyes was definitely not his type. Still, there had been *something* about her...

'Oh, I'm so sorry.'

Draco placed a steadying hand on the arm of the young woman who had not so accidentally collided with him. Blonde and stunning, she *was* his type.

His smile was automatic and lacking a spontaneity that the recipient appeared not to notice. Standing on one foot, she had grabbed his arm for support. 'Are you all right?' he asked.

'I wasn't looking where I was going. It's these heels.'

She rotated one shapely ankle, inviting him to look, and Draco, being polite, did.

'I don't know if you remember...?' The eyelashes did some overtime and the pout was good but he'd seen better, he mused. Now, if Green Eyes ever decided to pout, those lips would have given her a natural advantage. 'But we met at the charity gala last month.'

'Of course,' Draco lied. There had been many attractive women there and good manners plus boredom meant he had probably flirted with a few. 'If you'll excuse me, I'm pushed for time—' His grimace was a product of impatience but the recipient chose to interpret it as regret.

'Shame, but you've got my number and I'd love to take you up on that offer of dinner.' Before Draco could even pretend to recall any such offer, let alone extend or retract it, the blonde suddenly stopped, her eyes widening at him as she waved her hand wildly at a figure about to cross the road.

'Eve!' she shrieked, forgetting the sexy purr.

Eve heaved a sigh and, pasting a smile on her face, turned without enthusiasm.

She had spotted them fifty yards back, hardly surprising as the couple who were standing at the entrance to the underground car park where she had left her car were drawing attention the way only *beautiful* people did. Eve had nothing a*gainst* beautiful people in general—her best friend was one, after all. She didn't even envy them their head-turning good looks because being the focus of attention everywhere you went was the stuff her nightmares were made of. It was just that this man…talk about bad luck…and talk about a *stereotype*!

It had been no shock to see him with the blonde—just a massive shock to bump into him again. As status symbols went, an underwear model on your arm was right up there with a big flash fuel-guzzling car, for alpha men like her father. But, to be perfectly fair, this man *wasn't* her father and she was making judgements like this *because*…?

Because of the liquid ache low in her pelvis, because a man who had barely brushed her life had finally given her the faintest *inkling* of the sort of irrational attraction that her own mother must have experienced in order to make her forget the principles she had instilled in her own daughter and have an affair with a married man.

Keep it in proportion, Eve. It's been a tough week and it isn't over yet, she reminded herself as she averted her gaze from the long scarlet nails that were possessively stroking his sleeve.

Her heart was thudding so hard that she could hardly hear her response to the woman almost as famous for her rich and famous boyfriends as she was for her perfect body. If he was Sabrina's latest that made him rich...well, that explained the arrogant air of smug assurance that really got under her skin and, as for famous, well...these days who wasn't? Even she could type her name into a search engine and have pages appear.

'Hello, Sabrina.' She acknowledged the tall stranger from earlier with an unsmiling nod while she struggled against the effects of his brain-mushing charisma.

'Eve, it's so good to see you.' Eve got a whiff of heavy perfume as the air either side of her face was kissed. 'And perfect timing too. I can tell you in person...' The dramatic pause stretched a little too long before her announcement. 'I'm available.'

Eve always hated the feeling of walking into a conversation halfway through. Was she meant to know what the woman was talking about...?

Draco watched the expression on Eve's face; it was clear she didn't have a clue what the blonde was talking about. He fought a laugh with more success than he had fought the gut kick of lust he had no defence against when he had recognised the petite figure who, unless he was mistaken, had been about to make good an escape.

Draco wasn't used to women who crossed the road to avoid him—they did the reverse occasionally—and he wondered what he'd done to make her look down her elegant little nose at him. His ego remained intact—it was pretty robust most of the time—but his interest was piqued. What would it take to melt that stern disapproval into uncritical adoration? He was setting his sights too high, he realised; he didn't want adoration from her, just a smile. Although adoration might be nice after a long night getting to know her better...?

'You are?' Eve asked Sabrina.

'Yes, but my agent said he is *still* waiting for a call back from your office about the new campaign...so-o-o exciting. He said something about you not using models this time.' She rolled her eyes. 'But I told him it's obvious you think I'm still committed to the supermarket people, but the thing is I decided to call it a day with them as they were just going so *down market* and not the sort of thing I want to be associated with at all.'

'Sorry, Sabrina, but I've been out of the country so the agency has been doing all the recruiting.'

'But you'll have the final say...right?'

Eve was tempted to say she'd be in touch but her innate sense of honesty won out. It would be unfair to string the other girl along. 'Actually your agent had it right; we're not using models, just real women...not that you're not real, but you're not ordinary. What I mean is—'

'She means, Sabrina, that normal women can never aspire to looking like you do.'

Had anyone else made the intervention Eve might have felt grateful, but instead she found herself biting back a childish retort of *Don't tell me what I mean.*

'You're so sweet.' Sabrina pressed a soft kiss on his lean cheek.

Eve rolled her eyes and thought *perleeze* just as, above the model's head, the dark eyes found her own. His sleek ebony brows lifted and he smiled, the sort of smile that she imagined a fox might produce when contemplating a defenceless chick.

Eve narrowed her eyes and lifted her chin in silent challenge. She was not defenceless or stupid enough to smile at a man who could flirt with one woman while another was kissing him!

As she pulled away the model's complacent expression faded. 'But isn't that the idea? They all think if they buy the product they will look like me,' she said, looking confused.

Eve heaved a sigh. She had neither the time nor the inclination to explain herself to this woman whom she ungenerously stigmatised as totally self-centred. Her eyes slid of their own volition to her tall, arrogant companion... not a case of opposites attracting in their case, she decided waspishly, but like meeting like. 'Sorry, but I must run... lovely to bump into you...' She could hear the insincerity in her voice but didn't hang around to see if anyone else had. Head down, she headed for the entrance to the underground car park.

The brief encounter had left her feeling... She laughed, the sound echoing around the concrete shell, and shook her head. If there was ever a moment when she was allowed to feel weird it was today! Ignoring the fact her hand was still shaking, she fished her key ring out of her bag.

She had enough to deal with today without analysing the skin-tingling effect of a sexy stranger who represented pretty much everything she despised in a man. She was jet-lagged, facing the prospect of biting her tongue while her mother threw away her life and freedom and—she rubbed her shoulder and grimaced—she'd just had minor surgery. She was definitely permitted a little *weird*.

'I'm curious, why do you keep running away from me?'

Eve started violently, nearly losing her grip on her keys as she spun around. How on earth could someone that big make so little sound? He was standing a few feet away just beyond a sleek gleaming monster that was the motoring equivalent of him. If she cared about cars she would probably know what it was, but she didn't so in her head she simply grouped it under the heading of *look at me I have loads of money.*

She lifted her chin. 'There are laws against stalking.' She knew perfectly well that none of the adrenaline pumping through her body was the result of fear...which was too worrying to think about just now.

'And quite right too; speaking from experience it can be—'

Her hoot of derision cut him off. 'God, it must be so tough being irresistible to the opposite sex.' She only just stopped herself hastily adding she was not one of that number, but then actions always spoke louder than words and she hoped she was channelling contempt and not lust. There was no way in the world that he could know about the shameful heat at the juncture of her thighs.

'I'm flattered—'

'Not my intention.' She sounded breathless, and she definitely felt breathless as she fought to hold onto her defiance in the face of the suggestion of a smile her retort had produced.

She didn't know him.

She disliked him.

She had never felt such a strong reaction to a man. Ever.

'Relax, *cara*, this is my car.' He pressed his key fob and the monster's lights flashed.

Calling herself every kind of a fool—sure, you're so irresistible every drop-dead gorgeous man has to follow you, she thought scathingly—she wrenched her own car door open.

'Would you like dinner sometime?'

Draco was almost as surprised to hear himself make the

offer as she looked to hear it. It had been an uncharacteristic impulse kicked into life by the sight of her getting in that car and the knowledge he would never see her again.

'Well, it seems like such a waste...all this...' his long fingers moved in an expressive gesture that encompassed the space between them '...chemistry.'

Draco felt satisfied with this explanation for his uncharacteristically impulsive behaviour. She looked—he studied the small heart-shaped face lifted to him—less so.

The soft flush that covered her skin and the angry sparkle in her luminous green eyes made him tip his head in a nod of approval. There was passion there. He knew he'd been right about the chemistry.

'I'm assuming it's an ego thing with you...you have to have every woman your willing slave.'

He adopted a thoughtful expression as though considering the charge, then slowly shook his head. 'Slave suggests passive,' he purred, staring at her mouth with an expression that made her stomach quiver with a mixture of anger and lust she refused to acknowledge. 'I find passive boring.'

'Well, I find men who have massive egos boring!' she jeered, and slid onto the driver's seat. 'And there is no chemistry,' she yelled, before slamming the car door.

She could hear the sound of his low throaty laughter above the metallic scream as she crunched the gears before finding reverse.

CHAPTER TWO

THE TWO YOUNG women who stood waiting in the bedroom were both in their mid-twenties but there the similarity ended.

The girl who sat on the edge of the four-poster, one slim ankle crossed over the other, was an elegant, tall, blue-eyed blonde. The other one, who had spent the last five minutes prowling restlessly up and down the room, her heels making angry tapping sounds on the age-darkened polished boards, was neither tall nor blonde, and, even though the two women were dressed identically, she was somehow not elegant.

She was five three without heels and had chestnut-brown hair. Making no concession to the occasion—the dress was enough—she wore it as she always did: scraped into the heavy knot on her slender neck. It was not a style statement, though it did reveal the length of her neck and the delicate angle of her rounded jaw, just convenient. When exposed to even a sniff of moisture it fell into a mass of uncontrollable kinky waves and Eve liked control in all aspects of her life.

There had been a period when she had struggled to emulate her friend Hannah's effortless elegance, but no matter how hard she tried it just didn't happen. She always ended up looking as though she were dressing up in her mother's clothes. Gradually Eve had found her own style or—as an exasperated Hannah put it—*uniform*, which was a little unfair. Not all Eve's trouser suits were black—some were navy—and who had time to shop anyhow when they had a business to run? You couldn't afford to relax in this competitive world.

'Ouch!' She tripped over the skirt of her duck-egg-blue silk bridesmaid dress and banged her knee on the window seat. The pain made her green eyes film with tears.

'Well, if you'd come to a fitting it wouldn't be too long.' Harriet gave an affectionate smile and shook her head. The frantic last-minute pinning meant that Eve's dress had a sort of waist but the neckline of the fitted bodice still had a tendency to gape and slip down a couple of inches if Eve moved too quickly—and Eve moved quickly a lot. Her friend was never still mentally or physically, and just watching her made Hannah feel tired.

Eve gave another hitch accompanied by a hiss of exasperation. If she'd been more naturally blessed in the boob department it wouldn't be a problem, but even with the tissues tucked into the strapless bra that was chafing the partially healed scar on her shoulder blade she was one cup size short of keeping the bodice up.

On the plus side, while she was focusing on not exposing herself she wasn't thinking about her mother throwing herself away on a man who didn't deserve her! The furrow in danger of becoming permanent in her wide brow deepened because, impending wardrobe malfunction or not, she was thinking about it and had been ever since her mother had rung excited as a schoolgirl with the glad tidings. A week was not a long time but Eve had prayed her mother would come to her senses.

She hadn't.

'The measurements you sent must have been way off. Sarah said you've lost weight since she saw you last,' Hannah commented.

Eve felt a stab of guilt that intensified when Hannah made excuses for her.

'I know Australia is a long way to come for a fitting.'

'I didn't go there to avoid my mother!' Eve protested.

'I never thought you did.'

Until now, thought Eve, wishing she could keep her big mouth shut. 'I don't see what all the big hurry is for anyhow.' The way Hannah was looking at her made Eve frown. 'Well, do you?'

Hannah pressed a protective hand to her stomach, reflecting on how odd it was that Eve, who was super smart and intuitive in so many ways, could not have at least *suspected*. She had often felt a little intimidated by her friend's quick brain and focused drive, but for all her ability there were times when Eve couldn't see what was right under her nose and this was one of those occasions. Hannah swiftly changed the subject; now was probably not the time to voice her suspicions.

'Well, you made it back in time, which is the main thing. I'd have loved you to be at my wedding too,' Hannah added wistfully.

'I didn't get an invite.'

'I barely made it there myself.'

'Fine, be mysterious,' Eve grumbled, thinking that whatever the full story behind her friend's marriage to the Prince of Surana she had never seen Hannah looking happier or more beautiful—she was positively glowing.

'But you must be happy, Evie; this is what we have always wanted. For us to finally be a family.'

Eve swallowed the retort on the tip of her tongue.

She could hardly say to the man's daughter your dad is a sad loser and I never wanted him to marry my mum. I wanted her to wake up to the fact he was using her and end the sordid, secret affair.

She had no idea what had happened to make Charles

Latimer, not only acknowledge the long-term affair with his cook after years of hiding it, but propose to her and then invite half the world to the wedding. She glanced out of the window at the sound of another helicopter coming in to land—another VIP, she thought sourly. Charles Latimer certainly moved in glittering circles.

Her jaw set as she turned away. 'What's keeping her?' As far as Eve was concerned it was a disaster!

When the silence stretched Hannah's expression grew anxious. 'It's very romantic.'

Eve's brows lifted. 'You think?'

'You know, I agree with you totally that Dad has behaved very selfishly over the years to Sarah, but your mum is the best thing that has happened to him,' Hannah said earnestly. 'I'm just glad he's woken up to it. I can't wait for Sarah to be my mum.'

'She's a good mum to have,' Eve said, a lump forming in her throat as she thought of all the sacrifices her single mum had made over the years. She deserved the best and she was getting Charlie Latimer. Eve's small hands tightened into fists, her nails inscribing half-moons into her palms. 'I think she already thinks of you as a daughter.'

'I hope so.' Hannah's blue eyes filled with emotional tears, which she blinked to clear as the door to the interconnecting room opened to reveal the bride.

Her face almost as white as the dress she was wearing, Sarah Curtis stood for a moment framed in the doorway before taking a step and almost immediately grabbing onto a table to steady herself. Reacting faster than Eve, Hannah was on her feet in an instant, her beautiful face creased in lines of concern as she rushed to supply a steadying hand to the older woman.

'Are you all right, Sarah?'

Eve blinked. She wasn't seeing her mother's pale face as she was transfixed by the miles and miles of tulle her mother was wearing. The first sight of the outfit on its hanger earlier had rendered her literally speechless and it had been left to Hannah to make the necessary congratulatory noises. Somehow she had managed to sound totally sincere.

Hannah had to be a better actress than she had previously thought because the get-up was quite memorably awful and—what was worse—*inappropriate*. Eve didn't know what had possessed her mother to suddenly decide to channel her inner princess!

Sarah gave a wan smile. 'All I need is a bit of blusher.'

Hannah threw her a knowing look, her hands on her hips, and the older woman sighed heavily, suddenly looking sheepish. 'All right, I wasn't planning to tell you girls till later because I'm not quite twelve weeks yet and—'

It had to weigh a ton, Eve thought, sizing up the intricate beading on the mile-long train that was many a girl's dream. But not hers; she had never dreamed of wearing such an elaborate get-up. Did that make her weird? If so she was glad, she decided defiantly! How did a woman in her forties think that it was in any way appropriate to wear a white meringue wedding dress?

She dragged her gaze upwards just as Hannah, looking totally regal in her beautifully fitting dress—actually she was a princess for real these days, a fact that Eve still hadn't got her head around—walked over and hugged her mother. Both women were crying, to Eve's confusion. Had her mum finally realised that the dress was a disaster?

'You could always ditch the train,' Eve suggested, trying to remain practical and upbeat for her mother's sake. She knew she just had to suck it up today and be there for her mum in the future when things went sour with Charles, as they inevitably would.

Sarah, sniffing, laughed. 'I wish it were that simple. I didn't have any morning sickness at all with you, darling, but this time…' She rolled her eyes and accepted the glass of water that Hannah passed her.

Playing mental catch–up, Eve blinked. *Morning sickness*…? She must have misheard. You only got morning sickness when you were…*pregnant*!

A stunned vacant expression clouding her green eyes, she felt herself hit a mental brick wall. The impact made her mind go blank and she sat down with a gentle thud on the window seat. Paler even than her mother, she sat there not even breathing until finally her chest lifted in a long shuddering sigh and her lashes swept down in a concealing curtain. She stared at her hands and waited for the dull metronome thud in her ears to subside, but it didn't.

'There, that's better—all you needed was a bit of colour.'

A hand absently rubbing the nape of her neck, Eve looked up as her friend applied a finishing flick of blusher to the older woman's cheeks.

'You're p-pregnant, Mum. H-how?' Two sets of raised eyebrows turned her way and Eve blushed. She was regressing; she no longer stuttered or blushed. 'Well, I suppose that explains it.'

'Explains what, Eve?' Sarah asked.

Eve shook her head and thought why the rich scumbag Charlie Latimer had suddenly decided, not only to make his secret affair with his cook public knowledge, but to marry the woman who had been his mistress. It didn't involve a sudden attack of respect or love for Sarah; it was all about the possibility of an heir.

Not that Hannah looked as though she minded the possibility of being disinherited—her friend looked delighted.

'I knew it,' Hannah said smugly as she dabbed the moisture from around her soon-to-be stepmother's eyes. 'Whoever invented waterproof mascara deserves a medal—not that you'd know about that, Eve.' She flashed her friend,

who had been blessed with naturally thick dark lashes that
required no embellishment, an envious smile before turning back to Sarah. 'I said to Kamel last night that I thought
you might be but he said that just because I'm—' She
stopped and covered her mouth with her hand. 'I wasn't
meant to say anything until Kamel has told his uncle because of all this protocol. You won't breathe a word, will
you…?'

'Oh, Hannah, darling, Kamel must be thrilled!' Sarah's
waterproof mascara was once again being put to the test
as she reached up to hug Hannah.

'We both are, but Kamel is acting as though I'm made
of glass. He won't let me do a thing, and the man is driving me crazy,' Hannah confided with a laugh.

The expression in her friend's eyes when she said her
husband's name made Eve look away feeling uncomfortable, almost as though she had intruded. Eve was prepared
to like the prince her friend had married because he was
clearly as potty about Hannah as she was about him, but
the cynic in her wondered how long the honeymoon period would last.

'You're both having babies.' Eve was still playing mental catch-up.

Looking mistily ecstatic, Sarah clapped her hands. 'Isn't
that incredible? Our family is growing, girls.'

'A real family,' Hannah chimed in.

Eve cleared her throat. It was obviously her turn to respond, but what to say…? She managed a faint and un-
imaginative, *'Incredible.'*

She'd moved a long way on since she had lain awake at
night wishing she had a *real* family. Eve had pretty quickly
realised that not having a father, at least not one willing
to acknowledge she existed, was actually a blessing, not a
curse. Unlike the majority of her classmates she had been

spared the trauma of seeing her parents going through an ugly divorce or separation.

Her mum had not even had boyfriends until she came to work for Hannah's father. Hannah had caught on much sooner than Eve and she had been more concerned by the secrecy than the relationship itself.

For Eve, it hadn't just been the secrecy, it had been everything, and the longer the affair had lasted, the deeper her anger had grown as she'd watched helpless to do anything while her mother allowed history to repeat itself as she had become what amounted to the plaything of man who treated her like the hired help in front of his rich and powerful friends.

Charles Latimer might not be married but in every other way he was her own father—a selfish loser who used and humiliated her mum. Of course, back then Sarah had been a young impressionable student on her first holiday job—easy pickings for her unscrupulous rich employer.

What Eve could not understand was how her mother could let it happen again when she was now an independent, intelligent woman. How could she allow herself to be used and humiliated like this...? Where were her pride and self-respect?

Did Mum realise that he was only marrying her because of the baby? Eve wondered. Well, at least he was one step up the evolutionary scale of slime from her own father, whose contribution when he had learnt of her had been to write a signed note that included the words *get rid of it*.

Eve had never told her mum she had found the note while searching for her birth certificate, and she'd never let on she knew the identity of her father. Instead she had carefully folded it and put it back in the box that held her birth certificate.

'Having a baby at your age...' She sensed rather than

saw Hannah's look of warning. 'Not that you're old, obviously.'

Her mother managed a wan smile at the retrieval. 'Always the soul of tact, Evie.'

Eve watched as Hannah and her mum exchanged a look. She didn't resent the rapport that her mum and her friend had but, though she rarely acknowledged it, there were occasions when she did envy it. Eve was her daughter but Hannah was a kindred spirit.

'I just meant...' She paused and thought, What did you mean? 'Couldn't it be dangerous...for you, and the baby?' But not for Charlie Latimer. Eve felt the anger and resentment she had always felt towards the man deepen so that they lay like an icy block behind her breastbone.

'Loads of women in their forties have babies these days, Evie.' Hannah proceeded to tick off a list of well-known celebrities Sarah's age and older who had given birth recently.

'And I'll have a lot more support than I did last time around; your father has been marvellous, Hannah.'

Too little too late, Eve thought, before the guilt kicked in; it always did when she thought about all the things her mum had given up to be a single parent. She finally deserved some happiness but was she likely to find it with Charlie Latimer...?

Eve clenched her jaw. No, her mum deserved more—she deserved better after all the sacrifices she had made.

Wanting to give her mum the things she deserved had been behind Eve's choice to reject the prestigious university scholarship she'd been offered and instead start her own firm. It hadn't been easy. All the banks had turned the inexperienced eighteen-year-old away and in the end it had been a charitable trust set up to promote youth enterprise that had been convinced by her business plan and the rest, as they said, was history. Nowadays she was held up as one of the trust's success stories, and regularly mentored young aspiring entrepreneurs and helped raise funds.

It had been a year ago that Eve had been able to go to her mother and triumphantly tell her she didn't need to work for Charles Latimer, and that she, Eve, was able to support her while she did what she wanted: a university course, open her own restaurant…anything.

Good plan with one problem. It turned out her mum was already doing what she wanted: she wanted to waste her talents, to slave away for a man like Charles Latimer. Eve had been angry, hurt and frustrated. She knew that a distance had formed between them since that day. She had let it form.

Sarah's green eyes filled again as she scanned her daughter's face and asked anxiously, 'You're all right with this, aren't you, Eve?'

'I'm really happy for you, Mum,' she said quietly, thinking, If that man hurts you I'll make him wish he had never been born.

Maybe she was a better actress than she thought, or maybe her mum just wanted to believe the lie, but either way Sarah visibly relaxed.

CHAPTER THREE

THOUGH THE LAWN had been rigged out with a positive village of canvas to house the reception, the ceremony itself was being held in the timbered great hall of Brent Manor, Charles's country estate. The guests, entertained by a string quartet, were seated in semi-circular rows around a central aisle and the dramatic staircase was lit up to give everyone a good view of the bridal party as they made their big entrance.

The warm-up act was followed by a well-known soprano, who belted out a couple of numbers that reduced some people to tears. For Draco it felt like a visit to the cinema when the trailers went on for so long you forgot what you'd actually come to see.

Finally the wedding march started, but his sigh of relief earned him a poke in the ribs from his daughter, so he dutifully turned his head to watch the slow progression of the wedding party down the staircase. His interest was initially directed towards the tall bridesmaid who was the new wife of his friend Kamel.

Draco studied her as she walked past the row where he sat. Beautiful, he thought as his attention drifted for a moment to the second bridesmaid, who up to this point had been blocked from his view by the statuesque blonde.

He experienced a jolt of shock closely followed by an even stronger jolt of lust as he identified the slender creature as this morning's green-eyed Eve! While he did not believe in fate or karma or even coincidence, Draco did believe in not wasting opportunities.

She made Draco think of the Degas he had purchased several years ago: the big-eyed delicate-featured dancer in it possessed the same ethereal quality. Not that there was anything balletic about this woman's hunched shoulders and the expression in her wide-spaced eyes was less dreamy and more abject misery. As his glance lingered he realised that there was nothing joyous in any aspect of her body language, including the smile painted onto her face.

As she drew level with him he could almost feel the tension rolling off her in waves. In the hollow at the base of her white throat—she had quite beautiful collarbones, he mused—a pulse throbbed. It wasn't just tension rolling off her, he realised; it was a level of misery you would have expected to see at a funeral, not a wedding!

At the precise moment she drew level with him Draco got a glimpse of something else you didn't expect to see at a wedding! It happened so quickly that if he hadn't been staring at her he'd have missed it, and she handled the dilemma rather well. Without skipping a beat or looking to left or right she grabbed the bodice of her dress before it slithered all the way down to her waist so it was a bit of a blur, but he got a glimpse of a white lacy strapless bra through which he saw the faint pink outline of nipples and a birthmark shaped like a moon high on the left side of her ribcage.

As the service went on he found himself staring, not at the bride and groom, but at Eve... Was that really her name or a marketing tool? He was curious about her misery but a lot more interested in seeing that birthmark again... The white lace was pretty but in his head she was wearing pink tartan silk. He had felt instant attractions to women before but never one as consuming as that he felt when he looked at this woman.

His eyes didn't leave her all the way through the ceremony. Then, as the procession led by the jubilant happy couple returned down the aisle, she was briefly hidden from sight by the bride and groom. Draco, who had struggled to leave his cynicism behind, had time to think, I give them a couple of months, before he saw her come into view once more. Unlike the new Princess of Surana, who was smiling at every familiar face she saw, his bridesmaid was staring fixedly ahead. She radiated a sultry sexiness that he could almost taste.

She had actually walked right past him, when she suddenly turned her head. Their collision of eyes had such an impact that for a split second he stopped breathing and she stopped walking. The air whistled through his flared nostrils as he exhaled slowly, and watched the colour wash over her skin.

His wink brought a flash of anger to her dark-framed emerald eyes but did not lessen the tension in the muscles around his mouth and eyes... The hunger he was feeling was no laughing matter.

Once she'd accepted it was really happening, Eve just wanted it to be over. For the most part she managed to blank out the actual ceremony. There had been that wardrobe malfunction but she was pretty confident that no one had noticed. The eyes that hadn't been on the bride had been on the beautiful Princess of Surana, but just to be on the safe side straight afterwards she had slipped away below stairs—no guests here, just the caterers who had not made use of the big old-fashioned pantry—to stuff a few more tissues in her bra. Going braless in this dress had not been an option so she had to grin and bear the discomfort it caused her shoulder. Well, it was better than baring her all, which she almost had done!

She stayed in the pantry as long as she could without risking her absence being noticed; the dress dilemma hadn't been the only reason she had taken some time out. A memory of winking dark eyes came into her head and crossly she pushed it away, refusing to give him space in her head—refusing to give him the satisfaction. No man had ever looked at her with such earthy speculation and then to wink as though they shared some sort of secret…or was it that he thought she was a joke? She had maintained an air of cool disdain but inside Eve hadn't felt at all cool!

She had no clue who he was—and she wasn't interested enough to find out, she decided loftily. The guest list was as glittery as was to be expected when the groom was as wealthy and well connected as Charles Latimer, though in true lord-of-the-manor style he had invited all the estate workers and their families, among them a few girls she went to school with. She made no attempt to avoid them but neither did she speak to them.

A minor miracle—helped along by her resisting the temptation of the freely flowing champagne, as alcohol had a way of loosening her tongue—Eve managed to make it through the speeches while maintaining her assigned role of happy daughter of the bride.

By the time the bride and groom took to the floor for their first dance the knot of misery in her chest was a weight so heavy she felt as though it were crushing her, and her face muscles literally ached from the effort of looking pleased and proud while inside she was screaming *no*!

As the applause died away and the other guests began to drift onto the floor she pretended not to see Prince Kamel heading her way—the poor man nudged into doing his duty by Hannah, no doubt—and headed for one of the

flower-filled temporary ladies' rooms. The last thing she
needed was a sympathy dance!

But what about a sympathy something else…? For some
reason the face of one guest popped into her head along
with the maverick shameful thought, which she couldn't
even blame on alcohol. She gave her bodice a defiant hitch
and gritted her teeth, banishing the blatantly sexual features to some dark dusty corner of her mind.

The bathroom was empty—well, she was due a break!
Filling a basin with water, she stood there staring at her
reflection. What she saw did not improve her mood in
the slightest. It had been drizzling when they had trans-
ferred from the house to the marquee complex that had
been erected on the west lawn for the reception so her
hair was no longer sleek. It had frizzed and the strands
that had escaped around her hairline had turned into tight
corkscrew curls.

She sighed. 'Maybe I should invest in a wig?' Great,
now she was talking to herself. She propped her elbows
on the counter top and leaned in close so that her breath
fogged the mirror. Standing there with her eyes closed, she
patted her hair down as best she could with water, and listened to the soft gurgle as she pulled out the plug and the
water drained away.

If she'd had to make a list of the five worst days of her
life this one would have been right up there. It was the
keeping it in that made everything worse. She'd had to
smile through the knowledge that her mother was throwing herself away on a man who was not worthy of her, a
man Eve despised, while looking as if she were dressed
in a curtain and to top it all *that* man was here watching
it happen.

Now what were the chances of that? It was like some
horrible cosmic conspiracy! She had turned her head because she had literally felt his eyes on her, which was

crazy. But she hadn't been hallucinating; he really was there.

It had been the burst of energising adrenaline result-ing from that brief contact and that wink that had got her through the photo shoot, but any benefits had been can-celled out by the fact that every time she had glimpsed him since then he'd been staring at her.

He was rude, he was arrogant and she determinedly ig-nored him, which was not as easy as it sounded when even across the room and separated by dozens of other people she was painfully conscious of the primitive sexual aura he exuded that had struck her dumb earlier that day. It wasn't just his height or undeniable physical presence that made him stand out among the other men present, it was that rawness, the hint of danger he possessed.

It seemed crazy to Eve that some women were actually attracted by danger, that the whole bad-boy thing turned them on, but not being one of them she went out of her way to avoid him instead.

She opened her eyes and gave her reflection a stern look. 'Come on, Eve, this will all be a memory tomorrow.' Consciously straightening her shoulders, but not so much that it made her bodice slip down—she'd got the hang of it now—she headed for the door.

She had pushed it open a crack when she heard a voice she knew all too well. She peered furtively through the crack, knowing it wasn't one person, it was all three. They always had hunted in a pack and it seemed they still did.

The bullies from her school days no longer wielded the power over her that had made her life a misery but the thought of going out there and facing them right now... No, there were limits to how much 'suck it up and smile' she had left in her—a school reunion with the three witches was just too much to ask of anyone.

Lifting her skirt, she ran for one of the cubicles, closing

it just before the three women who like herself had had parents who worked on the estate came in.

'I just love that lippy, Louise.'

There was a clatter as make-up was emptied onto the counter top.

'So Hannah bagged a prince, lucky cow…'

There were murmurs of agreement.

'He's gorgeous, but I think she's put on weight.'

'Oh, definitely.'

'Look who's talking.'

In the cubicle Eve covered her lower face with her hand, not just to protect herself from the cloud of perfume that was drifting her way, but to stifle a gurgle of laughter. She wasn't surprised that her friend inspired jealousy but *fat*…! Hannah was perfect and everyone knew it.

'She's welcome to her prince—it's the hot Italian one I fancy. Now he i*s* fit…with those eyes and that mouth.'

You're obsessed, Eve chided herself. Just because the man is dark, why assume they are talking about him? Italian? Actually, one of the things that had struck her about him had been his Mediterranean colouring… Her green eyes glazed over as she conjured his voice in her head, hearing the slight husk in his deep, sexy drawl, but no accent.

'Is he Italian?'

'Have you never heard of Draco Morelli? Where have you been living?' came the pitying response. 'Honestly, Paula, I sometimes wonder what planet you live on. He's a multibillionaire or something, on all the richest lists.'

'So he's loaded? Better and better. Shame about the scar…but I suppose it isn't that bad.'

'Married?'

Someone giggled. Eve didn't know who by this point as their voices had blended into one high-pitched whine that grated on her nerves. At least one thing was cleared up: there was no longer any question mark over who they were talking about. Once they mentioned the scar she knew that the man the trio were discussing was the one whose stares she had been trying to ignore all day.

'Does it matter?'

The careless response made Eve's lips purse in a silent moue of distaste.

Marriage might not be something she personally aspired to, but if you were going to take vows—and she knew at least two of the women outside her cubicle door were wearing wedding bands—you stayed faithful to those vows.

If not, then what was the point?

She wasn't surprised, given he moved in the same circles as her new stepfather, that this—what had they called him? *Morelli*—had money, but, unlike the trio who were discussing him as though he were a piece of prime juicy steak they contemplated eating, Eve was not impressed.

You could recognise the quality of good tailoring without admiring the person who wore it! Her birth father had money and status and he was a total sleaze. Eve admired talent and intelligence, and there had certainly been intelligence in the dark-eyed stare that had followed her all day, but it had been the sexual challenge in them that had made her stomach muscles quiver.

'A definite plus,' someone admitted. Maybe Emma? Eve speculated. 'But I wouldn't throw him out of bed if he was broke. Imagine him stripped and ready for action...'

During the general laughter and crude comments that followed Eve found herself responding with a mixture of indignation and distaste... It wasn't so much that someone had hijacked her secret fantasy, although that was bad enough, it was that she'd been forced to admit she'd had one, that she had pictured a total stranger naked and sprawled on a bed that bore more than a passing resemblance to her own!

So you wondered what he looked like naked, Eve, big deal, she told herself. Did you think you were the only woman whose creative juices were switched on by his sexual charge?

'He's been staring at me all day, can't take his eyes off me. Have you noticed?' Louise boasted.

Eve's nostrils flared as she hung onto her temper. So he'd been eyeing up all the women—what a sleaze! It was just as well she hadn't felt special...well, not much. She could genuinely say she hadn't *wanted* his attention, but it was one thing not to want it and another to know he pulled the same tired trick with every woman in the room!

'You mean he came on to you? When?'

'I wrote my number on his hand.'

'No...how much have you had to drink? What if your Rob had seen?'

'What did he say?'

'He just looked at me and I went shivery! He's got the most incredible eyes... Then he said...'

'*What?* What did he say, Louise?'

The dramatic pause had not just her friends, but Eve in her hiding place, on tenterhooks.

'I could tell by the way he's been looking at me that he wants me. You always can...'

'Yes, but what did he *say*?'

'He said he had an excellent memory and if he wanted to remember a number he would, and then...'

'What? What did he do then?'

'Then he wiped it off!'

Louise had clearly decided this was encouraging. Her cronies, a lot less under her thumb than in the old days, were less sure. The subsequent squabble continued until they found a subject that they all agreed on—they were united in their contempt of the wedding.

'I think in this day and age when people are losing

their jobs and everything this sort of lavish display is totally insensitive.'

So why did you come? mouthed Eve from her hiding place. Someone seemed to hear her silent question.

'Yeah, but the champagne is good.'

'She's only the cook.'

'But good-looking. I wouldn't mind looking half as good as E-E-Eve's mum when I'm her age.'

'You've got to hand it to E-E-Eve's mum—she got her man in the end. My mum says they've been at it for years.'

With a militant light in her eyes, Eve reached for the door handle. No one, but *no one*, was about to bad-mouth her mother when she was around and get away with it.

'What about E-E-Evie? What does she think she looks like?'

Eve's hand fell away as she listened to the cruel malicious laughter. It brought the memories flooding back and for a moment she was the misfit stigmatised as a swot and taunted for her stutter.

'And that hair!'

'And the eyebrows, and she's still flat as a pancake, talk about molehills… Do you think she still stutters?'

'I don't know. The snooty cow walked straight past me and acted like I wasn't there. Well, whatever money she is supposed to have made I think that it's exaggerated as she hasn't spent any on make-up. I was right all along—she's definitely a lesbian.'

'You only have to look at her.'

'Definitely.'

'To think we got detention for saying it at school! The girl has no sense of humour.' There was the sound of rustling and another blast of hairspray before someone said, 'That's my mascara.' The sound of the door opening and then, 'She was always full of herself, looking down her nose at us, the little swot.'

Old insults and she'd heard them all before.

The door to the ladies' room closed with a dull clunk and the room fell silent, but Eve stayed inside the cubicle giving them another few minutes just to be on the safe side and let the tears dry.

She lifted a hand to her damp face... How crazy was that? She had sworn that they would not make her cry again, that the bullies who had made her life a misery had long ago lost their power to hurt her.

So why are you hiding in the loo, Eve?

Because she had nothing to prove.

'I'm not hiding.' She was about to slide the latch when a soft reply made her jump.

'I know but it's all right—they've gone.'

The kind voice didn't belong to any of the three faces from the past.

The only person in the otherwise empty ladies' room was a young girl. Even in her flat ballet pumps she was several inches taller than Eve and slender. The encouraging smile she gave when Eve stepped out lit a face that had perfect features.

Eve could feel the girl's warm brown eyes as she walked across to the washbasin. 'Are you all right?'

Eve smiled at the girl's mirror reflection and turned the tap, allowing the warm water to flow over her hands.

'Fine, thanks,' she lied, mortified to hear the wobble in her voice. This was crazy; she was a hard-headed businesswoman, so why was she fighting the sudden and utterly uncharacteristic urge to unburden herself?

The girl continued to look troubled. 'Are you sure?'

What a nice girl. She reminded Eve a little of Hannah at the same age. Not in colouring, as the teenager had raven-black hair, golden-tinged skin and liquid brown eyes, but in the confidence and innate grace that would set her apart from her contemporaries. Eve nodded and the girl walked towards the door.

Her hand was on the handle when she stopped and turned back, her expression earnest. 'My dad,' she began hesitantly. 'Well, he says you shouldn't let them get to you, or at least not let them *see* they get to you. It's the pack instinct—bullies react to the scent of fear, but underneath they're insecure and cowards.'

'Sounds like you have a good dad.'

'I do.' A grin flashed that made her look much younger all of a sudden. 'But he's not perfect.' The grin appeared again. 'Though he thinks he is.'

The girl's grin was contagious.

'Do you mind me asking…? Are you…?'

For the first time that day Eve felt the urge to laugh. She swallowed the tickle of hysteria in her throat, horrified to feel tears pricking her eyelids. 'A lesbian?' Eve finished for her.

'It's fine if you are,' the girl said.

The kid was so sweet, so kind, the contrast with the women's malice so profound that Eve felt the tears press hotly against her eyelids. She blinked hard and stretched a hand to lean heavily on the wall.

The mental exercise she'd employed to lock her emotions in a neat box required energy, and Eve's reserves were severely depleted. If she could have played the scene again she wouldn't have hidden but old habits once learnt were damned hard to break.

'No, I'm not.' The sob when it came emerged from somewhere deep inside her. Eve did not immediately associate it with herself, then another came and another… as all the emotions she had kept under tight control that day suddenly shook loose.

'Stay there. I'll get someone.'

'I'm f-fine…' Eve hiccoughed but the girl had vanished.

CHAPTER FOUR

EVE DIDN'T REALLY expect the girl to return at all but she did, and with the last person in the world she would have expected to see in a ladies' room.

Draco Morelli was the wise father— Oh, my God!

Eve backed away waving a warding hand as she fought to swallow a gulping sob. 'Go away!'

Draco made a swift assessment. 'Keep an eye on the door, Josie, and don't let anyone come in.'

'Okay.' She caught her father's hands and leaned forward to squint at his wrists. 'Did that woman really write her number on your arm? Don't look like that; Year Ten have pictures of you up in their common room. I've grown used to having a *hottie* as a father. Oh, and by the way, she's not a lesbian,' the girl threw over her shoulder as she whisked out of the room.

Draco didn't even blink. 'Always good to know.' He turned back to the weeping woman, who had backed into a corner, her face tear-streaked and her eyes red and puffy.

Marriage had given Draco a deep distrust of female tears. Clare had been able to turn them on and off like a tap and she had perfected the art so that they never smudged her make-up or gave her a blotchy nose. Her weeping was aesthetically perfect.

Comparing Clare's artistic weeping with the sobs that intermittently shook this woman's whole body despite her obvious efforts to control them was like comparing a spring shower with a monsoon. The emotions were genuine, he was conscious of that, along with a twisting of something close to sympathy in his chest, though if he'd been asked to put a name to it he'd have called it indigestion.

Draco had no desire to know the source of this emotional outpouring; he just wanted her to stop crying. In not one of the fantasies he had indulged in to get him through this long and interminably boring day had he pictured her like this.

He had imagined her many other ways, including wearing the striking lingerie, which a few casual enquiries had confirmed she actually designed, and also clad in nothing but an expression of passionate surrender.

His glance drifted over her face, heart-shaped, firm-chinned, her abundant warm-coloured hair springing from a high forehead. He liked his women well groomed and set the bar high, so it was surprising that, even now she was blotchy and tear-sodden, he still found much to please him about her.

He pondered the reason behind his fascination, and decided that the stubborn definition of her soft chin gave her face character and the generous defined line of her arched brows framed eyes that, when not bloodshot, were an almost unique shade of deep green. And of course the mouth that was fuelling his lust-filled fantasies... His wandering gaze stilled on the lush curves and he berated himself mentally after his first thought was about parting those soft pink lips and exploring their moist interior. At his side his long fingers flexed as he pictured himself tenderly brushing aside the curls that clustered around her face.

'I'm fine.' If being totally mortified counted as fine, she thought.

It was some comfort to Draco that she appeared to be gaining a semblance of control.

Maybe you should follow her example, suggested the sardonic voice in his head.

Hard to argue with when he was conscious of the heat pooling in his groin.

She struggled to pull in a deep breath as he continued to stare, making her skin prickle with heat. 'Will you go away?' She injected as much coldness into her voice as was possible while fighting another sob.

More accustomed to having women deliver responses designed to please rather than repel him, Draco took a few seconds to formulate a dignified response.

'I would like nothing better.' It ought to be true, but actually there were several things he would have preferred to do, though none of them was an option while his daughter was outside the door. 'Look, you don't want me here and I don't want to be here—'

'Then go away,' she hurled, wiping her face on her forearm and wishing the floor would open up and swallow her when she caught a glimpse of herself in the mirror behind him. Mortifying enough to make a spectacle of herself but to do it with this man as a witness made it a million times worse.

'My preferred option also,' he bit back, losing his patience. The woman might have a supremely sexy mouth but there were limits to what he was prepared to tolerate to look at it. 'My daughter came to me for help, and Josie retains a childlike belief in my ability to achieve the impossible. I struggle to keep the illusion alive.'

Dry-eyed now, she tilted her chin. 'Odd, she looked like a bright girl.'

She had anticipated an angry response so the appreciative humour that deepened the lines radiating from his spectacular eyes threw her off balance.

'That's better,' he approved. 'So what's the story?'

'What story?' She walked past him to the basin and turned on the water. 'Shouldn't you be going? Someone might come in and, as you see, I'm fine now.'

'Don't worry—Josie will give us some privacy.'

Privacy with this man was the last thing that Eve wanted! The thought sent a fresh flurry of prickles down her spine. 'So what do you expect her to do if someone wants to come in?'

He gave an indifferent shrug. 'She's a very resourceful girl.'

Eve stared at him in the mirror and shook her head. She could hear the pride in his voice; indifference was obviously the last thing he felt when it came to his daughter.

'And you're a really weird sort of father, not that I know anything about fathers.' Wishing the admission unsaid, she bent her head and splashed water on her blotchy face.

When she lifted her head again he was standing right there beside her, close enough for her to be conscious of the warmth of his hard, lean body, with one of the neatly folded individual hand towels that were stacked beside the linen basket in his hand.

She stared at it as though she'd never seen a towel before while the water from her hands dripped on the floor. She wasn't conscious of lifting her gaze, but as her eyes drifted slowly over the hard angles of his face she was suddenly aware of the increased volume of a low static hum in her ears.

This close she could appreciate just how evenly textured his golden-toned skin was, shadowed now by a light dusting of dark stubble that almost hid the scar next to his mouth.

She felt a sudden and almost uncontrollable urge to lift her hand and touch the place where she knew it was and trace the line...

'So, you don't have a dad, then?'

Like a sleepwalker coming to, she started, her raised hand moving jerkily and snatching the towel from him without a word. Under cover of a glare, she fought a debilitating wave of trembling weakness.

'What, is this research for your next book?' she snapped.

'Well, they do say everyone has one in them, but actually you just interest me.'

His comment whipped away her protective camouflage. Feeling horribly exposed and yet, more worryingly, excited, she dabbed her face with the towel. 'I'm not at all interesting, Mr Morelli.'

His sable brows lifted. 'You know my name.'

'It came up in the conversation.'

'Ah, yes, the conversation,' he mused slowly. 'So those charming friends of yours, what did they say that upset you so much?'

'Not friends,' she flashed, then, seeing his expression, she lowered her eyes and added more moderately, 'We went to school together, the little village school, and then—'

'Here, you missed a bit...' He took a corner of the towel she still held and, leaning in to her, dabbed a spot beside her mouth. Then he dabbed it again...and again...

Eve, who had been standing like a small statue, her eyes trained straight ahead, while admiring his very nice ears, heard a whimper escape her lips and hastily turned it into a cough.

'Secondary school,' she finished faintly.

'That cough sounds bad.' Draco was happy to go along with the pretence for now, but was curious why it apparently bothered her so much that there was such a dramatic level of sexual chemistry between them. Unless... A furrow indented his brow as he realised that just because she had no partner here did not necessarily mean there wasn't one somewhere in the background.

The possibility she was unavailable dragged the corners of his mouth downwards in a brooding, dissatisfied curve.

Her eyes slid away from his. 'A tickle in my throat.' It sounded less inflammatory than 'a starburst in my belly'.

'Relax,' he ordered.

Eve bit back a laugh.

'You might as well tell me what they said, you know, because otherwise Josie will, and if my daughter has been traumatised I'd like to know up front.'

'Traumatised!' She was shocked by the suggestion and then it dawned on her that his interest arose from parental anxiety and not, as she had thought… Well, what did you think, Evie—that he found you fascinating? That he wanted to know what made you tick or just that he wanted to get in your pants?

In your dreams. She sighed and then thought wryly that was probably the only way he'd ever appear in her bed! It was ridiculous to try and pretend that this man hadn't awoken some dormant responses in her or that he wasn't the domineering, controlling type that she was never going to get involved with. He might make an appearance in her fantasies but in real life—no way! He might make a lousy lover but at least he seemed to be a good and concerned father.

'Your daugh… Josie wasn't involved… I wasn't involved in what just happened in here.' Eve was horrified that he seemed to suspect that his daughter had witnessed some sort of slanging match. Or maybe even a brawl. 'Really,' she assured him earnestly. 'They didn't even know I was here and I didn't know your daughter was here either. It was just a case of eavesdroppers hearing bad things about themselves… We didn't get on at school either.'

'They look a lot older than you…'

He caught her look and added, 'Josie pointed them out

when she was dragging me in here. Why would their jealousy of you make you cry?'

God, why didn't Josie come and drag him out again—right now? Eve glanced at the doorway, willing the girl to appear, but it remained empty. She sighed again. The quickest way to get him out of here seemed to be to satisfy his curiosity and go three seconds without breaking down like some sort of neurotic basket case.

'That had nothing to do with them. It was just a combination of champagne, jet lag and...' She stopped, an arrested expression appearing on her face as she belatedly processed his comment. 'They aren't *jealous*.' Spiteful and insensitive, granted... 'Why would you think they were jealous of me?'

He looked amused by the question. 'Let me see. You are a success and you are beautiful and they are...' His lips twisted into a grimace of contempt as he recalled the blonde with the unlikely orange tan who had thrust her chest in his face and written her number on his hand, embarrassing all those who had witnessed the action.

Draco had not been embarrassed but he had been offended and annoyed.

'*Not*.'

He thought she was beautiful?

'And you did not drink any champagne.'

Her accusing green stare settled on his face; it was nice just for once to be the one on the offensive. 'How do you know?'

'I'm an observant man.'

Her eyes narrowed. 'You were watching me!' she flung, quivering with a combination of outrage and excitement that tied her stomach in knots and brought a flush to her pale skin.

'And you knew I was.' His retort was unanswerable for

someone who was not a good liar. 'It is the game men and women play, *cara*,' he drawled.

Eve felt as if she had just stepped out of the training pool into the deep end. She struggled to fight her way through the panic that was closing in on her and remain calm and in control. 'I'm not playing games.'

He looked at her for a long moment, acknowledging a flicker of uncertainty as the extraordinary possibility that she was telling the truth occurred to him. She could not be *that* inexperienced, surely? But looking deep into those big emerald eyes, he saw she wasn't trying to hide anything—or perhaps she didn't know how...?

A word popped into his head: *innocence*.

He straightened up, pulling away from her in more than the physical sense. He had thought they were on the same page but he had been wrong; he had seen that sultry mouth but not the emotional baggage that came with it. It was a good thing he had discovered his error now, before things had gone too far, he told himself.

She was high maintenance, and he was a bastard who had no intention of changing. Always better in his experience to call a spade a spade.

'Will you do something for me?' he asked.

He was not about to make an indecent proposal with his daughter just outside the door but even so her heartbeat kicked into a higher gear. 'That depends.'

'Smile and try not to look so tragic.'

She stiffened, her spine snapping to attention. 'Pardon me?'

'I'd like to stay a hero for as long as I can in my daughter's eyes, so I'd be grateful if you could suck it up and look like I waved my magic wand and made everything better. It's not as if you're the only one who doesn't like weddings. I suspect with me it's that they remind me too much of my own,' he admitted with a frankness she was beginning to find disturbing.

It was a day he was able to think about with a degree of objectivity now, but for a long time it hadn't been that way. Now he was able to admit that he had known halfway through exchanging his vows that he was making the biggest mistake of his life, and it was doubtful it would even have got that far if his parents hadn't been so against it, and delivered an ultimatum.

He had been twenty and had thought he knew everything. Their parental disapproval had been like a red rag to a bull, and what better way to display his maturity than to get married against their wishes and show them how wrong they were?

'Suck it up?' she repeated in a low, dangerous voice. 'Suck it up? What the hell do you think I've been doing all d-d-day? As for your marriage, I...I...spare me the details.' She glared at him, daring him to comment on her stutter. These days it rarely surfaced but she was always conscious that it could at any moment—and it was his fault that it just had.

Eve felt something snap inside her. 'You think you don't like weddings, let me tell you,' she huffed, 'about my day!' She reached inside the bodice of her dress and after a grunt produced a wad of tissues, which she waved at him. 'Did you have to stuff your bra full of tissues to keep your dress up? Did you have to watch your mother, who is the best, *totally* best person you know, marry a man who is so far beneath her in every way?' Eve's voice dropped a husky octave but shook with the strength of the emotion that gripped her as she concluded, 'And it wouldn't even be happening now if the scumbag hadn't got her pregnant!'

For about three seconds she felt the intense relief of getting it off her chest...and then she looked at the tissues in her hand and gulped quite literally. The wave of horror that followed made her want to vanish... What had she been thinking of, telling a total stranger such private things?

Her green eyes lifted to his face, her insides churning sickly. 'If you tell anyone I'll—'

'Be forced to have me killed. Don't worry—your secret is safe with me,' Eve heard him drawl with teeth-clenching sarcasm.

'The idea is growing on me,' she declared grimly.

Forgetting the cold shoulder he had intended to present to her, he grinned. 'I'm curious—have you got any more tissues down there or is what remains all you?'

She pressed her hand to the neckline of her strapless gown; without the extra padding to fill it he had a view all the way down to her waist and he was certainly looking.

'You're hateful!' Eve looked at the wad of tissues and threw them at him.

Laughing, he reached out and caught them. 'Seriously.' Actually he had been *seriously* impressed by the view of her small but perfect breasts like plump little apples in their lacy covering. He could just imagine them filling his hand—only they wouldn't because she was high maintenance. She was an innocent... Mmm, *how innocent, exactly...?*

He didn't want to know. All right, maybe he did—virgins of her age were a bit like unicorns: the things of fables.

'So what have you got against Charlie Latimer?' The guy was successful, solvent and as far as he knew had no major vices like drink, drugs or gambling, yet her animosity had been toxic in its intensity.

'So you don't know he's been having an affair with my mum for years? That makes you something of a rarity.' Could you sound any more bitter, Eve?

'I don't listen to gossip, but I do know that relationships

are complex and it's hard to judge what makes one work from the outside.'

'They didn't have a *relationship*. She was his bit on the side. She doesn't *have* to marry anyone, let alone him! I'd have looked after her. I *wanted* to look after her.'

'You're very possessive.'

'Protective,' she flashed back, angry at the inference and his sardonic expression.

'Don't you think that maybe your mother has earned the right to make her own decisions and her own mistakes…?'

She cast a simmering glance up at his lean face. 'What business is it of yours anyway?'

'None at all. I thought you wanted my input.'

'Well, I don't!'

'I stand corrected.'

She pulled herself up to her full height and, bristling with dignity, looked pointedly at the route to the door he was blocking. 'If you don't mind…? And don't worry.' She flashed him a wide insincere smile, her eyes shooting daggers. 'I will smile, but I'd prefer not to be seen coming out of the ladies' room with you.'

'It might make the world look at you in a different light.'

She narrowed her eyes and said with fierce distaste, 'You mean people will see me as a tart.'

'No, I mean they might think you actually have a life.'

She sucked in a breath of outrage. 'I have a perfectly good life already and I don't give a damn what people think.'

'If that were true you wouldn't give a damn what people think if we walk out that door together.'

Teeth clenched in sheer frustration, she glared up at him. He couldn't have looked smugger if…if… No, he simply couldn't have looked smugger. 'Just wait here.'

'Shall I count to a hundred?'

Responding to this with a disdainful sniff, she tossed

her head and pushed through the doorway, pausing only to fling a 'Thank you!' over her shoulder.

He didn't count to a hundred. Instead he thought about what had just happened. Running the scene through his head, little snippets of the conversation making him frown, others smile. It had clearly hurt her to say thank you, and Draco felt a faint twinge of guilt as he knew he didn't deserve it. The only cry of help he'd responded to was his daughter's. He'd only come in here for Josie, because he wanted her to think he was a good guy, but in truth he wasn't. If he had seen an hysterical woman crying in the bathroom, his instinct would not have been to wade in and help, it would have been to walk in the opposite direction very fast.

He had his life streamlined so that he could focus on what was important—he did not get involved.

The women standing outside reading the 'out of order' sign that was pinned to the door looked at him wide-eyed when he emerged.

Ignoring their astonished stares, he unpinned the sign written in the pink lipstick his daughter was wearing and nodded.

'Everything is back to normal.'

Which was a good thing. Eve Curtis had even more issues than he had imagined; the man who got her would need a medal and a degree in counselling.

CHAPTER FIVE

DRACO JOINED HIS daughter, who was sitting at an empty table beside the dance floor. 'The notice on the door was a nice touch.'

'Is everything all right, Dad?'

'Fine.' He reached out a hand to ruffle her hair but Josie got to her feet

'She's available; I checked.'

Draco looked down, not so very far now. Over the past ten months his daughter had grown ten inches and had gone from being a sweet, slightly chubby five-feet-one twelve-year-old to a slender, leggy thirteen-year-old; still sweet but to his parental eye worryingly mature, with the sort of coltish good looks that had already drawn two offers of modelling contracts.

Draco was just relieved he hadn't had to come the heavy parent over the latter; Josie had plans for her future that did not include becoming the face of anything.

'Who is available?' He glanced down and noticed for the first time that his daughter was holding a cocktail. He winced and blamed Eve for taking his eye off the ball. Just what was the woman's problem? He slung a quick glance across the room and sure enough she was still acting as if she were at a wake, not a wedding reception. God, no wonder she had been bullied; she was one of those people who simply couldn't blend into the background, and didn't try either. She stood out in a room of a hundred—or in this case nearer five.

He reached for the drink. 'I don't think so, angel.'

'You know something, Dad, you have serious trust issues. It's only a mocktail.' She turned the stick in the glass of brightly coloured but non-alcoholic contents and offered with a grin, 'Try if you don't believe me.'

His expressive lips twisted into a moue of distaste. 'I'll pass.'

'So about Eve, Dad.'

He shook his head wryly. *About Eve*—it was more a case of a detour around Eve. She was an emotional storm. He caught his daughter's look and said defensively, 'What about Eve?'

'I said she's available.'

His daughter was teasing, but under her smiles was she really…? He wasn't entirely sure, but one thing he was sure of was that this was a conversation he did not want to have.

'Is that boy a friend of yours?' He angled a narrow look towards the young man who was making his tipsy way across the dance floor towards his daughter. Recognising the warning, the kid abruptly changed direction.

'Good try, Dad.'

'Try at what?'

'At changing the subject.'

'What subject would that be?'

Josie rolled her eyes before directing a finger across the room to where Eve was standing. 'She's all alone and you should go and talk to her. Or are you scared?' his daughter, who thought she knew what buttons to press, speculated innocently. The hell of it was that five times out of ten she did and he could see those odds narrowing as she got older.

'I know a lot of men are scared of rejection,' she added. Draco, who didn't have much experience of rejection, looked amused; women's magazines had a lot to answer for. 'So how do you know that men are scared of rejection?'

'Clare told me.'

His half-smile faded. 'Since when do you call your mother Clare?' he asked sternly.

'She asked me to—she says now that I'm taller than her being called Mum makes her feel old.' Seeing his expression, Josie touched her father's arm. 'She can't help it, you know. Some people are just—'

'Self-centred and selfish.' Draco frowned, regretting the bitter words the moment they were uttered. After the divorce he had been determined not to bad-mouth his ex-wife to their daughter and always felt guilty as hell when he failed. He did not want to be the sort of parent who used their kid as a bargaining chip and asked them to take sides.

'Relax, Dad, you're not telling me anything that I didn't work out for myself years ago. So are you scared...? You've been staring at her all day—yes, Dad, you have. She is *the* Eve in Eve's Temptation. Brains and beauty. Oh, before you say it—'

'What was I about to say?'

'Beauty isn't all about long legs and boobs, Father.'

Always good to know that your daughter thought you were shallow and sexist. 'I am aware of that.'

'And you obviously fancy her so don't let me cramp your style. Go for it, Dad.'

'Thank you very much.'

His daughter ignored the irony. 'I think you need a challenge.'

'Being your father makes every day a challenge.'

'I'm a far better daughter than you deserve.' She grinned and for a moment looked more like his little girl again. Draco pushed away the wave of nostalgia and reminded himself that nothing stayed the same.

'I'm not going to contest that one.' He touched her

cheek. 'How about you let me worry about my social life, kiddo?'

Her childish brow furrowed. 'I just don't want to see you lonely. I'm not going to be at home for ever, you know, and you're not getting any younger.'

Feeling every day of his thirty-three years, Draco allowed his daughter to pull him onto the dance floor. Eve had already gone.

Having delivered the car and the keys to Draco, his driver squeezed his bulk into the passenger seat of the Mini beside his wife. Draco stepped smartly to one side as the Mini reversed, sending up a cloud of gravel, and shot off down the drive with a honk of the horn.

A smile played across the firm line of his lips as he watched the car vanish, narrowly avoiding a collision with one of the catering vans that were beginning to leave. On balance Draco was glad the husband and not the wife was his driver.

He strolled back towards the Elizabethan manor, which was impressively backlit now the light had faded by some state-of-the-art laser technology. Less high tech but equally attractive were the trees surrounding the house, which had been artistically sprinkled with white fairy lights for the occasion. There was no sign of Josie, who had said she'd be only five minutes when she had gone back to make up a doggie bag for her cousin, fifteen minutes ago.

Overhead a helicopter took off, and he sighed. It would have been easier to make the return journey by the same means of transport in which he had arrived, but the last time he had landed in the meadow at the timbered farmhouse where his ex-model sister lived the bucolic life of a hobby farmer with her banker husband, she had complained that her hens had stopped laying.

It did not seem very scientific, but then neither was

naming a load of hens who all looked identical to him and assigning them individual personalities, so rather than risk getting in her bad books again, as she helped out a lot with Josie, having her to stay when he was out of town, he had decided to drop Josie off by car before driving back to London himself.

Philosophical about being kept waiting by his daughter, he had positioned himself beneath the illuminated canopy of a tall oak to wait for Josie just as a minibus filled with guests from the village set off, leaving behind three figures on the gravel.

'Who is he calling drunk?' the one who had written her number on his arm slurred, waving her fists at the bus.

Another sat down on the floor and took off her shoes. 'My feet hurt. Louise, why did you have to swear at him?'

Moving back into the shadow, an expression of distaste twisting his lean, patrician features, Draco placed a supportive hand on his neck and rotated his head in an effort to relieve some of the stiffness afflicting his muscles.

The first exercise having failed, he was rolling his shoulders when a figure appeared in the illuminated doorway—not Josie, but one he recognised. It wasn't hard as she was still wearing the full-length bridesmaid dress, but now it was topped by a lacy shrug that had little cap sleeves that covered her bare shoulders and was buttoned up to her throat, concealing everything else.

He watched as she glanced to right and left as though looking for someone and then began to walk towards him, only not him, she couldn't see him, yet a man could be excused for thinking it was a sign.

A man could also be accused of spinning the situation because of the ache in his groin. He sighed and stepped deeper into the shadows. His trouble was he had gone too long without; there had only been the one night since ending things with Rachel.

There could have been more but he had not made the effort—not that there was much effort involved. He had the number on his phone of a young politician who was attractive, ambitious and discreet. She had a busy schedule, was opposed to cumbersome emotional baggage, and her Brussels base was an advantage, not a problem.

'Here she comes. E-E-E-Evie.' If the sniggered whisper was loud enough for him, the odds were that Evie had heard it too.

Draco slid the phone back into his pocket as he felt a sudden rush of anger. If he had paused to think, he would have been surprised by the white-hot intensity of it, but he didn't pause. Instead he stepped out of the shadows where two strides brought him to Eve's side. Without a word he grabbed her by the arm and jerked her towards him.

Soft and warm, she collided with him, her gentle curves fitting perfectly into the angles of his body.

She was too shocked to even cry out; her eyes flew wide, her pupils dilating dramatically as she looked up into the face of the man who held her. She let out a tiny fluttery sigh, stiffening as almost casually he slid his free hand around her waist, his fingers spreading across her ribcage from her waist to just beneath her breast, possessively, as if he had the right.

'What are you doing?' The question proved her brain was working... The rest of her body she wrote off, as it was clearly reacting independently. The heat that made her skin burn was seeping into her blood, so that she felt light-headed, and the sensual fog in her brain made it hard to think—so she just stopped trying.

Why bother when it was a fight she was going to lose? Because she really wanted to taste him, and it was all she could think about.

He bent in closer, brushing her cheek with his lips, holding her eyes all the time. His stare was hypnotic; she couldn't have broken eye contact even if she'd wanted to and there was a big…no, a massive question mark over that.

'I'm going to kiss you—are you all right with that?'

No…one word, how hard was that? That's all you have to say, she told herself firmly.

'Someone will see,' she whispered instead.

'They're meant to, so shut up, *cara*, and don't have another panic attack.'

The comment roused Eve to lethargic indignation. 'I don't have panic attacks. Let me go!' It was weak and way overdue, but at least she'd made a protest—she could tell herself later *I tried to stop him*.

Man up, Eve, take responsibility—you want this.

'What the hell do you think you're doing, Draco?' Saying his name had been a mistake as suddenly everything seemed intimate, more personal.

'Relax and don't hit me; we have an audience. I am once and for all going to lay to rest any doubts about your sexuality.' He touched the side of her jaw. 'Don't look.'

She lifted her gaze to his, and the dark passion-glazed look in her eyes sent a surge of power through his veins.

'Look where?' She could no longer pretend she wanted to look at anything but him.

Her voice had dropped a sexy octave, the sound possessing a tactile quality that made him hungry to feel her small hands on his skin…exploring…

'Do you have doubts about my s-sexuality?'

'Not a one,' he said against her lips. 'I hate the idea of you stuttering for anyone else.'

Her stutter was the bane of her existence and he was acting as though it were a gift! 'You don't have to do this.' But of course if he didn't she might die, although to the women watching them she knew it already looked as though they were kissing. 'I really don't care what they think.' But it might be nice to wipe the smiles off their smug faces.

'Actually I *do* have to do this,' he muttered raggedly.

They were both breathing so fast she could not separate the sounds or even the heartbeats. She gave a little nod, her breathless moan of anticipation barely audible.

'I have wanted to kiss you since this morning when you threw your bra at me.'

His eyelashes cast shadows along the crest of his cheekbones and through her half-closed eyes they looked like solid blocks of colour. 'That feels like years ago...' The words were soft sibilant sighs, hardly audible above her tortured shallow breaths. 'Well...?'

'Well what?'

'Are you going to find out...how it feels to—?'

The rest of her words were lost in the warmth of his mouth. He explored her mouth, his tongue probing and his lips moving against hers with sensuous expertise. The pressure of the kiss bent her backwards against his supporting arm and she straightened up again as his head lifted like a sapling when the wind died.

He was still close and breathing hard; they both were. Through the mesh of her lashes she could see the fine texture of his olive-toned skin, the darkened stubble thicker now on the surface of his jaw and lower face, the gold tips on the end of his thick jet-black eyelashes. A shiver of sensation rippled through her body, then another and another...

'So was that your good deed for the day?' she murmured.

Draco, who had really fought his baser instincts to keep the kiss under control, just nodded. It had been a mistake to kiss her; all it had done was make him realise what he was missing and that he wanted her more than ever.

'Yeah, and now that our first kiss is out of the way...'

He leaned in again, the gleam in his dark eyes warning her of his intent.

This time the kiss was very different. With considerably less finesse, less control, the wildness scared Eve on one level and on another excited her unbearably. She wanted everything he was doing and more. The knowledge shocked even as it made her arch into him.

She could feel his arousal rock hard against her belly as he moulded her against him, sealing their bodies at hip level. Then while he continued to plunder her mouth with a raw hunger of bruising intensity Draco's big hands moved over her body.

She could feel the heat of his hand through the silk of her dress as it moved up and down her thigh. While his other kneaded and moulded the aching peak of one small breast.

It didn't even cross her mind that they were standing in full view of anyone who happened by. She couldn't think beyond the throbbing ache of need between her thighs and when it became too much to bear and as what was left of her control broke she grabbed the back of his neck with both hands and pulled his face in closer.

Eve kissed him back with an urgency, a wildness, that matched his. She clung to him like a limpet as he staggered back, struggling to keep his balance while she pulled at his clothes with greedy hands, trailing kisses across his face, down the strong column of his neck then moving back to his mouth.

When she slid her hands under his shirt he gasped, then moaned. Eve felt his ribcage lift as he sucked in a breath then held it as he grabbed both of her hands, which were sliding down the corrugated muscles of his belly, and dragged them away.

He stood back, looking down at her for a moment, at the wanton picture she made. It had been the feeling of her eager hands sliding over his damp, satiny smooth skin that had almost made his control snap, and it was only the knowledge that his daughter could be one of those interesting passers-by to witness this that made him hold back.

'Well, I think that might have done the trick,' he gasped, still fighting for control.

Oh, God, oh, God, oh, God!

The cry was in the vault of her skull. Her lips thankfully stayed closed and trembling as Eve watched him drag his shirt together, tucking it into his trousers.

'Are you all right?' He felt a slug of unwelcome guilt, she looked so damned fragile standing there.

She took several shaky steps backwards, only stopping when her back made contact with a tree. Lifting her chin, she directed what she hoped was a look of cold disdain, but was more than likely breathless shock and confusion, at his lean face.

He wasn't touching her but there was a fierce intensity in his rigid attitude that made her stomach muscles vibrate.

'I'm not going to have sex with you to prove I'm not a lesbian.'

'Oh, I think you proved that already seeing as your friends have left. And it is always polite, *cara*, to wait to be asked first.'

She had no defence against the mortified rush of colour that bathed her body in a guilty glow. 'Pity you didn't ask first before you mauled me about like that. And you can quit with all that Italian *cara* stuff; it's incredibly cheesy.'

'To be accurate I think we should call it mutual... mauling,' he mused, the smouldering glow in his deep-set eyes sparking as he added, 'And to be honest that didn't go quite the way I anticipated. Sorry—' he glanced over his shoulder '—but Josie could be here any minute.'

Just when she thought she could not feel any more humiliated, she tossed her head. 'It was only a kiss.'

His brows lifted and he barked a dry laugh. 'If you think that was *only a kiss*, *cara*, I can't wait to see your version of *just sex*!'

'There won't be any just sex! No sex at all!' Turning on her heel, she could hear his soft laughter following her.

CHAPTER SIX

IF HER MUM had been around this wouldn't be happening because Eve knew that Sarah would have taken one look at her daughter's face and said, 'No way are you driving, my girl—you're in no fit state.'

It wouldn't have mattered what Eve said because that was what mothers did: they stopped their daughters driving even if they were perfectly capable—or she would have done if she'd been there and not off on her honeymoon with her new husband.

Eve gave a self-pitying sniff as she trudged on, finding it easy to lay her present predicament at the door of Charlie Latimer. She decided to give it until that next bend, because how frustrating would it be if she turned back only to later realise that she had actually been within a few hundred yards of the main road and hopefully some help or at least some place with a phone signal?

She was trying her phone again when she heard the car in the distance and felt a stab of relief. But by the time the distant light had become dazzling the relief had morphed into apprehension; if this were a crime drama she'd be the body in the first scene, the one that normally made her want to shout at the screen, How could you be so stupid?

She took a deep breath. This was real life, most people were not homicidal maniacs and she was not about to get into a car with a stranger. She just wanted to ask if they

could contact a local garage to come and pick her and her
car up…yes, that was definitely the sensible option.

The big low car slowed and, heart beating hard, Eve carried on walking, though more slowly, projecting as much
confidence as possible as you should when you were alone
in the dark in the middle of nowhere… For goodness' sake,
Eve, Surrey is hardly the last wilderness! she scorned.

'Are you totally insane?'

It was not the conversational comment that made her
spin around directing her wide-eyed stare at the driver of
the car, but the deep voice with that tactile 'once heard
never ever forgotten' quality. Her stomach reacted by going
into a deep dive while simultaneously every square inch
of her skin prickled with an appalling awareness that was
painful in its intensity.

Her head was immediately filled with thoughts of his
mouth crashing down on hers, his warm lips teasing, tor-
menting… With a massive effort she reined in her imagination and her indiscriminate hormones, managing to focus
on the here and now.

The painful truth here was that in some ways a homicidal maniac might have been easier to cope with.

The engine was still running as she took a deep breath,
lifting a hand to her face against the glare of the headlights as the driver's door was flung open and the occu-
pant vaulted out.

It was impossible to read his expression, but his body
language was less of a struggle. His tall, lean frame was
rigid, projecting none of the languid, mocking attitude that
got under her skin, but something that approached anger.

She squared her shoulders. Some people might con-
clude it was a sort of cosmic conspiracy or fate that kept
on throwing her into this man's path. Eve, who believed
a person was in charge of their own fate, thought it was
more of a bad day getting worse!

A lot worse.

'What are you doing here?' Not your loud voice, Eve, warned the critic in her head. As he took a step closer and she fought the urge to mirror his action with several back she got sucked in once again by the entire in-your-face physical thing he had going on. If his voice was hard to forget the rest of him was...she released a tight fractured sigh and thought...stupendous.

'I was passing...?'

She did not respond to the dry wit but then as a shaft of moonlight fell directly across his face she saw he wasn't smiling either; each fascinating hollow and carved sybaritic angle of his incredible face was set in a grim line of cold accusation that set her chin up another defensive notch.

'Are you stalking m-me?' It was not hard to visualise him as a sleek predator but she, Eve reminded herself, was not anyone's prey. Despite her intention to cloak her comment with a believable level of amused indifference, she finished on a stutter.

Cut yourself some slack, Eve. There probably wasn't a woman on the entire planet who could laugh at the idea of being pursued by this man...and they hadn't been kissed by him—or kissed him back.

She closed the door on that memory, but not before her insides had dissolved and her core temperature had risen several painful degrees.

'If I was stalking you, you're making it damned easy.'

'You're calling me easy?' Why not just leave your foot in your mouth, Eve? It will save you time and energy, she thought with an internal groan.

'Easy?'

The echo carried a note she tried to place as his dark eyes went from her face to the near-empty minor road. She turned her head, wondering if he had seen another car.

Five miles, Draco estimated, if not more since he had seen another vehicle, and that off-roader had turned down a farm track. He wouldn't be on it himself if he hadn't been dropping off Josie at her English cousin's house, and what would Eve have done then…?

Eve tensed as his attention refocused on her face.

'No, you're bloody hard work. Just get in the damned car.'

'That won't be necessary, thank you. I don't want to be a nuisance, but if you could inform a garage that I broke down. This is a short cut.' Hearing the defensiveness in her own voice, Eve frowned. For the past half-hour she had been contemplating turning back as each successive bend in the road did not reveal the main road—but there was no need to tell him that.

His brows lifted as he slid a phone from his pocket, wishing leaving her standing here in the middle of nowhere was an option.

Liar, said the voice in his head. He hadn't got excited by the idea of making out in a car since his teens, but for some reason this woman, with her prickles and her lush lips and her hungry eyes, had made him ache in a way that made self-delusion useful. After all, what was the point overanalysing something that was as simple as sex? Especially as with her he knew it would be stupendous!

'Ever heard of mobile phones?' Ever heard of avoiding someone with emotional high maintenance written all over her face? He detoured around his own internal question and waved his phone at her—trying to ignore the way the softening effect of the dark copper-toned curls that framed her face made her appear younger and more vulnerable.

'Ever heard of black spots where you get no signal?' she returned seamlessly. Did the man think she was a total idiot?

No, he just thinks you're easy, Eve—with good reason!

The door opened on the memory still raw, still recent, still mortifying and, yes, still wildly exciting, submerging her in a tidal wave of hot, lustful longing against which her only defence was to shove her trembling hands into her pockets and look away.

She could not remember feeling this out of control for... well, ever. She didn't like it, and she didn't like him. No, not liking him was too mild an emotion; she hated him.

Draco's ebony brows twitched into a line above his masterful nose as he slid the phone back into his pocket without looking at it. He was trying not to see the visible tremors that shook her slender frame under the double-breasted jacket that looked at least two sizes too big for her.

'Get in!' he snapped, fighting off an irrational surge of tenderness; combined with the lust that still circulated hotly through his veins, it made for a contradictory and uncomfortable mix. It was a massive mistake to equate small and delicate with vulnerable or in need of protection—she was as tough as nails.

Or she'd like the world to think she was.

Ignoring the mental addition, he added with silky sarcasm, 'Unless you would prefer to walk? Or possibly wait for a serial killer? They do say that they come along in twos, or is that buses?'

Her scornful glance swept upwards from his polished toes but she only made it as far as his waist and stalled. At some point, like her, Draco had changed. The dark jeans he now wore fitted just as perfectly as the tailored trousers of his morning suit, though the cut of the denim emphasised his lean hips and the muscularity of his thighs.

Swallowing past the sudden aching occlusion in her throat, she wrenched her eyes clear, gave a scornful snort and angrily retorted, 'You've never caught a bus in your life!' She stopped, frowning darkly as her accusation drew a startled laugh from him. 'And statistically speaking—'

The pistol-shot snap of Draco's long fingers made Eve jump and indicated his opinion of statistics and his diminishing patience levels. She was glad of the interruption as it was hard to focus on statistics when she was thinking how it felt to be plastered up close against those iron-hard thighs, feeling the shocking imprint of a rock-hard arousal on her belly.

He gave a sigh, intoning wearily, 'Get in, Eve. I've better things to do than stand here arguing the toss.'

Eve, who had been swaying slightly, blinked hard. She knew about red mists but the one that floated in her brain clouding good sense was darker and it had warmth and depth and— No, don't wrap it up, Eve, she told herself impatiently. It's just lust; get over yourself. So the man knows how to kiss?

'Thank you, but I've said if you could—'

He raised an ironic brow and she stopped, catching her full upper lip between her white teeth as she gave a sigh and surrendered, if not to the dark mist, then to the practicalities of her situation. So she accepted a lift from him— what was the worst that could happen?

She brushed a strand of curling chestnut hair from her eyes. The only thing she'd achieved when she'd looked in the engine earlier had been a bang on the head, which had shaken half her hair loose. Of course it had gone into frizz mode immediately. Her eyes went to his dark head. After they'd kissed his hair had been sexily ruffled. Now it was smooth and sleek and yet it was still sexy.

'That's very kind of you—' Her eyes connected with his and she stopped speaking, her heart beating hard and fast. There was nothing that could be even loosely termed as kind in his eyes right now; the feral glow made her insides dissolve.

She sounded like a prim schoolmistress and she looked— His eyes slid of their own volition to the full curve of her cushiony lips, and he groaned silently. He recalled how she kissed like a sex-starved angel, and gritted his teeth against the ache in his groin that packed the kick of a mule.

'I'm not kind.'

Eve gave her head a tiny shake, causing a curling tendril to attach itself to her mouth, and she detached the strands with an impatient frown.

In his seat before her Draco leant across, pulling away the jacket draped over the back of the passenger seat before she leaned back. His hand touched her shoulder as he slung it into the back, even that light contact sending an electrical surge through her body.

She survived the brush of his eyes, breathing through the moment and even managing to acknowledge his action with a slight nod despite the swirling confusion in her brain.

As he hit the ignition the space was filled with a classic jazz ballad. Eve exhaled, covering her mouth with her hand to disguise her sigh of relief—she wouldn't have to make conversation.

Then he turned it off.

They had driven a few minutes when he broke the silence.

'Will you fasten your jacket?'

She didn't fight the childish urge to challenge everything he said or question it too deeply. 'Why? I'm warm.'

The comment drew a rumble of laughter from his throat, but, bemused and desperately hiding her reaction to the nerve-shredding effect of being in close physical proximity to him, Eve turned her head and slung him a scowl.

'I'm missing the irony.'

'You make your living selling underwear but you don't wear your own products.'

She was tired and stressed and it took a few moments for his meaning to penetrate. When it did she grabbed the corners of her jacket and pulled them together.

'You mean I'm not an underwear model. Well, for the record, most women aren't and I make underwear for normal women.'

'Make but not wear.'

'I...I had a very minor surgery and the bra strap chafes.' The Australian doctor had been reassuring about the mole he'd said looked innocent, but to be safe he'd whipped it off and sent it for analysis.

'Minor?'

'A mole removal, but it was nothing sinister.'

His brow smoothed as he slid a sideways look at her face. 'With your skin you should plaster on factor fifty.'

'I'm not an idiot.'

'That's open to debate.' What wasn't was her delicious, soft, smooth pale skin; it would be nothing short of criminal to expose it to the harshening effects of the sun. 'Statistically speaking, someone with your colouring—'

'I am not ginger; it's chestnut.'

Colour aside, it was an essential part of his fantasies.

'Well, statistically—'

'Do you know how boring people who quote statistics are?'

He adopted an expression of unconvincing confusion as he consulted the rear-view mirror. 'I never quote statistics,' he explained. 'I make them up—no one ever knows the difference and you sound informed and intelligent.'

'Seriously?'

'Totally,' he confirmed. 'You should try it. You'd be amazed at how few people question a statistic.'

Eve bit her quivering lip, then, losing her fight, broke into peals of laughter.

She had a great laugh, when she wasn't feeling bitter

and twisted and sexually frustrated. He couldn't believe now that he had actually almost convinced himself she was a virgin. He realised that Eve Curtis could be fun outside bed, not that his interest in her extended beyond the bedroom, he told himself.

Wiping her eyes, she turned to him. 'So the next time I find myself losing an argument I should make up a statistic.'

'You have to keep an element of realism and you have to believe what you say.'

'You mean,' she cut back slickly, 'you have to be a good liar.'

'That goes without saying…'

'Like you.'

'I could say I'm always honest but I might be lying.' Eve recognised the crossroads they were approaching; it was the one where she always nursed a secret fear of taking the wrong turning and ending up in Wales.

She told him the area she lived in, fully anticipating he would ask for updates, but he didn't. Draco was obviously one of those people with a built-in sat nav. He was one street away from the building where Eve lived before he asked for further directions.

'It's the next turn…you just went past it. Our street lights are part of the council cuts,' she said by way of apology as he backed up.

She unfastened her seat belt, unable to conceal her palpable relief that her journey was at an end, though now it was she was able to concede she might have been overreacting. Alpha males were really not her thing; their earlier kiss was not her thing; nothing that had happened today was her thing.

Tomorrow happily was another day, a new start, a clean slate. Running out of clichés, she turned to Draco.

'Well, thank you.' Just to keep things unambiguous, she

added, 'For the lift.' The kiss was something she would
not forgive, but she had every intention of forgetting it or
at least mentally filing it under *of no importance*.

'I'll see you in.'

She struggled to sound amused by the offer and reached
for the door handle. 'That really won't be necessary. I can
look after myself...see, I have my key...' Her hand came
up empty from the pocket in her handbag where she always kept her key ring. 'It has to be in here somewhere...'

Several minutes later the contents of her bag had been
removed twice and replaced and it became clear that her
keys might well be somewhere but they were definitely
not in her bag.

'You lost your keys...it happens.'

His soothing words did not soothe.

'Not to me! I always... I had them when I was opening the car bonnet...' She summoned a mental image of
the keys on their Tempting Eve logo fob. She covered her
face with her hands and groaned. 'Oh, God, I left them
in the ignition!'

'It's only keys.'

Her hands fell and she slung him a look. 'You're not
the one locked out.'

'You have some spares, a neighbour with a key...?'

'Yes, but...' She shook her head. 'They have a baby and
James works nights.' She shook her head positively. 'I can't
knock up Sue and the baby at this time of night.' The last
time she had seen her neighbour she had been shocked by
her appearance.

Seeing her expression, Sue had grimaced, smoothed her
hair self-consciously and said, 'Sleep deprivation is what
they don't tell you about in antenatal classes.'

Eve couldn't believe it; she had crammed a lot of low
moments into this day and he had been there to witness
them all.

'Do you mind dropping me at a hotel?' She snapped open the mirror of her compact and closed it again without looking at it before sliding it back into her bag. There were some things it was just better not to know and how she looked at that moment was probably one of them!

Beneath the thin veneer of cheerful bravado she had clearly reached the end of her tether. Draco looked at her in thoughtful silence, tempted to do what she requested, and why not? She wasn't his responsibility and she had more in common with a feral cat than a needy kitten. Granted she'd had a hell of a day and it showed, but his hadn't been so great either—with a couple of memorable exceptions!

The internal tug of war was short-lived, and in the end his conscience won out, or was that his libido...?

'I know I've been a nuisance.'

He flashed a sideways glance her way. She looked dead on her feet, and he stifled a trickle of sympathy, killing it dead. 'Yes.' Without a word he started the engine.

Eve compressed her lips, feeling considerably less guilty. Charm really was his middle name! After the key debacle she surreptitiously checked her purse to make sure she had her credit cards, and she struggled against the temptation to check again. He already thought she was a total head case, so why confirm it for him?

Happily the journey back to London didn't take long driving in this powerful car, and Draco showed no inclination to make conversation, which was a mercy. She glanced periodically at his profile, responding to some sort of compulsion that she chose not to analyse; it was remote, his expression stony.

She didn't recognise the area they ended up in, a quiet and ultra-exclusive backwater. The building he drew up outside with its Georgian portico overlooked a green square. A place like this was bound to be expensive, but she was past caring.

'Great.' Eve unclipped her seat belt. 'I'm sorry to put you to so much trouble—' she began formally, then stopped. She was talking to an empty space.

Draco got out of the car before the tension building in him cracked his jaw. The cynic in him wanted to believe that she knew what all those hungry little sideways glances were doing to him but he knew that she didn't. The woman had no wiles whatsoever, which made her more dangerous. Not exactly scientific, but it worked for him and it explained the fact he was struggling to keep his normal iron control in check—she simply didn't slot into any of the categories that women usually did.

She caught him up halfway up the steps to the impressive entrance of the hotel. It wasn't until she saw him insert a key into the door that the penny dropped.

'This isn't a hotel.'

A ghost of a smile twitched his lips as he looked down at her, his height advantage even more pronounced than usual because of the step he stood on.

'I love a bit of intellectual debate as much as the next man but it's late, I'm tired and you look...' his glance swept upwards from her feet until it stilled on her heart-shaped face, the light sprinkling of freckles across the bridge of her narrow nose standing out stark against the pallor of exhaustion that tinged her skin '...terrible.'

'You don't look so hot yourself.' The retort had sounded cold and cutting in her head but it emerged sounding petty and childish.

It was also a big fat lie. The visible dark shadow on his face and the spikiness of his hair caused by his habit of running his hand back and forth across his dark head when he was exasperated did not detract in the least from his sinful attractiveness.

Her glance drifted to his hand on the door. He had nice hands, she mused, big and strong with long, tapering fingers. She averted her eyes but the heat continued to spread through her body. There was no way in the world she was entering that house.

'It's been a long day.'

'I don't see the connection between the way I look and you not taking me to a hotel.'

'I assumed, wrongly it would seem, that this would be more convenient for you.'

'So you made the unilateral decision and expected me to go along with it.' Staying the night under his roof filled her with a panic that was irrational. It wasn't as if he was going to demand her body in payment for bed and board. 'Call me a cab!' she demanded, panic making her sound imperious.

His eyes narrowed. Draco was sick of humouring her. 'Madre di Dio!' he gritted through clenched teeth.

Eve stared, her startled green eyes round. His accent was so perfect that she'd almost forgotten he wasn't British, but right at that moment his Latin heritage was pretty hard to miss, as the combustible quality she had sensed he possessed under the surface had smouldered into life—and it was pretty impressive.

'Suit yourself! Spend a night in a hotel room without so much as a toothbrush but spare me the histrionics and call your own damned cab!'

'I will!' She watched him step into the hallway and without warning her annoyance melted as the sense of guilt she had morphed into embarrassed contrition as she saw the day through his eyes. Images of herself flitted through her head; she really hadn't covered herself in glory today.

As first impressions went, chucking her bag of lingerie samples over him took the biscuit. Then sobbing all over him in the ladies' room, telling him God knew what; she really didn't want to remember. And then she'd turned what was meant to be a face-saving kiss into some sort of marathon kissing competition. Just when he'd probably thought it was all over, he'd had to rescue her from wandering around alone in the depths of the Surrey countryside. Taking a deep breath, she followed him inside.

'Sorry, you're right. I'm not that woman.' It suddenly seemed important that he know this.

'What woman?'

'The one I've been today. I don't usually do girly crying, I don't normally need rescuing and I can call my own cabs.'

'Can you also perhaps resist the temptation to cut off your nose to spite your face?'

Following a short silence and an internal debate to which he was not privy, she nodded. 'Thank you. I would be grateful of a bed for the night.' There had to be a dozen or so to spare. The place, if the hallway they stood in was any indicator, was enormous. Typically Georgian, very light, with a really beautiful staircase rising up all three floors.

'If it's not too much trouble for…?'

He watched as she looked around as though she expected an army of servants to materialise.

'Just us tonight. What's wrong? Are you afraid of being alone with me?'

'Don't be stupid.' If she had an ounce of sense she would be. If she had an ounce of sense she wouldn't be here at all; she'd be in a hotel room. Instead she had capitulated far too easily to his suggestion that she stay here—well, more than suggestion, really; he had presented it as a *fait accompli*.

Eve wished she were surer of her own motives but she had a feeling that at some level her impulsive choice to stay had more to do with her hormones than any practical reasons.

The memory of the hunger that had devoured her when they had kissed terrified her, but it also drew her and she had a horrible feeling that he knew it.

His attitude had been take it or leave it, but underneath all that did he think they'd end up sharing a bed tonight?

Do you, Eve?

She pushed away the thought. 'I just thought that someone might be waiting up for you?'

The idea seemed to amuse him. 'We have no live-in servants.'

'So nobody like my mother, you mean?' she fired back.

'Like...?' he echoed with a shrug. 'I don't know your mother and I wouldn't dream of judging anyone by what they do.'

She flushed at the reprimand. 'Well, that makes you unique, or maybe you like to think of yourself as egalitarian but if your daughter announced she was marrying the boy who stacks the shelves in the local supermarket you wouldn't be so tolerant, I suspect.'

'My daughter is thirteen. I wouldn't be happy if she said she was marrying Prince Harry. I'm curious—are you really such a cynic or is it that chip on your pretty shoulder showing again?' As he spoke he opened a panelled door to his right and after a short angry pause she accepted the silent invitation and walked past him.

The room they entered was not enormous. There was an original Adam fireplace filled with unlit candles, some nice artwork on the walls, and the furniture was an eclectic mix of expensive modern pieces and original Georgian antiques.

It was simple and uncomplicated, unlike the man who lived here.

Her covert gaze slid to Draco, who had walked straight over to a bureau and pulled out a bottle and a glass.

'I like to keep it simple. Mrs Ellis, the housekeeper, is full time, but she doesn't live in and she oversees the girls who come in, and my driver is—'

'I get the picture—simple.'

He poured himself a second finger of brandy and downed it in one gulp. 'Sorry, nightcap?'

She nodded. 'Please, thank you. You have a beautiful home. Have you lived here long?'

'Since last year. Before that I split my time pretty much fifty, fifty between here and Italy, but my sister's married a Brit and her daughter, Kate, is Josie's age. When I was looking for a school for Josie she recommended the one Kate attends.' He arched a brow. 'You don't want to know any of that, do you? What you're really thinking is, is he going to make a pass at me?'

She flushed to the roots of her hair and took a large sip of the brandy.

'Whereas I'm standing here thinking, is she going to make a pass at me?'

Her squeaked protest drew his lazy grin. 'You see—it's not so nice to have someone look at you as though they expect you to leap on them any minute, is it?'

She held the glass in both hands and looked at him over the rim. Her eyes watered as the brandy stung her throat and pooled with a warm glow in her stomach. 'You have a very weird mind.'

'And you have a very good body, and for a designer your dress sense is...*interesting.*'

An insult and a compliment. Which should she respond to? In the end she chose neither. 'It's late, so if you don't mind...?'

'I'll show you the way.'

Like everything else in the place the doorway was generous but even so Eve found herself hunching her shoulders to make herself smaller as she went through, as though touching him would ignite some invisible touch paper. Annoyed at herself, in the hallway she lifted her head and pulled her shoulders back. She was acting as though she were a victim of her own hormones; his touch would not release some sort of carnal chain reaction unless she allowed it to.

She followed him up the deep curving staircase, her heart beating, her emotions see-sawing.

He reached the upper hallway and, without turning, pointed to his right. 'I'm up that way. The guest suites are that way—take your pick. Except probably the last two. Clare uses the end one when she stays over and my mother leaves a few things in the one next to it.'

He caught her look and said, 'Clare is my ex-wife.'

An ex-wife who slept over: very civilised... Just how civilised, exactly? she wondered.

'No, we don't have sex.'

Her eyes widened at this fresh evidence of his ability to read her mind.

CHAPTER SEVEN

'RELAX, I'M NOT a mind-reader, you're just incredibly transparent and in answer to that thought nothing is going to happen between us tonight. Unless you want it to...?'

Eve recognised it was a taunt, not an invitation, but if it had been?

The question formed before she could stop it and dangerous thoughts swirled in her head. She felt caught between anger and... She shook her head, refusing to recognise that sensation in the pit of her stomach as excitement. The admission would open too many doors she didn't want to look behind.

'You said before you were not that woman, the one who cries and needs a shoulder, the one who gets rescued, that isn't you.'

She shook her head, wary of walking into some sort of trap. 'No.'

'So tell me, what *is* you?'

Eve looked away, avoiding his disturbingly intent stare, her negligent shrug masking her confusion. Before today she could have replied to that question with total confidence, but today had challenged a lot of things she'd previously taken as given and now wasn't the moment to think about them. She had to stay focused.

On what?

She felt a cold finger of unease trace a path up along her

spine. She was only one stumbling step away from panic; she had always known her aim and gone for it... It gave her purpose, stability.

She tilted her head back to look at him, releasing a sigh of relief as, no longer treading water, she felt her feet touch bottom. 'I am...sensible.'

She half expected him to laugh but he didn't. 'And is it fun being sensible?'

She was fully prepared to defend undervalued common sense, but as her glance locked with his dark eyes framed by those crazily long silky eyelashes she experienced a stab of breath-snatching, heart-racing lust. It was followed by an equally fierce flash of anger that made her lash out.

'I think your idea of fun and mine is very different.'

Draco genuinely didn't give a damn what people thought about him, which had proved an advantage over the years. Losing his temper was a distraction that he did not normally allow himself.

He did not react to insults, it was a mindset and usually it was not a struggle for him to keep his cool, but Eve's lip-curling contempt touched an exposed nerve and his temper spiked.

'Oh, I think we might find we have some common ground, cara.' He opened the mental door he had shut them behind and allowed the memories to come flooding in. Her small, eager hands skating over his skin, her nails digging in, the frantic little moans as she had kissed him sent a hard throb of lust slamming through his body, the strength of it making him catch his breath.

A threat disguised as an invitation or an invitation disguised as a threat? It didn't really matter to Eve. What mattered was her body's response.

It was sheer bloody-minded defiance that stopped her retreating as he took a step towards her radiating anger and arrogance and sheer *maleness*. Such a suggestion a short

time ago would have evoked a scornful response; now it
sent an illicit thrill surging through Eve's body. She licked
her lips and tasted brandy, but the buzz in her head had
nothing to do with the alcohol. His dark, predatory stare
was more potent and more mind-destroying than an entire bottle of liquor!

He saw her pupils dilate, the dark centre swallowing
up all but a thin rim of green, and gave a hard smile of
satisfaction.

Common sense, she called it. He called it pragmatism
and he could do with some now to counteract the lust
throbbing through his body. There were warning bells—
there had been warning bells since the moment he first
saw her.

He'd spent the day ignoring them and as he reached out
to curve a hand around the back of her head he carried
on doing so, thinking instead about her lush mouth. He
couldn't remember the last time he had wanted a woman
this much…the last time he had burned this way.

It was a kind of insanity… He thought he would go insane if he didn't have her, but she wanted him too; he could
see it in the flush on her skin, the tremor in the hand she
raised in a fluttery gesture to her lips and then let drop.

But most of all it was in her eyes, her *hungry* eyes, so
deep he could have drowned in them.

He slid his fingers into her silky hair meeting a barrier
of pins. He removed one and let it fall to the floor, and
then another.

Her eyes widened in alarm then half closed. A silent
sigh left her parted lips as she breathed in and out fast
and shallow, focusing on the mechanics of it, as if drawing air into her lungs and releasing it and not the fact she
was floating on a sensual cloud several inches above the
floor was the most important thing.

'I'm not having sex with you.' It was hard to force the

words out with her tongue stuck to the roof of her mouth, but it needed saying as much for her benefit as his. When she did finally have sex it would be with a man she felt comfortable with, a man she could—

'Good to know,' he slurred thickly. 'But this is okay...' He stroked a finger softly over the skin around her ear. 'Right?'

It felt so right it hurt.

She struggled to retrieve her previous thought: a man she could...? *Control.* She shook her head slightly and found her cheek against his palm as she thought, That sounds wrong.

She genuinely didn't want to control this future lover; no, she just wanted to be *in* control... Draco found another pin and a deep visceral shudder stronger than the rest shook her, making her body vibrate like a tuning fork.

In control like now, mocked the voice in her head.

She squeezed her eyes closed in an effort to close down the thoughts and felt the touch of his lips on her eyelids light as a breeze.

Hands framing her face, he lifted his eyes and watched as her hair succumbed to gravity and the weight of the shiny coils slid downwards in slow motion to settle against her narrow back.

His hissing breath caused her eyes to open. Her eyelids felt heavy, but she felt light, as though she were floating; it was surreal.

'This feels really strange.'

He bared his teeth in a smile that made her shiver. 'It's meant to feel good.'

She swallowed and, eyes huge on his face, whispered thickly, 'It d-does.'

'Sexy stutter.'

Stutters weren't sexy, but she let the comment stand; it

was more empowering than she would have believed possible to have this gorgeous man telling her she was sexy.

Again he replied as though she'd voiced her doubts. 'It is sexy.'

He kissed her then, slowly, deeply, his hands framing her face, his long fingers stroking her scalp. Her lips parted under the pressure and he sank deep into her mouth, taking his time, drinking her in, savouring the taste of her. The possessive thrust of his tongue made the heat that had been slowly building inside her spark and explode like a firework display.

She wanted him more than she had wanted anything in her life. Blinded by sheer need, her control a thing of the past, Eve reached for him, rising up on her toes.

This is so not you, Eve.

The voice in her head was wrong because it *was* her and they *were* her fingers wrapping themselves into the fabric of his shirt and she was the one kissing him back with a wildness and ferocity that he answered with equally wild, head-spinning passion. He wrapped one hand in her hair, the other, like an iron band, he placed around her waist, lifting her off the ground as he plunged his tongue deeper into her mouth, drawing a soft mewling cry from her throat as he withdrew and repeated the process.

She was barely conscious that they had been moving all the time, moving, walking, stumbling, kissing, his mouth on hers, his lips moving, his hands on her body sliding over fabric, under fabric, over skin, everything fuelling the wild desperation that pounded through Eve. The only thing stopping her from falling as she blindly allowed herself to be steered down the wide hallways was her grip on the fabric of his shirt at waist level. There was no underlying softness to grab as his belly was corrugated with hard muscle. When they hit a pedestal displaying a Chinese urn, the piece of porcelain went flying.

'No!' A finger on her cheek stopped her turning her head towards the smashing sound. 'It's nothing,' he rasped, desperate not to break the mood. She stared up at him, the urgency in his voice echoed in the starkly beautiful, strained lines of his face and the molten heat burning in his heavy-lidded, half-closed eyes.

She stopped thinking about broken china; she forgot thinking about everything except the here and now. Her entire world was here, his face, his heat, and if the ceiling had fallen on their heads she wouldn't have noticed. She'd have just carried on looking and wanting.

She wanted to touch him, taste him... She was quivering with need, shaking from head to toe.

The grip of fingers in her hair was tight but not as tight as the grip of his dark, glowing stare.

'It's fine...' he murmured as his nose brushed along the side of hers. The gentle nip at the soft curve of the trembling fullness of her lower lip sent her deeper into the sensual maelstrom that held her enthralled.

'I love your mouth.' His tongue traced the outline until she widened her mouth, inviting him to deepen his erotic invasion.

They had reached his bedroom door when the buttons of his shirt gave way under the pressure of her purchase and Eve stumbled, but before she lost her balance he was able to scoop her up and carry her into the bedroom.

His impatient kick set the door hard against the wall but he didn't register the framed landscape on the wall vibrating hard enough to crack the glass as he closed it with his foot.

He walked across to the bed and, pulling back the quilt to reveal crisp white sheets, he placed her on the cool silk.

Eve pulled herself into a kneeling position, her glorious hair tumbled about her flushed face and her emerald eyes glazed with passion. She looked so totally gorgeous that it took all his will power to resist the primal need to simply sink into her and feel her close around him, but her pleasure was as important for Draco's satisfaction as his own and he needed to be sure she was ready for him.

Instead he left the moisture from a slow trail of kisses he pressed to her throat and straightened up.

Kneeling there on the big bed, struggling to breathe past the tangled knot of emotion in her chest, she watched as he rid himself of his shirt.

A hot breath snagged in her throat. She wanted him, and how could anything that felt so good be wrong? A hundred examples came to mind and she brushed them all away with fierce determination and caught hold of the un-fastened ends of the belt that dangled from his belt loops.

He smiled as she tugged, not resisting the pressure that brought him to the edge of the bed where she knelt. Eve continued to gaze up at him; he was so perfect he made her ache.

Eve stared up at him with a mixture of fascination, awe and hunger. She had never seen anything so beautiful. There was not an ounce of spare flesh to blur the perfect definition of each individual muscle, and with his flat belly and broad powerful chest he made her think of a classi-cal sculpture, but his skin was not stone, it was deep gold.

He slid the belt she had held out of its loops and let it drop to the floor but left his trousers hanging low over his slim hips as he took her wrists.

'I'm going to undress you now.'

She felt a spasm of uncertainty, but quashed it. This man could have any woman he wanted and he clearly wanted her. She wasn't even sure he saw her nod.

She sat there fighting to breathe and trembling as he took hold of the hem of her top and lifted it over her head, let-

ting it fall to the floor. She had nothing but a thin camisole on under it.

'Look at me, Eve.'

When she didn't he sank down onto his knees on the
bed beside her and, taking her chin in his hand, forced her
face up to his. 'You are beautiful.'

She quivered as his hand cupped one breast, his thumb
rubbing across the turgid peak that protruded through the
thin fabric. The sensation, along with the expression in his
eyes, blasted all her uncertainties away.

She responded to the pressure of his hand on her breastbone and fell back on the pile of pillows. With an impatient grunt he pulled them out from under her head until
she lay flat with him over her. They kissed, deep, soul-
piercing kisses that left her aching and wanting more, so
much more.

'You shall have it. You shall have everything, *cara*,' he
promised thickly. 'First we do not need these.'

She lay there as he skilfully removed the rest of her cloth-
ing, exposing her to his hungry, burning gaze, and wondered
if she had spoken out loud or had he read her mind again?

Very soon it no longer seemed to matter. But as they
kissed and he caressed her until every cell in her body was
on fire Eve learnt there were benefits to having a man who
knew what you wanted before you did!

When she had reached a point where she was one ache,
he levered himself up into a kneeling position and slid
down the zip on his trousers, holding her eyes and only
breaking contact to slide them down his long legs, his box-
ers swiftly following.

'Oh, mercy!'

He laughed and touched the corner of her mouth with
his thumb, then met her lips with his, drinking in her sweet
flavour, savouring the taste, the erotic movement of her
tongue against his.

'I want to taste all of you.'

His voice was like smoke as it clung; it seeped into every corner of her. Above it was the thunderous clamour of her heart.

'Relax, enjoy it, *cara*,' he whispered in her ear.

The intimacy of his touch, the audacious and shockingly effective caresses of his mouth and tongue should have shocked her virginal sensibilities, but Eve felt only pleasure as she moved against his hand and his mouth, letting him drive her to the edge again and again.

As her hand closed around the hard, silky thickness of his shaft he gasped and groaned. 'I have to have you, Eve, now.'

She opened her legs in silent invitation and when he moved over her, she lifted her hips to open herself for him. The first deep thrust took her breath away but as he started to move she realised there was more…and with each successive measured thrust of his hips he drove her deeper and deeper into the heart of the heat that burned inside her, until she was the heat.

The climax when it hit her was so intense that her cry rivalled the feral moan that emanated from his chest.

CHAPTER EIGHT

'WHAT ARE YOU DOING?'

Eve glanced towards the bed and immediately regretted it as he was looking magnificently rumpled. 'Getting dressed,' she mumbled.

'So why are you wrapped in the duvet?'

'Because I'm cold.' She would be after a cold shower.

'Right, because for a minute there I thought you might be going coy on me.'

She felt the embarrassed heat climb to her cheeks. Draco was right: it was absurd. He had got out of bed stark naked earlier and been totally relaxed, but the idea of him seeing her naked in daylight had sent her under the duvet. 'Don't be stupid,' she scorned.

'Considering there is not an inch of your body I have not explored...of course if I missed anywhere...'

He hadn't; he had even kissed the small fresh scar from the mole removal and told her they both had one. His, she had learnt, was from a skiing accident. She had kissed it too... She pushed the memory away, but she couldn't push away the warmth that remained low in her pelvis.

'Look, last night happened and I'm not trying to pretend it didn't,' she said. The second time they had made love had been even more intense than the first as he had encouraged her to explore his body while he had tutored her in how to please him in a voice that embodied sin. 'But—'

'You regret it?' His tone was sharp.

'No, but today is another day.'

He loosed a long whistle through his teeth 'Wow, now that really *is* profound.'

Responding to his aggravating sarcasm—*only aggravating if you let him get to you, Eve*—she turned her head sharply, intending to deliver an acid response. At the same moment, like a lazy big cat, he stretched. Disastrously distracted by the ripple of taut muscle in his ribbed belly and perfectly defined chest, she almost dropped the quilt.

'You still haven't explained how I'm your first lover.' How a woman who was as innately sensual as Eve had reached this point without having taken a man to her bed defied logic and his powers of deduction, but he wasn't going to complain as it was to his benefit. 'Did it not occur to you that it is the sort of thing a man might like to know upfront?'

'I didn't think you'd notice.' Keeping one hand on the quilt, she stalked back to the bed. 'What's so funny?'

He looped his hands behind his neck, drawing her eyes back to the muscles of his lean torso. 'You are…'

Her scowl refused to stay in place, he was so incredibly gorgeous.

'But deflections aside—'

'I was not trying to deflect anything.'

'It's a simple question, Eve.' He grabbed her arm and Eve sat down on the bed. 'Better,' he murmured, easing closer until their faces were close. 'Nobody is a virgin at your age by accident.' He tugged the quilt, holding her eyes as it slid down to her waist.

'I've not had time for r-romance.'

'Last night wasn't romance, it was sex, Eve.' The best sex he had ever had.

She lowered her chin to hide the hurt anger she knew was written on her face. When she lifted it again she was smiling. 'You really don't have to spell it out to me, Draco. I hardly thought it was the start of a deep and meaningful relationship.'

Her laugh grated on him. Her entire attitude grated on him; it wasn't as though he was looking for deep and meaningful any more than he'd been looking for a virgin to take to his bed. A virgin…! Eyes half closed, he relived that moment when he had known…and felt again the equally powerful surge of possessiveness that had been too primal to deny and still was—he was her first.

'You're a passionate woman, Eve.'

She shook her head, not able to admit even to herself her secret fear of losing control with a man, that she might lose some of herself at the same time… Her eyes lifted, a furrow appearing between her brows as she wondered what it was about him that made it all right to lose control.

'I've been b-building a b-business.'

His dark brows lifted. 'That is a reason?'

She nodded.

'It is possible to have sex and run a business at the same time, I promise you, *cara*.'

'I don't want a full-time relationship and I'm not into one-night stands.' A bit late to remember that, Eve. 'And even if I was in the market, men who share my aims and ambitions are hard to find.'

'There is nothing stopping you looking for one of them while you have sex with me. But, believe me, one night with you would not be nearly enough for any man, *cara*. Actually,' he mused, smiling to himself at the blush that had spread to all parts of her body, 'I think you'll find you can go to bed with a man who shares your aims and ambitions and wake up with a man who is not even faintly interested in your mind… Most men will say anything to get you into bed.'

'But you're different, I suppose?'

'As a matter of fact I am. I am exactly the sort of man you need.'

'Is that meant to be a turn-on?' Eve had no idea if this arrogant pronouncement was intended to arouse her, but it did.

'Think about it. I can give you great sex—and it was great—with no strings, no emotional upheaval, just satisfying sex. You may have no time in your calendar for romance, but I think a clever girl like you could fit in great sex.'

'That sounds...'

'Perfect?'

'Immoral!'

His husky laughter rang out. 'Stay with me long enough, angel, and I will corrupt you; you do have a body made for sin.'

Dropping the quilt, she rose from the bed, swept her clothes up into a bundle and marched into the bathroom.

As the door closed on her beautifully rounded little bottom he gave a loud groan. There were in his experience few certainties in life, but he found himself faced with one total certainty: he had to get Eve back in his bed or die trying.

Eve always arrived at the office first. She enjoyed those few minutes alone with no interruptions to plan out her day and get her thoughts together. Today she had arrived when her assistant was already at her desk with sympathy, a herbal tea she said always worked for jet lag and a wistful expression she always wore when she talked about weddings.

Eve accepted the sachet of tea and told Shelley she hadn't taken any photos.

'None?' The girl couldn't hide her disappointment. 'I suppose you were too stressed about today to enjoy yourself and let your hair down.'

Eve lifted a hand to her head just to satisfy herself it was neatly subdued. Unlike her imagination. *Just glorious; I want to wrap myself in your hair...* The flashback, the throaty, sinfully sexy voice was so real she could almost feel his warm breath on her neck.

Swallowing, she lowered her eyes, willing the flush to stay below neck level as her fingers tightened hard enough around the herbal sachet to make the contents spill out.

'I'll just...' She took a step towards her office then stopped, a frown pleating her smooth brow as she turned back. *'Today?'*

Her assistant blinked and brought up a chart on her tablet. 'There hasn't been *another* delay, has there? They are still letting you know this morning...?'

Eve struggled to conceal her dismay behind a cheerful smile that made her face ache. She had a point to make or at least a reputation to preserve—a reputation for being calm and unflappable in a crisis.

'No, it's still this morning.'

Inside the office she closed the door and leaned against it. This was not just a disaster, it was a... What the hell was it?

She had forgotten!

How could she have forgotten?

For six months her every waking moment had been focused on this deal; she had invested all her time and energy on it; she had lived and breathed it, focused on a goal and gone for it. She told herself that failure was not an option but she knew it always was, and that knowledge had made her wake up in a cold sweat in the middle of the night on more than one occasion.

And now on the very brink, she glanced down at her watch, and then lifted a hand to her face in shock. Within minutes she'd be receiving that crucial decision and she'd completely forgotten about it!

What did they say? Pride came before a fall... She had
gone back to her flat that morning to change feeling pretty
smug. Well, actually more *relieved*. Eve knew she wasn't
like her mother or any of the other women she knew who
lost the capacity to be objective when there was a man in
their bed, but there had been a niggling doubt—what if
great sex stole her self-respect and made her willing to
compromise all her principles?

Well, she'd had great sex; to her shock, the sort of mind-
bending, head-banging sex that she'd had really did exist
outside novels! Her body still ached from it—in a good
way—and for a short time she'd stopped being the Queen
of Caution and allowed her impulses full rein. It had turned
out to be a totally liberating experience. Draco was an incredible lover but equally importantly in the cold light of
day he was still an arrogant pain in the neck, which might
for all she knew be what made him a great lover; the point
was, she knew he was. She wasn't making excuses for his
shortcomings; she wasn't about to put him on a pedestal
or keep her mouth shut when she knew he was wrong.

It was a relief to have her theory confirmed. It wasn't
sex that turned women into willing slaves; it was love.
She didn't love Draco, and the very idea of falling in love
after twenty-four hours made her lips twitch into a fleeting ghost of a smile.

Love... To be honest, she didn't even like him that
much. If she never saw him again, she wouldn't lose any
sleep. That was why in some ways he was right. He was
perfect as a lover—there was nothing between them but
unbridled lust, nothing complicated by emotions. It had
just been sex—very good sex, to be sure—but there were
a lot of men out there who were not Draco, men whose
hands weren't so skilful perhaps... An image of his long
fingers gliding over her skin drifted into Eve's head, ig-
niting heat low in her pelvis until she pushed the image

away and reminded herself that she was in no hurry to repeat their night of passion. Another uncomplicated moment might happen but she was not going out looking for it.

Uncomplicated or not, the unwelcome fact remained that a night spent with him had knocked the contract that she'd worked so hard for completely out of her head...

Maybe I'm the exception that proves the rule—the woman who can't multitask.

It's business success or sex; I can't do both.

Failing to summon a smile at her humour and not willing to acknowledge she was uncertain on this unfamiliar ground, Eve took a seat at her desk. She released a deep sigh, but the calm that the minimalist arrangement usually inspired, with no photos or personal items cluttering her working space, just the essentials, failed to materialise. She touched the row of pencils, taking comfort from the symmetry.

She needed to clear her head and focus.

Before she could do either, the phone bleeped and that was it. She gritted her teeth and lifted it, trying not to think of the people who had told her that she was running before she could walk.

Ten minutes later she replaced it.

She was shaking.

The deal was closed, and it was only now she could admit that there had been moments, though she had never said it out loud, when she had doubted the wisdom of her Australian trip. But the groundwork had paid off, and the exclusive department store chain with outlets all over the southern hemisphere was going to take her line.

This was the moment she had been working towards, pushing herself towards, the moment she had dreamed about.

A tiny furrow appeared between her brows. So where was the high...the euphoria...the glow of achievement?

Instead it was almost an anticlimax, but that, she told herself, was only to be expected. To be really appreciated this
was the sort of good news that deserved to be shared, and
a line in Charlie Latimer's wedding speech came back to
her: *Success means nothing unless you have someone to
share it with—I have the best person in the world: my wife.*

Eve had not tasted the wine in her glass or joined in
with the spontaneous ripple of applause and her eyes had
remained dry but, his insincerity aside, didn't he have a
point?

Who would be happy for her? Her mother was on her
honeymoon and her best friend was busy being a pregnant princess.

She pushed away the sudden sharp stab of something
she refused to recognise as self-pity, and thought, Buy a
cat, Eve.

Or take a new lover.

There was still some mileage in the one she had, she
thought wryly…or did she still have him? The situation
was so far out of her comfort zone that she was still feeling
her way…*all over his warm satiny textured skin.*

She looked down and saw her fingers stroking the desk.
The dreamy expression clouding her eyes vanished and
the furrow between her brows twitched back into life as a
comment Draco had made came back to her.

She had no idea what time it had been when she'd
woken, not in her own bed, but in a strange bed held down
by the weight of a man's thigh thrown across her hips,
his head between her breasts. The initial adrenaline-fed
panic surge had made her struggle for a split second but
then she'd realised where she was and relaxed against his
warm chest.

He'd unconsciously voiced her inner doubts out loud.
*What are you doing? Stop analysing—just enjoy. There's
no tomorrow, just here and now, you and me. I don't want*

*you to reach me emotionally. I just want you to touch me…
please.*

The tortured plea had made her feel empowered, hot
and out of control.

She laughed softly as she got to her feet. She wasn't
even a little jealous of her friend; the last thing she wanted
was a baby. She was far too busy with her career right now,
but perhaps in a few years' time…? Her body clock had
barely started ticking and she'd only just discovered sex.

She straightened the row of pencils on her desk one last
time and, humming softly under her breath, headed for
the interconnecting door to her PA's office. Shelley had
really put in the extra hours on this one; actually, not just
her PA, but everyone had, and though friends and family
would say well done it was only the small team who really
understood what this success meant to her.

Perhaps, she mused, she could take them for lunch at
that new Italian everyone was raving about. Her stomach
growled at the thought of food—toast and cereal had not
been on the breakfast menu this morning and she had refused to sample what was!

'How do you feel about Italian, Shelley?' Eve asked as
she opened the door to the outer office. She was used to
the terrible clutter on the younger girl's desk but this was
the first time she had found a man there.

And the man was Draco. His back was to her but there
was no mistaking the identity of the tall figure who sat
casually there. Him being here like this was wrong on so
many levels.

'Steady!'

She was conscious of him unfolding his long length
from the desk and then towering over her as she struggled
to regain first her balance and then her composure. She
grabbed hold of it in both hands and enclosed herself in a
shell of rigid formality.

Shell or not, it didn't protect her from the waves of whatever it was he exuded, and her jangling nerves made civility impossible. 'What the hell are you doing here, Draco?'

She sensed rather than saw her PA's wide eyes.

'There, didn't I tell you she'd be delighted to see me, Shelley Ann?'

Her assistant laughed, not her usual raucous giggle but a low sexy chuckle. The woman had a boyfriend whom she said she adored, so what was she doing? Eve slung her an exasperated look. Shelley could not be more obvious had she been salivating—but for Eve's interruption she'd probably be ripping off her top and screaming *Take me!*

Eve's generous lips tightened. She was all for women taking the initiative but there was such a thing as too eager. Not that she expected this view to be shared by a man like Draco. Her eyes made a scornful sweep over the tall, lean figure now propped casually back against the end of the desk. She had no doubt he enjoyed having women fawn all over him—in fact, he probably expected it and she was one in a long line of those who had helped build his belief in his irresistibility.

'I came to take you to lunch.' One corner of his mouth curled up in a slow intimate smile as his warm brown eyes moved over her face.

'How did you know where to find me?'

He produced a gilt-edged business card. 'You left it behind.' And the smell of her perfume.

Eve swallowed and hissed under her breath. 'I'm busy.'

'Actually the supplier emailed to cancel your meeting.'

'Thank you, Shelley Ann.' His smile made the younger girl blush and thrust out her not inconsiderable chest. 'So, you see, you're free, *cara*.'

Instead of asking him just what he was playing at Eve found her eyes drawn to his mouth. Free was the last thing she felt; she felt *compelled*! Willing her heart to slow, Eve brought her lashes down in a protective curtain.

'Did I hear you say that you liked Italian?' he asked.

'She adores Italian,' the younger girl cut back.

Eve winced, her jaw clenched, embarrassed for her assistant. 'It's not my favourite,' she lied.

'She loves it.'

Eve slung her another exasperated look and Shelley winked and directed a lascivious leer at Draco's back, mouthing an exaggerated, *He's gorgeous—go for it!*

I already did, Eve thought, and felt the colour staining her cheeks flame even brighter. 'I really am a little pushed for time today.'

He gave an exaggerated sigh and shrugged. 'Oh, well, if you can't make lunch, I suppose,' he conceded, 'we could discuss it here.'

Discuss…*it*…? Panic slid through Eve. Shelley was a great PA and totally discreet about work but when it came to less professional gossip…!

'Oh, no, take her to lunch.' Shelley pressed her palms together and rested her chin on her fingertips. Batting her eyes at Draco, she confided, 'It's her birthday.' She met her boss's glare with an innocent look. 'Well, he doesn't work here, does he?'

Thank God for small mercies!

'You said don't tell anyone in the *office*,' Shelley pointed out.

'Your birthday? Oh, well, that settles it,' Draco announced with satisfaction. 'I'm taking you to lunch.'

Eve would have loved to assure him that it settled nothing except the fact that he obviously couldn't comprehend a situation when a person wouldn't do what he wanted, but decided it was better to appear at least to give in gracefully than risk having her personal life discussed in front of an audience. The horror of this thought actually made her shudder.

Outside the building and away from the prying eyes of her assistant, Eve pulled away from the light touch of the hand he had placed between her shoulder blades as he guided her out of the building—as if she didn't know her own way.

'I am more than capable of—' She broke off, taking a sideways step to avoid being knocked over by a middle-aged man whose eyes were glued to his phone. Luckily the heavy line of traffic had ground to a standstill so all she did was step into a puddle, though Draco took the opportunity to haul her back to the pavement.

'We had sex.' Eve cleared her throat, privately congratulating herself on how matter of fact she had sounded when that statement sounded weird on so many levels.

He did not blink, just held her eyes with a stare that made her stomach muscles quiver with the same tension that shimmered in the air.

'I had not forgotten.' Though once he had felt her cool little hands on his skin he had forgotten almost everything else, but *that* he would never forget, if only for the reason Draco had never totally lost control with a woman before. He had always stayed in control of his passion, his lust. Ironically when he had lost it the woman who had disintegrated his control had been a virgin.

It turned out his initial suspicion regarding her innocence had been right after all. The shock had lessened but the sense of total mystification lingered. She was so sensual and so sweetly responsive that it made no sense she hadn't tried sex before, but the fact remained he was her first lover. In moments of honesty he admitted that he was not a worthy recipient of that gift, but in return he would teach her how to enjoy her own body.

Eve struggled to hold onto her antagonism. His deep

voice had a tactile quality and his heavy-lidded stare did dangerous things to her as the busy street around them receded; it was scarily easy for the world to vanish when she looked into his eyes.

'That does not give you the right to stroll into my place of work and flirt with my staff.' Somehow her comment made it sound as though the latter was the worst sin. 'I don't suppose you can help yourself,' she muttered.

'Lighten up, Eve.'

She compressed her lips, irritated by his amused response. 'I'm perfectly *light*, thank you.'

His eyes widened as if in sudden comprehension. 'Or is it one of *those* birthdays,' he commiserated.

Her expression froze. 'I'm not thirty for ages yet.'

He grinned and chalked up an invisible point in the air. 'It's reassuring to know that you have some of the normal vanities.' His dark gaze grew warmer and more intent as he touched a finger to her chin, tilting her face up to his. 'You look about eighteen, which can be a little disconcerting, especially when half the time you act as though you're middle-aged.'

He gives and then he takes away she thought, snatching her chin from his grip and rubbing angrily with the heel of her hand at the tingling area of skin where there had been contact. 'You say the n-nicest things,' she said with an insincere smile.

'You do take life seriously.'

Her jaw tautened as she tossed back a scornful response. 'That's the difference between you and me; I think life *is* serious.'

He gave a tiny nod of acknowledgement. 'Life is also sad and funny...' He stopped as his car drew up beside them at the kerbside and, nodding to the driver, he opened the rear passenger door for Eve. As she got in he wondered why the hell he was discussing the meaning of life with this woman. He could have asked himself why he was here with her at all, but that question was more easily answered, though no less strange.

He wanted her, not in itself strange but the compulsive nature of it was. If he had thought about it too deeply Draco might have been troubled, but he didn't; he mentally categorised it as an appetite like any other, and like any man when it came to sex Draco enjoyed the pursuit.

But when was the last time he'd actually rearranged his schedule to pursue any woman…?

Dismissing the question, he reminded himself that, no matter how intense the attraction between them or how seemingly insatiable the hunger this woman aroused in him, history would inevitably repeat itself and he would lose interest. He was unable to exactly recall his sister's recent exasperated assessment of his love life, but he did remember that she'd likened him to a child in a sweet shop.

All that instant gratification, Draco, but one of these days, brother, you'll lose your taste for sugar and realise that what you need is something with a bit more bite.

'It's a matter of balance, *cara*,' he mused out loud as he slid into the limo beside her. 'The tough times in life are made bearable only if you don't waste the good ones.' He leaned forward and gave the driver instructions, speaking in Italian. The man, who was as big as a bear, replied in the same language.

'What self-help book did you get that little gem from or was it a Christmas cracker?'

'My father died unexpectedly, and it was devastating for those of us left behind, especially my mother, but the thing she clung to and still does is that there was not a single day in his life that he didn't live to the full. Not that he did spectacular things—it was the little things he took pleasure from, be it a great bottle of wine or his grand-child's first step.'

She was instantly remorseful for her snappy retort. 'Oh, I'm so sorry.'

'As my father would have said, bad stuff happens but until it does laugh a little.'

She shifted uneasily in her seat under the directness of his penetrating stare. 'I get the feeling that you don't laugh a lot, which is a shame as you have a nice laugh. It sounds like your hair feels on my skin... Speaking of which, do you put it up because you like me taking it down?'

She swallowed and lowered her gaze in confusion. All it took from him was a couple of husky-voiced compliments and her heart was tripping like a steam hammer. 'I p-put it up because it gets in the way.'

He leaned back in his seat, crossing one ankle over the other. 'And you like things neat.'

'Is that a crime?' she flared.

'Do you want to know what I think...?'

'No!' she blurted, leaning forward in her seat and shouting. 'We're here!' The man ignored her. She turned to round to face Draco. 'Is he deaf?'

'I think you mean hearing-impaired, *cara*, and he wasn't deaf, but after you yelled down his ear like that it's certainly possible. There is parking around the rear.'

'Oh. Sorry.'

The car pulled into one of the parking spaces Draco had referred to and came to a standstill. Draco said something in Italian to the driver, who laughed.

'Are you talking about me?' she asked suspiciously.

'Not everything is about you, *cara*. Do you *really* want to eat?'

Eve stared at him. 'Wasn't that the idea?'

He looked at her for a moment and then gave one of his inimitable shrugs. 'It is an option certainly.' This time when he spoke to the driver it was in English. 'Thank you, Carl, we'll get a cab back.'

The restaurant was busy; people were waiting for tables. Eve felt relief that there was absolutely no way they were going to get one.

CHAPTER NINE

FIVE MINUTES LATER they were being shown to their table by an attentive Italian waiter who at Draco's request conversed in English.

'In case you thought we were talking about you.'

'Very funny. Is that man really your driver…?'

Draco looked at her curiously. 'Carl…? What do you think he is?'

'A bodyguard?'

Draco's throaty laugh caused several heads to turn. She covered her glass with her hand. 'I'm working.'

'It's your birthday.'

The battle was short, as the constant bickering was tiring. It might be better, she decided, to save her energy for the important points…and anyway a glass of wine might help soothe her jangling nerves.

She tipped her head. 'All right, just a small one.' Actually there were worse ways to spend your birthday than sitting in a really good restaurant with a man whom every woman in the room had stared at when he walked in, though she imagined that the novelty would wear thin pretty quickly and it might even cause the odd jealous twinge to be with a man so universally lusted after. She angled a glance at his face. Was he *really* as oblivious as he seemed to all the lustful stares…?

'No, Carl is my driver.'

'So you don't have a bodyguard?' she probed, unable to hide her curiosity.

'The best sort of security is the sort people don't see.'

She put down her fork and leaned back in her seat, cradling her glass. 'That's not an answer.'

His response to her indignation was a slow, lazy grin. 'It is the only one I am giving.' He sat back in his chair and watched her make serious inroads into the rustic pasta dish she had chosen.

'This is really good.' Eve took another sip of her wine, determined to make it last. She glanced at his plate. 'Steak is a bit safe.' He had only eaten half of it. 'How did we get this table anyway?'

'I know the owner.'

She had suspected it must be something like that. 'The one who owns the entire chain?'

He nodded. 'That's right.'

'They're everywhere now but when I was in Paris last year it had just opened, and the place was heaving.'

She broke off as the manager approached.

'Sir...' he tipped his head to include Eve '...miss, I hope the meal was satisfactory?'

'It was delicious,' she said.

'We're happy customers,' Draco added.

There was something she couldn't *quite* put her finger on it, but the manager's manner when he spoke to Draco and Draco's manner when he replied...and then it came to her.

She waited until the older man had gone before testing her theory.

'Are you the owner?'

He didn't even blink. 'For the past two years.'

Her dark brows knitted as she straightened her cutlery, once, twice and then once more. She was bewildered by her inability to hold eye contact with him without feeling shivery and self-conscious.

'It didn't occur to you to mention it?'

'No.' Elbows set on the table, he leaned forward. 'So are you going home?'

'Home?'

'For your birthday.'

Eve retreated behind her wine glass. 'I have no home.'

'Boo-hoo! Wow, you really do have a chip on your shoulder, don't you?'

She responded to the callous charge angrily. 'I lived at Brent Manor for t-ten years but it was never my *home*, we were just the help.'

'Yet being the help, as you put it, did not prevent you and Hannah becoming friends and now your mother is the mistress of the house.'

Eve was not about to satisfy his curiosity, but he was not the first to remark on the unlikely upstairs, downstairs friendship. Hannah Latimer with money, charm and princess looks, who went to a prestigious private school and the painfully shy cook's daughter who went to school in the local town.

For Eve it had been hate at first sight and she had gone out of her way to avoid the daughter of the house with her golden hair and her permanent smile. She'd had numerous hiding places on the estate and when she'd found Hannah in one of those she'd initially been furious—until she'd seen the tears.

The girls had discovered they had something in common a long time before they'd found out their parents were having an affair. They'd both hated school and had both been bullied, although for different reasons.

'People find the entire rags to riches story fascinating... not literally rags, I know that, but don't be surprised if you find details of your mother's life popping up in gossip columns. We all have skeletons,' Draco warned.

She stiffened, horror seeping into her at the thought of her parentage becoming public knowledge, and retorted defensively, 'What are you implying?'

Draco realised immediately from her reaction that there was definitely a skeleton in the Curtis family closet. Hell, all he'd wanted to do was steer the conversation in the right direction... Oh, well, that left the direct approach.

'There is a photo that has been posted online. I thought you should know about it.'

He pushed his phone across the table and watched her face as she looked at the explicit photo of the two of them in an abandoned embrace the night of the wedding. He saw the colour run up under her fair skin when she saw what it was, and then recede leaving her paper pale. 'One of your enterprising ex school friends I assume.'

Eve closed her eyes and for a long moment she said nothing. Then in a hopeful whisper said, 'Perhaps no one will see it.'

There was no gentle way to break it so he just said it. 'Sorry, but apparently it has already gone viral.'

She covered her mouth with her hand, and above it her green eyes registered total horror. How could he sound so calm?

'You have to stop them.' He shook his head and she added wildly, 'What if your daughter sees it?'

'The odds are she already has. On the plus side it is quite flattering.'

She closed her eyes. Flattering? Was he insane? She was an intensely private person and the idea of that photo out there made Eve... 'I feel sick.' She waited until the strong wave of nausea had passed before asking, 'So what are we going to do?'

He arched a brow. *'Do?'*

'A plan.'

'There is no plan beyond damage limitation. Take my word for it—I have been here before.'

'Well, I haven't!'

'My best advice is to laugh it off, or maintain a dignified silence...'

A hoarse laugh was shaken from her throat. She could see precious little dignity in having pictures of yourself in a passionate clinch posted on the internet. It wouldn't just be strangers who would see it, but people who knew her: her mother, her friends, people she worked with.

'Or I could deny vigorously that there is anything going on between us.'

She exhaled. 'Good.'

'Which will convince them that something definitely is and prolong the interest in us.'

Eve clenched her teeth, her body rigid as she fought the urge to rush around the table and shake him. She firmly believed that violence never solved anything but on this occasion it might make her feel a hell of a lot better!

He met her eyes. 'Tell me what you want me to do?'

'I don't kn-know,' she admitted miserably.

'Then shall I tell you what I want to do? I want to get up and leave this place.'

'What about coffee?'

'Then I want to take you back to my place and do what I badly wanted to do with you this morning. I can promise you a birthday present you will not forget, *cara*.'

He...*they* had a problem and his solution...? Seduce her right here in a public place! Where anyone could have heard the things he'd said.

It was laughable; he was ridiculous.

Only his voice, the rich, rich bitter chocolate with that curious tactile quality, was not something she found herself able to laugh at. Their glances connected and a faint sigh left her parted lips. Desire zinged along her nerve endings, closing down her logic circuits and opening her pupils wide.

The seconds ticked away and with each one the sexual tension that crackled in the air mounted and the clenched core of desire in Eve's belly tightened. Draco just continued to stare at her with the same soul-stripping intensity, the carnal message in his eyes very clear.

She took a deep breath. 'Yes…'

They both got to their feet in unison, Draco almost knocking his chair over in the process.

He flung a handful of notes on the table without even glancing at the denominations, grabbed her hand and growled.

'Let's get out of here.'

He didn't roll away but remained heavy and hot above her. His face was pressed against her neck, his breath warm and moist against her skin. She liked it, everything about it, the skin-to-skin contact, his weight, the musky smell of sex mingled with soap.

They were lying naked on a massive leather chesterfield in Draco's study. They hadn't managed to make it up the stairs; they had barely even made it out of the cab.

The room was littered with the clothes they had ripped off in a mutual frenzy of haste for skin-to-skin contact.

The frenzy had passed but Eve's breath still came in a series of shallow gasps; her ribcage lifted with each gasp, making the breast not compressed by Draco's head quiver. One arm curled over her head and the other in his hair, she lay on her back, staring, eyes half closed, at the ceiling. Her body was gently humming still in the aftermath of a climax that had rocked her body with wave after wave of intense pleasure.

'How did this happen?' she murmured.

'Do you want bullet points or shall I run through it step by step?' She heard the smile in his voice.

'Neither, but happy birthday to me.'

He curved a hand over her breast. 'I'll second that.'

'Draco…?'

'Give me five minutes.'

She laughed. 'I have to go.' She tried to push him off her but he resisted.

'No,' he groaned.

She arched a brow. 'Please, Draco, I have to.'

With a show of reluctance he rolled away.

Eve felt his eyes on her as she got dressed. His dark stare made her feel self-conscious but also empowered. She could be naked in front of him; she could stutter and not want to die… Was that bad…good…dangerous? She gave her head a tiny shake. Eve just knew it felt good. To have a man like Draco act as though he couldn't get enough of you was a pretty ego-enhancing experience.

Midway through fastening her shirt, she stopped and tilted her head to one side in a listening attitude.

'There's someone here.' She could hear the sound of a door closing and voices…female voices?

'No, I told you—' This time Draco heard them too. He closed his eyes then sat up with a sigh.

'I think there's more than one of them,' she confided in a hushed whisper.

He left the chesterfield in one lithe motion. Reaching for his trousers, he angled her a carnal look that made her insides flip and her eyes glow.

'Hold that thought,' he commanded thickly.

'*That* wasn't what I was thinking.'

He dragged his shirt together; some lies were just too obvious to justify a response. 'Stay here—it'll be safer.'

The comment sent her imagination into overdrive. 'Safe

from what? Do you know who it is? Should I call the police?'

'It's nice to know you care, but I can handle this.'

Eve wanted to yell she didn't care after him, but suddenly she had an awful feeling it would be a lie.

CHAPTER TEN

BEFORE HE LEFT the room Draco buttoned up his shirt and dragged a hand through his hair.

The three females who were standing at the far end of the hallway didn't immediately see him when he walked through from the library, and it was Josie who first spotted him.

Her expression was a revealing mix of guilt and relief, which cut a long story short for him.

'Hello, kiddo, so let me guess —your mother sprang you from school to do something educational like—?'

'Shopping in the sales,' Josie supplied with a sheepish shrug.

'Good afternoon, Clare. You look gorgeous, as usual.'

'Draco.' She moved forward to offer each cheek in turn to him for a kiss. 'And you look…' She stopped, a speculative look entering her eyes as she looked at him. 'And you look…' responding to the warning flash in his eyes, she glanced at her daughter '…gorgeous too, darling. Something *definitely* agrees with you.'

'Mother,' Draco greeted Veronica.

'Draco, you should not wander around the house in your bare feet. It gives the wrong impression.'

'To who?'

'Standards,' she responded somewhat mysteriously.

'And I suppose you were just passing…?'

'Do I need a reason to visit my own son?' Veronica broke off, frowning, as a loud noise came from the library. 'Is there someone in there, Draco?'

In the library with the shoe she hadn't dropped clutched to her chest, Eve closed her eyes while the moment stretched and thought, Please, *please*, say no. Hearing the mumbled conversation and not being able to make out what was being said had been frustrating so she had been moving towards the open door when she had dropped her shoe.

'Yes.'

She opened her scrunched eyes and clenched her fists. Would it have killed him to lie?

'Eve, *cara*, come out and say hi to Josie.'

Short of hiding behind the curtains, which did not seem such a terrible option to her at that moment, Eve didn't have much choice. She glanced at her flushed face in the mirror.

'She knows Josie?'

Besides Draco's daughter there were two women in the room. The older one had jaw-length dark hair streaked with silver, and as she glanced her way Eve received the impression of energy and simple elegance. She realised she was looking at Josie in forty years' time—*lucky girl*.

The other was a stunning blue-eyed blonde whose impressive curves were displayed in a tight bandage-style red dress that nipped in her minuscule waist and displayed a cleavage that would have made her a perfect model for Eve's Temptation.

Yes, *stunning* about described her, Eve decided. Her face, figure, her long river-straight blonde hair, everything more than deserved that accolade—stunning.

'Eve!' With the energy of youth but none of the awkwardness, Josie was across the room in moments, her admiring stare on Eve's hair, which fell in a rippling curtain of pre-Raphaelite waves down her narrow back. 'Wow, I just love your hair that way.'

Eve lifted a self-conscious hand to her hair. 'It has a life of its own.'

'Mother, this is Eve Curtis.' Draco took her by the arm and drew her forward. 'Eve, my mother, Veronica Morelli.'

'Mrs Morelli…'

'And this is Clare.' Eve felt his arm go around her shoulder and stiffened.

'I'm his ex-wife,' the blonde said, gliding forward on her five-inch heels and displaying a wide friendly smile. 'It's really nice to meet you, Eve. So where have you been hiding her, Draco? And how long have you two been together?'

'We met yesterday morning,' Draco said evasively.

'All right, I know it's none of my business,' Clare replied.

'I need to get back to the office,' Eve said abruptly.

'Office?' Veronica enquired.

'Eve runs her own company, Mother.'

'Really?' We must have coffee sometime and you can tell me all about your business.' It was obvious from her sudden change of attitude that his mother was now viewing her as potential bride material.

She was embarrassed but Draco had to be hating it. He could have simply outed her there and then as a casual fling but he hadn't, and she even felt a little guilty as she would not have expected this sort of consideration for her feelings from him.

'I guess if you're your own boss you can spend the afternoon…?'

At another warning look from her ex-husband, the blonde subsided.

'Sorry, but I must go—' Eve started.

'And Josie needs to get back to school.'

Josie pouted at her grandmother's pronouncement. 'But

Clare said that I could have the day off—we were going shopping and getting our nails done.'

'I'm sure your mother realises that your schooling comes first—and you call your mother Clare now?' This disapproving addition from Veronica drew a wry look from her son.

'Would you mind dropping Josie off at school on your way back to your office, Eve?'

Startled by the request, she nodded. 'Fine.'

The older woman grabbed Josie's hand. 'Come along, Josephina. You need to get into your uniform. We must not keep Miss Curtis waiting.'

'Sorry about the interruption, you two.' Clare smiled as her daughter left the room with her grandmother. 'Sex in the afternoon is just so beautifully decadent and naughty, I always think.'

'You're embarrassing Eve,' Draco chided.

'Really!' Her astonishment seemed genuine. 'Sorry, Draco, it's just when you strolled in here looking all...' She gave a reminiscent little sigh. 'I remember that look.'

Eve felt a sharp stab of something too near jealousy for comfort. She closed her eyes and thought, I have to get out of here. She'd heard of amicable divorces but this was ridiculous!

Veronica Morelli reappeared with a neatly uniformed Josie at her side. 'She couldn't find anything and I'm not surprised. Why you insist on living in this cramped doll's house I will never understand.'

Eve's jaw dropped. If Draco's mother thought this was cramped what was she used to? It must be a castle at least.

'Very nice to meet you both,' Eve lied as she left.

In the taxi Josie was talkative. 'You have no idea how glad I am that you're with Dad.'

'I'm not—' Eve encountered the teenager's questioning

look and closed her mouth. You couldn't tell your lover's teenage daughter that you were just having casual sex with her father, rather than a meaningful relationship.

As she recalled Draco's comment about his daughter trying to find him a wife a worried frown pleated her brow. She didn't want to encourage the girl's fantasy but brutal honesty was obviously not an option. 'I'm glad you're glad.'

'And you're nothing like Dad's usual type...'

Tell me something I didn't already know, Eve thought, an image of his incredibly gorgeous ex-wife drifting into her mind. There had to have been a lot of Clare clones since, and then me.

'I'm not supposed to know he has a type, which is kind of unrealistic but because he never brings them home he thinks I don't know.'

That got Eve's attention. 'He *never* brings them home?' She told herself firmly that she was not going to read anything significant into that.

'You think he does when I'm not there, like Lily's dad?' Josie shook her head vigorously. 'Lily said she could always tell when her dad's girlfriend had been in their flat as she could *smell* her and things got left behind and moved— and she was right as they got married last month.'

Did Draco's bed smell of her?

'I'm sure it's very hard when a parent decides to remarry.'

'Gosh, no, I'd love it, and Gran would too. She's always nagging him about it, but she doesn't think anyone's good enough for him and Mu— Clare is really bitchy about the ones he dates sometimes. But you're different and if you did marry Dad or even if you were his girlfriend, they wouldn't be able to send me to live with Mum and her fiancé, cos you'd definitely be a stable female influence in my life, wouldn't you?'

Eve digested the stream of artless confidences in silence, finally asking casually, 'Is there a chance of you going to live with your mum?'

Josie shook her head. 'No, Dad promised he won't let it happen, no matter what.'

She sat in the cab until Josie had gone through the school gates, then gave the address of her office to the driver. The cringingly embarrassing scene she had endured had been playing in her head on a loop like background noise since they had left the house, only this time, in the light of Josie's revelations, it took on a very different slant.

They said knowledge was power but Eve didn't feel powerful; she felt grubby and used. The worst part was she had really thought Draco had been sparing her embarrassment, that he had allowed the assumption they were in a relationship to stand uncorrected out of consideration for her feelings.

And I stood there like a puppet feeling...grateful. She felt her temper rise and didn't fight it.

An expression of grim determination spread across her face as she suddenly leaned forward in the cab. 'Change of plan.'

By the time the cab drew up outside Draco's home, in her head Eve had verbally demolished him and made a dignified exit. She was still riding the crest of a wave of righteous anger when she battered on the door with her fist, glaring at one of the several strategically placed cameras above her head that zoomed her way as she did so.

When the door was finally opened Eve, who had been leaning up against it, almost fell inside, narrowly avoiding a collision with the smartly dressed middle-aged woman who had opened it.

'Can I help you?'

Of course he didn't open his own door, she fumed. He

probably saved himself for the fun stuff in his life like manipulating and lying.

Eve didn't waste time on small talk. 'I want to see Draco.'

There was a short silence. 'I'm afraid you have the wrong address.'

The outright lie made Eve blink, but she refused to be put off. 'I know he lives here.'

'Now, here is a nice surprise.'

The drawled comment made both women turn their heads as Draco, wearing sweats and a vest, emerged through a door. He had a towel slung around his neck and his skin glistened with a layer of sweat.

Eve reacted to the testosterone-fuelled sight and, forgetting every word of the cutting and incisive speech she'd prepared, she stabbed an accusing finger in his direction and barked, *'You...!'*

Wow, said the voice in her head. *Powerful stuff, Eve, that's really telling him.*

After holding her eyes for a long simmering moment, he turned to the older woman. He unhooked the towel and dragged a hand through his damp hair.

'Thanks, Judith.' The smile was for the older woman but his eyes only left Eve's face for a split second. 'I'll take it from here. You get off and go straight home after your appointment.'

'Are you sure?' The older woman cast a doubtful glance Eve's way as she stepped towards the open door.

'What time is your dental appointment?'

The reminder drew a click of her tongue followed by a wince. 'Gracious, is that the time? You're sure...?'

Eve endured the other woman's suspicious glance, able to be more philosophical about being cast as a dangerous lunatic than she was about her visceral reaction to the raw power of Draco's sweaty body post workout.

Eve waited until the door closed. 'That woman said you didn't live here.'

'She's very protective. She popped in to see if I was all right on her way to the dentist.'

'Do you expect all your staff to lie for you?' All the self-discipline in the world couldn't stop her eyes drifting over his powerful muscular frame. She swallowed and licked her lips, managing to inject the scorn that had been absent from her lustful stare into her voice as she sneered sarcastically, 'You being so weak and defenceless.'

An army of housekeepers couldn't have defended him from the lust that had slammed like a hammer through his body at the sight of her standing there looking mad and so desirable it physically hurt.

Hurt…! Talk about self-delusion!

It seemed amusing to him now that midway through his workout he'd actually convinced himself that he was totally in control and he could go back to feeling smugly superior to men who allowed their hormones to rule their actions.

'I was heading for the shower.' And possibly therapy! It was one thing to recognise all the warning signs of a dangerous addiction, but it was another not to feel the need to fight it.

Why fight something that was so pleasurable? he mused.

Enjoy it while it lasted seemed a much more pragmatic approach to something that was so hot it would inevitably burn itself out soon enough, he told himself.

'If that was an invitation to join you, I'll pass.' She choked, her cheeks heated from the vividly arousing images of water sliding off his slick muscled body.

Ashamed of the heaviness and ache low in her pelvis, Eve dragged her gaze free of the invitation in his heavy-lidded eyes and pretended to look around.

'Your guests gone?'

His glance was drawn to the tears glazing her eyes. 'Are you all right?'

The fake concern after what he'd done brought her teeth together in a silent snarl of disbelief.

'No, I'm not bloody all right. I'm furious.' With him for being a manipulative liar, but mostly Eve's anger was aimed at herself. 'How d-dare you use me? I swore I'd never let any man use me the way my father used mum. You planned it all, didn't you?' she flung wildly. 'It was all cold-blooded calculation.'

The last comment drew a laugh from him. 'Nothing between us is cold-blooded, *cara*. Who is your father?'

Her face froze. 'A bastard like you.'

She saw the flash of anger in his dark eyes and lifted her chin, welcoming the thought of confrontation…then watched incredulously as he began to stroll across the hallway to the central staircase.

'You're walking away?'

'I'm taking a shower before my muscles seize up and we both say things we might regret later.' He had been headed for the shower in the well-equipped basement leisure suite when he had seen her image on one of the security cameras.

'I don't regret anything!'

She'd yelled at him in a way he did not tolerate from anyone else; she'd flung accusations, called him a bastard to his face and created the sort of emotional scene he hated and yet he found he could reply with perfect honesty.

'Neither do I. Feel free to join me,' Draco murmured as he heard her heels clacking behind him on the marble floor.

Eve was panting with the exertion of chasing after him, but only a second behind as she followed him through the door of his bedroom suite. It wasn't until the door swung shut with a click that sounded awfully final behind her that she questioned the wisdom of her actions. A second later she was definitely panicking.

'What do you think you're doing?' A shrill note crept into her voice as she watched him peel the vest over his head. His back was to her and as he stretched his arms her eyes were riveted to the play of muscle under his olive-toned skin; each ripple and contraction made her stomach flip and quiver. He was perfect anatomically and aesthetically.

He turned to her with an expression of innocent surprise on his too handsome face and as his hands dropped to his sides, his feet slightly apart, his attitude was one of blatantly sexual arrogant challenge and there was nothing contrived about it—this was him.

Her breath snagged in her throat as, still holding her eyes, he dropped the vest he had peeled off onto a chair. 'I told you, I'm taking a shower.' His eyes glittered with sardonic humour but he managed to sound mildly surprised by the question.

'I want to talk to you.' She struggled to maintain an air of subtle disdain while under the cold surface her hormones had gone into dramatic free fall. Whatever else he was, Draco was the most beautiful thing she had ever seen with more raw sex appeal in his little finger than most men had in their entire bodies.

'Nothing stopping you, *cara*.' He bent to unlace his trainers, even this casual action made riveting by the casual animal grace that characterised all his actions. He kicked off one shoe and then the other.

Watching him through the utterly inadequate shield of her lashes, Eve felt as though she were going to explode. What, she speculated, lifting a hand to her head, would the autopsy report as the cause of death...fury or lust?

Both would be accurate as this man somehow managed to tap directly into her most primal urges. He was the incarnation of everything that she had sworn to herself she would reject.

'So if you change your mind about joining me…the offer's still open.' Holding her eyes, he smiled and reached for the cord tie on his sweat pants.

Her eyes dropped and she felt the blush begin. Turning on her heel and presenting her rigid back to him, she missed his smile of satisfaction.

CHAPTER ELEVEN

'A TEMPTING OFFER, but I'll pass.'

Unwilling to admit even to herself, *especially* to herself, how true this was, how much she was tempted to join him in the shower, Eve picked up a cushion from the pile thrown artistically on a chaise longue set against the far wall and began banging it. When it was battered out of shape she moved on to another, plumping it so enthusiastically that his response was barely audible above the thwacking.

'Suit yourself.'

She waited a few moments then risked looking over her shoulder. The discarded pants lay in a crumpled heap on the floor and with a deep sigh she let herself fall back on the cushions. She concentrated on steady breathing in and out, but the tension that tied her muscles in knots stubbornly persisted.

This was not going as she had anticipated.

Midway through telling herself she'd have to up her game, she heard the shower start up in the adjoining bathroom. A glazed expression slid into her eyes before she let them close, but that made it worse. Images crowded into her head of a steam-filled room, water sliding off slick brown skin, droplets gleaming on the sprinkling of chest hair that became a thin directional arrow down his flat belly.

The memory of the open invitation he had issued echoed in her head, feeding the ache of need that throbbed through her. She lifted a despairing hand to her head where increasingly vivid carnal images were playing on a loop and wondered how it was possible to be so furious with someone, know perfectly well they were using you, and yet still want them so badly... Her eyes opened and her hand fell limply away.

Was she finally becoming the person she had never forgiven her mother for being? The thought worked better than a cold shower and coincided with a sudden silence as the water in the bathroom went off and a switch in her head went back on.

She went pale at the thought of how close she'd come to running towards temptation and opening that door. Where Draco was concerned she appeared to have no shame or self-respect. Genes will out, she warned herself, and, shaking her head, she surged to her feet. Recognising a weakness in yourself meant you could do something about it—there was always a choice.

Her mother had had a choice and she'd made the wrong one—twice. Eve had no intention of repeating Sarah's mistakes.

She weighed her options, and it didn't take long to make her decision. She'd pass on the satisfaction of having the last word and put a safe distance between herself and Draco.

Run away. She released a slow measured breath. It was a plan—definitely a plan.

But before Eve could put this plan into action or even place one foot in front of the other Draco, whistling softly under his breath, strolled into the room barefoot and her urgent need to escape immediately became less urgent—a lot less urgent.

His dark hair had been slicked back messily with his

hands and was still dripping water, leaving dark patches on the white shirt he wore.

Emotions raw and her senses heightened to a painful degree, Eve knew with total certainty that that image, this vignette, had imprinted itself indelibly in her memory. For as long as she lived she would remember the way he looked and the way she felt.

'Did you miss me?' he asked, tucking the dangling tails of his shirt into the waist of dark trousers as he watched the expressions flicker across her face. When her mask was down she had the most expressive features he had ever encountered.

She tipped her chin. Sometimes the truth, however unpalatable, was the best defence. 'With every fibre of my being.'

The sexy husk in her voice sent a visceral shudder through his body, and his nerve endings tingled the way they had when her hair had brushed his bare skin.

'Right, now I'm all yours.' His grin flashed as he held his arms wide in invitation and drawled, 'Double entendre totally intended, in case you were wondering.'

'I wasn't.' Suddenly Eve was fed up with the games and the smart talk. She was glad now she hadn't made good her getaway; she would have always regretted not telling him what she thought of him.

Holding his eyes, she planted her hands on her hips, unwittingly drawing his attention to the gentle curves, and looked him up and down. See how you like it, she thought.

Problem was, he did seem to like it! There was a glimmer of admiration in his slow appreciative smile as he purred, 'Like what you're seeing, *cara*?'

She flushed and thought, Who wouldn't? Draco was the epitome of virile alpha-male perfection.

'You used me.' She swallowed, recognising that it was irrational that the knowledge hurt. After all, there was no trust between them, no bond that had been betrayed—just her own stupidity.

The quiet accusation caused his smile to fade. Jaw clenched, his dark brows drawn into a heavy line above his eyes, he sketched a frown that deepened as, unable to resist the compulsion, he let his glance drift over her body, seeing the smooth sleek lines and soft curves beneath the clothes, remembering the silky softness of her delicious skin that made his core temperature climb.

The powerful kick of his libido scored the angles of his carved cheeks with dark colour. The cold shower he had just endured had provided a temporary relief from the insatiable hunger, but now it was back and he could barely think past the desire to sink into her, feel her close tight as a silken glove around him.

'I think there was some mutual using,' he husked. 'And the way I recall it you had no complaints.'

She narrowed her eyes, folded her arms across her chest in an unconsciously self-protective gesture and angled a look of simmering contempt up at his lean, handsome face.

'You know exactly what I'm talking about!' she charged furiously.

Know?

He almost laughed. He knew nothing except that this had never happened to him before. It wasn't just his body; this woman had taken up residence in his head. He shrugged, refusing to acknowledge the surge of panic that slid through him. This thing between them would run its course, burn bright, and then become a delicious memory.

'How about you spell it out just to be on the safe side?' he suggested.

'Spell...let me see.' Finger on her chin, she pretended to think about it. 'B A S T A R D, exclamation mark. You are afraid of losing custody of Josie so I'm a token girlfriend... a female influence, a—' she sketched quotation marks in the air and drawled with disgust '—"stable relationship" to waft under the nose of your ex… No wonder you wanted me out of there before I could tell them the truth.'

'And what truth is that?'

'I'm just another of your one-night stands.'

'Bitterness…yet I seem to recall you wouldn't have it any other way, *cara*. Or are you moving the goalposts now?'

'I'm not bitter, I'm mad!'

'If you say so…and to be accurate it was not just at night—we already did night and day.'

Feeling an errant nerve jump in her soft jaw, Eve looked away.

'And you look about as stable as a diva having a melt-down,' he teased.

But, hell, it suited her! Eve had been repressing her passionate nature so long she probably believed that she was the tight-lipped, buttoned-up robot she liked people to think she was—it was a role she preferred to hide behind. To know that he was the only man who had seen behind the façade made him feel… He frowned, struggling to condense and compress all the emotions this woman shook loose in him into just one word…one sentence…one book!

'If I'd known you wanted to make friends with my mother and ex-wife I'd have taken Josie to school myself, though for future reference, just in case your paths cross again, I feel you should know that intelligence agencies all over the world have adopted my mother's interrogation techniques. And how was I meant to introduce you, by the way? This is Eve—we're just having sex?'

'So you were being kind.'

'There was a certain amount of self-interest involved,' he admitted.

'You used me,' she insisted, clinging tightly to her righteous indignation even though what had seemed like a legitimate accusation on the taxi drive back now sounded a little bit hysterical. 'You set it all up, got me here knowing that your ex would—'

'Would what exactly? You seriously believe I arranged to have my ex-wife, my mother and my teenage daughter walk in on me naked with a woman in the middle of the afternoon?'

She had, but when he put it like that... The sliver of doubt in Eve's head widened as, unable to admit she was totally in the wrong, she conceded, 'I don't suppose you expected your mother to be there too.'

'Thank you for that.'

His sarcasm made her teeth ache.

'For the record, I never expect my mother. She believes strongly in the advantage of surprise. Since my father died she is bored and I have become her project. Or, more correctly, getting me married to someone suitable has become her project.'

'So you admit it. You let her think that we are...are... are... Will you stop looking at me as though I'm a bug under a microscope or something?'

'In a relationship?' he finished her earlier sentence.

'We're not in a relationship, we're having sex!' she bellowed before adding through gritted teeth. '*Were* having sex.'

Eve would have preferred her over-the-top reaction to make him angry, not curious, as she struggled to retain her defiance in the face of his searching scrutiny.

'Why is the distinction so important to you?'

Wanting to aggravate him, she deliberately misunderstood. 'I like good grammar.'

'Not that distinction, the one between having sex and being in a relationship. Is this to do with your mother and Latimer...?' he pressed shrewdly.

Feeling the pressure of his stare and reacting defensively, she stuck out her chin. 'This isn't about me, it's about you; and anyway, I don't think you're anyone to lecture me about relationships. According to your daughter you change women the way most men change their socks.'

Draco recognised classic deflection when he heard it; he used it himself on occasion. But unlike Eve he did so consciously. He might not be guilty of contriving the situation earlier as she'd accused, but he had felt no compunction about taking advantage of it. For the first time in months, his mother had left without dropping heavy hints about moving in to take care of Josie.

'You didn't have to pump my daughter for information, Eve. You could have just asked me if you'd wanted to know anything about me.'

Eve rolled her eyes in response, while Draco made a discovery that utterly shocked him. He had meant what he'd said.

He had become adept at recognising the warning signs when a woman wanted more than he was prepared to give, and even the suggestion that they were looking for weaknesses in his emotional barriers was usually a signal to walk away—but now he was inviting Eve in to walk around his head!

'I didn't pump!' she exploded, her eyes flashing green fire at the charge. 'You're Josie's favourite subject.'

He arched an ebony brow. 'Not yours?'

'Oh, I find you fascinating,' she trilled, taking pleasure from the flicker of something that might have been unease she saw move at the backs of his eyes.

'So you have been discussing me with my daughter.'

'You know how it is when girls are together...'

He responded to this with a veiled look that made it impossible for her to read his reaction—was he worried...? She hoped so!

'Don't play games with me, Eve.' For the first time

his low voice held a thread of anger as he took a step towards her.

'Am I meant to be scared?' The adrenaline rush that sharpened all her senses to a painful degree made her respond in an uncharacteristically reckless fashion—though compared with the reckless steps she'd taken recently this one was fairly innocuous.

He reached out and took her chin in his fingers, tilting her face up to him. 'Some people are.' Power, which for Draco was a by-product of his financial success, not an aim in itself, meant he was used to seeing the fear and envy that was often behind people's smiles. They saw the public image and not the man and he had no problem with that; he had no wish to be understood or universally loved. 'Not you,' he said positively.

There was no escape from his searching stare—the truth was Draco himself didn't frighten her. It was the way he made her feel that was beginning to scare Eve witless...

Still resisting the possibility she had more in common with her mother than she was prepared to or could admit, Eve shook her head and countered, 'Should I be?'

His hand fell from her face to her shoulder, where his thumb moved restlessly back and forth over her collarbone as he stared down into her face feeling a sudden surge of protectiveness.

'Probably. I don't want to hurt you.' But that didn't mean she wouldn't be collateral damage in what passed for his love life. He felt a sudden knife thrust of anger at himself. She was not meant to be so vulnerable but she was—and he'd seen it right from the beginning.

She watched him warily. His honesty had finally drained all the anger from her; maybe he deserved some in return.

'I thought you had planned it all,' she admitted in a small voice.

Even though his hand fell away he remained so close that she imagined she could feel the warmth of his body.

'After Josie told me about the custody battle and that your ex is using the emotional vacuum of what passes for your love life as leverage…' Her eyes lifted. 'No insult intended.'

The tension in his jaw relaxed as he read the sincerity in her face.

'I decided that when you came to my office this morning you knew exactly what was going to happen…I mean…'

'That we'd end up having wild sex in my study and my family would walk in on us.'

On the receiving end of his dark intense stare, she felt her temperature shoot up several degrees. 'I'm trying to apologise.'

His eyebrows rose incredulously.

'I can now see that it was—'

'Spontaneous?'

She frowned fiercely at the interruption. 'A series of co-incidences.' He saw a flicker of guilt move like a shadow across her face. A soft heart could be a major disadvantage in the business world, and it made him wonder how she had got so far.

'Apology accepted. You had the details about Clare's custody claim from Josie… Is Josie worried about it?'

He'd thought his daughter could tell him anything…but for the first time Draco stopped to consider the suddenly shockingly real possibility that his daughter really was losing out not having a stepmother she could bond with. He didn't like the thought of Josie opening up to someone who was almost a total stranger, *needing* to open up to another woman as she had done with Eve.

His little girl was growing up and did the awful, boring Edward have a point? Was she lacking a female role model?

'Josie has total faith in your ability to sort it.' And just about anything else that might crop up. When the teenager spoke of her father, even when she was complaining, it was obvious that she adored him and had complete trust in his ability to keep her safe.

The way her own mother had kept her safe... Had Eve always appreciated it?

Draco nodded, feeling a surge of relief, his concern allayed slightly, yet the doubts that had been awoken remained there just below the surface.

'Are you really not worried about the custody claim? I mean, don't courts normally favour mothers?'

'Potential custody claim.'

The smooth correction drew a frown from Eve. 'You don't think she'll go through with it?'

Was he really as confident as he sounded? Or was this an example of his feelings for his ex-wife clouding his judgement?

In his place, with a great kid like Josie to protect... But she wasn't in his place, Eve reminded herself, and Josie wasn't her child. Which meant she could be totally objective, unlike Draco, and probably any other male when it came to a woman like Clare.

'Josie has never lived with her mother?'

'No, never.' He arched a brow. 'Do you think that's wrong?'

A few minutes had been long enough for Eve to see that the beautiful woman was the last person in the world that should be given charge of any child, let alone one as special as Josie who, in her opinion, deserved a lot better.

'I think that depends on the mother and the circumstances,' she said tactfully.

'Clare walked out when Josie was a baby.'

'How could she have done that?' In Eve's mind a woman

was hard-wired to care for her baby before anything else, and there were women who gave their lives for their babies.

She supposed women like Clare were the flip side of the coin. Yet she still couldn't see how any woman could walk out and abandon her baby and she never would.

'Was there…someone else or was it post-natal depression, perhaps?' she suggested tentatively.

'No, she just got bored.'

Watching her face, he sank down onto a sofa. 'Take the weight off,' he said, patting the arm in invitation.

'I'll pass.'

He grinned and Eve almost responded, making up for the near slip with a really fierce frown. She needed her anger to hide behind… Her eyes widened in alarm before she lowered her eyelashes protectively to mask her expression… Where did that thought come from?

'Clare loses interest in things very quickly.'

Shocked by the suggestion, Eve looked up. 'Even in her own daughter?'

He ran a hand down his jaw. 'In anything.' A fact that Edward had yet to learn.

Eyes on her face, he didn't miss another flicker of repugnance as he let his broad shoulders relax into the buttoned leather back of the chesterfield, giving a grunt as he stretched his long legs out and crossed one ankle over the other.

His fitness regime was pretty brutal but the previous night followed by today's session with Eve had left him with some muscles he hadn't known he had aching. Eve in his bed beat a treadmill any day!

'So you no longer think this afternoon was part of some dastardly plan of mine.'

She shifted uncomfortably and shrugged. 'Maybe not,' she admitted.

His brows lifted. 'Maybe?'

Maybe she deserved to squirm a little...? 'All right, *definitely not—*'

'This custody thing.'

'That's worrying you now, isn't it?'

The question in Eve's mind was, why hadn't it been worrying him all along?

'Look, this isn't Clare, it's her fiancé who is driving this campaign for custody of Josie, and he has his own political agenda. What he doesn't realise is that Clare is *allowing* him to manipulate her. Don't let the ditsy blonde stuff fool you; Clare is smart and when she needs to be, she's totally ruthless.'

This chilling assessment made Eve shiver, all the more so because it came from Draco. He clearly still had feelings for the mother of his child—nothing else in Eve's opinion made sense of the fact he seemed to tolerate and make excuses for Clare doing just about anything. The question was how deep were those feelings?

'And you're all right with that?'

'She loves Josie.'

But do you love Clare...? Eve just stopped herself voicing the question that loomed large in her head. What would be the point when she already knew the answer? No man could make so many allowances for a woman who had left him literally holding the baby unless he had real feelings for her. Maybe he couldn't admit it, but it was obvious to her that the only reason that Draco had not been in a real relationship since his divorce was that he was still hooked on his beautiful, selfish ex-wife and the mother of his child.

Eve was glad she was not competing with that!

'No, I'm not in love with Clare.'

Her eyes flew wide. 'I w-wasn't thinking that!'

His brows lifted in a sceptical arc.

'Look, I know you don't want to know what I think.'

Draco arched a sable brow. 'But you're going to tell me anyway...?'

'Maybe you shouldn't be too complacent about this custody issue; courts can be unpredictable.'

He looked thoughtful. 'You think I'm complacent?'

She thought he was gorgeous. 'There's no harm taking precautions.'

He nodded slowly.

'Look, if you want them to carry on thinking that we are...together in the short term, obviously while we are still...'

'Having sex?'

'If we *are* still having sex?'

'For Josie's sake?'

He was not making this easy. 'For *my* sake,' she admitted. 'Then that's fine. If, of course, you *are* up for it.'

'Come here and I'll show you how up for it I am.'

It took very little persuasion to make her fall into his lap.

CHAPTER TWELVE

EVE WAS APPLYING a final sweep of mascara when Hannah swept into the room. She spun her stool around to face her friend, who was already in full regal evening dress, the empire line not quite disguising her pregnancy bump.

'How is Kamel?'

'Oh, fine, according to him.' Hannah's eye roll could not disguise her concern for her husband's health. 'But in the real world he has a temperature of a hundred and two and looks like death warmed up in a gorgeous way... He's impossible! Why can't he do man flu like every other man instead of...? God, but I wish I could stay with him.' Her friend took a deep breath, pasted on a bright smile and muttered, 'But duty calls and the doctors swear that the antibiotics should have kicked in by the morning. He's very lucky it's not pneumonia...and if he'd left it any longer...'

'He'll be fine.'

'Of course he will...you have no idea, Eve, how grateful I am that you're here. This is the first time I've ever done one of these things on my own and Kamel is the charity patron, so it matters just having a friendly face in the room. I hope I'll—'

'You'll do amazingly, and I know you're grateful because you've told me about ten billion times, which was unnecessary, as was the makeover. Or maybe it wasn't,' she admitted, glancing down at the designer gown she had

selected from the rail of similar garments her friend had
wheeled into the room.

'You look stunning, Evie.'

Eve looked up, a faint flush on her cheeks. A few weeks
ago she wouldn't have believed Hannah, nor for that matter would she have had the confidence required to wear
the dramatic full-length red dress that clung to her body
like a second skin, hugging her breasts, emphasising her
tiny waist and softly curved hips before flaring at the knee
flamenco style.

Being with Draco over the past weeks had done that,
had given her that confidence in her own sexuality and sensual allure. That was the plus, that and great sex, and his
earthy laugh... The downside... She pinned a smile on her
face and promised herself she wouldn't go there tonight.

Who was she kidding? She carried it with her like another layer of skin. She had fallen in love with Draco and
she had to hide it, disguise it, bury it. There was simply
no other way of dealing with this situation.

She had fallen, deeply, for a man who was everything
she had spent her adult life avoiding, and they weren't
even in a real relationship. But the important thing was,
it was on her terms.

She squeezed her eyes closed as she experienced a moment of scalding self-disgust. At least Mum had been honest. On her terms, indeed...!

In reality this meant she wasn't available when Draco
clicked his fingers, even if she was. Even if this meant she
spent some really miserable nights when she could have
been sharing his bed lying alone. She repeatedly told herself it was worth it, because it meant that she was in control.

She recognised the self-delusion but she wasn't brave
enough to admit it.

'And I can't remember the last time I saw you with your
hair loose. I hardly recognised you,' continued Hannah.

'I hardly recognise myself these days,' Eve admitted quietly as the two women left the room.

With cameras recording every inflection and under the glitter of chandeliers Hannah gave the speech on her husband's behalf with charm and dignity. In fact, she was so good that for about ten seconds Eve even stopped wondering about Draco.

What was he doing?

Who was he talking to?

What would he have thought of her in this dress?

Draco was putting in a token appearance towards the end of the evening because Kamel was a good friend and he had always despised men who forgot their friends the moment they became romantically involved—and he wasn't. Eve and he had a civilised relationship; while it was different from his other liaisons in many ways, it was still not permanent.

Josie having recently opted for the weekly boarding option at school was the only reason Eve slept over at his place, though not quite as often as he would have liked. Eve had a life he wasn't part of; he had a life she wasn't part of... He was just telling himself how well this situation worked for him when these worlds meshed.

It was totally unexpected. He simply turned his head to see what the titled blond-haired guy he had been introduced to when he arrived was staring at, and it turned out to be a who. *His* Eve, looking totally at ease, smiling, charming, in a red dress that was slinky and sexy and... He felt his core temperature jump as his eyes followed the sinuous curves of her body. This was not an outfit she should be wearing outside the confines of their bedroom!

Not even conscious that he had blanked an ambassador who had been approaching him with his hand outstretched, Draco strode across the room.

'What the hell are you doing here?' he thundered in Eve's ear.

It was Hannah, standing beside her friend, who blinked as her gaze moved from Eve to the tall figure who stood there glowering like some dark avenging angel.

Eve's shock gave way to indignation. 'Is there any reason I shouldn't be here?' she retorted with deceptive calm.

'You might have mentioned it to me.'

Her feathery brows lifted. 'You're here; did you mention it to me?' She lifted a hand to cover her mouth and said softly from behind it, 'There's a film crew here tonight, Draco. Do you really want to broadcast this to the world?' Removing her hand and raising her voice, she added brightly, 'You know Hannah, of course.'

Draco tipped his head, his eyes not leaving Eve as he said, 'Princess. I am sorry to hear Kamel is unwell.' Then to Eve, he added, 'I'm going home. Are you coming?'

Hannah's gasp was audible.

Draco flashed a look her way then back to his lover. 'You didn't even tell your best friend we are together?' He thought women shared everything...everything that mattered anyway. It felt like a betrayal. Was she ashamed of him or didn't he even rate gossip?

Eve narrowed her eyes. 'No, I'm not coming.'

He gave a magnificent shrug. 'Fine. I'm leaving for New York on Friday.'

'Have a good flight.'

'You will be back for my birthday?' Josie asked over the phone.

In his hotel room Draco left the window and the view of Central Park. 'Aren't I always there for your birthday?'

'Just checking. It should be a good party. Aunt Gabby is cooking all my favourite food.'

'You're being good for your aunt Gabby, I hope.'

'I'm always good and she loves having me. Ask her if you like—she's here.'

'I'll take your word for it. Josie, I was wondering if you've seen—' He stopped suddenly.

'Have I what…? Sorry, Dad, the line's not so good.'

The line was working a hell of a lot better than his brain! He was so desperate for news of Eve, any scrap or small detail, that he'd been about to milk his teenage daughter for information on her.

What the hell was he doing?

He had lost count of the number of times he had picked up the phone, hungry to hear her voice, but he'd never dialled the number. And why? Because he'd been proving a point. They had not spoken since the night of that damned charity ball.

Pathetic!

All he'd actually proved was that he was gutless. What else did you call a man too afraid to admit he needed a woman, needed to hear her voice, see her smile, watch her fall asleep?

His chest lifted in a silent sigh; he was afraid to admit that he'd finally fallen in love. The admission came with a certain sense of relief; love had made a fool of him once and he'd sworn it would never happen again. But it had.

'You still there, Dad?'

Draco stared at the phone in his hand blankly for a moment before lifting it to his ear.

'I'm fine.' He wasn't but he would be, he thought.

'I said do you mind if I ask Eve…to my birthday party… please?'

'That would be fine.'

Eve had been nervous about meeting Mark Tyler, but it wasn't nearly as awkward as she had imagined. By the time they were drinking their coffee they had discovered they had a lot in common and were talking as though they'd known each other all their lives.

If things had been different they might have. As the thought registered in her brain, she looked at the hand he had laid on hers and sighed.

Across the table Mark looked concerned. 'Are you all right?' He caught the direction of Eve's gaze and, flushing slightly, went to move the protective hand he had instinctively placed over the smaller one that lay on the table, but as he lifted it her wrist turned and her fingers curled around his.

Their eyes met and clung, and her voice was thick with the same emotions that shone in her eyes as Eve shook her head.

'I'm fine; it's just…I…'

'I know,' he acknowledged.

Coffee finished, the bill paid, Mark suggested he walk her back to her flat rather than call a cab. As it was a beautiful clear evening and she wasn't ready for it to end yet, Eve agreed.

Outside the pavement was wet but it had stopped raining and the night sky was bright and clear, or at least as bright and clear as it ever got in the City.

Eve walked straight into a puddle, splashing her new shoes and tights.

'*Singin' in the Rain*,' they both said in unison and then laughed.

'One of my favourite films,' Eve said.

'A classic,' Mark agreed. 'So you're not sorry you came?'

Eve had admitted to him how nearly she hadn't, how even at the last minute she had almost choked. She still hadn't got over the shock of being contacted by a half-brother who hadn't known she existed until he had been going through his dead father's things and who now wanted to meet her.

'I'm glad we met. I don't know why I always assumed you knew about me...probably because I knew about you, even though I'm not meant to,' she said.

'I was scared stiff,' her half-brother admitted with a laugh.

'You were?'

'Amy encouraged me; she said it was the right thing to do and then when I saw you at the charity thing the other week—well, Amy made me come over.'

Eve smiled. Mark had brought his wife into the conversation constantly; he clearly adored her, which was wonderful for him. The relationship she had always envied him with his...*their* father had been pretty awful, apparently. Lord Charlford had bullied his son and heir, taking every opportunity to belittle him. It was his wife who had given Mark his confidence back and given him the strength to escape his father's toxic influence.

'Tell me to mind my own business, Eve—Amy always says I'm too pushy!—but do you...have anyone in your life? The man I saw you with...Morelli, perhaps?'

They had reached her building and Eve paused and turned around to face her half-brother. 'There is someone,' she admitted. 'But I'm not sure—'

'If he's *the* one?'

'We've only been together a couple of months but... oh, yes, he's the one for me. I'm just not sure...' Eve's voice terminated on a tearful wobble and she was horrified to feel her eyes fill as she gulped past an emotional constriction the size of a boulder in her aching throat '...if I'm the one for him. He's...' She stopped and shook her head, the lamp light picking out the tear that escaped and slid down her cheek.

Since he'd left for New York after that night almost three weeks ago now, she hadn't heard a word from Draco other than a pretty terse text when he had landed. She had told herself she hadn't expected more, but of course in reality she had.

She'd had a lot of time on her hands to think about her expectations regarding Draco and recognise how unrealistic they were. She had finally admitted to herself that she wanted all the things that she had once scorned. She wanted to love a man to distraction and she wanted to be loved the same way, and it very much looked as though she was not going to get either of those things, as Draco couldn't give her what she needed.

Self-respect and simple common sense had told her that this was a crunch point in their relationship. When Draco returned she owed it to both of them to be honest with him and if he couldn't give her what she needed it was time to move on. She understood now, if her mother really did love Charles Latimer as she loved Draco, why she had stayed with him. Eve could see herself slipping too easily into the same sort of arrangement, but dying a little more each day as her self-respect was eroded.

The thought filled her with utter horror but so did the prospect of never seeing Draco again and that was what it would involve. There were no half measures.

Mark lifted a hand and blotted the tear with his thumb, smiling down into her tearful face. 'You're unhappy. I'm sorry.' His handsome face tightened with anger as he added softly, 'Whoever he is, he's a fool.'

'Don't be nice...' she sniffed '...or I'll cry. I don't know what's wrong with me just lately.' Only yesterday she had had to leave a meeting because she'd started to cry when someone had shown her a picture of a litter of kittens her friend had rescued after someone had tied them in a sack and thrown them into a rubbish skip.

'Don't worry, I'm used to tears. Since she's been pregnant Amy cries at anything and everything.'

Her mother, Hannah and now this Amy were all pregnant. Sometimes it felt as though she were the only person in the world who wasn't!

She went still, and her legs began to tremble as a coldness crept over her body, invading every cell with a terrible dread as the feelings swirling through her coalesced into one question!

'Oh, God!'

'What is it?' Mark watched in alarm as the last vestiges of colour left her face.

His concerned voice shook Eve out of her daze. She struggled to act normally, forcing a smile and shaking her head. 'Just a thought, that's all. Something I should have considered but I didn't... Silly, really.'

Silly was perhaps not the most appropriate word to describe a potentially life-changing event, and the more she thought about it, the more... No, she thought, closing that door. She would not and could not think about it now. She needed to know for sure first and that couldn't happen until tomorrow unless...?

She scrunched her brow, trying to remember if the supermarket on the corner stayed open twenty-four seven and, if they did, did they stock pregnancy-test kits?

'Look, I'd invite you in for coffee but I'm a bit tired.'

Mark nodded, kissed her cheek, then hugged her. Eve planted a reciprocal kiss on his clean-shaven cheek and hugged him back.

'You will come to Charlford to visit, won't you? Amy is longing to meet you. The place is upside down as she's ripping out and tearing down everything that reminds her of Dad—she always said he made her skin crawl. But after I found out about you... She says the best way we can punish him is by having good lives.'

'Amy sounds...I'd love...' Her voice trailed away.

Mark, his hand on her shoulder, turned to follow the direction of her wide-eyed, shocked stare. He turned just in time to see the fist that a moment later connected with his jaw and sent him sprawling.

With a cry Eve was on her knees beside her brother. 'Mark, are you all right?'

Holding his jaw, Mark shook his head. 'Fine. He took me by surprise, that's all.' The glazed expression in his green eyes was replaced by one of anger as he looked up at the tall man who stood over them. It was mixed with a healthy helping of fear as the man was big in a lean, athletic way, a real tough customer.

'What the hell are you doing, Draco?' Eve demanded, fitting a clean tissue to the blood seeping from the corner of her brother's mouth as she sat back on her heels to glare up at him.

The red haze that had descended when Draco had seen the guy touch Eve's cheek and then tenderly embrace her was slowly receding, leaving an anger that was equally lethal but as cold as surgical steel.

'I would ask you the same question but it's very obvious,' he bit out.

'Oh, I am so, *so* sorry, Mark.'

Mark took the tissue from her.

'And he's sorry too, aren't you, Draco…?' Eve said.

'No.'

The unequivocal response drew a glare from Eve, who lifted her head to tell him exactly what she thought of him but he was gone… She turned her head to see him walking away down the street. 'Stay there and don't move,' she said to Mark. Her jaw tightened with determination. 'I have something I need to do.'

Mark caught her arm. 'Leave it, Eve. The guy is dangerous.'

Eve let out a scornful snort. 'I'm not scared of him!' she declared.

He was walking and she was running but it took her

fifty yards before she caught up with Draco. As she drew level with him she caught his arm.

She was panting to catch her breath as Draco swung back, his lips curled in a snarl, his eyes as cold as ice chips.

Her eyes searched his lean face. 'Are you mad?'

One corner of his mouth lifted in a sneer. 'Not any more.' For weeks he had fought the knowledge that he loved her, then finally admitted that he was afraid. He'd felt he had moved forward when in reality it turned out he'd been right all along. Loving someone always ended badly.

His cryptic reply just added another layer to all the other layers of confusion in her head—him being here when she knew he was in the States, his attack on Mark, his attitude now as he looked at her as though she were something unpleasant he had stepped in. She was too shocked to be angry or even hurt.

'You're not even here.' Stupid thing to say, Eve, she told herself as her eyes travelled the long, lean length of his broad-shouldered, muscle-packed frame, seeing but still not quite believing he was here. That this was happening.

'Yes, I can see how that might be inconvenient for you,' he drawled.

There was a heavy beat of silence as she waited, fully anticipating that any second now a light would go on in her brain and she'd understand what was happening. But there was no light, just the aftertaste from the acid bite of his sarcasm. She saw his hands clench into fists, and the tension that was rolling off him in waves had a physical presence.

'What are you doing here?' If she could work that out maybe the rest would fall into place but, no, it wouldn't, because nothing would explain him hitting Mark and nothing, she thought, feeling a stab of anger, would excuse it.

His jaw clenched as he realised he'd nearly made the

mistake of his life. 'Spoiling your evening. I suppose you
do know he's married.'

Her green eyes still shocked and glazed like someone
who had just been jolted out of a trance, she blinked. She
followed the direction of the sharp, contemptuous movement of Draco's head to where her half-brother had got to
his feet and was walking towards them.

'Mark? Yes, I know.'

Forehead furrowed, she tried to figure this out. What
was the relevance of Mark's marriage? Did he know her
half-brother? Was there some sort of feud between them,
though she had not imagined until now that Draco was
the sort of man who resolved feuds with his fists. Up to
this point she had only seen Draco be controlled and cool,
the last man in the world she had imagined losing control.
Not that he didn't have a passionate nature, but outside the
bedroom he kept those passions on a tight leash.

She was relieved to see that her half-brother seemed
all right, no thanks to Draco. Worried for his safety if he
followed after her, she waved her hand and yelled, 'No,
Mark, it's fine.' The last thing she wanted was to be in the
middle of a brawl.

Had Draco thought she was in danger? The idea might
have worked if he hadn't walked away immediately afterwards, and if it hadn't been for that look he'd given her,
the coruscating contempt in his eyes in that last dismissive glare...

Turning back to Draco, she said in a fierce voice, 'You
lay a finger on him, you bully, and I'll...just don't...' She
expelled a shaky sigh. 'You hit him, you really hit him!'
That part still didn't seem real; none of this seemed real.

She knew the man was married and she had been totally brazen about it. Draco searched Eve's face for some
sign, some little spark of guilt, and saw none...nothing.
How could he have got it so wrong?

Mark reached them, the bruises already coming out on one side of his face, the sight of which made Eve feel sick. She moved to stand between the two men. 'Leave him alone,' she warned again.

Draco's jaw clenched at her protective gesture. 'I'm curious…is it the title?'

Eve blinked. 'What are you talking about?'

'Is that the attraction?' He slid a look of smouldering contempt Mark's way and she felt her brother take an involuntary step back. Eve for one didn't blame him. Draco was being positively intimidating! 'Or do pretty blond boys do it for you now?'

'Pretty?' What on earth…? Mark, he meant Mark, who was not pretty, but definitely handsome, in a much less aggressively masculine way than Draco. When illumination came it was dazzling, and with total clarity she finally realised what Draco had seen—or rather what he thought he had seen.

Draco thought that he had caught her in an assignation with a lover!

Ignoring Mark's restraining hand, she stepped forward, her hand extended towards Draco.

'Or does your deceitful little soul enjoy the illicit thrill of sneaking around?' Draco accused.

Her hand fell away.

The shocked hurt in her eyes made him pause, anger, guilt and jealousy twisting inside him, but only briefly. Had she considered his feelings when she got into bed with his pretty lordship? She had zero loyalty and did she ever consider anyone's feelings but her own? He'd seen qualities in her that weren't there, the same way he'd felt a deeper bond where there wasn't one. There was just sex, as she'd always insisted.

'Or is it just a case of like mother, like daughter? Where is your father in all of this?'

Eve was not even conscious she had raised her hand until the whiplash crack made her jump back in shock. Only she hadn't jumped; Mark had pulled her back after she'd slapped Draco across the face.

Mark held her back with a protective arm, anger making him feel brave as he faced Draco. 'He's dead. Her father is dead; *our* father is dead.'

Draco froze, the blood draining from his face as his gaze moved between the two faces staring back at him with similar expressions of disgust and loathing.

'He's your brother? Charlford was your father?' he said in a strangled voice. He was struggling to take in the information as panic slid through his body, freezing his brain. He had messed up big time! 'I thought...'

'You thought that I was cheating on you and you also implied that my mother has questionable morals,' Eve said coldly.

'I didn't say that!'

Even as he protested he realised that it didn't matter what he said; there was no going back. She would never forgive him—he had insulted her mother, and he'd punched a man...her brother!

She was looking at him with loathing in her beautiful eyes and he deserved it.

The shame of having lost the control he prided himself on, the shame of acting like some sort of Neanderthal was a bitter taste in his mouth, and the words he wanted to say wouldn't come. Maybe that was for the best. So far what he'd said had only made things worse.

'As good as!' she charged furiously. 'I'm really glad I discovered before it was too late what an intolerant, evil-minded jerk you are!'

His lean profile clenched. She was saying nothing that he didn't deserve. The furious jealousy he had felt when he saw Eve appear with another man had ripped away any claim he had to being civilised. He had never experienced anything like it before, and he never wanted to again.

'Well?'

He arched a brow and said quietly, 'What am I meant to say?'

'Sorry?' she suggested in an icy voice.

'I am sorry,' he said, including Mark in his response.

'Is that meant to make things better?' she shrilled, not to be placated. 'I never want to see you again ever!' she yelled wildly, then, grabbing her brother's arm, she stalked off towards the entrance to her building, not pausing until they were in the communal foyer. 'Is he coming?' she asked her brother through clenched teeth, adding urgently, 'Don't look!'

Mark, who was already looking, turned back. 'Don't worry, he isn't coming. He's gone.'

Eve expelled a long shuddering sigh. 'Gone?' she parroted blankly.

'Yes.'

Mark's smile died as his sister burst into tears.

CHAPTER THIRTEEN

SITTING AT HER desk as Draco walked into the office, his PA beckoned him wildly. 'It's him!'

'I'll take it in my office.' He didn't ask who the him was; there was only one person he had seen make his unflappable middle-aged secretary blush and that was Kamel, the Prince of Surana. He'd be lucky if he got any work out of her for the rest of the day, he thought sourly.

'Hello, Kamel. What can I do for you?'

'Grow a pair.'

It was an answer that only a good friend could have uttered, but even so the harsh suggestion made Draco's eyebrows rise dramatically. 'Have I done something to upset you?'

'You've done something to upset my wife, which amounts to the same thing. No, actually, it's worse.'

Draco, who could only recall having exchanged half a dozen words with the princess at her father's wedding or at the charity evening, waited for an explanation.

'Eve is Hannah's best friend, Draco. They're sisters now! Your name is a dirty word in our home. What the hell is wrong with you, man? Eve is a… Actually, this is none of my business.'

'You're ringing to tell me it's none of your business or that I'm a loser?' Kamel wouldn't be the only one. Josie had stopped asking him about Eve but he could see the disappointment and disapproval in her eyes every time she looked at him.

His best friend, his daughter… Was there a message in there he ought to be hearing…? No, Eve had made her feelings very clear, and, even if he did jump through hoops to get her back, who was to say it wouldn't happen again? There was a limit to how often a man could reinvent himself. He was who he was and if she didn't like him warts and all what was the point?

The point is you're lo… No, he wouldn't even allow himself to think the word. His life was full, busy, and *loneliness* was a state of mind reserved for people who indulged in self-pity.

'Both, but, no, I'm ringing you regardless, and God knows I hope I'm doing the right thing here… You know Hannah is pregnant?'

'Congratulations.'

He heard the hissing sound of exasperation echo down the line at the interruption. 'The thing is the doctors won't allow her to travel right now and I'm not leaving her.'

An icy fist suddenly reached into his chest. 'Has something happened to Eve?' On his feet, he dragged a hand through his hair and thought, I should be with her.

'Not Eve, no, not in that way.'

'Eve is all right, isn't she? She's not hurt or ill or…'

'Eve is well. It's her mother, Sarah, who's been rushed to hospital. We've had Charlie on the phone and the man is totally distraught, falling to pieces, as I would be in his place. Sarah has been admitted with severe pre-eclampsia.'

The medical term rang a warning bell in Draco's mind. 'That's bad?'

'Very bad,' the other man confirmed. 'Apparently they're going to deliver the baby early to give her a fighting chance.'

'Charlie told you this?'

'No, Eve did. She took the phone off him and it was just as well as he was sobbing and not making much sense. Hannah is worried sick about Eve, her father, and Sarah, and she feels guilty as hell she can't get there and she's mad at me because I won't leave her and come over to take control of the situation. There's no question that my place is here with her, but if I could tell her someone is there with Eve, and that she isn't alone coping with it all…?'

Draco's jaw tightened. 'I'm the last person Eve would want there.'

'This isn't about you.'

The comment hit Draco with the force of a below-the-belt kick delivered with perfect accuracy.

It was something he had needed to hear. He'd been going through the motions for weeks, telling himself that he was better off alone, but what about Eve, what was best for her? Eve might not want him in her life and the choice was hers, but, *Dio*, he would be a fool not to try to convince her to change her mind. But that was for the future. The priority now was to be there for her, take some of the burden off her slender shoulders.

Halfway out of the door, his keys in his hand, Draco said to Kamel, 'I'm on my way.' He was about to toss the phone to his secretary when he realised he didn't know where he was going. 'What hospital?'

Every second of the record-breaking fifty-mile journey Draco sat with his jaw clenched and his hands white knuckled on the wheel. He tortured himself with imagined images of Eve alone in pain and distress, having to cope with a disaster that was a whisper away from being a tragedy and having a man far too heavy use her as an emotional prop.

Her mother being in a critical condition was not his fault but everything else could legitimately be placed at his door. His friend thought he was a fool and he was right. If Draco had not been a total fool he'd have been there with Eve right now and she wouldn't be facing this *alone*. *Alone*... The word kept reverberating through his head.

Well, she wouldn't face anything alone again.

He was going to be there for her whether she wanted him or not. He was not going to let her out of his sight and, short of a restraining order, she couldn't stop him.

That's right, Draco, just bulldoze your way in because that has worked so well so far! How about showing a bit of humility, saying sorry and letting Eve decide if she wants you there? he told himself.

She'd sent him away but it had been pride and fear of rejection that had stopped him asking her for a second chance. His mouth twisted into a grimace of self-disgust as he caught a glimpse of himself in the rear-view mirror.

'You gutless wonder, Draco.'

She was the best thing that had ever happened to him.

The hospital was a maze of corridors but he finally found someone who could, if not answer his questions, at least show him a visitor's room. The nurse's grave face did not send out a positive message.

If anything had happened to her mother Eve would need a lot of support. It hurt to admit he might not be the person she wanted at such a time, but had anyone contacted her brother?

'Mr Morelli?'

Draco stopped pacing and turned his critical glance on the white-coated doctor who had entered the room. He stifled the impulse to demand to be taken to Eve immediately and tipped his head in acknowledgement.

'Is there any news?'

'You're family?'

It took a supreme effort but despite his frustration at the delay Draco showed no offence at the question. 'I am Draco Morelli. Eve Curtis is my fiancée.'

The younger man's face cleared as he offered a hand. 'Sorry about that but we had an incident earlier. Some enterprising reporter got wind of this and got as far as outside Recovery dressed as a porter.'

'Blood-sucking vampires.'

The medic responded to this heartfelt observation with a nod of his head. 'Unfortunately Mr Latimer's own security overreacted to the situation and we have also had to exclude them. I'm George Robinson, part of Mr Stirling's team. I'll get a nurse to show you to the SCBU. Miss Curtis is with her brother.'

'A boy?'

The doctor nodded. 'Very small, as you'd expect, but his condition is stable. It is the mother we are more concerned about at this juncture.'

In the special care baby unit and feeling very much out of his comfort zone, Draco nodded his thanks when given a gown to put on, and, after washing his hands, he was shown the way to a glass-panelled side room.

The nurse who escorted him was speaking, something comforting, he thought, but Draco, who nodded absently at intervals, was only catching one word in three. His heart nearly stopped when he saw Eve through the glass sitting side on to the door. She was enveloped in the same sort of gown he was wearing, but on her it reached the floor. As he stared she reached forward, her eyes trained on the tiny scrap of humanity in the incubator, attached to tubes and wires that bleeped. The baby appeared smaller than Eve's hand, and the loving expression on her face as she gently touched her finger to the baby's thin cheek brought a film of moisture to his eyes.

Eve heard the nurse enter but didn't take her eyes off the tiny figure in the incubator. Babies should be plump and pink but her baby brother was tiny and wizened, his skin shiny. It looked so fragile that she was afraid to touch him even though they had said that the contact was good for the baby.

'Sorry I let the tea go cold.' Logically she knew the baby couldn't hear her, that his sleep was controlled by the drugs being fed into him and the machines that breathed for him, but she struggled to raise her voice above a whisper. 'He's not in pain, is he?' It didn't seem possible that the tubes protruding from his fragile little body could not cause him pain.

Slowly Eve withdrew her hand and turned her head, her eyes widening when she saw him.

Draco had anticipated many reactions from her and he had as many responses ready. He knew the one he should have used six weeks ago—*he was staying.* But it was the reaction he had *not* anticipated and that he was not prepared for that was the one he actually got.

Something else he was not prepared for was the strength of the feelings that broke loose inside him at the sight of her. She looked so vulnerable and so beautiful that in that second he knew he would have died to save her a moment's pain.

Far better, though, to live for her.

She looked like someone in a trance as she got to her feet, not shouting at him, not rejecting him, but with a tremulous smile on her face and a glow in her green eyes made even more dramatic by the dark shadows beneath them that sent a surge of relief through him.

'You're really here?' It was like a dream but the past few hours…Eve had no idea how many…had been a complete nightmare.

Unconscious he had said her name, Draco took a stride towards her and with a cry she flung herself at him, her arms going around his middle as her face burrowed into his chest. Draco did the only thing possible: he wrapped his arms around her and pulled her in close to his body as she sobbed and clung to him.

'Just came to say I'm off duty if you—' The midwife, nodding with benevolent approval, took the emotional scene in her stride, having seen many, and left them to it.

'Sorry,' Eve mumbled into his chest. The sobs that had shaken her had stopped but she stayed where she was, leaning heavily into him and unable to summon the strength or the will power to pull free. 'I missed you.'

It was only because the hand stroking her hair stilled that she registered belatedly what she had said. She lifted her head, too tired to be appalled by what she had admitted and, with her hands flat against his chest, pushed away until she was standing a few feet clear. Head tilted to one side like a curious bird, she angled a cautious look at his face.

Draco stood there holding the red ribbon she had hastily tied her hair back with when she had got the call in the middle of the night; it looked incongruous in his fingers. Unable to shake the idea that if she looked away he'd vanish, her eyes clung to his face, which was crazy. He wasn't a mirage, he was real, and her body reacted to the reality by coming alive... Her nerve endings tingled and her heart began to thud hard.

Draco's presence filled any room he entered, but in this antiseptically white box it was overwhelming but also intensely comforting. She had been feeling desperately alone, unable to stop the negative thoughts filling her head, and weighed down by a terrible sense of impending doom.

And now she wasn't alone... She pressed her hand to her stomach, thinking she was never alone and never would be again. Not the time, not the place, though, so *very* not the place to mention the new life growing inside her when another new life so close by was clinging on so tenaciously to his.

If she hadn't known before, the past few hours had brought home dramatically to her how precious the life she carried was, and how terrifyingly vulnerable. She had never had more admiration than she did now for her own mother, who had carried that responsibility of motherhood alone, had brought her up all by herself.

She would tell her—if she got the chance.

Her lips trembled as she felt tears press at the backs of her eyes. 'My mum might die, Draco.'

The fear shining in her eyes pierced him deeper than a blade. The muscles in his throat worked and the rush of tenderness he felt was so strong it took his breath away. He would have given anything to be able to tell her that nothing bad would happen to her ever again.

He touched the side of her face gently, his fingers brushing over the peachy softness of her smooth cheek before he captured both her hands in his. Drawing them up, he placed them against his chest.

'Why assume the worst when the best could still happen? Your mother is in the best place and you torturing yourself like this is not helping her, is it?'

Eve swallowed. 'You're right, I know, but—'

'It isn't my mother.'

'No, it's just this place is…' She looked around the room filled with the hum and mechanical bleep of the machines that were monitoring her brother.

'What you need is a break,' he said firmly.

'You can't help yourself, can you?' she said.

He was taking charge again, she thought with a small inward smile. But this time, rather than displaying his usual unstoppable energy, the lines bracketing his mouth were deeper, and those fanning from his incredible eyes were more sharply defined, and his cheekbones pushed tighter than she remembered against his bronzed skin.

'You look tired,' she exclaimed, then winced. 'Sorry, I didn't mean to say that out loud.'

You look beautiful, he thought. 'Hannah sends her love.'

Eve gave a tiny smile and tipped her head in acknowledgement. Hannah's love was good, but it was Draco's
love she needed, Draco's love she craved, Draco's love
she woke up in the middle of the night feeling the lack of
like a big black hole in her chest.

Draco couldn't take his eyes off Eve. There had been moments when he had pictured her pining for him, regretting sending him away. But if she had been missing him
it didn't show. Of course the day had left lines of strain
around her lovely eyes and soft purple bruises under her
eyes but her skin was glowing with health and her magnificent hair was gleaming and glossy.

The feelings Eve had been holding inside for weeks
threatened to burst out. She wanted to tell him about the
baby, but she tightened her control. This was not the time
or place and he was only here because somehow Hannah,
from her palace, had asked him to come.

'Have you seen Charlie?' It was odd to be worrying
about someone who for so long had been the focus of her
loathing, but she was. She had never really believed that
Charles Latimer truly cared for her mother, but the first
words he had said to the doctors had been, *My wife...what-
ever it takes, please save my wife.*

He'd said the same thing over and over and he was still
with her right now rather than standing over his heir.

Draco shook his head. 'No, I haven't.'

'This is very hard for him.' Fear, she learnt, made her
stepfather loud and aggressive, and it was a miracle he had
not alienated the people who were trying to help Sarah with
his accusations of negligence and dire threats of litigation
if she didn't survive.

Eve had had to control her own fear in order to calm
him down, and when she'd succeeded his tears and remorse

had been in many ways more difficult to cope with than what had preceded them.

'I missed you too.'

The husky words made her eyes fly to his face. If you miss me so much, she wanted to say, why the hell did you go away and not come back? Instead she bit her lip and asked, 'Is Hannah all right?'

'I didn't speak to her.'

Eve suppressed a genuine sigh of relief. When Hannah had rung last, Eve had been feeling particularly emotional and Hannah, who could be quietly persistent, had pushed until the whole story had come tumbling out. It was very possible, she realised guiltily, that her friend had gained quite a one-sided version of the situation.

'Kamel rang and he gave me quite a talking-to. He says she is frantic about you all and very frustrated that she can't be here with you.'

'I don't know why they rang you. You didn't have to come.'

The expression in his dark eyes was tender as he brushed a strand of hair from her face. 'We both know that's not true.'

She stared at him for a long moment and then without a word looked away and retook her seat by the cot, her expression dismissive, her body language distracted.

Typical mixed messages he thought, his scrutiny moving from her remote profile to her fluttery hands. His jaw clenched in frustration. He didn't know what response he had expected but *anything* would have been better than this silence.

Had he not been clear enough?

Did she want him to crawl?

What did she expect?

Maybe a bit of humility?

As quickly as it had erupted his frustrated anger faded.

The fact was he would do whatever it took to get Eve back…and, admittedly, his timing was bloody awful.

We both know that's not true…he'd said! If she hadn't forgotten how to, Eve might have laughed.

The fact was she felt she knew nothing, and understood even less! Her head was literally buzzing from lack of sleep and the unremitting stress of not knowing if her mother was okay. Her hormones were all over the place and last but not least was the fact that her secret lay very heavily on her conscience… Draco *might* be saying what she wanted to hear or she could be totally misconstruing a simple kindness.

Eve couldn't trust her own judgement and this was too important to make mistakes and open herself up to ridicule or, even worse, pity!

Draco moved a little closer, lowering his voice as he approached the glass cot with its high-tech attachments. 'How is he?'

'They say he is a fighter.'

It seemed to Draco that he would need to be, but he kept silent. 'How long have you been here?'

'I've no idea,' Eve admitted dully.

'You're exhausted.'

'I'm fine. It's Charlie who's a wreck… He really loves Mum but I never thought he did. I thought he married her because of—' her eyes slid to the incubator '—the baby, but I was wrong, so wrong, about so many things. If Mum dies I'll never be able to say sorry.' Her lips trembled as she blinked away the fresh rush of tears that threatened to overflow from her luminous eyes.

He took hold of the back of her chair. 'Your mum is having the best possible care here.' She turned her head slowly to look up at him, the shadowed sorrow in her incredible eyes wakening every protective instinct he possessed. He just wanted to hold her…for ever.

He touched her cheek lightly with one thumb, curling his hand to frame the side of her face, not touching but close enough to raise the sensitive, fine downy hair on her skin.

'I j-judged Mum because of her affair with Charlie, but I always thought that she had been trapped into it, that she felt she had no alternative. That if she finished with him, she would lose the security of her job and her home. I told myself that was what kept her with him.' She shook her head. 'It made me feel better about their relationship somehow. Does that sound crazy?'

'It sounds very normal.'

'It never occurred to me to ask her, and we never spoke about it. It was one of those things she knew I knew, and I knew she knew I knew...' The sound of a high-pitched alarm made her flinch and stare fearfully at the cot, panic building inside her. 'Should we do ...?'

Before she could finish a uniformed figure entered the room. Eve felt the comforting pressure of Draco's fingers on her shoulder as they watched the midwife glance at the baby before she pressed a few buttons on the array of glowing dials and the noise stopped immediately.

'Is he...?'

'He's fine. All our parents get spooked at first but after a while they read these things better than we do. The parents' room is down the hall if you fancy a coffee or a break. Oh, I'm Alison, by the way. I've just come on shift and I'll be looking after...any ideas of a name yet?'

Eve shook her head.

'See you later, then.' The rosy-cheeked midwife angled a questioning look at Eve's face. 'You OK, Mum?'

She didn't trust herself to speak, let alone correct the mistake. It might be a mistake now but in the not so distant future she would be able to claim that tagline...*Mum*.

What if I'm bad at it?

Oh, God, she was so not ready for this!

If I'm not ready, imagine how Draco will feel.

Eve had imagined it; she imagined his reaction a dozen times a day.

She had worked through every possible emotion he might display, every accusation he might fling in the heat of the moment and she had her responses worked out... cool, calm understanding. She wouldn't be hurt; she would be grown up. You're going to be a mother, Eve, she told herself. It's about time you grew up, don't you think?

CHAPTER FOURTEEN

SHE WAS READY and totally prepared.

Every night she had gone to bed thinking she would contact Draco tomorrow, and on the following morning she had woken up and thought of a perfectly valid reason to leave it another day...and on the one day she had actually picked up the phone and dialled his number it had gone straight to messaging. Determined not to wimp out once she had got that far, Eve had rung his office, where she had got through to a particularly superior-sounding female who had left her on hold for what felt like hours and then told her Mr Morelli was not in the office today.

The moment she put the phone down Eve thought of the things she could have said...and *thank you* was not one of them! She had worked herself up into a state of fury, mostly aimed at herself for being so damned meek and not telling that snooty woman where to get off!

Why settle for the messenger? she had asked herself. *Out of the office indeed!* Sure he was! The man should do his own dirty work and someone should tell him that. She had actually got as far as putting on her jacket to go and confront him about avoiding her, when she lost her courage.

She'd have to find it again pretty soon!

'I'm sorry about not correcting that midwife's assumption we were the parents,' she said.

Hearing the tears clogging her voice, he took a long deep breath and exhaled, expelling with the warm air the images the nurse's comment had inserted in his head. As a parent he knew that empathy could take you only so far. Happily Josie had always been a healthy child, but the couple of times she had been really ill...not times he wanted to relive.

Sombre-eyed, he looked at the cot. What if they *were* the parents and this *were* their baby lying there?

'Sorry, I know I should have explained to her but—'

A hissing sound of exasperation left his lips as Draco moved around the chair until he faced her, then, squatting down on his heels, he looked into her pale, unhappy face.

'Will you stop apologising and will you stop imagining everything is your fault? It isn't.'

'Isn't it? I had no idea how Mum felt. I just decided how I thought she *should* feel... I made it up as I went along.'

Draco gave a dry laugh. 'Pretty much like being a parent...I've been making it up for fourteen years.'

She looked at him, her chest swelling with the level of love she felt when she looked at him. 'You're a good father.'

And he would be to their baby too. In her calmer, more rational moments Eve knew that, and she also knew that when he got over his anger and got used to the idea, which might take a bit of time, he would step up.

But Eve didn't want duty; she wanted love.

'I *really* believed that if I could give Mum an option, get her away from him, that she would take it,' Eve admitted sorrowfully. 'It seemed simple then; totally black and white.' She gave a sniff, inviting his incredulity, anticipating his contempt. Unable to meet his eyes, she continued in husky-throated self-disgust. 'I was such a kid.'

'No, you were and are a daughter who loves her mother very much. Just what is the point in beating yourself up like this, Eve? There comes a point when guilt simply becomes self-indulgent. You are not responsible for what has happened,' he said firmly.

Head down, she gnawed at her full lower lip as she listened. 'Don't make excuses for me; I'm a horrible person.' She lifted her head and scowled at him. 'Why are you smiling?'

'Because you are not a horrible person and even if you were I'd—' He shook his head and stopped, the words *still love you* staying unspoken because if ever there was a wrong time to say I love you, this was it.

'Well, I am. Do you know how many times I've made an excuse not to see her? And when I knew about the baby...' her tortured, self-recriminatory gaze went to the incubator where her brother fought for his life '...I couldn't be happy for her.'

'Well, you're here for her now, and you're here for Charlie and the baby.'

She nodded. 'Yes.'

'And it might be a long haul, so why don't we follow the nice nurse's advice—?'

'She's a midwife.'

'The nice *midwife's* advice and take a break?'

'I couldn't.'

'Come on, I'm not taking no for an answer. You need a break.'

'Since when did you ever take no for an answer?' Except when she had told him to go and he had gone, she thought bleakly.

'Then why bother arguing if I'm going to ride roughshod over your wishes anyway?' he teased gently.

She shook her head mutely and looked at the baby. 'He can't even breathe for himself.'

'He doesn't have to. You can't do anything here and they'll let us know if there is any change. Charlie is with your mother. She's doing well.'

'They said that?'

Draco couldn't bear to see the hope in her emerald eyes die. 'I spoke to one of the doctors when I arrived.' However he spun it, what he said would have no bearing on the outcome, and if it made it easier for Eve to bear right now, then as far as he was concerned a white lie was a no-brainer.

'All those tubes and he's so tiny...' Her voice husked with emotion as she compressed her lips and looked away. 'Charlie couldn't even bear to look at him.' The confession came in a rush as she expelled a shaky breath, gulping as she remembered the expression on her stepfather's face when they had asked him if he wanted to see his son. 'And if anything happens to Mum, the baby will be all alone.'

'You can't think that way, Eve.' Emotion roughened his voice.

Her shadowed green eyes lifted; he made it sound so easy! 'I can't not.'

'You mean you *won't*.'

'You make it sound as though I'm enjoying this.'

He looked from her angry, resentful face to her clenched fist and shrugged. 'Hit me if it makes you feel better.'

'Not all of us feel the need to resort to violence!' The remorse she felt was instantaneous at her reminder of his actions towards Mark and she began to mumble an apology but he cut across her.

'He won't be alone—he'll have you and Charlie. The man is just scared right now. Whatever happens, he'll love his son. How could he not?'

'My father didn't love me.' Her tired voice had a singsong quality as she continued. It seemed to Draco that she had forgotten he was there. 'He wanted Mum to have an abortion and he sent a letter telling her. I found it... I never told Mum. I just put it back. Mum was only a student and she had a holiday job on his estate. He treated her as though she were…and me, I was just rubbish to be got rid of.'

Draco could see it clearly, the girl who had carried the secret of her father's rejection with her into adulthood. The image made his heart ache for her, and awoke his anger. If Charlford were here now…but he wasn't.

He'd died and he was a small loss to the world, to Draco's way of thinking, but it had robbed him of the satisfaction of confronting the man with his desertion…though what good would it have done? He had met the type before and when confronted with their misdeeds they were more often than not incapable of accepting their guilt, let alone feeling any remorse.

He sighed out the anger, and as he looked at Eve he felt an upsurge of pride. 'You were better off without a father like that.'

'That's what Mark said too.'

Suddenly the memories of their last meeting were there between them, seemingly making the air heavy.

'Your brother is not an idiot. Was he all right after I…?'

'He was fine.'

'Good—I said things to hurt you that night.' He gave his head an angry, self-admonitory shake and decided to cut a long story short. 'I was jealous.' It turned out to be easier to admit it to her than it had been to admit the glaringly obvious fact to himself.

Her green eyes widened at the admission. 'That's what Mark said too,' she mumbled, shocked to think what this admission might mean. 'I told him that he was being stupid and that you're not the jealous type at all.'

A ghost of a smile touched Draco's lips. 'You're right, I'm not the *jealous* type *except*, it turns out, where you're concerned.' His stare made her flush. 'I'd like to tell you that I'll never act like that again, but I think if I see you

kissing another man I would… Actually I think you can
pretty much guarantee I would. You do know you've been
driving me crazy from the first moment I saw you.' He
stopped and raked a hand through his hair. 'I can't speak
of these things in here.'

Eve got to her feet slowly, her thoughts in total chaos.
She was confused, shocked, excited. She glanced towards
her brother, torn between what she perceived as her duty
and her desire. 'I feel like I'm deserting him.'

'It's fine, I understand. I need a break. Can I bring you
something…?'

She shook her head and watched him leave, tension
translating itself into a rigidity in his normally fluid gait.
The door had barely closed before it opened again and the
midwife from earlier came in, looking a lot fresher than
the colleague she had replaced.

'I've just got some charts to bring up to date and I'll
make the little one comfortable. Why don't you go for a
break with your man? It can be really hard on them, you
know, the ones who keep tight hold of their emotions.
The little one won't be alone—I'll be right in here or out
by the desk.' She nodded through the glass panel where
the nurses' station and its constantly ringing telephone
was sited.

Eve stood there for a moment and then nodded, smiling
her thanks before blowing her brother a kiss.

Still struggling with the white gown, which appeared
to come in only one size—massive—she caught up with
Draco outside the parents' lounge, coming out of the door,
not into it.

'Aren't you…?

He turned his head and looked at her, and Eve forgot
what she was saying; she forgot everything except that he
was the most gorgeous man on the planet, the shape of his
face, his eyes, his lips, the scar…everything! It seemed

unbelievable that there had been moments when she had convinced herself that they were better off apart. When she wasn't lying to herself she had been literally aching for the sound of his voice.

She was aching now, for more than his voice.

She took a deep breath. It was her turn. She leapt into the unknown and the words came in a rush, falling over one another to get out of her mouth before she changed her mind and chickened out.

'When you walked away that day, I felt as if you'd taken a bit of me with you.' She lifted her hand, intending to press it to her heart to illustrate the empty space and let out a squeal of sheer frustration as the tie on the gown responded to her impatient tugs by tightening painfully around her neck. 'Oh, God!' she groaned in a mixture of frustration and discomfort. 'Can you give me a hand here? This thing is trying to strangle me...I can't reach.' Holding the neckline, she couldn't lift her head to look at him without it digging into her neck and she let out another squeal of frustration.

'Stay still.'

It was hard to read anything in his voice and his fingers were steady as they brushed the skin of her nape. Eve wasn't steady at all; she was shaking and even the lightest touch sent electric shudders through her helplessly receptive body.

'Done.'

Eve kept her head down as she pulled her arm out of the sleeve. 'I have terrible timing,' she mumbled as she finally rid herself of the garment.

His lazy laugh was warm and husky. 'I have always found your timing impeccable.'

She lifted her gaze, wanting to see in his face what she had heard in his voice, but it wasn't there.

Nothing was there. His face was pale and strangely

stiff, his unblinking stare was fixed on…? She glanced downwards.

Realising as she did so that she was wearing her pyjamas, as she had only had time to pull on a pair of boots and throw a thin jacket over the top.

'It might not catch on,' she admitted ruefully, 'but I was in bed when I got the…' Her voice trailed away as it hit her that it wasn't her clothes he was staring at, it was her. Or more specifically the small but definite bump of her belly. For weeks it had been the subject that had dominated her every waking moment and now of all times— she had forgotten.

Slowly, very slowly, her eyes left the soft curve of her belly and when they reached his face they were wide and wary, but there was still nothing to see in his face—nothing. In all her scenarios there had definitely been an explosion…not this…this *nothing*!

Was he even breathing?

The knowledge of what he had been given was totally overwhelming. The life, the life they had made together was growing inside her…and that feeling of total glorious rightness was quickly followed by an insidious fear that spread its roots like a cancer. He had so much to lose, in this place right now, how could that not scream at him? It was all so fragile—this happiness could be snatched away from him at any moment.

'I can see this is a bit of a shock and I understand, but what…?'

His jacket still held the heat of his body as without a word he draped it around her shoulders. He still hadn't said anything to her, and she wondered if that was going to be his response—ignore it and it'll go away!

The knot of hurt in her chest tipped over into anger. 'Aren't you going to say *anything*?'

His muscles along the angular line of his jaw clenched

as he carefully closed the door to the sitting room behind him. 'Not in there. I need some fresh air and the people in there at the moment...' His eyes brushed the closed door. Symbolically closing his own internal one on his fear, Draco chose instead to embrace life and love and... He fought down the urge to crush her against him and claim that mouth for his own. 'Need some privacy.'

And I need some answers or questions or both... She needed something from him; after weeks of not knowing she still didn't know. 'Why?'

He angled a brow and said quietly, 'Think about where we are, Eve. Parents get to make some tough decisions in here.'

'Oh!' Even in her emotional state she had noticed the couple sitting beside an empty cot when she had arrived. Their faces had stayed with her, a mixture of fear, resignation and anger that had fed the sense of dread that lay like a cold stone in her chest.

Unconsciously her own hands went to her stomach where there was a slight but defined bump to curve them around. Her size had resulted in a few raised eyebrows during her recent first antenatal appointment and the phrase *big for dates* had been bandied around. Eve was totally confident that her scan the following week would confirm her dates. There was only one time it could have been, as Draco had always taken care that way. There had just been the one time when the condom had split.

Rather naively she had imagined that one time would be OK.

She tipped her head, her eyes sliding towards the closed door. It certainly put things into perspective. 'All right, but I can't be away from my brother for long.'

'What I have to say won't take long.'

They were words Eve struggled to take any comfort from as she also struggled to keep up with his long-legged pace. All the corridors seemed the same to her, the place was a maze, but Draco seemed to know exactly which way to head.

Probably in the daytime the gravelled quadrangle with its tubs of flowers and benches would be popular, but not surprisingly at this time of night it was empty.

As they stepped outside Eve took a deep gulp of fresh air and looked up at the light-filled rows of windows surrounding them. She shook her head.

'How do people work here day in and day out, seeing all that...grief?' She had forgotten the exact percentage in the recent article she had begun to read. Eve had scared herself so much she had stopped halfway through—it had been about survival rates in very premature births, but the numbers had horrified her and it seemed that many very young babies that did survive had long-term medical problems.

'I suppose there are coping techniques. I imagine they learn to balance compassion with objectivity...and I'm assuming that the good days make it all worth it,' Draco replied.

This was not a good day. 'I was going to tell you about our baby,' she said.

'When?'

'Six weeks ago.'

'That's very specific.' His eyes dropped to her belly. It still hadn't sunk in...*a baby*. A sense of warm anticipation flowed through him as he pictured her with their baby at her breast.

'I rang your office. After they'd put me on hold for ages and they told me you weren't available because you were out of the country...' Her eyes lowered, she recalled the hurt and anger she'd felt, and it was still there in her face when she said with careful neutrality, 'I got the message.'

His eyes narrowed. 'Well, I didn't.'

And the culprit would be the temp who had seemed to feel it beneath her to do anything much but file her nails, and offend at least two clients. It did not surprise him to learn that she had picked and chosen the messages she had passed on.

Did not surprise but did anger him, and he had already made it clear to the agency who'd supplied her that he had been dissatisfied with her work. The person he had spoken to had been very apologetic, explaining that he was in a difficult position because the temp in question was his wife's sister.

Draco had made the man's position easier by dispensing with the services of his firm.

'When did all this happen?' Draco asked.

'It was Tuesday the sixth.'

'I *was* in the country that day. That's the anniversary of my father's death, and it has become a tradition for us all to go to his favourite spot. We take a picnic, remember him and raise a toast.'

'Oh.'

'So when are you due?'

'Christmas.' She placed a self-conscious hand on her stomach and said defensively, 'I know I'm enormous.'

'You're beautiful, and you'll be a perfect mother.' He had never in his head associated a pregnant woman with sexiness, but looking at Eve and knowing that his child, their child, was growing inside her did not diminish his desire in the slightest; it simply added a new dimension to it.

'Are you all right?' she asked. He was obviously not if he thought she looked beautiful. 'Do you want to sit down?' Looking concerned, she nodded towards the bench that was set against the wall.

He laughed and sat down, pulling her down beside him. 'I would much prefer to lie down.'

The warmth of his hungry, all-encompassing gaze made

her shiver. She started in surprise when his hand went to her stomach, curving over the gentle mound.

'And I am the one who should be asking you that question. Are *you* all right?'

None of this was going according to her script. 'I think you might be in shock, Draco.'

'No, I'm in love.' And there was no might about it. 'I thought I had lost you,' he said, his voice thick and unfamiliar with emotion. 'I just lost it when I saw you with Mark. I wanted to kill him! What the hell are we doing living separate lives pretending we can function apart? I can't, I know I can't. I need you, Eve, to be a whole person and not some cardboard cut-out. I need you.'

Eve stared at him, her heart thudding fast, and whispered, 'You don't have to say that.'

'I *do* have to say that,' he countered firmly as with a smile that made her heart flip he took her wrists and pulled her gently to him. Wrapping her hands around his neck, he kissed her tenderly and with infinite care.

Eve was weeping tears of joy. 'Say it,' she whispered, needing to see it in his eyes when he said the words; then and only then would she allow herself to believe it.

'I love you, Eve. Will you give me a second chance?'

'Idiot!' she said, lovingly touching his cheek. 'Oh, Draco, I've been so unhappy without you. I love you so much.'

With a groan he hauled her to him and kissed her deeply. His smile faded as he drew back and saw the sadness in her eyes.

'What's wrong?'

She shook her head and sniffed. 'It just feels wrong to be this happy at a time like this.'

'Would your mother want you to be happy?'

She nodded tearily.

'Then let's be happy. The real celebrations can wait, but

the important thing is we have each other and whatever happens, here or anywhere else, you know I'll be there for you, don't you, Eve?'

Her eyes shone with happiness as she looked into the face of the amazing man she loved so much. 'I do know.'

He kissed her again before they went back in—together.

EPILOGUE

'IT'S SNOWING! IT'S snowing…!'

Josie rushed into the drawing room where her father was placing the angel she had made when she was six on top of the tree. It had lost a piece of wing and the leg surgery had left her lopsided but she always had pride of place.

Eve, looking almost as excited as her stepdaughter, bounced to her feet. 'Snow for Christmas—what could be better?' She gave a contented sigh.

'How about an hour's sleep?' her more pragmatic mate suggested.

'We had three hours last night.' Sleep deprivation had become a way of life but, sleep-deprived or not, her husband was still the handsomest man on the planet and since the birth two weeks earlier he had been at home to help.

She had needed it. Her dating scan, with Draco there beside her, had shown very clearly the reason for her 'large for dates' size. The sight of the two little hearts beating had reduced Eve to tears. Draco said it hadn't hit him for weeks and when it had his reaction had been to go out and buy a house in the country—*as you did*!

'Impulse,' he'd admitted. 'But I drove past on my way to Gabby's and I just thought, I can see our family there— but if you hate it…?'

Eve hadn't hated it, she had loved it, so home for them

was now a Victorian vicarage five miles from where his sister lived. Josie was delighted to be so close to her cousin.

During Eve's pregnancy, she and Gabby had grown close and since the birth of her healthy twin sons Gabby had been a real support, as had Josie, who was delighted with her twin brothers. The custody threat hanging over them had gone. Clare had dropped all thoughts of having Josie live with her after she channelled her maternal instincts into her latest project—a donkey sanctuary.

So different from a year ago, when Eve had worked in an empty office on Christmas Eve.

'The snow is sticking—do you think Mum and Charlie will get here?'

They would have a lot of people around the table tomorrow, although Veronica had chosen to stay with Gabby. Their turn to have her next year, she'd promised, but they were all coming over for lunch. And of course Eve's little half-brother Joe, who was now a sturdy little chap who had suffered no long-term ill effects from his shaky start, would be there too. Sarah had spent four days in Intensive Care and there had been times when things had looked very black but she had finally pulled through and had come home a week before Joe.

'They'll be fine.'

Draco came to stand behind her, his hands on her shoulders. Eve leaned back into him, feeling safe, warm and cherished.

'Our first Christmas together... I wish Hannah could come,' Eve said wistfully.

'They'll be here for New Year.'

'I can't wait to see the baby.' Hannah had given birth to a gorgeous little baby girl called Cordelia and she had already asked Eve to be godmother to the baby royal. 'It's so peaceful,' she sighed, staring out at the snowy scene.

On cue the speaker in the corner flooded the room with loud baby squawks.

Eve turned and buried her face in Draco's sweater. 'I shouldn't have tempted fate!' she groaned.

'Davide or Dario?' he asked. Their twin sons already had very distinct personalities but to him their cries were as identical as their faces and it amazed him that Eve could identify them.

She turned her head and listened for a moment. 'Davide.'

She started for the stairs and he pulled her back. 'No, you sit there and we'll bring them down to you, won't we, Josie?'

Always a willing helper, Josie jumped to her feet.

At the door Draco turned back. A question in her eyes, Eve watched him approach.

'Have I told you how much I love you today?'

She smiled as his lips brushed hers. 'Once or twice,' she murmured against his mouth. 'But,' she admitted, reaching up to frame his face with her hands, 'you can't have too much of a good thing.' And her husband was the *best*!

Coming back into the room to see where her father had got to, Josie rolled her eyes.

'Not again! You're meant to be the responsible adults here. Get a room!'

* * * * *

Join Britain's BIGGEST Romance Book Club

50% OFF your first parcel

- **EXCLUSIVE** offers every month

- **FREE** delivery direct to your door

- **NEVER MISS** a title

- **EARN** Bonus Book points

Call Customer Services
0844 844 1358*

or visit
illsandboon.co.uk/subscriptions